D0899465

TO CATCH A FALLING STAR

On a muggy August day in 2002, Alexandra Lind was unexpectedly thrown backwards in time, landing in the year of Our Lord 1658. Catapulted into an unfamiliar and frightening new existence, Alex could do nothing but adapt. After all, while time travelling itself is a most rare occurrence, time travelling with a return ticket is even rarer.

This is the eighth book about Alex, her husband Matthew and their continued adventures in the second half of the seventeenth century.

ANNA BELFRAGE

To Catch A Falling Star

SilverWood

Published in 2015 by the author
using SilverWood Books Empowered Publishing®

SilverWood Books
30 Queen Charlotte Street, Bristol, BS1 4HJ
www.silverwoodbooks.co.uk

Copyright © Anna Belfrage 2015

ISBN 978-1-78132-243-7 (paperback)
ISBN 978-1-78132-244-4 (ebook)

British Library Cataloguing in Publication Data
A CIP catalogue record for this book is available from the British Library

Set in Bembo by SilverWood Books
Printed on responsibly sourced paper

This book is dedicated to my three sons,
true brothers of the heart. May you always be there
for each other, no matter where life takes you.

Chapter 1

Isaac Lind should not have drunk quite as much as he did that evening, but flushed by the success of his latest exhibition, he allowed himself to be dragged along, to be toasted in pint after pint of lager.

By the time he left the pub, he was unsteady on his feet, but in a mellow mood. He stood for some moments by a high brick wall, sniffing at the lilacs that hung over it into the narrow little street. Late April was a nice time of the year, and even here in London, it was difficult to miss the advent of spring, the heady scents of flowering shrubs competing with the permanent smells of stone, exhausts and muddy tidal waters.

Isaac continued on his way, strolling towards the river. It was going to be a long walk home to Notting Hill, but the night was warm and Isaac was in no particular hurry. Veronica and Isabelle would be asleep anyway, and, knowing Veronica, it might make sense to walk off some of this agreeable buzz before showing up back at their little apartment.

He stood for a moment with elbows on the stone parapet and decided that someday he would paint this – a silhouetted London lapped by the returning waters of the Thames. He yawned and looked at the swirling waters below: multiple little maelstroms, murky waves slapping in irritation at each other as they jostled for space. He yawned again, his mind drifting over to his latest piece. An urge built in him to hurry to his studio, not his bed, and look at it again. So, instead of continuing on his way home, he turned to the right, making for the attic space he rented for his painting.

The eye-scanner at the main gate let him through with a loud beep. He shrugged off his leather jacket as he took the stairs, making for the top floor. More security, and when he swiped his thumb on the keypad, the door swung open on well-oiled hinges. Yet another swipe, and the space came alive with lights, a soft whirring informing him his computer was back online. His fingers flew over the screen and music flowed out of the two narrow speakers, a slow monotonous Gregorian chant.

Paintings leaned against the walls, bursts of vivid colours that implacably drew the beholder's eyes into whatever little detail was hidden in the depth of the heaving brush-work. One was a study in reds and oranges, and in their midst one could vaguely make out a burning, twisting figure, mouth wide as it screamed out its anguish to the world. Isaac extended a finger to touch it and laughed nervously. He could feel his skin blistering with the heat.

"How can you do this?" his agent had said, shaking his head in admiration. "How on earth do you make it so vibrant? Hell, I can even smell the stench of roasting flesh!"

Isaac wasn't sure how he did it. His fingers worked, and he slipped into a subconscious state where colours flowed together on the canvas, and all according to an inner voice. It scared the hell out of him, but that wasn't something he was about to admit – not even to himself.

He flicked off the old sheet that covered his latest work, a painting that was very different from anything else in the room. Just looking at it filled him with unwelcome sensations of vertigo, a niggling feeling that he was walking a tightrope over forbidden zones – like he'd done all those years ago when, as a boy, he had painted the picture that allowed his grandfather to dive from this time to another. Impossible, of course, and yet it had happened.

He caressed the wooden frame of the picture, a depiction of a somnolent courtyard, an empty stone-flagged space, surrounded by arched walkways in whitewashed stone. In the middle a fountain, a constant welling of water, and Isaac knew exactly what the water would taste like and how cool it would feel to his fingers. In olive greens and muted browns, with the odd dash of whites and startling blues, the water spilled over the fountain's edge to fall in transparent drops towards the ground.

Isaac reared back, and in his head he heard a mocking laugh. Too afraid to look deep into your own work? Well, yes, he was. Sweat broke out across his forehead, beaded his upper lip, and made him wipe his damp hands against his jeans. He tried to break eye contact with the falling water, but now he heard it as well, the pitter-patter of drops on wet stone, the trickling sound of water running through a narrow channel, and there, just where he had painted it, a minute point of white beckoned and promised, entrapping his eyes in a shaft of dazzling light.

Carlos Muñoz was walking back to his room when he saw the stranger lying sprawled half in, half out of the fountain. With a soft exclamation, he hurried as well as he could to the groaning heap of a man. Carlos wrinkled his nose. The man was drunk, but how on earth had he ended up here, in the monastery's secluded courtyard? He swept the cloister walks but they were empty, most of the monks hastening back to their beds from matins for a few more hours of sleep.

Carlos kneeled clumsily on account of his peg leg and turned the stranger over. He yelped and dropped the man back onto the cobbles, scrambling back a few feet. Ángel? Here? But no, it couldn't be – his cousin had died two years ago on Jamaica, hanged by the neck for spying on behalf of his royal Spanish majesty.

"Fucking hell," the stranger groaned, and Carlos scooted backwards, got back up.

"*¿Inglés?*" He hadn't spoken English since he returned from the New World. "*¿Es Usted inglés?*"

"No," the stranger moaned and sat up. "If anything, I'm Scots." He spoke passable Spanish, understandable but heavily accented, and looked about himself with trepidation. "Bloody, fucking hell," he cursed in English, and Carlos thought the young man reminded him of someone – apart from being a disconcerting copy of himself.

He extended his hand to help the man stand, and they

were nose to nose, of remarkably similar build – albeit that the stranger was a couple of inches taller – both with a soaring quiff of dark hair over the right brow, both with dark, lustrous eyes that were saved from being doe-like by strong, dark brows.

The stranger gaped. At one level, Carlos supposed it was most droll, this meeting between two men so alike as to seem twins, no doubt with identical expressions of disbelief painted on their faces. At another level, it was so disquieting it made Carlos' good leg dip, causing him to have to hop for a couple of steps to regain his balance. The stranger inhaled, barked a laugh, and, to Carlos' bemusement, pinched himself – multiple times.

"Where am I?" the stranger finally said.

Carlos studied this double of his in silence while smoothing down his cassock. Might the man be an English spy? But no, if anything, the stranger seemed utterly confused.

"*En Sevilla*," Carlos said.

The stranger groaned, tore at his hair and groaned some more. "Bloody, bloody, bloody hell! This can't be happening, I'm just drunk – really drunk – and soon…oh God!" The man swayed, steadied himself against the nearby wall, thereby coming to stand in a patch of moonlight.

Carlos had never seen a man dressed like this before. With interest, he took in the wet, long breeches, the odd footwear in some kind of fabric, and the rather more normal shirt, even if it was narrow in fit and had small buttons down the front rather than laces. One of the sleeves was burnt, the skin below looking red and irritated. A leather belt but no knife; no sword – not even a pouch; no cloak; no hat; and hands as narrow and long as his own, but with the fingers liberally smudged with ink and paint.

The stranger folded his hands together under Carlos' open inspection. "I can't get it off," he muttered.

"Are you a painter?"

The man nodded and looked about the courtyard. "I got it just right," he muttered, and a shiver ran through him. "The arches, the fountain – shit, even the crumbling plaster is just as I painted it."

Painted it? Carlos followed the man's eyes round the small courtyard, smiling as he always did when he took in this his favourite place: the arches in soft sandstone, worn to smoothness through very many years, the whitewash of the walls, the irregular stones of the walkways – all of it spoke of permanence. A huge stand of ivy clambered its way up to the latticed first-floor shutters, in a circle surrounding the fountain grew straggling roses and high tufts of lavender, and set into a niche in the wall stood the abbot's pride and joy: an ancient statue of the Virgin.

"What is this place?" the man asked.

"A Dominican monastery," Carlos said. "San Pablo el Real." He shifted into English, and the stranger's eyes grew round with astonishment. "My home for the past two years, a resting place for a battered soul." He nodded at the man. "It would seem you are in need of some rest as well."

"Rest? No way! I have to find a way back home." The stranger scowled at the surrounding walls and went over to stare intently into the waters of the fountain, as if he were looking for something in the shallow basin.

"Hmm," Carlos said, and then recalled his original question at finding the man. "How did you get here?"

The man shrugged. "I have no idea, I just—" He broke off. "I just fell."

"Fell?" Carlos looked at the sky. There was nothing to fall from.

"I know," the stranger said, his eyes full of anguish. He shook himself like a wet dog and extended his hand. "I'm Isaac, Isaac Lind."

"Carlos Muñoz," Carlos replied and grasped the hand. Isaac Lind? He recognised the name. He tried to place it but came up with a blank.

"Muñoz, you say?" Isaac said, and it seemed to Carlos the name had some relevance for him. Ah well, in truth not an uncommon name.

"Yes, Carlos Benito Muñoz." Not Muñoz de Hojeda,

11

like his uncle and his cousins, not for a bastard this illustrious name. His throat tightened as it always did when he thought of the shame that clung to him like a wet cloak – something dear Uncle Raúl never let him forget.

"Pleased to meet you," Isaac said.

"Likewise," Carlos replied.

Isaac shoved his hands into his pockets and turned his back on Carlos, the slow, casual pivoting of a man taking in new surroundings.

"This may seem a strange question," he said, "but what year is it?"

Carlos gave the slender back a surprised look, and all along his arms his hair rose to bristle in fear. What was this man, dropping out of nowhere in strange vestments to land in their courtyard? He crossed himself.

"1688," he answered as calmly as he could.

Isaac closed his eyes. A strangled sound escaped him, and his frame bowed. Carlos was well familiar with dejection, and saw it now in every line of the man before him. His heart filled with compassion, and he decided that for now the important thing was to get this unexpected visitor dry and out of the beady eyes of the abbot, who would shortly be about.

"We had best get you out of those…err…clothes." Carlos gestured at Isaac's strange and rather revealing breeches.

"My clothes?"

"They are somewhat conspicuous – and wet."

"Oh." Isaac ran a hand down his thighs, and followed Carlos in under the cool arches, up some stairs, down others, along a straight passage and into Carlos' little room.

As always, Carlos was washed with a sense of contentment upon entering this little space that was only his. At most sixty square feet, it contained his bed, a desk, a chair, a stool and a heavy wooden crucifix. Leaning drunkenly along the desktop were his precious books, propped up on one side by a heavy inkstand, on the other by the wall itself.

"Are you a monk?" Isaac asked, taking in the little space.

"No, I'm a priest. The monks are not accorded the luxury of private accommodations."

"Luxury?" Isaac studied his surroundings pointedly, making Carlos irritated. There was a pitcher and a basin, a chamber pot tucked into a corner, and even a window, albeit set too high up to allow any kind of outside view. Few men aspired to such comfort, and even fewer achieved it.

Carlos chose not to comment, busying himself by digging through his chest. With a satisfied grunt, he produced breeches and a shirt.

"We are of size," he commented, handing the garments to Isaac.

"Of size?" Isaac began to laugh, a high nervous laughter. "Yeah, I would say so. You could bloody well be my twin!"

"Yes," Carlos agreed, unnerved by the shrill sound, "we are uncommonly alike."

They inspected each other again, and in the dim light of Carlos' little room, the likeness was even more extraordinary. Had Isaac worn his hair as long as Carlos did, it would have been difficult to tell them apart – bar the wooden leg, of course.

"What happened to your leg?" Isaac asked, shedding his strange leggings.

Carlos gaped at the revealed undergarment: short of leg, in silk it would seem, deep blue, and decorated with flowers. He made even bigger eyes at the heavy gold chain that had lain concealed under Isaac's shirt. Not an entire pauper, Carlos reflected, noting the gold rings and the strange, thick metal bracelet round one wrist.

"Your leg," Isaac repeated.

"I lost it," Carlos said.

"I can see that. I was more curious about the how."

"It was in the colony of Maryland," Carlos answered, frowning as he considered the issue of shoes. He himself only had one, no longer being in need of pairs. "I spent some time with the Indians. A wound I had festered, and so..." He shrugged.

"...and so?" Isaac prompted, inspecting the breeches narrowly before stepping into them.

"A woman I know cut it off." Carlos sighed, but then

13

smiled at the memory of this remarkable woman. "Alex Graham, *que vayas siempre con Dios*." And your daughter as well, he added silently. May the Lord always protect Sarah Graham, wherever she goes.

"Alex?" Isaac croaked. "Alexandra Graham?" He tugged at the shirt, entangling himself in the laces around the neck.

Carlos threw him a cautious look. "Do you know her?"

Isaac laughed again, making Carlos want to clap his hands over his ears. "Know her? Well, if she's the Alexandra Graham who's married to Matthew Graham, then she's my mother."

"Isaac, Alex's son? But you're dead!" Carlos reeled back against the door.

"Not last time I checked." Isaac broke out in yet another bout of hysterical laughter.

"But Alex…" Carlos stopped and peered at him. "Oh my God!" he exclaimed and sat down with a thud on the bed beside Isaac.

"Yes?"

Carlos shook his head. Alex had known his father – she'd spoken so warmly of Don Benito whom she had met aboard a ship to the colonies. Carlos grimaced, his mouth filling with bitter bile as it always did when he thought of his father, a Catholic priest who broke his vows, and as a result Carlos had been born, taken in by his paternal uncle. *Quizás*…maybe… He eyed the man before him. Yes, that would explain the uncanny likeness, but it would also mean that Alex had bedded his father while married to Matthew, and somehow Carlos couldn't get his mind around that.

"How old are you?" he asked, and Isaac's eyes tightened at his tone.

"Thirty-two."

Carlos gaped. He was not yet thirty, and he would have taken the man before him to be younger, not older. His hand found his rosary, recited his way through a decade, two decades, and finally opened his eyes again, somewhat more in control of himself.

"I don't understand."

"Welcome to the club," Isaac muttered. "Who the fucking hell does?" He rested back against the wall and closed his eyes. He yawned, he yawned again, and just like that he was sunk in sleep, toppling over in the direction of Carlos.

Chapter 2

"Stop! I…" With that, Alex Graham slid off the horse, picked up her skirts, and ran back towards the main house and the people assembled before it. She didn't want to do this – how on earth was she supposed to survive leaving her home and more than half of her family behind?

She slowed her pace, surveying her home for the last twenty years, and she had to clench her jaws to stop herself from screaming out loud that Matthew could ride off on his own, without her, because she was staying here, where she belonged.

Her eyes flew up the slope to the graveyard where her father and one of her sons lay at permanent rest. A choked sob burst from her. Who would now go and sit beside Jacob to tell him of what was happening in the lives of his family? Who would make sure his headstone was kept free of moss and lichen? Who would decorate his grave with a freshly cut rose on the date of his death?

A small, hunched figure detached itself from the group of people and came towards her at a brisk trot. For all that she was almost eighty, Mrs Parson was still quite agile, and stout enough to cope when Alex threw her arms around her.

"I don't want to do this." Alex buried her nose in Mrs Parson's starched linen cap. "I don't think I can."

"Aye, you can. You have to, no?" Mrs Parson disentangled herself and gave Alex a brief pat on the cheek. "And you'd be right unbearable company should you remain here while Matthew sets off on his own. You'd wilt with anxiety."

Alex nodded reluctantly, her eyes flying up to the graveyard.

"I'll take care of Jacob, and of Magnus." Mrs Parson kissed Alex on both cheeks and shoved her towards the waiting horses. "Go on with you."

"I—" Alex hated it that the tears she had kept so tightly under control now were bursting from her. "Oh God," she moaned, "I can't."

She cried and cried, hands wringing at her skirts, and there was Naomi, eyes as red as her own, and Alex hugged her daughter-in-law to her chest as if she'd never let her go. Mark's children came next – Hannah, Tom, Lettie, Rosie and baby Peter. And there was Ian's wife, Betty, wild hair firmly braided, and more grandchildren, four more little bodies to hug. Maggie was crying and begging her not to go, Grace and Timothy clung to her skirts, while Christopher retreated to stand with his cousins, eyes bright with tears.

Alex kissed them all repeatedly, and when she reached Mark, she just held out her arms. Mark pressed her to his chest, and her nose was too clogged for her to be able to draw in his scent, so instead she ran her fingers through his hair, down his cheeks, to memorise him and carry him forever with her, imprinted in her skin.

"Mama," he whispered, and she could hear how close he was to crying. "My Mama." He smiled down at her and ran a gentle thumb under her eyes. "You'll be back," he said, but neither of them knew if that was true, and Alex didn't want to let him go.

"Alex?" Matthew's hands closed on her upper arms, turned her to face him, and she could barely see the dark of his coat through her tears.

"What are we doing?" she groaned. "How can we even think of splitting ourselves apart like this?" She leaned out of his attempted embrace, slipping away from his hold like she'd been doing for the last few weeks, punishing him with her distance for a decision she had allowed him to take.

"I thought we were in agreement," Matthew said.

No they weren't, not really. But how could she deny him this? And so they had decided that this was what they should do, but now, on the day of departure, she didn't want to – no more than she had wanted to during the long, tortuous countdown. This was her home, here were her roots, her family, and to ride away from all this was like tearing a limb off.

"I have to go. I must see Hillview again." Matthew took a step away from her, and his hands slid down her arms to clasp her hands. "I don't want to go without you, but if you don't think you can do this, well then…" Eyes a bright hazel burned into hers, a wordless plea that she come with him.

"Will we come back?" she said.

"I've said so a thousand times. If you want to, we will."

If? There was no if about it, and he bloody well knew that, didn't he?

He tried to gather her close, but she stepped away from him, dried her face with the end of her shawl, drew in several steadying gulps of air, and turned to face her family.

"Don't you dare die before I come back," Alex said to Mrs Parson.

"I'll do my best." Mrs Parson smoothed at her apron. "Last I looked, I was as healthy as I've been these last twenty years or so, no?"

"Hmm," Alex snorted, "pure luck, in my opinion. It's not as if you actively do anything to keep hale and hearty, is it?"

"I eat, sleep and knit. Seems to be working, no?"

"Obviously." Alex leaned forward to hug Mrs Parson once again. "And be gentle with Thomas, okay?"

"That is none of your business, lass," Mrs Parson said huffily, shaking out her skirts. "We are both old enough to know what we are doing." She threw a look at where Thomas Leslie was sitting on his horse, waiting for the cavalcade to set off, and grinned at Alex. "It will do him good, to be away from here for some days."

"Poor man," Alex muttered, feeling composure return to her in leaps and bounds with their habitual bantering. "You're wearing him to the bone."

"And feeding him back into shape," Mrs Parson reminded her with a chuckle, guiding her gently but insistently towards the horse.

Mark offered her his hands, and she stepped into them and sat up behind Matthew, looking down at her son. She leaned over and brushed at a strand of dark chestnut hair, letting her fingers linger for an instant on his cheek.

"I'll be back," she mouthed. Mark just smiled and nodded. She threw one last look at him when she reached the top of the lane. Her son was clinging to his wife, Naomi's arms tight around his waist.

She didn't speak to Matthew during the day, and once they stopped to make camp for the night, she chose to sit with Ian, ignoring Matthew's extended hand.

"Bloody Luke," Alex said, using a long stick to poke at the glowing embers. "This is all his fault."

"But it's a generous gift. Hillview restored to Da, and on top of that, he's paying for the passage."

Unfortunately, in Alex's opinion, as otherwise they would not have been in a position to go.

"Well, we did save his beloved Charlie from certain death," Alex said, unimpressed.

Luke Graham, viper that he may be – and in Alex's book her brother-in-law remained a dangerous, unknown quantity – had done very well out of life, and was, as far as she could understand, filthy rich. She doubted his generous gesture had made much of a dent in his purse, and surely his son was worth it.

Having survived eight months in gaol after the Monmouth rebellion, Charlie Graham had been transported to serve out the remainder of his life as a slave in the West Indies, but Matthew and Alex had found him two years ago and managed to buy him free, returning to Maryland with a skeletal young man, permanently marked by his ordeal.

"Are you saying you wish he hadn't given Da Hillview?" Ian said, keeping an eye on where Matthew was conversing with Thomas Leslie.

Alex hugged her legs. "Yes, I really wish he hadn't. But I can never tell your father that, can I? The moment I saw him holding the deed to Hillview in his hands, I knew that he'd go back." She uttered a small, strangled sound. "I have to go with him, there's no choice in that. But Jesus, Ian, it's tearing me apart."

"But you said how he has promised that you'll come back." His voice shook, making him clear his throat.

Alex hitched her shoulders, overwhelmed by a longing for chocolate, something she could binge on to keep the anguish that was growing in her belly at bay. She looked across the fire at her husband, and he smiled in her direction before resuming his conversation with Thomas.

It pissed her off. Here she was, so obviously split in two, and he was so elated by the thought of finally going home that he had been uncharacteristically obtuse when it came to picking up on her distress. To be fair, she hadn't exactly told him, because she couldn't put into words just how much it scared her to be leaving most of their children here. Even if they'd agreed that this was not necessarily a permanent return to Scotland, it wasn't exactly a sedate little Sunday outing, was it? No, it was month after month on a creaky wooden ship that, in Alex's considered opinion, made it over the sea due to sheer luck and nothing else, and who was to know they didn't drown or get boarded by pirates? She swallowed hard and turned her wedding ring round and round, her eyes lost in the flames.

Ever since Luke's letter reached them last April, they'd planned for this. Or, rather, Matthew had planned for this, his eyes acquiring a distant look whenever he thought of his home, the grey, weathered manor in Ayrshire that they had been forced to leave back in 1668 on account of the persecution of men such as he, Covenanters to the core and stubborn enough not to want to give in when the King requested they bow to him and the Anglican Church.

So they had come here, to Maryland, he and Alex with five live children and one in the making, and for the first few months, she'd been worried Matthew would never get over the loss of his home. But that was twenty years ago, and the children that came with them were adults, they had grandchildren and friends, and had built a new life for themselves here. And if Luke hadn't waved that tempting deed at him, Matthew Graham would've been content with what he had.

Alex slumped: she didn't want to go, she wanted to stay

here. Instead, in less than a week, she'd be aboard a ship destined for Edinburgh with her husband, his nephew and their three youngest sons, the latter presently sitting some distance away, discussing the merits of muskets over bow and arrows.

Ian put an arm over her shoulder and pulled her close. "You have to come back."

"Tell your father that," Alex said.

"Oh, I have, Mama. All of us have."

"And what did he say?" Alex asked.

Ian didn't reply at first. "That you'll be back – God willing."

"Hmph," Alex snorted, but was glad all the same.

Once in Providence, Alex succeeded in evading Matthew all the time. Not that hard to do when she could escape into fussing about Ruth, big as a bloated cow in the last month of her pregnancy. When she wasn't with her daughter, she had errands to run, friends to visit, studiously ignoring his silent presence.

At night, she retired before him and pretended to sleep when he came to bed. In the mornings, she flew out of bed on the pretext of helping Ruth – a major lie as their red-headed, capable daughter needed no help in running her household.

Matthew grew more sombre with each passing day, constantly attempting to corner her. Alex was having none of it, so when she saw him coming yet again in her direction, a determined look on his face, she wheeled, deciding then and there that she had to visit the apothecary.

She bumped into Kate Jones on her way into the little shop. As always, Kate looked gorgeous, her silvered blond hair swept into a becoming knot and only nominally covered by a rakish blue hat. Dark brows rose in well plucked arches over dark eyes. The facial skin was albeit somewhat flaky, the mouth surrounded by a fine web of shallow wrinkles, but, all in all, Kate Jones looked younger than her fifty-odd years.

"You have to come back." Kate gave Alex's hand a little squeeze. "This would be quite the dreary place without your occasional visits."

"Mine and Matthew's, right?" Alex said, following

Kate's eyes to where they had locked on her husband, loitering a few yards down the street.

"Well, he's a good dancer, is Matthew, and, yes, I'll miss him too, of course I will – as will Simon."

Alex smiled obliquely. Kate Jones was since some years involved in a relationship with Simon Melville, Matthew's widowed brother-in-law, a relationship Matthew seemed to have difficulties accepting, no matter that he assured Alex he didn't care that Simon was bedding bonny Kate.

Yeah right. Alex would now and then catch Matthew looking at Simon with a displeased expression on his face – and all because once, very many years ago, Matthew had been Kate's lover. It still made Alex swallow down on a rush of jealousy, and she narrowed her eyes, making Kate squirm.

"Alex," Kate sighed, "that was ages ago. And we both know it only happened because of circumstances."

"Huh," Alex said, even if she knew this to be true.

"He's a man – a man that at the time was close to death, a sick and hurting man, holding on to life in whatever way he could."

"Maybe," Alex shrugged, "but I still don't like it."

"No, that's very apparent." Kate laughed. "I suppose I should be flattered, that you still see me as competition for a man so totally yours."

"You think?" Alex smiled, taking in Kate's impeccable exterior with substantially more warmth.

"Alex Graham, that man eats out of your hand. Always has, always will. Now," Kate continued, "if you're hoping for a miracle cure for seasickness, I'm afraid you won't find one here either."

She propelled Alex further into the dark shop, and together they spent the next half-hour discussing potential remedies for greensickness with the knowledgeable wife of the apothecary. In the end, Alex exited with a small twist of paper containing a piece of ginger and some dried mint.

"Probably better to drink myself silly," she grumbled to Kate who laughed, kissed Alex on both cheeks, and hurried off.

"Promise," she called back over her shoulder.

"Promise what?" Alex asked.

"That you'll be back!"

"I promise," Alex said, throwing eye darts at her husband who was still waiting for her. She swivelled on her toes and walked the other way.

She was crossing the small square by the meeting house when she heard a shriek, a loud sound of pain, and without thinking overmuch, she picked up her skirts and hurried over to where three boys were huddled round a fourth.

"He fell, mistress," one of them stuttered. "He just fell. We never did him no harm."

"Hmm," Alex voiced, too experienced a mother to be taken in by the wide round eyes of the three boys. The fourth boy was lying on his back, eyes squished shut, one arm at an odd angle.

"From the tree," one of the other boys said. "He fell off the branch." He pointed at a tree some yards away.

"Oh dear," Alex said, hands examining the hurt boy. A dislocated elbow, no more. She helped the boy to sit, took a firm hold of his forearm, told him it was going to hurt, and pulled, ignoring his high-pitched yelps as she eased the elbow joint back into place. "There," she said with a smile, "as good as new."

The boy snivelled, cradling his arm. He needed some sort of bandage, and seeing as she had nothing else at hand, Alex hiked up her skirts and tore off a piece of her worn petticoats. The boys gawked at the exposed legs, and one of them tittered, but Alex ignored him, concentrating on tying her makeshift bandage into place. Only when the combined shadows fell over her did she realise she had adult company, and she stood up hastily.

"Well, well, if it isn't Mrs Graham," Minister Macpherson said, small eyes travelling from the bandaged boy to Alex and back again.

"Minister Macpherson." She nodded and made as if to pass him by.

He blocked her with his considerable bulk, shaking his

head at her. "And what, pray, were you doing, exposing yourself to these boys?"

"Exposing myself? What are you on about?"

"We saw," the minister's companion said, and at the sound of his voice, Alex started, turning to properly inspect the small, reedy individual.

"Saw what?" Oh my God! Richard Campbell himself, much more worn than when she last saw him fifteen years ago, but as self-inflated as always, his lower jaw jutting out in a way that gave him an uncomfortable resemblance to a human toad – very much in line with his general character, according to Alex.

"How you bared yourself." Richard Campbell sniffed, looking her up and down.

"You have a shallow mind, Mr Campbell," Alex said coldly, "but then that's nothing new, is it? I was helping the boy with his dislocated elbow."

"Oh? And how would you know that it's dislocated? Are you perhaps a physician?"

"I'm the mother of several boys. Anyway, what are you doing here? Last I heard, you were in Boston."

"Called to serve, Mrs Graham," Richard Campbell said, expanding his chest as far as it would go. "Sent here to further strengthen the morals of our little community, what with the upcoming final battle with the papists."

"As tolerant as ever," Alex muttered, looking this her least favourite minister ever up and down.

"As wayward as always," Richard Campbell snapped back, "consorting openly with papist priests, even to the point of having your youngest daughter lured away from the true faith."

Alex's cheeks heated. "When Sarah had need of God, it was a Catholic priest who helped her."

"Had need of God? And why was that? Everyone knows, Mrs Graham, how she brought it on herself. Wilful and disobedient, she was." Minister Macpherson shrugged.

"From her mother," Richard Campbell commented with a sigh, "undisciplined and wayward."

"Get out of my way," Alex hissed. "Get out before—"

"See? I told you. Aggressive and lacking in respect towards her betters." Richard Campbell shook his head. "It is fortunate that she's leaving – no longer our headache."

"My wife has never been your headache, minister," Matthew said from behind them. The ministers jumped, backing away from the forbidding look on Matthew's face. "If anything, she's mine. And I won't have my wife – or my daughter – vilified by two tight-hearted, uneducated boors, be they ministers or not." With that, he bowed, extended his hand to Alex, and without another word led the way towards the harbour.

"If Richard Campbell's here, it almost makes me consider never coming back," Alex joked weakly once they were back at Julian's house. "Almost," she added, before retaking her hand and with a mumbled excuse about seeing to their packing, darting inside.

"Alex," she heard him call, "Alex, we must talk."

Too late, she thought, escaping up the stairs to their little room.

"Will he fly away from me, at sea?" Adam asked, stroking his pet raven over its gleaming back.

"Given that he so far has proved himself quite intelligent, I doubt it." Alex gave her twelve-year-old a brief smile before going back to rolling together clothing as tight as it went prior to packing it into bulging bags.

They were leaving tomorrow, and Alex had retreated into a functional mode, packing, repacking, ticking off items on her long lists, inspecting the two cabins that were to house them for the six- to eight-week journey, counting the coins she was to carry in her pouch, sewing in the ones that were to be hidden in hems.

She kept her distance from Matthew, and instead talked to Ruth and Sarah, repeated her constant admonishments about washing and cleaning your teeth, eating vegetables and drinking milk, until her daughters hugged her into teary silence. She hugged Malcolm, Ian's eldest, she kissed her baby grandchildren, and all the time, Ian hovered in her periphery, and Alex had no idea how she was to survive saying goodbye to him.

And then it was dawn, and the tide was turning, and Alex felt her mask crack wide open as she cried in Ian's arms, unable to let go of this her beloved boy.

"I...oh God!" She swiped at her eyes and attempted a smile. "I love you, Ian Graham, but you already know that, don't you?"

"Aye," he said thickly, "but mothers always love their bairns."

"Yes, we always do. And especially when we have sons like you." Her best friend, the one she whispered all her secrets to, including the ones she couldn't share with Matthew, the stepson she had welcomed into their family as a twelve-year-old and since then loved with the protectiveness of a lioness.

She stood on tiptoe to smooth at his hair, rested her hand against his cheek, and hated Matthew for putting her through this. A long steadying breath, yet another, and she was capable of giving him a blinding smile. "My son, the child of my heart."

Ian didn't speak. He just smiled down at her, a slow smile so like his father's. Alex kissed him one more time and whirled away, convinced her heart was actually breaking, so much did it hurt.

Ian stood apart from his sisters, his eyes never leaving the swiftly disappearing *Diana*. He could still see Mama, the dark cloak fluttering like a banner behind her, and he stretched out his hand, fingers splayed in a last attempt to grab her and hold her here, with him, with them all.

"Carry them safe," he said, "and please God, carry them home, back to me." Especially her.

Chapter 3

Isaac woke slowly. A flicker of an eyelid, a huge yawn and with a groan he sat up. God, no! He scrubbed at his eyes, at his face, he blinked and blinked, and still his surroundings remained the same: a narrow little room very different from his own bedroom. He looked down at the coarse breeches he was wearing, stroked the sleeve of the worn linen shirt, and pressed his mouth closed round an urge to scream.

The painted fountain, Carlos Muñoz... Fucking hell! Isaac shoved his hands in under his legs and sat like that for a long time, drawing in breath after steadying breath. Not that it helped – not much – but his heartbeat dropped, the tightness in his throat receded, and with a loud, protesting rumble, his stomach informed him it was hungry – starving, actually.

Light streamed from the little window, and on the table someone had set a tray containing a piece of bread, a thick wedge of cheese, and watered down wine. Isaac wolfed it all down before moving towards the door.

He wasn't sure if he dared leave the room. What was he to do if he was confronted by someone other than Carlos? He cracked the door open and peered out into the corridor. Empty, very empty, and in the distance, he could hear the sound of men singing, a steady rising and falling of voices that transported him back to his studio and his Gregorian chant music. Not surprising. This was a monastery, and he presumed the brothers were busy with Mass. He had only a vague idea of monastic life, but seemed to recall that there were six or seven services a day – very excessive, in his opinion.

Isaac took a step out onto the cool tile floor. He took another but, when he heard a door bang open close by, scurried back inside, the door still at a crack.

Carlos was coming down the passage, accompanied by a man Isaac supposed to be the abbot, a tall man who walked with his hands clasped behind his back while he listened to what Carlos had to say.

"A relative?" the abbot was saying just as they came up abreast with the door.

Isaac retreated to lie on the bed, his back to the room. He heard the door open. Thick cloth rustled when two cassocks swung into the room, and then the men were leaning over him.

"Hmm, yes," the abbot said in a hushed voice, and Isaac was so glad he had taken Spanish instead of French in school. "Astounding!" the abbot added. "One could almost take you for twins."

"He looks very much like my dead cousin," Carlos said.

"And he's from the colonies, you say?" the abbot asked.

The colonies! Isaac almost sat up to tell the old man that he was absolutely not from any colony. He was from Scotland – 300-odd years in the future. And if you do, you burn, he admonished himself. They'll tie you to a stake and burn you for a witch.

"Yes, from somewhere over there," Carlos replied.

"But he's of the faith, I hope," the abbot said, and Isaac could swear the man was sniffing him as if there was a common scent to all Catholics.

"Of course." Carlos sounded affronted.

"And he does what?"

Carlos' finger touched Isaac's right hand, tapped lightly at his paint-stained fingers. "He paints."

"Ah." The abbot sounded interested. "He's welcome to stay, Brother Carlos. And once he wakes up, bring him to see me."

"Yes, Father," Carlos answered.

The door creaked shut.

"So now I'm related to you and from the colonies." Isaac rolled over and opened his eyes.

"Well, I had to tell them something." Carlos sat down

on the bed and with a relieved grunt, took off his peg. "It chafes in the heat," he explained, and proceeded to jump quite nimbly on one leg to where the pitcher and basin stood, dipping a linen towel in the water with which he first washed his stump then hopped back to clean the cup of the peg. "As per your mother. She is most adamant when it comes to hygiene."

"She is?" Isaac shrugged. "I wouldn't know. I haven't seen her since I was seven."

"She thinks you're dead."

"She does? No, I don't think so."

Carlos shook his head. "Alex Graham would never abandon a child of hers. There must have been a reason. A good reason."

Isaac buried his head in the pillow. He didn't know whether to laugh or cry. A sudden thought struck him, and he opened one eye to squint at Carlos. "You're a priest, right?"

Carlos nodded that yes, he was.

"And if I tell you things, you can't tell anyone else, can you?"

"What you tell me under the seal of confession remains between the two of us and the Lord," Carlos said.

"No matter what?" Isaac was by now sitting up, eyes locked into eyes identical to his own.

A worried crease appeared between Carlos' brows. "Are you a Catholic?"

"Yes," Isaac lied. Not too much of a lie given that his grandmother, Mercedes, was from Spain and definitely Catholic. After all, the poor woman had converted already in the 1470s together with the rest of her family. As always when he thought about Mercedes, which was very rarely, he had to stop himself from bursting out in high, incredulous and panicked laughter. His grandmother a time traveller as was his mother, and now so was he. With a sidelong look at Carlos, he settled himself on the bed, took a deep breath, and began to talk.

Carlos was so pale Isaac worried he was about to faint.

"Born in 1999?" he squeaked. "And – *Dios mío* – Alex was born in 1976?" He shook his head, slowly.

"Just as I told you, a young woman falls through time and lands well over 300 years before her own birth. She meets a man – the love of her life, apparently – and she doesn't even try to return to her own time and her own people. Consequence is one abandoned child, me. Not that I ever truly missed her. I was only three at the time."

Carlos had stopped shaking his head, and was now opening and closing his mouth instead. "Does Matthew know, do you think?"

Isaac nodded. "Of course he does. And I know that for a fact, having met him myself."

"What?" Carlos clutched at his rosary, cross lifted high enough to give the impression he was warding off demons or something.

"I..." Isaac had to clear his throat. "Well, I found a magic painting and fell through it to where Mama was."

There was a sound like that of a horse neighing. Carlos was laughing – or crying – the sound clambering further into the higher registers with every breath he took.

"That's impossible," he said once he'd regained some control.

"And yet..." Isaac spread his hands.

"How can you fall through a painting?" Carlos hiccupped.

"Trust me, you can," Isaac said darkly, and went on to describe the last time he'd seen his mother, a long gone summer when he was seven and had plunged from 2007 to land in 1663.

Carlos moaned, hiding his face in his hands. And when Isaac explained that Alex had found another of those magical paintings and so had been able to help him back into the future, Carlos stumbled to his feet and retreated to stand as far away from Isaac as possible in the little room. Isaac pretended not to notice.

"But who?" Carlos said. "Who can paint such pictures? It must be a witch or a necromancer."

Isaac decided not to share his own obscure talents with

him, and just nodded. He supposed telling the priest about Mercedes would be too much. It was she who had painted the majority of those small blue and green time portals, in her desperate attempts to get back to her time: fifteenth-century Spain.

"And now? How do you come to be here, now?" Carlos asked.

"Another painting." Isaac fiddled with one of his rings. "I have a daughter, she's four." Isaac had to bite his lip to stop it from wobbling. Veronica and Isabelle – would he ever see them again? He raised his face to stare at Carlos. "I want to go back, God, how I want to go back."

"Of course you do, but instead you're shipwrecked here, in a time and place very far from your own." Carlos looked at Isaac for a long time. "And your father? Is he still alive in the future somewhere?" The priest's voice had regained its normal timbre, making him sound remarkably unperturbed.

"My father?" Isaac shook his head. "I've grown up with my adoptive father, my Dad, John, but my real father was a most unsavoury character called Ángel Muñoz who…well, I don't really know what he did to my mother, except for kidnapping her."

"Oh." Carlos swallowed. "A future relative." He gave Isaac a wavering smile. "No wonder Alex in her more unguarded moments regarded me with apprehension."

"Not your descendant at any rate, right?"

"No," Carlos said, "most definitely not."

Once the initial shock had worn off, Carlos bombarded Isaac with questions, and Isaac patiently replied, describing a life that had Carlos making huge eyes. Electrical light, central heating, water at the turn of a tap – luxuries Isaac had always taken for granted, but that had Carlos muttering 'I don't believe it' over and over again. Even more, he gaped when Isaac told him that, in the future, man could fly.

"Fly?" Carlos said. "Up there, in the sky?"

"Mmhmm." Isaac nodded.

Carlos wet his lips. "And God? Have you…have you been able to fly all the way to Heaven?"

Isaac nearly burst out laughing, but the intensity in the other man's eyes stopped him. "No," he said instead, "that high we can't fly."

"Oh. As it should be. Man is not meant to stand before God's magnificence while alive," Carlos said in a relieved tone, and shifted the conversation to more practical issues.

"Your cousin tells me you're a painter," the abbot said to Isaac some time later.

"Yes," Isaac said.

A slight frown appeared on the other man's face, and at Isaac's side, Carlos nudged him.

"Yes, Father," Isaac amended, and the abbot's brow smoothed itself out.

"And what do you paint?" the abbot asked.

Isaac considered this for some moments, trying to recall what kind of pictures were being painted in this day and age. "Family groups, city lives, and, on occasion, a painting or two of the Virgin, Father."

"Hmm," the abbot said, his hand fingering the crucifix that hung round his neck. Under his sharp eyes, Isaac tugged at the sleeve of his borrowed shirt, trying to cover the tattooed Celtic cross that decorated his left forearm.

The abbot placed his hands on his desk and rose, overtopping Isaac by an inch or so. "I've already told your cousin you're welcome to stay. I understand you had a harrowing experience getting here."

"Yes, Father." For now, that was all Isaac could say. He had to talk to Carlos first.

"And while you're here, well then, maybe you can help me with a small matter." The abbot was already leading the way out of his little room. In the open courtyard, he stopped and indicated the wall opposite the entrance, behind the fountain. "I'd like there to be a mural of the Virgin there."

"There?" The artist in Isaac was doubtful. The wall was far too much in shadow, and damp would quickly harm a mural, he explained, suggesting instead the western wall.

"I'm not sure," the abbot said.

Isaac moved closer. "There, and the morning sun will hit it squarely."

The abbot rather liked that, Isaac could see, tilting his head this way and that as he considered the suggested location. He submitted Isaac to an endless stream of questions, and Isaac explained about pigments and plaster, did a cursory structural inspection of his chosen wall, and at the end of all this, the abbot told Isaac to order whatever he needed.

"And how will you depict her?" the abbot asked.

Isaac was stumped. The Virgin Mary was generally depicted with the Holy child or, perhaps like Michelangelo's Pieta, the adult dead Jesus cradled in the despairing mother's arms. Hesitantly, he said as much.

"We have plenty of those." The abbot waved him off. "I want something different."

"Ah." Isaac nodded and creased his brow in frantic thought, dredging through his scant knowledge of religious things. "Maybe when the Holy Spirit came to her?"

The abbot thought about that for some time, and then nodded, twice. "Yes," he said, "I like that." With that, he was off, cassock flaring round his legs to reveal a long undershirt in bleached linen.

"How the fuck did I get myself into this?" Isaac hissed to Carlos once the abbot was out of earshot. "I have no knowledge about all this stuff."

"Stuff?" Carlos gave him a stern look.

"Well, you know, about the Virgin, and how she was impregnated by the Holy Spirit." Isaac made a slight face.

"Haven't you read the Bible?" Carlos asked, and at Isaac's head shake looked horrified. "Ever?"

"Never."

Carlos took him by the arm, towed him up a flight of stairs, and flung open a door to one of the most beautiful rooms Isaac had ever seen.

"Oh!" he exclaimed, stepping reverently into the monastery's library. Smooth arches rose up along the walls, embracing high, narrow windows that flooded the reading carrels with light. Along the further wall, tomes of huge books lay open, displaying a brilliance of colour on vellum that had Isaac knotting his hands round the need to touch them.

The floor was of small, well-worn tiles, a mosaic of blues and whites; the massive bookshelves were of polished wood; and all along the wall ran a line of sconces, each of them decorated with what Isaac assumed to be the statue of a saint.

Isaac gawked, craning back to peer up at the roof, several storeys higher up. So many books... He drew in the smell of dust and leather, smiled a greeting at one of the brothers, who was busy at one of the desks, and followed Carlos to the carrel furthest from the door.

"Here," Carlos said and opened a gigantic Bible, "read and learn."

Isaac peered down at the text. "It's in Latin."

Carlos muttered something about ignorant but after some rooting about and a heated discussion with the librarian, he returned with a Bible in Spanish.

"Thanks," Isaac said, not about to admit he found this very difficult as well. Instead, he bent over the illuminated pages, and, word by word, made his way through the story of how a young girl was chosen to carry the son of God.

Chapter 4

"Lucky you," Alex said, smoothing Samuel's dark hair off his brow. "You're the only one to have inherited my propensity for seasickness." Five days, and the bloody ship was still cavorting over the waves, making Alex's guts flip over at least once an hour.

"Ugh," Samuel said, clutching his basin like a drowning man grips at a floating spar.

"Come on." She helped Samuel to stand. "Let's puke outside instead."

Samuel protested that he didn't think he could move, but Alex was determined, and ten minutes later, they emerged on a windblown, sunny deck that tilted disconcertingly this way and that.

"Close your eyes," Alex said. "Just enjoy the wind on your face."

Samuel gave her a baleful look. "That just makes it worse."

"Well then, keep them open." Alex subsided with her back against one of the masts.

She'd cried for most of the first day. Hiding in her berth, she had cried for most of the second day as well, but when Matthew attempted to talk to her about it, she just waved him away.

She was angry with him for having forced this choice upon her, and even more she was angry with herself for not having had the guts to say that she didn't want to go. It irked her to see Charlie's joy at finally being on his way home; it irritated her that her sons considered this an adventure, no more; but, most of all, it bothered her to see Matthew more or less bolted to the prow, his eyes to the east. She resented that he should be on his way back home while she was on her way from home, and once again she cursed

Luke Graham for his oh so generous but double-edged gift.

A sailor tripped over her, and she pulled her legs in, muttering an apology. Samuel had fallen asleep, curled like a shrimp by her side, and she scanned the deck for her other sons. David was halfway up the rigging, and when he saw her, he grinned and waved. At fifteen, he was tall and fluid, hazel-eyed and dark-haired like his father and most of his brothers, and about to embark on a career as a lawyer – or rather the required studies.

"Better?" he asked, dropping down beside her.

"A bit," Alex hedged. It wasn't as if she was planning on eating anything anytime soon.

David sat down on the other side of Samuel and gave him a worried look. "Is he no better, then?"

"I think he is." Alex smiled at the protective tone. "He's sleeping."

David nodded and reclined back on his arms, studying his brother. Only one year younger, Samuel was of a size with David, but ever since the day eighteen months in the past when a tomahawk had sliced off Samuel's ear and permanently damaged his right shoulder and arm, David had decided his brother needed a constant bodyguard: himself.

"It isn't easy for him," he had explained to Alex, "being back with us. He misses his Indian family, and at times the other lads tease him on account of not having an ear."

"And what do you do then?" Alex had asked.

"I clobber them."

The part about Samuel missing his Indian family was more problematic, and much more infected. Alex looked down at her son, asleep on the deck, and she just had to touch him, reassure herself that he was back with her, that she no longer had to walk around with her heart in shreds as she'd done during those long, unbearable months when her Samuel had been White Bear, adopted son of the Indian chief Qaachow.

Sometimes, she'd admit that she was glad he had been so badly injured in that Indian raid, thereby returning him to her, and then she'd be terribly ashamed that she should wish something so awful on her son. But at times he still donned buckskins and moccasins, disappearing for days, weeks, months, into the forest, driving Alex nuts with fear.

"I just have to," he said when she berated him. "I miss them."

He had at first refused to come with them on this voyage, but neither Matthew nor Alex were about to leave him behind, and so Samuel had spent the last few weeks with his Indian family in a long, protracted goodbye. Alex stroked his cheek. She hoped he'd grow out of them but deep inside she knew he never would.

"Hello there," Alex said to Hugin when he landed on her shoulder. The bird cawed an affectionate greeting and used his beak to inspect her ear for edibles.

"Nope, no luck this time either." She dug about in her petticoat pocket and offered him a dried apricot which he daintily took and flew away with. "He probably doesn't want to hurt my feelings by refusing it," she said to David. "I suspect he just drops it into the sea."

David laughed but agreed: the corbie preferred meat.

"Have you talked to Da?" David asked.

Alex's eyes drifted over to her husband, and despite her mood, her heart filled with pride. Tall and motionless, he was standing several yards away, his short, mostly grey hair ruffled by the wind. The narrow fit of his breeches accentuated his long, strong legs, and the warm day had him wearing only his shirt, the linen snug over the width of his shoulders.

"How talked to him?" she asked. Their children had antennae the size of the Eiffel Tower for any kind of discord between their parents, and apparently David's warning system was telling him all was not well between Matthew and Alex.

"You haven't sat together or walked together much lately," David said.

"Aye," Samuel put in, eyes still closed. "Not for the last month or so."

"And how would you know?" Alex asked. "You weren't home all that much, were you?"

Samuel just shrugged. "We all know. It grows. Every day, the silence between you grows."

"Marriage counsellors, the lot of you," Alex muttered once David and Samuel had finished listing suggestions as to how to begin talking again.

"We'll move Samuel into our cabin," David said, "so you'll have space to be alone and talk."

"You're going to be very uncomfortable, crammed four into one cabin," Alex warned, although she very much liked the idea of having the cabin to themselves.

"Adam isn't that big yet." Samuel grinned and glanced at his youngest brother, standing some distance away.

"And Charlie doesn't sleep there anyway," David added.

"He doesn't?" Alex asked.

"Nay," David said. "He doesn't like being below deck on a boat."

"Ah." Alex nodded and supposed that probably he wouldn't, given his recent adventures. Just to be on a ship must be bringing back a lot of unwelcome memories of weeks spent in chains and shivering in the hold together with his fellow rebels.

"And he's right fearful," Samuel added. "Afraid that mayhap they'll be waiting for him when we land and cart him off to hang."

"Oh." Alex hoped that wouldn't happen. Just in case, she decided this was a matter best discussed with her husband, choosing to ignore her sons' amused glances when she shared this with them.

He'd seen her emerge from their cabin with Samuel in tow, had watched her converse with their sons, and kept a discreet eye on her progress towards him – rather unsteadily, as Alex had yet to find her sea legs. At one point, she overbalanced, near on landing on her knees before regaining her feet. He should go to her, offer her his arm, his hand, but he feared such a gesture would be waved aside, angry blue eyes burning into his.

Matthew shifted on his feet, was washed by a wave of

shame at what he was putting her through – a recurring and discomfiting emotion these last few months. From a distance, he'd watched her grapple with the consequences of a return to Scotland, and they'd had no words to discuss this, with her sidestepping every time he tried to raise the subject – which, he admitted to himself, wasn't often. He exhaled, eyes on the beckoning east. He was overjoyed to be returning home while she so obviously was not, only doing this for him. Behind him, he heard her mutter a curse, and then she was standing beside him, close enough to touch for the first time in weeks.

He listened while she voiced her concerns over Charlie's safety.

"Nay, I don't think you need to worry. That's why he's coming with us to Edinburgh. Besides, how is anyone to know he's a convicted Monmouth rebel?" He gestured in the direction of Charlie, in everything a respectable young man, with no huge R branded on his face.

"Well, that's a relief. Maybe you should tell him."

"I already have," Matthew said, "but he doesn't believe it."

He peeked at her. She looked pale, but was no longer green around the mouth and had gone to some trouble with her appearance this morning, a sure sign, in Matthew's experience, that she was feeling better. But she still avoided eye contact with him and stood with her arms crossed over her chest, making it difficult for him to take her hand.

He did anyway, insisting gently when she at first tried to tug herself free, and they stood side by side holding hands for some time. His thumb travelled in slow circles over her wrist, rediscovering her skin, her pulse. He couldn't recall when last they'd gone so long without each other, and was suffused by a wave of longing for her. Her fingers touched his, they widened and braided themselves around his, and Matthew expelled a long breath. God, how he had missed this!

"I didn't expect it to be so difficult," he said.

"Hmm?"

"To leave the bairns behind."

"You didn't?" Her tone signalled he had to be a right daftie not to understand that.

"Nay, I thought the fact that they're all grown and have families of their own would somehow help. But it didn't, did it?"

"No, it most certainly didn't."

"You wish he hadn't given it to me."

"Yes," Alex replied. "I think this was a terrible choice to have to make."

"But we made the choice together," he pleaded.

Alex kept her eyes on a strangely shaped cloud and nodded. "I couldn't take this opportunity away from you," she said with an edge of recrimination. She gave him a small, insincere smile. "And you're happy, aren't you?"

"And you're not?" Too late, he chided himself, you should have asked her this before, but you were too craven.

"No," she replied. "Not if it's forever." He stood staring towards the east, and she turned so that she looked to the west. "That's where I have my roots now," she said, throwing him a look from under her lashes.

He made a vague sound. She'd change her mind once they were at Hillview, of course she would. Alex disengaged her hand from his, and he could sense that once again she was disappointed in him.

"I've promised, haven't I? If you wish it, we'll go back."

"And if I want to and you don't?" she asked.

"I've promised," he repeated dully.

"Good to know." She stepped away from him and stood waiting until he turned to face her. "I thought you had your roots there as well," she said, nodding towards the west. "That you were tied closer to what you and I have built together than to the home that was yours long before I became part of the picture. But it seems I was wrong." She smiled sadly. "It makes me feel inconsequential, somehow." Once again, she folded her arms over her chest, and once again, Matthew found her hand and took it.

"Come here," he said, and when she shook her head, he drew her towards him until she stood close enough for

40

him to gather her to him, close enough that she should feel the whole length of his body pressed against hers. It helped. Slowly, she relaxed against him. She slipped her arms around him and rubbed her cheek up and down his shirt front while he picked at her hair, drawing out the odd strand to float and curl in the wind. He leaned back to see her face.

"Are you that unhappy to be going back, then?"

"Oh, Matthew..." Alex gave him an exasperated look. "What do you think? Of course I want to see Scotland and Hillview again, but it's just—" She broke off for an instant. "Adam! Get down from there now!" she called, pointing towards the deck.

"You heard your mama," Matthew said, and Adam nearly fell from the rigging at his tone, landing on his knees. Matthew returned his attention to his wife, still warm and soft in his arms. "It's just..." he prompted.

"It's not home. Not to me." It came out very blunt. Nay, he knew that. Where he still had a large piece of himself sunk in Scottish earth, Alex had transplanted entirely to the fertile soil of their new home. "Besides, no matter whether we stay there or go back, I'm going to end up having children on either side of the Atlantic, and I hate that. It leaves me ripped apart to think of leaving David and perhaps even Adam in Scotland."

"Bairns always leave, Alex. They grow away from you – as they must. But it's always you and I. As it was in the beginning, it will be at the end."

"Whoopee...two geriatric, half senile people wandering around on the Scottish moors?"

"Why not? You like walking."

"Not in the rain and the cold," Alex said. "I'm far too old to find that anything but disagreeable."

"The sun always shines in Scotland." Matthew smiled.

"In your dreams, Mr Graham. It's called selective memory."

He laughed, more out of relief to be back to talking to her than due to anything else, and with her hand still in his, led her towards where their sons were sitting on the deck.

★

Not that their recent discussion had resolved anything, but it felt good to hold hands with him, and Alex felt her shoulders relax for the first time in months. She leaned towards him, inhaling his familiar scent, and was about to suggest they repair to their cabin when they were intercepted by their captain.

Jan van Verdhoed was a rakish former pirate turned law-abiding citizen – although Alex knew for a fact he did the odd privateering when opportunities arose. And with his new ship, the *Diane*, he had the wherewithal to take on larger vessels, being the proud owner of eight cannon. As always, Othello the dog padded at his heels, pink tongue a garish contrast to the black and white fur. And behind Othello came one of the other passengers, a young woman Alex had not properly met before.

"Mrs Graham, somewhat improved today?" Captain Jan smiled, showing off teeth that were a startling white in contrast with his coppery skin. A ring in his left ear, a short well-trimmed beard, eyes fringed by long lashes – Captain Jan was a walking poster boy for interracial reproduction, having inherited his Dutch father's height and general features while from his Carib mother came the colour of his skin and eyes, the darkness of hair and beard.

The woman at his heels was his absolute opposite: no more than five feet, with hair so fair it seemed white; large, light blue eyes and skin so pale Alex suspected a regular use of arsenic powder – at least on the exposed chest and neck. Alex waited for the girl to curtsey and introduce herself, but instead the young woman fluttered long, straight lashes at Matthew and wondered in a sultry voice if Mr Graham might have the time to further introduce her to the game of chess later today.

"Maybe," Matthew said, and with some interest, Alex noted the heightened colour that crept up his cheeks.

"I suggest you ask one of our sons instead," Alex said. "They would be more of an age with you."

"Your husband is such an excellent teacher, Mrs Graham,"

the young woman purred. "We've whiled away quite a few hours the last few days, what with you being indisposed."

"Really? Well, now I'm back on my feet, as you can see." And if you try out anymore seductive pouts on my husband, I'll punch you in the mouth, Alex thought.

"This is Nan," the captain introduced.

"Nan? Just Nan?" Alex asked, bending over to give Othello a little scratch behind his ears.

"I need no other name." Nan smiled. "I am quite unforgettable as it is." With that, she dropped them a little curtsey and wandered off in the general direction of Charlie.

"I see you've been adequately entertained while I've been confined to our cabin," Alex said.

"Chess, Alex. No more, no less, no matter what that wee strumpet might insinuate."

The captain laughed. "Nan has been flustered to find her charms so blithely ignored – and not only by your husband but also by me." He pulled his brow together in a slight frown. "I keep well away from prowling she-wolves, and that Nan she is constantly hungry." He leaned towards Matthew. "You best keep an eye on your nephew. It would not do for us to wrest him from certain death in Barbados to lose him to a fortune-seeking courtesan."

"Courtesan?" Alex said.

"Sounds much better than whore." Captain Jan clicked his fingers, and Othello lumbered to his feet, following his master towards the bow.

"I see you giving her chess lessons, and I'll not let you touch me once during this trip," Alex growled.

"Oh aye? And how would you stop me, Mrs Graham?" A hand slid down her back to pinch at her posterior.

"Watch me," she said, but she didn't protest too much when he gripped her by the arm and steered her towards their cabin.

Chapter 5

"She had to make a hasty departure from Jamestown," Matthew said, stretching out full length on the floor of their cabin.

"She did?" Alex poured a generous amount of oil on his back, rubbed her hands warm, and set to work, massaging her way up his back.

"Came aboard just as we were about to sail, and handed over a sizeable purse to the captain for him to take her along," Matthew said, his voice muffled in his arms.

"Well, maybe the wife found out."

"The wife?" Matthew laughed into the blanket below him. "The wives, more likely – as I hear it, wee Nan had quite the circle of eager admirers."

"Clients, not admirers. Or maybe you think she just sat around and served them tea while playing chess." Alex dug her fingers into his buttocks, and he yelped, rearing up from the floor.

"God's truth, woman!"

"No pain, no gain, and it's been a long time." Far too long, she thought, softening her touch to trace the familiar outline of her man. For a man just fifty-eight, Matthew Graham was in very good shape, for all that he only had four toes on his left foot, bore scars after floggings and weapons, and had a disfiguring brand on his buttocks. Strong, long muscles, not an ounce of surplus fat, and when he flipped over, it was quite obvious all other parts were in working order as well. She gave him a deep look, laced with promise, and his hand came up to drift down her neck, over her chest.

"Will you lie with me, sweetest wife?" he whispered.

Alex nodded, and when he rose to his knees, she sat perfectly still as he undressed her, each piece of clothing taking an unreasonably long time to slip off her body and fall to the planking.

"Almost a month," she breathed against his cheek when he laid her back.

"Twenty-four days," he said, brushing his nose against hers. "Too long."

"Much too long," she said.

Samuel and Adam were involved in a card game when Alex emerged on the deck, feeling rejuvenated by the last few hours spent only with Matthew. David was once again clambering like a monkey in the rigging; Matthew strolled over to talk to the captain, and on the opposite side of the ship, Nan was standing close to Charlie, head thrown back to reveal a slender, very long, white neck. She placed a narrow hand on Charlie's sleeve, stood on her toes to whisper something, and just as Charlie was bending his head towards her mouth, a small man exploded from the galley and charged in the direction of Nan, cleaver held high.

"Whore!" he screamed. "Adulterous slut, now you'll finally pay!"

Nan took one look at him, wheeled and darted off, nimble like a weasel as she made for the relative safety of the captain. The cook – well, Alex assumed he was the cook given his stained apron – gained on her, and for a horrifying moment, Alex was certain he intended to bury the cleaver in Nan's head. At the last moment, he twisted the implement, bringing down the flat of the blade with such force that Nan tottered and fell, a slow, graceful collapse onto the deck.

Charlie grabbed the cook from behind, one of the sailors took hold of his arm, and the cleaver fell to the deck.

"For shame, Patrick," Captain Jan said.

"I had to," the cook blubbered, tears and snot mingling on his broad face. "She has to pay."

Alex looked up from where she was examining Nan. "Pay for what?"

The cook blew his nose in his apron and wiped at his face with his sleeve. "I curse the day we found her. How

45

I wish that the sea had swallowed her before we came upon her!"

"Came upon her?" Charlie said.

"She was shipwrecked off the Breton coast," the cook said. "We found her and two other survivors clinging to a rock." He glared down at Nan whose eyelids fluttered open. "So young and sweet, with a silvered tongue and those big blue eyes."

"Well, I never looked at you, did I?" Nan said, groaning as she sat up. "No woman in her right mind would."

Patrick the cook seemed about to burst but, with surprising dignity, turned his back on her and directed himself to his captain.

"She should have been left to die on that rock. All she brought us was misfortune." He scrubbed at his eyes and, after yet another black look in Nan's direction, settled down to tell his story.

"...wait, wait. Brothers? And all of them pirates?" Alex was trying to bring some structure into this complicated story of love and betrayal.

"No, cousins," Patrick repeated patiently. "Black Jack and Red were cousins, and Sean was Red's half-brother. A giant of a man was Sean."

"Is," Nan muttered, and a shudder ran through her. She was sitting with her back to the railings, a handkerchief pressed to her head. Blood was seeping through the linen, staining her hair pink, but all in all, Alex wasn't too concerned: head wounds always bled, and little missy seemed perfectly fine in all other aspects, what with how she kept throwing soulful looks at Matthew, Charlie and the captain. Only Charlie responded, coming over to crouch beside her as if to protect her.

"We'd been sailing together for nearly a decade by then," Patrick continued, "but the day we found her it was only Black Jack on board while Red was off up the coast with Sean to find himself a new vessel."

"Oh, just like that?" Alex asked, and all of them turned irritated eyes at her.

"He was a pirate," Matthew said. "So he didn't stop and ask permission."

Patrick snickered. No, Red had set off in one of their long boats and returned with a hijacked ship, a tidy little sloop that was right fast in the water. But it took him several weeks, and by the time he hailed his cousin and best friend, Black Jack was a lost man, wed to the siren he had dragged from the sea.

"He always called her that," Patrick said. "My siren, he'd say, and she'd go all doe-eyed and pouting."

Nan looked away, muttering that no one had asked her, had they, and suddenly she was married, Black Jack claiming ownership to her.

"How married?" Alex interrupted. "I don't suppose you had a priest aboard, did you?"

"It takes all sorts, ma'am," Patrick replied.

"Ah." Alex swallowed back on a gust of laughter at the image of a cassocked priest with a cutlass in hand.

"The moment she laid eyes on Red, she wanted him. He had that effect on women." Patrick's mouth stretched into an almost imperceptible smile. "A handsome man was Red, with long, bright hair, and eyes the colour of the sea."

"Most poetic, however imprecise," Alex said, and Charlie frowned at her.

Matthew's mouth twitched. It stopped twitching, settling instead into a disapproving gash when Patrick went on to describe how, one night, Black Jack had come into his cabin to find his wife cavorting with his cousin – in his bed. Matthew's eyes strayed to Charlie, that uncomfortable copy of his father, and Alex tightened her hold on his hand.

"He's not Luke," she told him in an undertone. "He can't help it that he looks like him."

Matthew gave a slight nod, and she relaxed her hold. After all these years, it was still a festering sore in Matthew that his first wife had cuckolded him with his brother.

With an effort, she returned her attention to Patrick's tale, at present a long and colourful description of the vengeance Black Jack had wreaked on his cousin for impugning his honour. Charlie shifted on his feet and sneaked a look at Matthew, but his uncle had locked his light eyes on Nan, and she sat frozen in his ice-cold beam.

"He killed him," Patrick ended. "He threw him in the sea, and Red couldn't swim."

"Oh God," Alex said.

"No God," Patrick hissed. "This was her, the hussy, setting cousins up against each other!"

Nan shrank beneath his eyes. "I didn't mean it to end like that."

Patrick spat at her. "At the next port, Black Jack had her taken up on deck. Her chest was bared before us all, and he branded her for the adulteress she is. And then he threw her overboard, as he had done with his cousin, but there, in Port Royal, there were men to succour her as there had been none to save Red.

"He never forgave himself," Patrick sighed. "For the sake of a false woman, he killed his best friend, his cousin, and it gnawed at his insides daily." He raised his face to look at Captain Jan. "I left. I couldn't stand to see him sink deeper and deeper into despair. He was my brother, and there was nothing I could do to save him. But when I saw her on board, earlier today, I just had to make her pay – or try to, at least." With one last burning look at Nan, he shuffled off towards his galley.

"His brother?" Alex said.

Nan nodded. "Black Jack was his eldest brother." She wound her arms tight around her middle. "Sean found me in Jamestown, so I had to run, leave everything I had and flee."

"Oh dear," Alex said, hitching her shoulders.

"Oh dear? It was five years ago, and it wasn't my fault, was it?"

"No, of course not. Red just happened to land in bed with you below him."

"Look!" Nan screeched, took hold of her neckline and tugged, thereby baring a set of small but pert breasts and a branded A. "I've paid enough," she said, covering herself.

"Don't you agree?" Large, luminous eyes turned this way and that, locking at last on Charlie, who nodded and helped her to her feet.

"Of course you have, and I'll kill anyone who says different." Charlie glared at the assembled men as if daring them to disagree.

"Shit," Alex muttered. She'd seen how Charlie's eyes fixed on the ugly A, and with a little sigh, she resigned herself to yet another acrimonious discussion with her nephew.

Just as she'd expected, Charlie came to find her once he'd accompanied poor tottering Nan to her cabin.

"I've told you, haven't I?" Alex said, looking at Charlie with some compassion. "It's too dangerous to try and get them off you." Charlie's eyes narrowed into a stubborn look that made him an exact copy of Ruth, and Alex's breath hitched in her chest with longing.

"I can't walk about like this!" he said, waving his hand in the general direction of his shirt front.

"As long as you're in your shirt, no one sees it," Alex tried.

"But I know! I feel them all the time! Just like she, poor Nan, does."

"They'll fade," Alex said. "With time, they will fade."

He clearly didn't believe her, his thick brows coming down to form a bristling line of red over green eyes.

"What will my father say?" he half groaned.

"He'll say you're lucky – it could have been someone swiped your nose off instead." Oops, not the right thing to say given that Luke had gone noseless through most of his adult life, courtesy of a close encounter with an enraged Matthew and a knife. Most well-deserved, in Alex's opinion, given what Luke had done to Matthew.

If possible, Charlie's brows sank even lower. Alex mumbled an apology, and beckoned for him to follow her into her cabin.

"They're too big," she said, as she always did, inspecting the four-inch branded S and B that decorated his chest. The S bore signs of self-inflicted damage, but both letters were clearly visible against the pale skin on Charlie's torso.

"I could burn them off," Charlie suggested – he always did. "Or flay the skin off." He gritted his teeth.

"No, you can't." She found a stone jar of goose grease ointment, but Charlie shook his head.

"I don't need that. I need someone with the courage to excise these goddamn brands once and for all!"

"Not me. I'm sorry, Charlie, but I'm not taking any chances, okay?"

"No, not okay," he replied, and crashed out of the cabin. With a muttered curse, she followed him outside, finding Matthew by the railings.

"I've told him a thousand times! To burn them off is to invite infection and all other kind of nasty stuff." She glowered over to where Charlie was standing as far away as was possible on a ship no more than 140 feet or so, glowering back at her. "I just hope he doesn't try something silly but if he does, he can bloody well salve it himself." She turned away to look out across the sea instead. "Well, in some weeks, we'll turn him over into the tender and loving care of his father."

"Aye." Matthew's jaw worked; his fists clenched and unclenched. He looked down at her, eyes shifting in green through gold in the low afternoon sun. "What do I say – do – when I meet Luke?"

"Pretend it's a stranger. After all, he is, isn't he? It's more than twenty years since you saw him last."

Matthew scowled. "I dare say I'll recognise him."

"Well, I don't know. Maybe he's fat and bald."

"Bald?" Matthew began to laugh and gave her a quick hug. "Aye, mayhap he is." He chuckled and went over to talk some sense into his nephew.

Chapter 6

...Today we woke at two (we always do), stumbled off to hear matins, slept some more, and then it was up at dawn, this time for prime. It's always up at dawn here – unless you're lying at death's door, you're expected to look bright and chirpy from five thirty and onwards. Otherwise, nothing much has changed since yesterday – oh yes, I've actually managed a full body wash in hot water and was even able to wrangle a clean shirt from Brother Luís. Everyone stinks, Dad. It's like walking around with a jockstrap over your nose – okay, okay, perhaps an exaggeration, but you get the general picture, don't you? And the food... I had no idea beans could be served under so many guises.

Isaac was taken over by this new life of his, lulled into a daze by the combined effect of the strictly regulated hours of monastic life and the unfamiliarity of it all. He rose with the others for services, sat through Mass, mumbled along in prayers he had never heard before, listened with closed eyes to the soothing chanting of the choir, and in between these religious activities, he divided his time evenly between the library and the mural. Not that he wanted to – he wanted to be left alone to mope in bed – but Carlos wouldn't let him.

"I can't paint in full sunlight," he explained to the abbot. "The pigments flake if they dry too fast." So he painted in the afternoons and read in the mornings. Well, read was perhaps an exaggeration: it was more looking at the pictures, his long, dexterous fingers turning pages in books the size of a briefcase but twice as thick at times.

"We have a famous library." The abbot beamed when Isaac expressed how impressed he was. "Some of these books are rarities. Most of them donated, like this one." He produced an old book, dusty and quite thin. "Bartolomé de las Casas, his history of the destruction of the New World."

"Oh," Isaac said, although he had never heard of the writer in question.

"A Dominican friar," the abbot continued with some pride, "and his voice actually did stop some of the maltreatment of the poor natives."

"Oh," Isaac repeated.

The abbot handed him the book. "Read it. It should interest you, seeing as you're from over there somewhere."

"Ehh," Isaac said, but the abbot was already swishing down the central aisle of the library, making for the door. Isaac sighed. Knowing the abbot, he'd be back in a couple of days to interrogate him on the book, and with a face, Isaac added it to the pile he had on his carrel. At least his Spanish was improving at an impressive pace.

It was the afternoons that he lived for: the moments when he stood and mixed his paints and tried to pull from his mind an image that would paint him back home. He tested by painting small swirls of blue and green, but his brain refused to cooperate.

Isaac flung the brushes away from him. When he truly needed to paint himself through time, his talent seemed lost, and the small funnels he created were flat and one-dimensional, not the heaving, living thing that was time caught on canvas. Maybe that was why, perhaps painting on a whitewashed wall precluded acquiring the depth he needed. But he had canvas and paint, and Carlos wouldn't mind if he painted in the room they shared. Isaac muffled a nervous laugh. He probably would mind if Isaac disintegrated before Carlos' eyes.

Later, Isaac decided. He'd think about all this weird stuff later. Instead, he concentrated on the depiction of the ecstasy of a young girl taken over by the Holy Ghost. He unsnapped his wristwatch and set it on a small stool before losing himself in the creation of a dark, lustrous eye.

"You're very good," Carlos said, startling Isaac out of a pleasant daydream in which he was back in his studio.

Isaac hitched his shoulders. So far, he wasn't that

impressed, even if by now the flowing lines of what would be skirts and hair were beginning to take shape, as was the face. The light was going, and Isaac began to pack away his pigments and oils. With a huge yawn, he stretched and turned to Carlos only to find the priest stiff like a board beside him.

"What?" Isaac said.

In response, Carlos hunched together and, with a hissed 'hurry', led Isaac at a run from the courtyard.

"Wait! My watch!" Isaac wheeled and ran back towards the fountain, and smacked straight into the man presently retrieving his Rolex from the stool. "That's mine," Isaac said, snatching it out of the stranger's hand. His mouth dried up completely when the man turned to face him, and his own shock was clearly mirrored in the older man's face.

"¿Ángel? ¿Mi hijo?" the man stuttered, taking a step towards Isaac. An older copy of himself, this had to be Raúl Muñoz, the man who had taken Carlos in as a baby and hastily turned him over into the keeping of the monks in an attempt to bury the shame of having to raise his priest brother's bastard.

"No," Isaac said, and since he had no idea what to say to this man, he fled.

"Raúl Muñoz is a generous patron of this order," the abbot reprimanded Isaac later, "and I won't have him treated with anything but the utmost courtesy."

"I was in a hurry, Father," Isaac said, hating having to stand subservient before the seated abbot.

"No excuse! And according to Don Raúl, you rushed away without even bidding him a good day! He's most upset, and let me remind you, he's the patriarch of your family here in Seville, and you must accord him due respect."

"I must? I don't know the man from Adam, and, as far as I know, he's never done anything for me." Quite true, as Don Raúl was floating dust by the time Isaac had been born. The only thing the rich, well-dressed man had achieved was to sire a line that ultimately would result in Isaac, but that wasn't something Isaac felt particularly grateful for. The abbot stared at Isaac, his fingers drumming slowly but steadily against his desktop. "You'll apologise to him tomorrow, and as he has requested you spend time with him, well, so you will." With a wave of his hand, the abbot dismissed him, and to Isaac's own surprise, he obediently left.

"You'll have to do as he says," Carlos said. "The abbot has quite the temper on him, and should you question his authority, you may find yourself scourged or thrown out on your ear." He gnawed at his lip. "Uncle Raúl will never believe our present story, and should he begin to dig, God knows what he'll unearth." Carlos shivered. "He has contacts everywhere, even in the Inquisition, and he'll not hesitate to throw you to the wolves if he considers it necessary."

"What?" Isaac squeaked.

Carlos nodded and deflated further. Isaac would break in less than half an hour, he said morosely, just as he himself would. And should it come out that Isaac was from another time and that Carlos had harboured him knowingly...

"They'll burn us both," Carlos said.

Isaac's toes curled in reaction to what those potential flames would feel like. "So what do we do?"

"We lie."

Don Raúl opened his mouth, closed it, opened it again, and snapped it shut, looking from Carlos to Isaac and back again with a flare of desperation in his eyes.

"Half-brothers?" he croaked, digging into his velvet sleeve to produce a handkerchief.

"I'm afraid so," Carlos said.

"And his mother?" Raúl waved his hand at Isaac. "Yet another court whore?"

Isaac bristled, but Carlos gave him a warning look.

"I don't think she'd agree," Carlos said. "She's married since many years back."

"To sleep with a priest!" Don Raúl spat.

"Maybe she didn't know," Isaac said, "or maybe she didn't want to."

If possible, Don Raúl shifted to an even paler hue, and his fingers groped for his rosary. Hypocrite, Isaac thought, to sit there and pretend aversion at your brother's potential sins when, according to Carlos, you've littered the countryside with your bastards.

"I chose not to tell the abbot," Carlos said. "I thought you'd prefer it that way. So now, Isaac is a second or third cousin, great-grandson to your grandfather's brother who spent some time on Hispaniola."

Don Raúl mopped his brow and stuffed his handkerchief back out of sight. "That was wise. It's enough to have one bastard sired by a priest in the family."

Carlos flushed but held his tongue.

"And why are you here?" Don Raúl swung his head to glare at Isaac. "Why didn't you stay, over there?"

"I'm a painter," Isaac said, "and so I decided to come here and paint. Not remain in obscurity forever."

"Obscurity?" Don Raúl laughed. "Are you so good that you think to lift yourself into the public view here? Here, where we have Herrera and Zurbarán? Murillo?"

"Yes." How presumptuous. Isaac swallowed. Could he produce something of the stark brilliance of Zurbarán? His fingers twitched, electricity jolted through his arm, and he folded his hand around an imaginary brush. Yes, he could. In his fingers lived the talent to create flesh out of pink and grey and green, to anchor the sunbeams forever to his work, and capture life between breaths.

Don Raúl snorted and got to his feet. "Well, we shall see." With a curt nod, he walked away, his polished boots echoing on the tiled floors.

"Asshole," Isaac muttered, grinning when Carlos laughed.

It rained the next day, and after having spent a fruitless morning attempting to recreate a blue and green time funnel on a small piece of canvas with no success whatsoever, Isaac slouched off to the library.

On the top of the pile was the book the abbot had given him, and, with a sigh, Isaac opened it, trying to read his way through convoluted sentences in archaic Spanish that told of death and strife in the Spanish colonies. He gave up on the text and was studying the detailed pictures when Carlos came to find him.

"I thought you might enjoy seeing the city of Seville," Carlos said. "It's three weeks and more since you arrived, and however an enchanting place the monastery is, you must find it boring."

"Boring?" Not quite the word Isaac would use, not when he was stuck in a time not his own without a clue as to how to get back. Terrifying would be a better description. All the same, he readily agreed to go, and a few minutes later, they stepped outside the gates.

Isaac blinked at his surroundings. Straight ahead, he could make out the imposing finger of the Giralda, the former minaret converted into the cathedral's bell tower, and he was standing on a cobbled road filmed with mud after a full day's rain. Not only mud, he noted with distaste when they turned right and made off in the direction of the river. He hurried after Carlos, and soon they were by the river, leaning over the parapet of the Puente de Triana.

"We live over there," Carlos gestured downriver, "close to the Royal Palace, the Alcázar."

"We?"

"They, my uncle and cousins." Carlos frowned at the waters swirling by beneath them. "It must have rained heavily to the north, and if it continues, it will flood. The abbot is already having the cellars emptied."

"That happens a lot?" Isaac asked, fascinated by the muddy waters of the Guadalquivir.

"Far too often."

At first, they strolled along the river, enjoying the afternoon sun that had broken through the rain clouds, but soon they were walking through narrow alleys and winding cobblestone streets. Isaac gawked at girls in long, sweeping skirts and faces hidden by hats and mantillas, at urchins in threadbare clothing that ran in packs, and when they reached the sunlit square by the cathedral, he halted. So many people…Men in rich, dark clothing and cloaks, sometimes accompanied by women but far more often alone. Priests, nuns, scruffy street vendors, beggars, beggars, beggars, and everywhere children. A woman with her hair uncovered smiled invitingly at Isaac. Carlos barked something at her and hurried them along, nodding at a few acquaintances, and then they were back in the shade of the buildings.

"This used to be the *Judería*," Carlos said as they walked deeper into a warren of small streets, courtyards and imposing houses.

"*Judería*?"

"The Jewish quarter, before they left."

"Left? They were expelled," Isaac said, "and avaricious Christians stood by to pick up what they were forced to leave behind."

"Hmm…well, yes. All for the better, given that they refused to embrace the single True Faith."

Isaac chose to remain silent, concentrating on his surroundings. It struck him that this was where Mercedes had been born. Here, among these somnolent courtyards, she had lived out her childhood, first as a Jewess, then as a convert to Catholicism. It must have looked more or less the same 200 years ago, he supposed, staring at the whitewashed walls, the flowers and the glimpsed courtyards, havens of green and shade that beckoned from behind half open doors.

Isaac had never met Mercedes, nor had they spoken much about her at home – not that strange, given the sheer impossibility of her life – but as he walked these ancient streets, Isaac felt an affinity with his unknown grandmother, a painter like him, a reluctant time traveller like him. What had her life been like, he wondered, thrown back and forth through time in her repeated efforts to get back home?

Carlos came to an abrupt stop. "There," he said, and Isaac took in a house in ochre with iron-wrought railings at the gate and windows. The house was three storeys high but narrow, forced into a corner of the small square they were standing in. "The family home. It used to belong to

Hector Olivares," Carlos continued. "He was given it by the Catholic Kings in recognition of his diligence in the service of the Church." He made a face and crossed himself.

"Hector Olivares?" Isaac croaked.

Carlos looked at him strangely. "You know of him?"

"No, no," Isaac assured him, "I just got something stuck in my throat." But he did know of him. He gave Carlos a cautious look out of the corner of his eye, bursting with the need to tell someone.

"For some reason, Hector Olivares gave the house to one Juan Sánchez, and his granddaughter married a Muñoz, and so the house came to us." For an instant, Carlos' brow darkened. "But it came at a price, unfortunately. Hector Olivares died at the stake, and with him died his accomplice, Juan Sánchez's grandmother. Even worse, the woman was a *Marrana*, a Jewish convert, and both her father and her sister burnt at the stake for false conversion."

What? Isaac steadied himself against the wall. Such coincidences don't exist, he told himself. No way can he be talking about Mercedes. Or can he? He had to squat, place a hand on the ground to stop the world from spinning round him.

"Are you alright?" Carlos crouched beside him.

"Dizzy. The sun, I suppose."

Carlos helped him up and motioned towards the courtyard. "Plenty of shade there."

"So why did Hector Olivares end up burning to death? I thought you said he was a servant of the church," Isaac said, standing in the centre of the shaded patio – a restful place with a sprawling fig tree on the southern wall and a rose that exploded in deep dark reds clambering through the screens of the first-floor gallery. After a full day of rain, the air was fresh and full of moisture, making Isaac's hair curl wildly – just like Carlos'.

Carlos looked about with a slight frown, his voice dropping to a whisper. "We don't talk about it."

"Why not?"

"The shame!" Carlos hissed.

"Shame? Why would you feel shame?"

Carlos eyed Isaac from under his brows. "It's an incredible story – ungodly, some would say."

"Try me," Isaac said drily. "It can't be more incredible than my own story, can it?"

"It is much, much worse!" Carlos chewed at his lip for some moments before exhaling, loudly. "Well, since you're family, I suppose you're entitled to hear it." He sat down on a stone bench and beckoned for Isaac to do the same. "They disappeared, the two of them, Hector and his Jewish mistress."

"Mistress?"

"That's what they say, that they were lovers, but who knows?" Carlos shrugged. "There was much talk of sorcery, and even more so when very many years later the Jewess returned, landing one evening in her grandson's house. She slept like the dead, desiccated and covered in wrinkled skin as dark as that of a prune. Her grandson kept her return a secret – well, he tried to. And then Hector returned as well, a frail and badly burnt shell of a man that screamed in constant pain. His family tried to hide him too, but it is difficult to hide a man who wails like a demented wolf through the days, and the priests decided he was possessed – by the devil."

"Or maybe he was in pain," Isaac said.

"He was over a hundred years old! He should have been dead long before – as should she, the witch."

"Witch?"

"What else do you call a woman who sleeps for close to two decades and then one day wakes up, screaming in an incomprehensible language, calling for a magus?"

Not magus, Isaac thought. She'd been calling for Magnus, for her husband, his grandfather.

Carlos crossed himself. "My ancestor was appalled when he discovered his new bride's family was hiding this living corpse – even more when he understood the old crone was a former associate of Olivares – so he informed the Inquisition."

"How nice of him," Isaac said.

The sarcasm was lost on Carlos who gave Isaac a serious look. "Nice? He was doing his duty by the Holy Church, as any good Christian should. Anyway, the Inquisition decided to act, and despite their apparent frailty, the Jewess and Olivares were taken in for questioning, accused of sorcery – rightly so, for how else to explain their abnormally long lives, their disappearance? After weeks of interrogation, they admitted they were the creatures of the devil, and the Tribunal condemned them to death."

"Good for them," Isaac muttered, feeling rather sick.

"You shall not suffer a witch to live," Carlos said. "They had to die, their evil purified by fire."

"How utterly primitive."

"Do you want me to go on?" Carlos sounded angry. Isaac waved for him to continue. "He had to be carried to the stake, incapable of walking on his own, and as to the woman, she might have been old like Methuselah but it took four men to drag her to the stake and fetter her to it."

"Oh God." Isaac needed a whisky. Not about to happen.

Carlos lowered his voice. "They held hands when the kindling was lit. There was a rush of white heat, a burst of fire, and just like that they were gone, pulverized to ashes. No agonised screaming, no suffering. The devil claiming their own, right?"

"The devil?" Isaac tried to laugh. "There's no such thing as the devil."

"How would you know?" Carlos crossed himself. "Anyway, that's how she died, my Jewish ancestress, and you can imagine just how bitterly my great-grandfather regretted having married Juana Sánchez, polluted not only by her Jewish blood but now also by the taint of sorcery."

"What happened to her?" Isaac asked.

"To Juana? She took the veil. She was made to see that was the best – for her, and for her son." Carlos grinned lopsidedly. "My family has a long tradition of using the Church to hide away its least desirable members."

"Ah." Isaac regarded a lizard darting up the shadowed

wall. "So what was her name?" Not that he needed any confirmation, but he needed to hear Carlos say it out loud.

"Hmm?"

"Your Jewish ancestress – surely you know her name?"

"No, we don't. All we know is that her father was a Benito Gutiérrez."

Isaac turned to look Carlos full in the face. "That wasn't his name. His real name was Benjamin ben Isaac, and his daughter was Ruth until she was baptised Mercedes."

"How do you know?" Carlos asked in a breathless voice.

"Because she's my grandmother," Isaac said, and Carlos looked about to faint – a most understandable reaction. Any further conversation was cut short by the arrival of Don Raúl, who seemed less than thrilled to find them in his patio.

...He's quite the character, actually. Not the bloke you'd share your Friday pint with, but full of himself and therefore quite amusing, in an unintentional way. We stayed there for some hours, and, with wine, Raúl mellowed, telling us anecdotes of his childhood, of his business life. It would seem that of his three sons one is dead – for espionage, no less – one is set up to take over the family business, and the youngest, confusingly also called Carlos, is at present in Madrid. From what I hear, not meeting them is no major loss.

We walked back in absolute silence, and, unless Carlos asks, I don't intend telling him about Mercedes – it sort of makes an incredible tale, doesn't it? Shit, Dad, I'm not even sure why I'm writing this. Maybe to remind myself that you're still there, somewhere. But you're not, are you? Strictly speaking, as I write this, you don't exist, and neither do I, and yet I do, and God, Dad, I want to go home! Why, oh why did I paint that fucking fountain?

Chapter 7

The last days on the *Diane* were interminable. Matthew counted the minutes, nay seconds, he pestered Captain Jan for estimates of their time of arrival, and in between he stood in the bow, willing the land of his birth to rise before him. But, not being blind, he couldn't help noting the one-sided courtship being played out on deck, with Charlie a constant fawning presence at Nan's side. It made him frown, the way his nephew gawked at the lass, and even more when the wee baggage tossed her head and pouted, sending long simpering looks in his, Matthew's, direction instead.

There was no question the lass was right bonny with her heart-shaped face and fine, delicate features. And the size of her, like cupping an egg, he supposed, so fragile, so breakable. He threw Nan a considering look: not his type of woman, he liked them round and strong, but Nan was strangely alluring somehow. An elbow dug into his side, making him redirect his eyes.

"Not the daughter-in-law Luke is hoping for," Alex said. "She has him eating out of her hand like a trained pigeon."

Matthew smiled at the likeness. Charlie might resemble a lot of things, but decidedly not a rotund pigeon. "Daughter-in-law? He's but dallying with a pretty lass – the only lass on the ship."

"You think? He's hooked, falling over his own feet in his eagerness to adore sweet Nan. It's probably on account of her brand."

"What?" Matthew was surprised.

"Well, he's so self-conscious about his own brands that meeting someone equally disfigured fills him with relief."

"She was branded as a consequence of her actions. That wee hussy deserves her A, but Charlie didn't deserve it."

"Of course he did," Alex said. "In the eyes of the law, he deserved much more than that. He was condemned to die as a slave." He scowled, and Alex put a hand on his sleeve. "You know I don't agree, but let's face it. If she deserved the A then he deserves a huge R somewhere – R as in rebel." She snuggled in against his side, and together they stared out towards the west where the sun was setting in streaks of orange and reds, adorning the sea with shimmering golden bands.

"He's falling in love with her," she said.

"He's hoping to bed her, no more."

Alex laughed softly. "Wanna bet?"

Two days later, Matthew stood surrounded by wife and sons as Captain Jan guided the *Diane* in towards Leith.

"Welcome to Scotland," Alex said, and turned to smile at their sons who were looking at the emerging darker grey in a day made entirely grey by a combination of wet fog and no wind. But it smelled of home, of Highland mists, and peat fires and bogs, and Matthew would gladly have dived off the ship to swim the last stretch, so eager was he to stand anew on the granite ground of his homeland.

"It's not at its best," Matthew said to his lads, inhaling the fresh June air.

"Oh yes, it is," Alex replied.

Matthew took her hand in his, and they were as silent during the approach to land as they had been the day twenty years ago when they had stood on the poop deck and watched their homeland recede and finally drop below the horizon.

The breeze picked up, the veils of mist were torn apart, and when the *Diane* finally berthed, Edinburgh had reappeared before them, the castle atop its crag a brooding presence to the right.

"It's wet," Adam said. Hugin ruffled up his feathers and shrank closer to Adam's head and the protection of his hat.

"And grey," Samuel added.

"That's because of the rain, lad." Matthew smiled down

at him. "Once the sun comes out, you'll see how green it is."

"If the sun comes out," Alex muttered.

"Alex," Matthew began, but was distracted by the lonely figure standing to the side on the quay.

Vaguely, he registered Alex leaning against him, but Matthew wasn't really aware of her because there, in a cloak that fluttered in the wind, the weak light glinting off his silver nose, stood Luke.

"So he received the message then," Alex said.

Charlie had written a note to his father when the *Diane* anchored in Falmouth appraising him of their expected arrival in Edinburgh. It had been all they could do to keep him from disembarking there, and only Matthew's harsh reminder that in England he was still a convicted rebel, had made Charlie sullenly remain aboard.

"Father! Father!" Charlie yelled, swiping off his hat to wave it in the air. In response, Luke spread his arms wide, and the dark red silk lining of his cloak became visible.

He looked disturbingly rich. From the cut of his long coat to his silk stockings and silver-buckled shoes, Luke Graham appeared every inch the man of worth Matthew knew him to be, and it irked him that a man so lacking in morals – at least when it came to his brother – should have such success in life as to be able to dress like a nobleman. Lace dripped off cuff and neck, gold decorated his chest and fingers. The ostrich plume in his hat had been dyed a dark purple, the waistcoat glittered like amethysts in the sun, and Matthew heard his sons draw breath, a hushed murmur of admiration as they took in this unknown but dashing uncle.

"Quite the peacock," Alex said.

If his sons were stunned by the apparition that was their uncle, Nan's reaction was far more worldly-wise, those big eyes wandering up and down Luke repeatedly. With a little smile, she sauntered over to where Charlie was still leaping up and down with joy.

"She just fell in love as well," Alex whispered to Matthew. "But not with him, with his money."

Matthew frowned. Wee Nan placed her hand on Charlie's

sleeve and said something that made him nod, grinning down at her as if he'd lost his wits. Charlie took Nan's hand and gave it a little squeeze, and bent forward to whisper something in her ear before reverting to waving at his father.

"Luke's headache, not ours." Alex's breath tickled his cheek.

"He doesn't even know the lass exists," Matthew replied.

"So we tell him and leave it at that," Alex said, and then it was time to disembark.

There was no stopping Charlie. In a welter of long limbs, he near on fell down the gangway, stumbled for a few paces, and fell into Luke's receiving arms. For a long time, they clung to each other, their voices low murmurs, no more. Luke stood back, but his hands remained on his son's arms, refusing to relinquish their hold on him. And Charlie was weeping and laughing, he was dancing on the spot, while Luke's hands seemed soldered to the live flesh of his son.

Matthew took his time ensuring his family and belongings were properly landed, hoping that Luke would leave in his haste to carry Charlie off somewhere to dine and rest. But he didn't, and Matthew straightened up, sharing a quick look with his wife before striding over to greet his brother amicably for the first time in thirty-five years.

He stopped some yards away, having no inkling as to what to say to the man standing before him. Still very much Luke, with hair that was now a lighter shade of its original vibrant deep red, streaked liberally with whites and greys. The eyes that regarded him warily were as green as they had always been, but the face was much, much older.

Matthew bit back on a surprised gasp. He'd shaved that morning, and was familiar enough with his own reflection to know that he looked younger than his brother, despite being five years his senior. Mayhap Alex was right when she insisted they eat greens and fruit, because when he saw himself mirrored in his brother's eyes, Matthew saw a strong and vigorous man, still in his prime, while Luke, although as yet tall and strong, was a man with a foot on the last incline of life.

It pleased him that Luke should be so taken aback, eyes flying repeatedly over him.

"You look well," Luke said.

"So do you," Matthew replied, and it wasn't a lie: it was just that he himself looked so much better.

They studied each other some more, and Matthew scuffed at the ground with his toe while Luke fidgeted with his cravat. Should he extend a hand, attempt a handshake or a half-hearted hug? But no, he couldn't countenance such, so Matthew kept his hands clasped behind his back.

Luke shuffled his feet. "I…" he began, eyes bright with unshed tears. He cleared his throat. "I can never thank you enough. Never. My son, wrenched from certain death by you." His voice broke, his eyes overflowing.

"Aye well, he's a good lad," Matthew said, looking at anything but his brother.

"So changed." Luke nodded in the direction of Charlie who was conversing with Nan. Luke's gaze lingered on Nan, mouth compressing as he studied the lass. "Who's that?"

"That, brother, is Nan."

"A woman with designs on your son – or rather your money," Alex said, coming over to join them.

Luke swivelled on his toes to greet her, a hissing sound escaping him as he stared at her. Ah yes, Matthew had forgotten just how alike his Alex and Margaret were, and from the way Luke was studying Alex, it was clear Luke was most disconcerted by this living reminder of his dead wife.

Alex made no effort to smile. Instead, dark blue eyes bored into Luke, conveying that she had neither forgotten nor forgiven the iniquities Luke had put his brother through. It amused Matthew to see how Luke shifted under the weight of her stare, one hand straying to his silver nose. Alex gave him a sarcastic smile, one eyebrow shooting up in ridicule – a lost nose was nothing in comparison to all those lost years.

Luke flushed. He flicked at some lint on his waistcoat, cleared his throat, but something to the right of Alex made his mouth snap shut. Matthew followed his eyes. Two men, converging upon them, and from the way they were dressed, Matthew concluded they were soldiers of some sort – officers, even, given their sashes and swords.

"I must…" Luke muttered, retreating a couple of paces. "Charlie, they might be after Charlie."

"You think?" Alex turned to frown at the men.

"Go," Matthew said, his eyes never leaving the approaching men.

"Mistress," the older of the two men said once they got close enough. He inclined his head in a polite nod, and Alex curtsied back. "And you are?" the man asked Matthew.

"Who wants to know?" Matthew said.

The younger man looked Matthew up and down. "Times are a trifle uncertain, and it is the mayor's wish that all newcomers be interrogated."

"Newcomers?" On purpose, Matthew slipped back into a heavy brogue, but the elder of the two just shook his head.

"You're from the colonies. So what brings you back?"

"Business matters," Matthew said. "I have land here."

"Ah. And the pistols?" The younger man pointed at the polished butt visible just to the right of Matthew's belt buckle.

"As you said, gentlemen, the times are restive, and I have wife and bairns to protect."

"Bairns? Strapping lads, rather." The older man frowned. "I need your names, sir."

Reluctantly, Matthew told him, giving him their destination as well.

"Cumnock?" The younger man straightened up. "You're not one of those Covenanters, are you? We've had our bellyful of such."

Matthew looked away.

"Well, are you?" the older man said.

"I've come to see to my lands," Matthew said. "Nothing more, nothing less."

"That is not what we asked, is it?" The younger man crowded Matthew backwards.

"Now, now," his companion said, "give the man room to answer."

"I am of the Scottish Kirk," Matthew said stiffly,

"A Covenanter, then." The young man spat before Matthew's feet. "A plague on you, and all your sort."

Matthew was sorely tempted to clap him over the head, but Alex was leaning heavily on his right arm, and from the expectant expression on the man's face, Matthew could see he was spoiling for a fight. For all that Matthew was lean and fit, the officer was in glowing health, with arms as thick as Matthew's thighs so with an effort, Matthew composed himself.

"No longer," Matthew said. "I may have been, in my youth, but now I keep my own counsel when it comes to matters of faith."

"Hmm." The older man pursed his mouth. "We'll be keeping an eye on you, Master Graham. The King does not hold with rebellious subjects." With that, they walked off, and Matthew was left gritting his teeth.

It took the lustre out of his homecoming, this abrupt recall to a reality where the people of his faith were defined as rebels, dangerous elements best contained by force or deportation. On the long trudge from Leith, he said scarcely a word to his family, and it was only once they had passed the Nor Loch and entered the city proper that some of his buoyancy returned to him.

"He looked old," Matthew said some hours later, unable to keep a satisfied tone out of his voice.

"Who?" Alex said, sinking deeper into the hip bath. The room they'd taken was full of sleeping lads on pallets, but she had insisted on taking a bath, curtly informing Matthew that as far as she knew, all her sons had seen her naked before and weren't about to die of shock.

"Luke."

"Yes, he did, didn't he?" she said, lathering her hair. "He does, however, look very wealthy."

"Let me," Matthew said, sinking his fingers into her

scalp. "He is wealthy, and for all that he spent a year in house arrest, it hasn't damaged his standing in court over much."

"How do you know?" Alex asked.

"I'm not entirely without contacts, even if quite a few of my erstwhile companions are dead by now." Matthew rinsed her hair, handed her a couple of towels, and sat on the bed to watch her step out of the tub, pink and glowing. "The King was right in placing him under house arrest." This was information he had pieced together from several letters arriving not only from London but also from Edinburgh and even from Amsterdam. It would seem Luke had very much on purpose sent Charlie to Amsterdam, hoping the lad would become a well-known face at the court of William of Orange. Unfortunately, he had been dazzled by the Duke of Monmouth instead, thereby becoming an enthusiastic participant in the rebellion three years hence that nearly cost Charlie his life.

"You think?" Alex tugged a clean shift over her head and came to join him on the bed.

"Aye, he's politically astute, my wee brother, and just like you, he doesn't see the English taking to a line of Catholic kings."

"Well, to be entirely honest, I know, don't I? I know James will be out on his ear shortly." She hunted about for her comb. "It's just that I can't recall exactly when. I should have paid more attention in history class."

"When do we leave for Hillview?" she asked some while later, wrenching Matthew out of private musings as to how close to the fire his brother might be flying.

"In some days. I have deeds to notarise, and then we must find ourselves horses and such."

"Some days?" Alex gave him a penetrating look.

He averted his face from her, muttered something about having the maid empty the hip bath and cart it away, and escaped the room to yell down the stairs. Alex retreated behind the bed hangings when the door swung open to let in the harried maid and the yard lad.

"You're scared," she said once they were alone again.

"Nay, not afraid precisely, more…I've never been away this long from it before, and it may have changed." He twitched the bed hangings closed, enveloping them in a musky, deep red glow, the candle on the headboard flaring in the resulting waft of air before settling down to burn steadily again.

"I seem to remember having had this conversation with you before," she said, curling up against his chest.

"But that time it was only three years. This time, it's twenty." He closed his eyes, imagining all kinds of destruction. Mayhap someone had moved the barn, or torn down the stables, and where the dovecote had stood since time immemorial he might come home to find a pigsty.

"A pigsty?" Alex laughed and shook her head.

"Or a privy."

"The ground's too rocky for a privy there, and pigs like mud, not stones. Besides, you can always change it back." She nestled into him. "You don't think they'll have touched the graveyard, do you?" Despite her casual tone, he knew this was her secret fear, that they'd return to find the headstones gone, the rowan tree cut down, and they'd have no idea where their wee daughter lay at rest.

"Of course not, that would be desecration. And Magnus said, didn't he, how the rowan was still there when he visited Hillview last." It made him smile – albeit crookedly. His father-in-law had been to Hillview before his longing for Alex drove him to attempt some time travelling of his own – successfully, as it happened, even if the mere thought of those accursed painted time portals had Matthew breaking out in a cold sweat. Magic: black magic, even.

As always when they touched upon the sheer improbability of his dear wife's life – born in 1976, fallen back to land in the seventeenth century with him – he felt her tense, her hands gripping his shirt.

He tightened his hold on her shoulders. "I won't let time take you back, lass. You're staying with me 'til the end of our days and well beyond." He threw her a teasing look down the length of his nose. "Although I fear that means I must join you in hell."

"Not if God is fair and unprejudiced. I do as well as I can."

"But we all know that God is selective as to who gets in to heaven. Most of us are not accorded grace."

"Not my God. He has plenty of room up there in His rolling meadows for all the truly good and kind souls." She propped herself up on an elbow to smile down at him. "And I bet you He has tea and cake as well."

"Tea and cake?" Matthew laughed out loud. "What will a soul want with tea and cake?"

"Let me tell you I have no intention spending an eternity just wafting about and looking adequately spiritual." Alex grinned. "I'm planning on eating and drinking and having lots and lots of sex."

"Sex, hmm?" Matthew rolled her over, lowering his voice to a seductive rumble.

"As much as I can get," she said, tugging his shirt out of the way. Her hand found his balls, she ran a nail up his member, and he dipped his head to nibble her ear, smiling at the responding gooseflesh that flew up her thighs. "Although I think we can manage that in hell as well," she went on, "it will just be that much hotter."

"You shouldn't jest about it," he said with attempted severity.

Her eyes stared up at him, mostly black in the night. "I don't care where I go after death, as long as it's with you."

It still made his heart flutter when she said things like that, a heartfelt, silent thank you buzzing through his brain. For my life and my bairns, for my health, but most of all for my wife, my miraculous Alex, I thank you, Lord, every day, I thank you.

Chapter 8

"I didn't remember it as quite this big," Alex said next morning, "or quite as full of people."

Humanity thronged around them, houses rose to amazing heights along the narrow side streets that gave onto the High Street, and Alex was terrified of losing one or more of their sons in the general press of people.

"Here?" she said when Matthew took a left. She peered down the dark close, wrinkled her nose at the sharp scent of urine, and hurried after him with their sons in tow.

"Why do they build them so high?" Adam asked, craning his head back to attempt a glimpse of the sky.

"I think the relevant question is how," Alex replied, eyeing the tottering ten- and eleven-storey tenements with misgivings.

"It's the wall," Matthew replied over his shoulder.

"Oh well, that explains it," Alex said.

"It's the Flodden Wall. It sets the city limits, like, and so they must build upwards due to lack of space."

"Let's just hope there isn't a major fire or an outbreak of the plague or something," Alex said.

"Stone doesn't burn." David leapt out of the way when a barrow boy came rushing out from a gate.

"No, but furniture does, and wooden floors and ceilings and wainscoting and shutters and—"

David just rolled his eyes at her and extended his stride to come abreast with his father.

"I don't like it here," Samuel said, shadowing Alex as well as he could. "It's dirty and dark, and all those people! They reek, Mama, don't they?" Yes, they did, and stared – mostly at Samuel and his missing ear.

"Quite." Alex slipped her hand under Samuel's arm as if

she was being supported by him. "And the smoke is awful." It hung like a haze over the city, a brownish smog of burnt wood and peat that made eyes sting.

Her two younger sons shared a look. This was not the Scotland they had heard Da go on about, Samuel muttered. This was a dirty place with slippery streets and a damp fog that seeped through their clothes. And the food...they had not much liked the rabbit pie yesterday, and there were no greens, none at all, and why was it all so salty?

Alex ruffled Samuel's hair and laughed. "You'll like it better when we get to Hillview."

"Simon has taught David well," Matthew said to Alex once they exited the lawyer's chambers. "He has a good grasp of things, the lad does, and he's a quick reader as well." He smiled proudly at his son, who grinned back.

"And I can read upside down," David informed them. "Uncle Simon taught me that, saying it's a useful and valuable talent."

"I can imagine it is." Alex liked – no, loved – Matthew's brother-in-law, and on top of that Simon Melville was an excellent lawyer, a drafter of deeds and contracts that, according to Matthew, were at once iron-clad and full of loopholes – if you knew where to look for them. Two years working for Simon had given David a more than adequate grounding in his chosen career.

"You really want to be a lawyer, don't you?" she asked David, receiving a beaming smile in return.

"I take to it easily." After ensuring his father was out of earshot, David added that it was far, far better than being a minister.

"Shush," Alex said, "and hopefully Daniel is as happy with his career choice as you are with yours."

"Except that he didn't choose, Mama, did he?" Samuel kept a cautious eye on Matthew. "Da wished him to be a minister, and that was that."

"And do you think he's unhappy?" Last time Alex had seen Daniel, May a year ago, he had seemed quite content, happy with his pregnant wife. And now he had a son, a little Magnus Alex had never seen.

"Nay," Samuel replied, "I think he's satisfied with his life." He grinned and a sparkle of vivid green lit up his eyes. "He isn't all that happy about having a papist sister, though."

"No. Well, that's as it is, right?" Alex said, squirming somewhat.

It wasn't only Daniel having problems with Sarah's conversion to Catholicism, it was Matthew as well, and at times she suspected that he blamed her, Alex, for allowing their daughter to spend so much unsupervised time with her pet Catholic priest, Carlos Muñoz. Alex chose to rationalise: Sarah had fallen in love with a Catholic man, and had converted before marrying him.

Her mind wandered all the way to Spain, hoping that Carlos continued at peace in Seville and that he was keeping both stump and peg clean. She had a soft spot for the young priest, the double of her future son, even if he was quite squeamish at times.

From Carlos, her thoughts passed on to Isaac, safe in the future. She rarely thought about him, on occasion she dreamed about him, but all in all, he was a faded image, and the few times he did pop up in her head, it was as a contented man, secure in his world and his art. It was with relief she dismissed concerns about his well-being. He was surely healthy and successful, and there was nothing she could do to help him anyway.

By the time they reached Grassmarket, the cloud cover was beginning to thin, and weak rays of sunlight filtered through to sparkle on the odd stand of wet grass, puddles and cobbles. The boys perked up at the sight of so much livestock, and after ensuring Alex was sitting safe and sound with a warm pasty in her hand, Matthew took his sons and dived into the market proper to find them horses. Alex leaned back against the worn granite of the water post and regarded the scene before her.

In one corner, poultry was being sold, just in front of her were the sheep, and for some minutes she exchanged belligerent stares with a heavy ram before someone bought him and led him away. She strolled across the open space, meandering around warm piles of dung, small children, huge muddy patches, and the odd gipsy selling lucky charms. Voices rose and fell around her, people laughed and haggled, and it was all quite agreeable. Until the damned horse tore itself loose from the temporary smithy and set off like an enraged bear through the crowds, with a man hanging on to its reins.

"Bloody hell!" Alex wheezed, trying to get off the ground. Her cap had been knocked off, she had sat in something suspiciously soft and warm, and her back was soaked through.

"Uuuuuhhh," the man on top of her said, and heaved himself up on his knees. He looked a sight. His right side was caked in mud, and blood flowed freely from his nose, dripping down on Alex who shoved at him.

"Help me up!" she said, and the man somehow got back on his feet and extended his hand to her. Shit, how it hurt! Her ribs ached, she seemed to have cracked the back of her head against something, and her hip...

"My sincerest apologies," the man said in a deep, cultured voice.

"As if that will go very far in covering the costs for new clothes." Alex twisted round to confirm that, yes, she had landed in a cowpat. She glared at him as she adjusted her bum roll: quite the gentleman, with his dark wig knocked askew to reveal long dark hair beneath it, substantially less curly than the impressive, if somewhat bedraggled, hairpiece.

He righted his wig, looked about for his hat, and swept her an elaborate bow, incongruous given the state of his fine embroidered coat and matching velvet breeches.

"You saved my life, ma'am."

"Let's not exaggerate," Alex replied edgily. "All I did was cushion your landing." He pointed, she swivelled, wincing at the accompanying twinge that flew up her back. "Oh." She had, in fact, saved his life. If he hadn't crashed into her, he would have ploughed head first into the water post.

The man looked her up and down with interest. "Not

only my saviour but a most handsome one at that," he said gallantly, using a muddy handkerchief to staunch the blood welling from his long, narrow nose.

"Not only a moron, but blind as a bat," Alex riposted, and the stranger laughed.

"I can assure you, mistress, that there's nothing wrong with my eyesight."

"So you live a life of delusions – poor you." Alex had by now assured herself that all of her was in working order, even if she suspected she might have sprained her wrist. "What happened to the horse?" she asked, gingerly moving her hand back and forth.

"Treacherous creature!" the man spat, but it was obvious he didn't agree with his own assessment, his face shining up when a boy came leading the horse.

"And who's the lucky one?" Alex muttered. "Not a bruise or a scratch or even a dab of mud on you!"

It was an impressive horse, seventeen hands or so, and with a hide that shifted in all shades of grey from a pearly almost white to the nearly black of graphite. The horse scraped with its hoof and jerked at the reins, making Alex back away.

The man said something in a low voice to the horse before turning back to Alex. "John Graham of Claverhouse, at your service."

"Alex Graham, but, as far as I know, we're not related."

"Now we are," he laughed. "After all, I owe you my life." He was a few inches taller than she was, with a longish face in which the nose and two dark brows were the main features. The mouth was a bit too small and prim, but the eyes… She was flustered by his open and admiring look, even more so when Matthew grabbed her from behind.

"Alex? Are you alright?" He frowned at John Graham, his free hand dropping to the hilt of his sword.

"What? Oh, yes, yes, I'm alright. A bit dirty, but quite alright." Alex nodded in the direction of John. "This is potentially a relative of yours. Mr John Graham, no less."

"I know who he is, and I can assure you he's no relative,"

Matthew said, his voice dripping ice.

John seemed to find it all slightly amusing, raised his brows, swept Alex yet another bow, and, after promising to compensate her for her ruined clothes, walked away, leading his horse.

"That was rude," Alex said.

"He was rude, to barge into you like that." Matthew wiped at her clothes.

"It was an accident. It was the horse that took off." She could still see the unknown Graham, now back at the smithy, and when he smiled at her she smiled back. "I quite liked him, despite that ridiculous wig."

"That's the man responsible for much of the despoilment of south-west Scotland. Bluidy Clavers, they call him, and for good reason."

"Despoilment?"

"Aye, he has chased Covenanters across the moors for years." Matthew spat, tightened his hold on her arm, and led her away.

"That's not entirely fair," Luke remonstrated when they met him over supper in a warm, stuffy little inn just off Lawnmarket, "and his wife is of respected Presbyterian roots." He waved his hand in a no at the proffered soup, but nodded at the lad to replenish his wine glass. "Claverhouse was given an impossible task, and he has attempted to urge moderation."

"Aye, tell that to John Brown's widow," Matthew said.

"John Brown? He's dead?" Alex dropped her spoon in surprise. "Why didn't you tell me?"

"I didn't think it would interest you. You barely knew the man."

"I knew his brother," Alex said. There was a moment of embarrassed silence in which both Luke and Matthew concentrated on their food and drink. Brown's brother had been murdered twenty-odd years ago by an accomplice of Luke in a desperate attempt to discredit Matthew and thereby have him hanged and fined from Hillview. Alex shifted her stool closer to Matthew, her eyes sharp on Luke.

"John Brown died due to his own foolhardiness," Luke said to break the quiet. "He meddled in treason, and he refused to swear the oath."

"What oath?" Alex asked, wondering what on earth they had returned to if men were killed for not taking an oath.

"An Oath of Abjuration, a pledge of loyalty to the King, and a promise never to take up arms against his liege," a dark voice replied, and there was John Graham in person. "Luke," he bowed, "Mrs Graham, Mr Graham."

Luke half rose as did Matthew, but John waved them down. There was an air of suppressed excitement about him, his mouth pressed tight around a huge smile that tugged at the corners of his mouth. In clean clothes, flashy silk stockings and without his wig he was quite handsome, Alex reflected, taking in well-turned legs, elegant hands and broad shoulders. For an instant, her eyes met his, a shared look of frank curiosity that made Alex's stomach contract pleasantly while Matthew's long mouth set into a displeased line.

"What is it, John?" Luke said. "You look fit to burst."

"It'll keep. First, I wish to lay at rest the cast aspersions on my character." He gave Matthew a flinty look, fully reciprocated. "I've never allowed my men to loot. I haven't killed randomly. All I've done is to uphold the King's peace and justice, and root out those among you who refuse to swear allegiance to our king. And as to John Brown…" He shook his head. "Like a stone, the man was, refusing to speak words he had already spoken before. So what was I to do? Allow a man openly a rebel to our king to live on? A man at whose home we found a cache of weapons?"

"John Brown was a godly man," Matthew said, "and he didn't deserve to die, shot like a dog."

"No one deserves to die like that," John retorted, "and yet men do all the time. But it was his actions that condemned him, not mine."

"That isn't what I've heard," Matthew snapped.

"Nay, you wouldn't, would you? But I don't lose sleep over it, for I did what I had to. God knows that, and so does my wife."

"Your wife?" Alex was confused. "Was she there?"

Luke chuckled and offered John some wine. "I rather think John here is referring to the fact that the Cochranes are stout Covenanters, the lot of them, including his sweet Jean, and had his wife considered his behaviour despicable, surely she would have let him know. I've often wondered what made you wed someone like her," he said, receiving a look of mild dislike in return.

"I don't think that's any of your concern, and I'm happy in my wife." A softness came over John's face, the small mouth relaxing for an instant into a faint curve. He drank deeply of his wine and leaped up to stand on the table beside theirs, glass held aloft.

"A toast!" he cried out. "A toast for the Prince of Wales! A royal, lad, y'hear? Born four days ago, and lusty and strong."

"A prince?" Alex whispered to Matthew who shrugged.

A half-hearted cheering broke out, and John Graham raised his glass to the innkeeper. "Whisky, man, we must toast the lad in whisky! Break out a wee keg and set it on my account, for now we drink the health of a bonny prince, James Edward Francis Stuart. May your life be long and fruitful. May you live to reign in peace!"

"Hear, hear," the crowd called out, filled their glasses with whisky, and loudly hailed the birth of the prince – or the advent of more whisky.

"Shit," Alex said.

Luke raised a brow. "No rejoicing?"

"He's a Catholic," she hissed. "This will be like tinder to the powder."

Luke nodded in reply. Something gleamed in his eyes, something hastily hidden in his cup of wine.

Chapter 9

"Perfect timing," Alex said when they made their way back to their lodgings. "We no more than land here, and lo and behold, upheaval stands at the gates." She pursed her mouth, an uncomfortable sensation growing in her gut. Hadn't there been fighting here, in Scotland, when the last of the Stuart kings was ousted? But, no, that was in the eighteenth century, wasn't it? Vaguely, she recalled a long lesson spent doodling while Mr Gower went on and on about the fallen clans, somewhere just outside Inverness – that had been in the 1700s, of that she was sure. "Luke wasn't too thrilled about the prince, was he?"

No, Matthew agreed. His brother had, if anything, looked most dour.

"He knows," Alex said, coming to an abrupt stop. "He's involved in something."

"I told you. He's often seen in the company of men with vociferous and staunch Protestant views." Matthew tucked her hand into the crook of his arm and resumed their walk, keeping an eye on their sons a few steps ahead. "The King did himself no favour in Luke's eyes by the treatment of his precious son."

"Probably not." Something whirred in her head, small cogwheels turning round and round. "But he could be hedging his bets."

"He could? How?" Matthew steered them round a beggar.

"You're here now, and everyone knows you're not a friend of the Stuarts, Commonwealth man that you once were. So, if the little scheme fails, how convenient that Luke has a Graham scapegoat in residence up here in Scotland, recently returned from abroad."

Matthew went still. "No, not again, he wouldn't do it again."

"He won't need to this time – James II is toast – but if he had to, yes, he would."

"Fantasies, Alex, you make him sound as devious and amoral as a serpent."

"Oh, and that's news to you, is it?" Alex gripped him hard as they walked by the Tolbooth, staring at the dirty brick façade and the narrow windows.

Matthew's mouth thinned into a gash. "We'll ask him on the morrow."

Either Luke was an accomplished actor or he was truly taken aback.

"Preposterous!" Luke was half out of his seat, "How can you even think...? Sweetest Lord! You saved my lad!" He wheeled to glare at Alex, swivelled back to stare indignantly at his brother.

"Well, you've done it before, haven't you?" Alex said.

"When I was a young man!" Luke snarled. "And it was because of Margaret." He glowered at his brother. "You shouldn't have touched her! She was mine, and you—"

"She never said, did she?" Matthew replied just as heatedly. "It was her throwing herself at me, wee brother." Just like that, the veneer of civility between the brothers cracked apart, revealing how unhealed their differences were. Luke looked as if he was about to throw himself at Matthew, while Matthew's hands were gripping the table with such force his fingers looked white around the edges.

"You lie! She wouldn't do such! She loved me, she did, and you...you took her!" Luke's face had turned a dark shade of red. "She hated it when you touched her. She told me how it made her shrivel up inside when you forced your attentions on her."

Matthew rose, the muscles on his forearms bunching when he leaned over the table towards his brother. "I never did! It was she, not I, that made the first move, and if she shrivelled, she hid it very well, yowling like a cat in heat in my arms!"

"Nay, that she didn't!" Luke brought the flat of his hand down so hard on the table Alex jumped.

"How would you know? You weren't there!" Spittle flew from Matthew's mouth. "I bedded her and she enjoyed it. Whatever she told you afterwards, she enjoyed it!"

Alex regarded him – hair on end, eyes a dangerous, glinting green – and she was overwhelmed by the familiar jealousy she always felt when picturing him and Margaret together. Had he enjoyed it as well, the bedding? As much as when he made love to her, to Alex? Bloody Margaret had been so picture-perfect, a storybook Snow White with skin like rose-tinted ivory, hair like ebony, and the blue eyes she had in common with Alex. She returned her attention to the men, now nose to nose across the narrow table.

"She told me she loved me and was honoured to be my wife, she danced through our wedding, she—" Matthew broke off and shook his head. "I loved her, God help me, I loved her and the lad, and all of it was torn away from me by you – by you and her, false whore that she was!"

Good description, Alex agreed silently. Margaret had claimed Ian had been fathered by Luke, and so she'd left Matthew not only without a wife but without a son – a son that she had known was Matthew's all the time.

For an instant, Luke had the grace to look ashamed. "We couldn't help ourselves."

"Of course, you could," Alex said, making both men start as they recalled her presence. "If nothing else, you could have had the guts to tell Matthew you lusted for his wife."

"Lusted? I didn't lust for Margaret! I adored her. She was mine, she was always mine, and he shouldn't have touched her. She was part of me, she belonged with me, and if it hadn't been for Da and his straight-laced morality..." Luke stretched for the earthenware pitcher and with a shaking hand, poured himself some more beer and drank. "I just took back what was mine," he said with attempted calm, setting down his drained mug.

"Yeah, first you fucked his wife – in his bed – and then you decided that wasn't enough. He had to pay with his life, so you accused him of treason. Quite the little Cain." Alex very much wanted to spit in his face.

"He had it all," Luke said. "He came home from his wars, the beloved eldest son, and I was but the second son, the spare, and now that the heir was back, I was relegated to obscurity. And then he took the single thing he shouldn't have touched: my Margaret."

"Your Margaret? Idiot! You were sent away, and she sank her false little claws into Matthew to ensure a feathered nest!"

"You don't like it, do you?" Luke sneered. "She was so beautiful, and you're still jealous that she had him first."

Alex felt herself blushing, angered by his perceptiveness.

It made Luke laugh before returning his attention to Matthew. "You were such a fool," he taunted. "So easy for her to handle. A simper and you rushed to do her bidding, and she and I laughed at you behind your back."

"Bastard!" Matthew growled.

"All those months when you left her to sleep alone on account of her being unwell, who do you think spent every night with her? And you didn't even suspect it!" Luke sidestepped an angry swipe. "Cuckold!" he jeered. "You were cuckolded for months – in your own bed!"

"If only I had killed you then and there, nothing of what came after would have happened!" Matthew's eyes narrowed into burning green slits. From nowhere, his arm shot out, the big hand closing round Luke's throat. "You took my dignity, you took years of my life, but most of all, goddamn you, most of all, you robbed me of my bairn!"

"You got Ian back," Luke managed to voice, his hands clawing at Matthew's grip.

"Not that bairn! The unborn wean you pummelled out of Alex, miscreant that you are." With an oath, Matthew threw him against the wall and retreated a couple of paces. Luke used the wall to lever himself back up on his feet. His silver nose had slipped out of place, baring a disfiguring hole.

"And this?" Luke's fingers shook as he replaced the cap. "What of my nose?"

"It should have been your balls, and it was only Alex's pleading that stopped me from gelding you." Matthew seemed on the verge of launching himself at his brother again.

"What have we here?" The dry voice made Alex jump, turning to see the younger of the two officers who had accosted them in the harbour. The officer strolled into the room, and at his back came two more men. "Disrupting the peace, Master Graham?"

"This is a private conversation," Matthew said. "None of your concern."

"Tsk, tsk. Of course, it's my concern. A Covenanter threatening a law-abiding citizen? No, no, Master Graham, I fear this will cost you time in the Tolbooth." He gestured for his men to take Matthew, but Alex blocked their way.

"Don't be ridiculous!" Alex said. "This has nothing to do with religion or politics."

"I dare say I'm a better judge of that than you are, ma'am. Now, move out of the way or we will take you along as well."

"Stop this, officer," Luke cut in, stepping forward. "This is a matter between my brother and myself."

"Brothers?" the officer said, eyes travelling from the elegant, if somewhat dishevelled apparition that was Luke to Matthew in his broadcloth coat and breeches.

"Yes," Luke sighed, "brothers. Not always on amicable terms, but definitely brothers."

"Hmm." The officer bounced up and down on his toes a couple of times. "Should he threaten you, you have but to call. My men and I will remain close."

"That is not necessary," Luke said.

"No? And yet I hear that Matthew Graham is a man who doesn't shy from violence. They say he killed two soldiers on the moor back in the sixties, and hanged an officer from a tree."

"He did what?" Alex succeeded in laughing through a very dry mouth.

84

"If I did, why was I not tried and hanged already back then?" Matthew said.

"Proof," the officer muttered. "It was a matter of proof."

"Ah." Matthew nodded. "And do you have proof now? Or should I mayhap haul you before a magistrate and accuse you of slander?"

"Everyone knows you did it!" the officer said.

"I think not. It may be that everyone *says* he did it, but the man rarely lives up to the myth." Luke waved a hand at the officer. "Be off with you. And heed my brother. Slander him and be prepared to take the consequences."

"Where's Charlie?" Alex asked later, sniffing at the fish stew set before her. After the officer had left, the brothers had busied themselves with their clothes in an effort to regain some kind of composure, and both had jumped with alacrity at Alex's suggestion that they go and find somewhere to eat. Luke had led them through the Netherbow gate and veered a sharp left into a close as narrow and as smelly as all of them were, even if the buildings here were somewhat lower, and finally opened the door to the small tavern in which they were now sitting.

"I'm not sure," Luke said. "I haven't seen him since just after breakfast."

David choked on his food, was clapped on the back by Samuel.

"I take it you have," Matthew said, studying his three sons, all of whom were suddenly very interested in scraping their pewter dishes clean of food.

"At a distance, no more," David said.

"Oh aye? And?"

David squirmed and muttered that it had been from far away.

"And?" Luke repeated Matthew's question.

"He was with her – with Nan," David muttered.

"Nan," Luke said in a tone that indicated just how little he liked it. He frowned down at his fish. "What does he see in her?"

"A victim," Alex said.

"Ah." Luke nodded.

"A temptress." Matthew sopped up the last of his oyster soup with a heel of bread.

"Temptress?" Alex said. "I must say I find her very ordinary."

"She isn't bad-looking," Adam piped up.

"Aye," Samuel agreed, "a pity about the brand."

"The brand?" Luke looked from one nephew to the other.

"She's branded," Samuel explained.

"With an A," Adam filled in, "for being an adulteress."

"How quaint," Luke muttered. "A wee slut." With a snap of his fingers, he had the innkeeper scurrying over. "I excuse myself. I have a son to find." He let a shilling coin, some grouts and a sixpence fall into the innkeeper's hand, and stood, grabbing for his cloak and hat.

"I can come with you," Matthew said, sounding rather reluctant.

"Or I," David suggested. He gave his uncle an eager look, and already had his hand on his cloak.

"I'll manage on my own, but thank you all the same, lad." With a sketchy bow in Alex's direction, Luke departed, leaving David to sit back down, grumbling under his breath.

"I found him with her," Luke said to Matthew next day, "cavorting with the lass in her rented room. Nay, my rented room, for it appears my son has used my name to find her board." He had hoisted Charlie out of bed, he added, threatened him with all manner of punishments, chief amongst them to have Nan thrown out on her ear, and then dragged his most unwilling son back to their own lodgings.

"Ah," Matthew said. "And now? Where's Charlie now?"

"At this precise moment, he is sulking, distressed because he can't return with me to London – at least, not yet."

Matthew nodded and looked out at the street where banners and the steady sound of drums accompanied the official rejoicing at the birth of a royal heir. Yesterday, the castle cannon had been fired in salute, but there were very few people participating in the procession that was winding down towards Holyrood Palace, headed by Edinburgh's mayor who carried the town's gift to the newborn prince.

"It doesn't sit well, does it?" Luke said. "A Catholic prince, the start of a Catholic dynasty."

"It wouldn't, would it? Not here, not where the Kirk is still strong. Up in the Highlands though…" Matthew tilted his head. "Is Claverhouse Catholic?"

"John? Oh no, John is an Episcopalian. But first and foremost, he's the King's man, just as he was his brother's man before. A loyal heart, John Graham has, and God save him for it."

"Or at least reward him," Matthew said.

Luke laughed. "God? He doesn't care one way or the other, I suspect."

"You sound disillusioned," Matthew said. "You know as well as I do that God is always there for the needy man."

"He is? And when two men claim to have God on their side, what is the simple man to believe?" Luke lowered his voice until Matthew had to concentrate to hear him. "William of Orange is a God-fearing man, and as to his wife, Mary is a devout Protestant, shocked by the defection of her father to popery." Luke sighed and straightened up, twirling a spoon round and round. "And the King, God help him, he's a most God-fearing man as well – and just as devout as his daughter. Religion! How it sours our lives!" He looked Matthew full in the face. "You would know about defection, what with your youngest lass and all that."

Ah, but he knew how to twist a knife! Matthew met his brother's glittering eyes, but chose not to reply. His Sarah had converted two years ago, and the wound was still raw. Every day, he prayed to God to forgive his lass, explaining over and over again that the lass had been distraught and in love, too young to know what she was doing. He was relieved when Alex came hurrying into the room.

"You'd best come quick," she said, and they rose to follow her out into the inn's cobbled yard.

"You've done what?" Luke's voice squeaked.

"I've wed her," Charlie said defiantly, and his arm came round Nan's narrow shoulders.

Luke looked her up and down in silence. "You've married that? A woman dishonoured by her own actions?"

Charlie flushed, blood mottling his skin in patches all the way up to his hairline. "Too late now. She's Mrs Charles Graham now."

"Oh, she is, is she? And how will you keep her?"

"Keep her?" Charlie gave his father a confused look. "Why, she stays with me."

"And you stay where? On what means?" Luke balanced forward on the balls of his feet, bringing his face close to his son's. "You have no money of your own. You have no income, no occupation – nothing but what I give you. Did you tell her that?" He slid a glance over to where Nan stood rigid, her mouth half open. "It seems you didn't."

"You can't!" Charlie spluttered. "I'm your only son!"

"Unfortunately," Luke said. "A son who disregards my wishes, who marries behind my back, who has already cost me considerably over the last few years to bring him home, safe and sound. A fool, it would seem: fool in his choice of friends, fool in his choice of wife. Do you see her in the salons of London? Will you show her off among your friends with the branded A peeking out of her neckline like a quaint decoration?"

Nan was now as deep a shade of red as her new husband, small hands twitching over the green velvet of her skirts.

"Father," Charlie moaned.

Luke just shook his head. "I don't want to talk to you for the moment, son. I'll see you at seven sharp tonight – without your slut of a wife."

"Father," Charlie repeated, and they all winced at the abandonment in his voice.

"Go," Luke slurred. "Go before I say or do something I'll live to regret.

"God spare me!" He sank down to sit, his eyes on the bright head of his son, still discernible a hundred yards or so away. "How can it be that I have a son as impetuous and ill-advised as that?"

"Maybe he takes after his mother," Alex said, which earned her a cold look from Luke. "Well, it's common, that the boys more resemble their mothers, and the girls their fathers."

"Our daughters resemble their mother." Matthew flashed his wife a look, thinking that his Sarah most certainly did. He wasn't quite as certain about Ruth.

"So do mine, although…" Luke shook his head. "It's Joan, I think, that is most similar to me in how she acts and thinks."

"A budding female Machiavelli," Alex muttered in an undertone Luke didn't catch, even if Matthew did. "See?" she said loud enough that Luke should hear her. "I'm right. Besides, I find it all rather romantic."

Matthew snorted. "Oh, you do? And you think the lass loves him?"

"No," Alex said, "but then I don't think he loves her either."

"Then why, for the love of God? Why wed her? He's already bedded her!" Luke exclaimed, giving Alex a demanding look as if she should be able to explain this whole irrational affair.

"Maybe because you so clearly disliked her?" Alex said. "Or maybe because, with her, he doesn't need to feel ashamed?"

"Ashamed?" Luke asked. "Ashamed of what?"

"For what was done to him, for the scars left on his skin by floggings and beatings, by brands and by months walking in fetters. It doesn't only mark you on the outside, dear brother – as I am in a position to know." Matthew sank his eyes into Luke, his skin itching with remembered floggings, his head swimming with unwelcome memories of his own humiliation at the hands of his overseer, all those years ago in Virginia – and all because of his treacherous brother. To his satisfaction, Luke broke eye contact first.

"My only son," he sighed. "My only son, and he has the wits of a befuddled hen."

"That's not entirely fair," Alex said. "He just lacks in self-preservation."

"Even worse than a hen, then," Luke said, making Matthew smile.

"Look at it from the bright side," Matthew suggested. "It's fortunate that he married her here, in Scotland."

For an instant, Luke looked confused, but then his brow cleared. "Aye," he nodded, "aye, that it is. What God has joined let no man put asunder − except here in Scotland where, thank the Lord, there is divorce."

Chapter 11

...Do you have any idea of how bloody hot it is in Seville in June? It's like trying to breathe in an oven, and on top of that, guess what? No pools, no long, cooling showers, no air-conditioning, no ice-cold drinks, no beer – or rather no good beer – no wandering around in shorts, no girls in bikinis. Make that no girls, full stop, but that may have something to do with this being a monastery. At least the church is relatively cool – luckily, given the hours I spend there. Very tedious, all these services, but not attending isn't exactly an option.

The day Isaac declared his mural to be ready for unveiling, a buzz swept through the congregated brethren. For the last weeks, he had worked behind a primitive tent, refusing anyone to see his work until he was done, and even if some of them had now and then attempted to peek, it was impossible to see more than the few inches just before your nose when heavy linen flapped all around you.

"Now?" the abbot asked.

"Oh no," Isaac replied. "Tomorrow, at dawn."

He had thrown himself into his work after his visit to Carlos' home, partly as a result of a sudden surge of inspiration, but just as much because, since Isaac's revelation regarding his grandmother, Carlos avoided him, scurrying off to pray whenever Isaac came into their little room.

Isaac couldn't exactly blame him. In this day and age, everything Isaac had told him was borderline witchery – and in any day and age it was entirely impossible. So Isaac spent his mornings in the library, the afternoons and evenings in the courtyard, and, in between, he did nothing much except miss his home and family. Every afternoon and every evening, he tried to coax life into a succession of small squares of blue, attempts that ended in curses and tantrums, with canvases being sliced apart by his palette knife.

At least his mural was brimming with life, from the hair that seemed to lift in the wind, to the blush rising over her cheeks and the thick eyelashes that were lowered over eyes as dark and promising as a forest tarn. Isaac raised his marten brush to set three final dots of brilliant white, and there it was: the Virgin and the Holy Spirit, entwined like lovers for all that she was fully dressed and the Spirit entirely invisible. Or was it? Something shimmered across the surface, and a frisson travelled up Isaac's spine. He corked the small stone jars in which he kept his mixed paints, cleaned his brushes, and with one final look at his work, dropped the sheet into place and went to find some food.

Isaac had quite the flair for the dramatic, standing silent before the expectant brothers just after prime, with the abbot self-importantly holding one end of the sheet while Isaac held the other.

"Not yet," Isaac said, keeping his eye on the eastern roof. "Not yet." A slice of sun became visible. A ray of light cut through the air and with a decisive yank, Isaac and the abbot uncovered the Virgin.

"Ooooh!" gasped the brethren. "Aaaaah," they added.

They bloody well should, Isaac decided, taking a step back to properly see his creation.

She was delectable, a girl child, almost a woman, that stood with her hands stretched out. The dark hair wafted in the breeze, a smile hovered on her face and those beautiful, seductive eyes, shielded by her innocently lowered lashes... A rush of air stood around her, a presence captured as an imprint on her clothes and skin, invisible but tangibly there. Closer up, the mural shimmered with golden light, glittered with water, and quivered with air.

"A wind," one of the monks whispered. "He came like a wind to her."

"No, no," another of the monks protested, "he's there in the light that surrounds her."

The abbot stood silent for a long time before clasping one

of Isaac's hands. "You've given us a treasure," he said, "for no one who sees this will ever doubt the absolute joy with which the Virgin received her heavenly burden." From the assembled monks came a murmur of agreement, and Isaac felt like he always did when he had a successful exhibition: alive all the way from his toes to the crown of his head.

He remained in the courtyard for some time afterwards, settling himself in one of the arches opposite the mural. He dozed, soothed by a high-pitched humming. With a start, he realised that the sound was coming from the mural, and when he opened his eyes, he saw that the halo he had so carefully hinted at round the Virgin's head was glowing. He stumbled towards her. The humming increased in volume, the halo burnt brighter and brighter, and already from several feet away, he could see the chasm of time, a narrow, bottomless chute of transparent colours, of pouring light. Yes! A way home!

He stretched out his hand, he stretched out the other, and his fingers were brushing at the wall when an arm came round his waist, yanking him away, and even if Isaac tried to tell whoever it was that was interfering to let him go, not a sound came over his lips. He fell back against a velvet coat, he caught the scent of lemons, and screamed inside because he had been so close!

"What were you doing?" Don Raúl barked, shaking Isaac hard by the shoulders. "Sleepwalking towards the Madonna like that?"

"I saw…" Isaac mumbled and decided that was all he was going to say.

"You saw? What did you see?" Don Raúl had been joined by the abbot who helped Isaac to sit on the brink of the fountain.

"I saw…" he repeated, thrashing about in his mind for a feasible explanation for his odd behaviour. He hid his face in his hands and groaned. "I saw her."

"A vision," the abbot whispered. "You have had a vision."

Isaac nodded. His Veronica – so close, her violet eyes smiling at him.

"*Santa María, proteja sus servidores,*" the abbot muttered, and Raúl fell into the prayer.

They had to support him back inside because his legs wouldn't hold him, either out of dejection or pure exhaustion. The abbot helped him into bed, a reverential look on his face as he used a damp linen cloth to wash Isaac's brow.

"Did she speak to you?" he asked. Isaac shook his head, and the abbot nodded: she would speak only to the truly deserving. "I shall leave you to sleep," the abbot said, and left the room with Don Raúl in tow.

The scraping of Carlos' quill over paper woke Isaac some time later. Carlos turned on the stool to regard him. "Are you feeling better?"

Isaac grimaced. His head was banded with pain, and he was fiercely thirsty. He blinked, his throat clogging with tears. He could have been back in his old life, with Veronica and Isabelle. Dad, he moaned silently, wiping at his wet cheeks.

"So fucking close," he said out loud.

"Close?" Carlos' voice sounded hesitant.

Isaac just nodded, mumbling that he had seen them, his woman, his child – for a brief moment, a portal through time had opened.

Carlos clutched his cross. "What happened?"

"Your uncle, that's what happened!" Isaac managed to sit up, surprised that he should be so weak, shivering as if with fever. "I have to go out and look at it again. Maybe it's still there."

But even as he said it, he knew it wouldn't be. The maelstrom of this morning had been the result of several coincidences: the completed painting, the sun striking the mural at a precise angle, and the reflections of the fountain's water on the wall.

Carlos accompanied him, sitting unobtrusively in one of the arches while Isaac paced, walked backwards and forwards, came at the mural from the right and from the left, but nothing happened, nothing at all. He sank down beside Carlos, and his body bowed under the weight of still being here, trapped in a time not his own.

"Tell me," Carlos said after what to Isaac seemed like an hour of absolute silence. "Explain how it is that you know of a woman that lived here in Seville 200 years ago, and how it is that she came to be your grandmother."

"I would have thought that rather obvious. She fell forward in time, not back." Isaac glanced at Carlos, sighed and stretched out his legs before him. He hated seeing himself in breeches that left his calves bare, he hated that they were scratchy and ugly and had to be tightened around his frame with a belt. He hated how his genitals hung free inside of them, how he was forced to wear the same shirt for well over a week, how he was reduced to cleaning his teeth with a bloody twig.

"I suppose that must have been much more of a shock than it is to go the other way," he said. "After all, I have some perceptions as to what 1688 might be, but how could she, coming from 1486 or so, understand the world she landed in?

"Her name was Mercedes," Isaac began, keeping his eyes on his hands, "María de las Mercedes, and she was a… hmm…a Jewish Catholic?"

"A *marrana*," Carlos said.

"That term only applies to the false Jewish converts," Isaac reprimanded him, and Carlos looked away.

"Her father burnt for false conversion."

"Yes," Isaac said, "on the say-so of Hector Olivares, who first raped Benito's daughter Dolores, then turned them over to the Inquisition – all this when he was being a loyal servant to the Church."

"How do you know?" Carlos asked, wetting his lips.

"Mercedes wrote it all down," Isaac said.

In some detail, he told Carlos the sad story of Mercedes and Dolores, two pretty girls in a long gone Seville, and the warped infatuation Hector Olivares developed for Dolores, culminating in a night when he and some friends entered the Gutiérrez home and raped Dolores in front of her pregnant sister and helpless father. The next day, both Benito and Dolores were gone, and Mercedes couldn't find them, no matter where she looked. Not until the *auto de fé* some months later when her father and sister admitted to being heretics and were condemned to burn.

Carlos had gone pale. "If they admitted it, it was probably true. The Inquisition is very thorough."

"Undoubtedly," Isaac said sarcastically. "But if you torture someone long enough, they'll admit to anything. And then, of course, there was Hector's testimony, and everyone believed him, what with him being such an upright citizen. Bastard! How often do you think he brought false testimony against potential heretics, walking away with all their worldly belongings as his reward?"

Carlos muttered something in an undertone.

"It happens now as well, doesn't it?" Isaac said. "A word here, a well-phrased calumny there, and an innocent man might find himself in the claws of the Inquisition, and who benefits materially? His accuser."

Carlos hitched his shoulders in assent.

"Mercedes was delivered of a son. She tried to resume her life, but all of her craved revenge, and so she began to paint – magical paintings such as her grandfather had taught her to paint."

"Her grandfather?" Carlos said.

"Yeah, some sort of wizard painter."

Carlos moaned, raising his hand to his mouth.

"Anyway," Isaac resumed, keeping a concerned eye on Carlos who had gone from pale to slightly green, "one day, she succeeded in painting a hole through time, mesmerising blues and greens that twisted together into a funnel, and right at the bottom, so small it was almost impossible to see, an elusive, winking point of light, an entry point to other worlds, other times."

"¡Ay Dios! *Santa María, Madre de Dios, proteja me, por favor, proteja me.*" Carlos swayed where he sat. "So it is true. She was a witch," he moaned. "An evil, evil witch, and her blood taints mine."

"And mine," Isaac said with an edge. He shifted on the cool stone and resumed his story. "One day, Mercedes tricked Hector into looking at her picture, and when he did, well, he just faded away." Isaac had to swallow a couple of times, overwhelmed by memories of his own painful drop through time. He cleared his throat. "Unfortunately for Mercedes, Hector somehow dragged her along, and after that they bounced through the ages, him chasing, she fleeing, and both of them trying desperately to return to their time." He had no idea for how long Mercedes had hopscotched through time, but one day she met Magnus Lind, and with him she found the one true love of her existence.

"They must have been a handsome couple," he said. "He tall and blond with eyes the blue of forget-me-nots—"

"—like his daughter's eyes." Carlos smiled.

Isaac gave him an irritated look. "Whatever. Anyway, one day, Alex was abducted by this Ángel Muñoz, and we think Mercedes set out to free her." He shrugged. "She never came back, and when they found Alex, she was tied to a chair in a room with two unknown dead men and a pile of soot on the windowsill." Isaac smiled crookedly. "Mercedes left a little boy behind when she fell with Hector, Juan Sánchez, and apparently her great-something granddaughter married into your family." He was suddenly struck by the disconcerting fact that, ultimately, it was a descendant of Mercedes who had fathered him on Alex, that he had Mercedes' blood from both sides. Maybe that was why he had inherited her accursed gifts.

"What I don't understand is why Hector deeded her family the house," he said, more to himself than to Carlos. "And why the bloody hell did she hold hands with him when they died?"

"Maybe she was afraid," Carlos said.

"Yeah." Isaac decided he had talked enough for now, rested his head against the low wall behind him, and scraped at a blob of paint on one of his nails.

★

Carlos sat back, stunned. Those ancient stories were true: he had a witch up his family tree, a Jewess who dabbled in black arts, and in his chest welled hysterical laughter. He regarded his relative out of the corner of his eye, his mind working furiously.

"You painted the picture through which you fell," he stated.

Isaac shrugged. "It came to me in a dream, a courtyard with sandstone arches against whitewashed walls, with a clambering vine in one corner and a fountain – a shallow fountain in its midst. And there was a niche with a worn statue of the Virgin, but it was the fountain and the water welling from it that I kept on seeing in my head. So I painted it, fool that I was." He threw a pebble at the fountain and stuck his tongue out at it.

"It was meant to happen." Carlos nodded.

"Meant? How meant? Of course it wasn't meant to happen! I don't belong here, I hate it here! I want to go home. Jesus, how I want to go home!" Isaac pulled his legs up and rested his head on his knees, hiding his face from Carlos. "I miss my woman," he said hoarsely. "I long for my daughter and my dad, but most of all I want Veronica."

Carlos put a tentative hand on his arm, worried that it might be shrugged off, but instead Isaac began to weep. Carlos remained where he was, his hand light on Isaac's arm, and the shadows lengthened. Vespers came and went, the compline bell was rung, and still they sat together in the dark while high overhead, a timid moon peeked down at them. Finally, Isaac raised a swollen face to Carlos.

"I'm hungry."

"So am I," Carlos replied, and smiled.

Chapter 12

"You've painted pictures such as that of the fountain before," Carlos said when they were making their way to the refectory the next morning. "You must have. How else did Magnus Lind come to end up buried in Maryland? Or was that one of M...?" He took a big breath. "...Mercedes' paintings?"

"No, it was mine." Isaac hunched together. "Offa was ill, very ill. He wanted to see Alex again, and I tried to paint what I remembered from when I fell through time. It worked, it would seem."

"It would, yes," Carlos agreed, sounding remarkably casual.

"I never set out to paint one again. I promised Offa I never would." This time it had just happened, without him fully noticing what he was doing. He mumbled a 'thank you' at the monk serving them bread and boiled eggs, and followed Carlos to sit on one of the benches furthest from the lectern where Brother Mauricio was finding his place in the large Bible. They didn't talk as they ate, listening instead to Mauricio's beautiful baritone voice as he read from the Book of Psalms.

When they came out, one of the novices intercepted Carlos and told him he was requested at the nearby convent where one of the nuns was ailing. Carlos hurried away, leaving Isaac to his own devices.

He didn't feel like attempting to paint, drained after the last few weeks of massive effort on the mural, so instead he set off in the direction of the library where he hadn't been for a number of days. He was in a somewhat better mood today, Carlos having procured a hip bath for him yesterday evening as well as a clean shirt and clean – well, relatively – breeches and a pair of rope-soled sandals that Isaac could almost pretend were flip-flops. It was unbearably hot in the sun, and Isaac was thankful for the thick walls and small windows, for the coolness of the corridors with their tiled floors.

He entered the library, stood for a moment to admire its elegant proportions, and went over to his own little carrel. At the top of the pile balanced a Bible, and tucked some way down was the book he had attempted to read some weeks back about the Conquest. Isaac was too tired to attempt to understand it, but he unfolded the detailed map of the New World and was perusing it when the abbot paused by his side.

"How are you today?" the abbot asked.

"Better," Isaac replied. "I think I was shocked."

The abbot nodded his head gravely in agreement. "Some say it's an augury of impending death to see the Virgin, but I hold that to be nonsense."

"Well, that's a relief," Isaac answered weakly, and the abbot smiled at him and moved on down the library.

After Mass, Isaac decided to sit outside for a while. He wasn't thrilled to see Don Raúl loitering in the courtyard, and even less when he realised Raúl was waiting for him, covering the yard in long strides the moment he saw Isaac.

"You're coming with me." Raúl's hand closed on Isaac's upper arm.

"I am? Why?" Isaac dug his heels in as well as he could, which was difficult with rope-soled sandals that only slid along the tiles.

"I have something to show you." Raúl propelled Isaac towards the door.

"And Carlos?"

"Carlos? Oh no, just you." They were almost by the door when the abbot came along.

"Father!" Isaac called. "I'm to accompany Uncle Raúl for some hours. Please let Carlos know when he arrives back, will you?"

The abbot beamed at him, and assured him that of course he would, inclined his head at Don Raúl, and hurried on.

"That was unnecessary," Raúl said once they were out in the sun. "I intend you no harm." He handed Isaac a hat and a cloak, muttering something about a Muñoz de Hojeda having certain standards to live up to, even if one was bastard-born.

"Did you know your father?" he asked.

Isaac shook his head. No, neither the Ángel Muñoz that had sired him nor his purported father in this time and age.

"He was a good man," Raúl said. "Weak, but good. It surprised me to hear he had fathered one bastard with that little maid of honour, Louise, and it surprises me even more that he should have broken his vows of celibacy again – and with a married woman, no less."

Go fish, Isaac thought snidely. I have no intention of spreading any light on this for your behalf. "Umm," he said, and squirmed as if embarrassed, "I don't know what happened. It's not an easy subject to raise with your mother."

"Mmm," Raúl agreed, and set off towards his home.

Seville in the midday heat of late June was painfully hot. To breathe was to risk burning your lungs, and things weren't exactly helped by the sheer stink of the place: drying mud along the river, offal and garbage in the streets, the stench of a bloated carcass that Isaac thought might have been a cat. He could feel the heat blistering his feet through the thin soles, and had it not been for the wide-brimmed hat, Isaac was convinced his brain would have shrivelled and expired there and then.

The city was eerily silent, shutters closed against the obnoxious sun as the citizenry retreated to their beds and their patios to pant their way through the baking hours of noon. A few mangy dogs skulked around, keeping to the shade as much as possible, but apart from them and two or three beggars huddled under the orange trees that lined the cathedral square, they met not one living thing. A donkey brayed in the distance, and from behind a balcony came the unmistakeable sounds of a man and woman making love. Isaac wondered how on earth they managed that without melting away.

"A remarkable mural," Raúl said out of the blue. He slid Isaac a look. "Near on other-worldly."

"You think?" Isaac hitched his shoulders.

"*Sí,* one could almost suspect magic at work."

Isaac managed a little incredulous laugh, and was very grateful when Raúl didn't pursue the matter further.

It was blissful to enter the shaded courtyard of Raúl's house, to be served cooled wine to drink. Isaac gulped it down, and then there was a plate with sliced melons and clusters of grapes, and for some minutes they just ate.

With a grunt, Raúl sat back, took off his hat, and undid the elaborate buttons of his coat. He dragged his hand over the silver of his bearded cheeks before calling for his wife to come and meet their guest. Isaac stood up and bowed.

The woman before him regarded him from eyes as dark as his own, gasped and turned away, speaking in rapid Spanish to Raúl.

"*Ya, ya,*" Raúl said in irritation, "*no volverá.*"

"Why not?" Isaac asked once his hostile female relative had excused herself. "Why doesn't she want me to come back?"

"You're too much of a reminder of our son," Raúl said shortly. He peered at Isaac and sighed. "It's quite distressing, and even more for a tender-hearted mother."

"Yes, I suppose it would be," Isaac agreed, even if, from what Carlos had told him of his childhood, this particular woman lacked sadly when it came to being tender – at least to the bastard nephew of her husband.

He followed his host indoors, up the stairs to the first-floor rooms – three rooms with dark wooden floors, dark wooden furniture, dark panelling halfway up the walls, and a collection of singularly depressing paintings, all of them in dark wooden frames. Well, at least he was consistent, Isaac reflected, trailing Raúl from one room to the other.

Finally, they entered a room that Isaac assumed was Raúl's sanctum. Surprisingly bare after the opulence of the preceding rooms, it was pleasing in its simplicity: a desk, a well-worn armchair, a low upholstered stool. On the wall was a woven tapestry depicting the Most Catholic Kings, Ferdinand and Isabella, and Raúl proudly explained that this was an heirloom, a precious item.

"Handed down from eldest son to eldest son. It was woven by the Queen's women in recognition of my family's services to Their Royal Majesties."

Isaac made appropriate sounds.

Raúl gestured for him to sit on the stool, closed the door, and rooted around in a small chest before sitting down with a carefully wrapped object in his lap. "I don't know what Carlos has told you of our roots, but like all families we have our share of skeletons. For all that it brought us this house, at times I wish my forefather had not married Juana Sánchez. For with her, nephew, came the tainted blood."

"Tainted?" Isaac asked.

Raúl nodded. "In her veins flowed the blood of Jews, and so it matters not how I toil, or how well I serve my country and King. I'll never be awarded *la Cruz Roja*. Never will I be installed in the Order of Santiago."

"Oh," Isaac said, not fully understanding.

"I forget, you've been raised God knows where." Raúl narrowed his eyes at Isaac who kept his face blank. "The Order of Santiago is an order of knights, and because of my impure blood, I'll never wear the insignia, the red cross on my chest, over my heart."

"Oh," Isaac said again. "And that matters a lot?"

"Matters? We come from a family who have served the kings of Spain since before Spain was Spain! My son died for his king in Jamaica some years back, my grandfather fought against the Turks, my youngest son is presently in Madrid serving the Queen Mother, and you ask if it matters?" He scowled, and Isaac mumbled an apology.

"Anyway," Raúl went on, once he had calmed down, "I didn't bring you here to tell you details of our family history. Of course, as a bastard, you have no claims on the greatness of the Muñoz de Hojeda family, but it may be some comfort to know whence you come from. A family of upright, loyal men – men who gave their word and died for it. Well, with the sad exception of my brother." He squinted at Isaac and shook his head. "Blood will tell, but if you apply yourself, you may be able to overcome the innate weakness of Benito."

"The fact that I didn't know my father doesn't mean that I'll allow you to slander him," Isaac said, heartily disliking Raúl. Poor Carlos, to grow up having this crammed down his throat – maybe he'd been better off with the monks after all.

Raúl's lip lifted in a slight sneer. "As you said, you didn't know him – I did."

He cut off any further discussion by unfolding the grey linen and placing a canvas on the desk. "This is why I bid you come. When I saw your mural yesterday, it niggled at something in my brain. I had seen another painting with that same vibrancy as in your mural. I thought it might interest you to see – an inherited talent, no less."

He shoved the canvas in Isaac's direction, and for a moment, Isaac thought he was going to throw up. He recognised it: several times a day, he walked by the photograph that must have been this painting's source, but how could it possibly be? The photograph had been taken in 2002 – three years after Mercedes disappeared. With a careful finger, he urged the painting closer, looking down at Alexandra Lind, with her hair short and wavy, eyes as blue as her father's, and in her lap sat a naked Isaac, the hair rising in its signature quiff.

It was different from the photograph in that more of the background was visible. He could see the moors, make out the granite that pushed through the heather and gorse, and just as Raúl said, the painting breathed life. Any moment now, the restive child would push himself free of his mother's arms and run towards the painter, and the fabric of Alex's clothes billowed for an instant before subsiding into painted stillness. Her hands at the child's waist shifted, and soon, soon, the boy would come running through the heather.

Only in one important detail did it differ from the original, and that was in how Alex was dressed. She was in full skirts and a striped bodice, not the jeans and shirt she wore in the photo. As if the painter knew that she'd been thrown back in time...He almost said 'Mama', but caught himself, making an effort to compose his face before raising his eyes to Raúl.

"What's this?" he asked, succeeding in sounding only mildly interested.

"I found it in an old trunk. Beautiful, isn't it? Look at the boy, all of him is Muñoz, from the way his hair grows to the mouth." He retook the canvas. "Pity about the hair on the woman. One wonders what crimes she may have committed to have it so brutally hacked off."

"Maybe she was ill," Isaac said.

"Ill?" Raúl laughed and looked down again at the canvas, fingers caressing the painted Alex. "That woman exudes health – health and happiness." He was right, and that was also a difference versus the original photo, because there Alex might be smiling, but there was something dark shading her eyes, while here she was radiant.

"So who painted it?" Isaac asked, even if he already knew.

"I have no idea," Raúl replied, "but he was very skilled. He signs himself with an M." He tapped at the scrawled letter, placed the painting face up on the old linen, and proceeded to wrap it up.

"It could be a woman."

"A woman? Paint like that?" Raúl laughed so hard he began to cough, and once he began coughing he couldn't stop, his face turning a worrying shade of purple before Isaac clapped him firmly on the back a couple of times, dislodging a huge glob of phlegm. Raúl concentrated on breathing for some minutes, and then stood to put away the painting.

"Why do you keep it hidden?"

Raúl shrugged. "It's too alive, too bewitching. Like your mural. In some months, the abbot will cover it up to keep the monks from coming there to gawk when they should be at prayers or Mass." He pursed his mouth and sharpened his eyes. "Man should not be able to paint like that."

"And yet I do." Isaac got to his feet. "A divine gift, perhaps."

"Or the work of the devil," Raúl muttered, making a hasty sign of the cross.

Too right, Isaac sighed, his guts twisting with longing for Veronica.

Isaac walked back alone to the monastery. Mercedes may have slept away a decade or two once she got back, but she had apparently been awake for long enough to paint a boy she had never seen before the Inquisition took her away. It made the hairs along his arms rise in alarm.

"I hope you are at peace," he whispered to the air. A sudden breeze danced across his skin.

...When I got back to the monastery, Carlos was waiting for me, and in his hands he held a letter, urging that I read it. From Mama, no less, telling him that Matthew and she were going back to Scotland. I don't know what Carlos expected me to do. Smile and start packing? He seemed a bit put out when all I did was shrug.

Chapter 13

They set off early on a June morning, leaving Edinburgh behind as they headed off in a south-westerly direction. Charlie had bidden them a sullen goodbye, Nan had been nowhere in sight, and Luke had confided that he aimed to take both son and daughter-in-law with him to Amsterdam, Charlie to attempt to re-enter the royal circle while Nan would be kept neatly at heel by a restricted budget and Luke's presence. Hopefully, she'd grow bored and do something that gave Charlie grounds for divorce.

"Not that I'm sure it will work," Alex said to Matthew once they were safely on their way.

"Mayhap not. None of our concern, is it? Luckily, his lasses seem more sensible than their brother."

"Tell me about it." Luke had almost bored them to tears the previous evening with his detailed descriptions of his two daughters – one of them safely married to a well-to-do mercer in the city and already great with child.

They were lucky in the weather, and the boys agreed that Scotland had a certain charm to it, even if the woods were more shrubs than trees, and the land looked remarkably barren.

"This is the moor," Matthew said. "It's all rock and moss and patches of meagre soil that will support gorse and heather, the odd stunted tree and brambles, and not much else. But it's bonny."

Yes, it was, Alex agreed silently, taking in the openness and the muted greys and greens of the rolling landscape, here and there dotted with stands of impressive stones. At every spring, Matthew had to dismount and drink, muttering that he was thirsty. But Alex knew. He couldn't get enough of it: the cold, slightly irony taste of the water that proclaimed to his taste buds that he was home, just as the kites in the sky and the surrounding moor confirmed to his other senses that he was finally back in the country of his birth.

"We'll be riding through Lanark, right?" Alex asked, having no real idea where they were at present. "I promised Mrs Parson to go to St Kentigern and check on her family." Well, the family was long gone, but at least she could verify if the tombstones were still standing.

"Tomorrow," Matthew said. "We cross the Clyde there anyway."

The plodding pace lulled Alex half to sleep. The boys were silent as well, not, Alex suspected, out of awe at the surrounding landscape but more out of a combination of being tired and hungry. She yawned and rested her cheek against Matthew's back. He was humming, a soft sound, wordless and happy. Abruptly, he stopped humming, and from close by came sounds of fighting, of men's voices raised in anger and fear. A shot went off, another followed, and their horses danced from side to side.

"What?" Alex asked.

"Cavalry." Matthew nodded at where a group of ten mounted soldiers had surrounded a smaller group of men.

"And the others?" Alex tried to make them out, but at this distance all she could see were that they were no more than five or six.

"Highwaymen," Matthew told her after studying them for some minutes.

Alex squinted. The men being herded together had an unkempt air to them, and when they rode closer, she supposed he was right, given how they bristled with knifes and swords and pistols.

Suddenly one of the horses squealed, detached itself from the others, and came barging over the ground towards them, ignoring its loudly cursing rider's attempt to bring it to a halt. Their mount snorted, pawed at the ground, and shied.

"Oops." Alex clutched with her thighs and the horse shied again, just as the other horse, which Alex now recognised, ran straight into them, eyes rolling, nostrils bright red. Dratted animal, Alex managed to think before their mount bucked, and just like that she was flying through space.

She hit the ground hard, landing on her knees before further collapsing forward. At least there were no cowpats, but the ground was strewn with stones and pebbles. She remained prone, dragging air into her lungs, before levering herself up on her knees.

"Hellspawn would be a good name," Alex suggested, glaring up at the restive roan and its rider, John Graham. "Or why not just call him Satan?" She rose, tentatively flexing her knees. "I still have bruises from our last encounter, and now I'll have a couple of new ones. Maybe you should change your mount to something that you can control."

A fair distance away, Matthew had brought his horse to a halt, and was wheeling back towards her.

"One of the accursed captives kicked him just below the hock. I can assure you I'm quite capable of handling him otherwise," John Graham said.

"Not so that you'd notice, and you still haven't compensated me for the ruined clothes, have you? And now I have a tear in this skirt as well."

John looked abashed. He ordered one of his men forward, weighed an extended pouch in his hand, and lobbed it over at Alex who caught it neatly. She eyed him for a moment, opened the pouch to peek into it, and looked back up at him.

"I want the horse instead."

"My horse?" John stared down at her. "And what would you do with Caesar?"

"Serve him up on a bed of salad with anchovies and bread croutons?" she said, laughing at her own joke.

"Eat him?" John stuttered.

Alex exhaled and took a limping step towards him. "Of course not eat him! I aim to make a gift of him to a real horseman. Someone who'll teach Caesar manners or cut him, whichever comes first."

"Cut him?" John Graham spluttered. "Have you any idea what this stallion is worth?"

109

"At present, he's a bloody hazard to innocent women, that's what he is!" The horse snaked out its head at her, teeth bared, and she rapped him firmly over the nose. "You bite me, and I'll bite you, okay?"

Caesar stamped his front hooves and proceeded to do a series of stiff-legged jumps on the spot, combining this with a quick rearing motion and some more jumps, and John Graham was no longer in the saddle but sprawled on his back at Alex's feet.

"Hello." She grinned.

John wasn't at all amused, getting back on his feet slowly. His cuirass had been knocked askew, and he muttered something about stupid women that hit high-strung horses across the nose.

"Hey, that horse of yours has cost me two – I repeat – two close encounters with the ground in less than four days." She handed him the hat he'd lost in his fall, and indicated the horse with her head. "I still want him, and if he doesn't behave, I can always make sausage out of him."

"What would a farmer's wife want with a war horse?" John Graham asked, smoothing back his hair – no wig today: all in all, a major improvement.

"You never know when they might come in handy," Alex said with a little sigh.

"No," John Graham said softly, "you never know."

He looked straight at her, and Alex smiled at him, liking the way his eyes lightened in response. He studied her openly, and she was conscious of how her hair had come undone to fall in untidy curls around her face. He had to be at least ten years younger than she was, but he seemed to like what he saw, and Alex sucked in her stomach and stood somewhat straighter. His gaze lingered on her chest, and Alex lifted her breasts that much higher, back curving. His eyes met hers, his smile widened, and Alex smiled back, thinking that his eyes were very beautiful, dark and soft like melted chocolate. There was the soft thud of feet dropping to the ground, and Alex whirled towards her husband who came towards her with a scrap of white in his hands.

"Here," Matthew said, handing Alex her cap. He stood watching as she collected her hair and pinned it back up, remained where he was until she had replaced her cap, and gave her the straw hat as well. She flushed at the look in his eyes, at the silent reprimand in how he held himself. Without saying anything, he conveyed the message that she should adjust her shawl over her chest, and not until she was properly covered up did he turn to face John Graham.

"Highwaymen?" he asked.

"A scourge on travellers like yourself, but these wretches will hang come next market day." John nodded his thanks when Samuel came up leading Caesar, and looked over at Alex. "I'm afraid I won't part with my horse this time, but should he aggravate you a third time, then he's yours."

"I'll hold you to it," she said, "and the best way for that not to happen is for you to stay well away from Cumnock."

John grinned. "I will keep it in mind, Mrs Graham." He tightened the girth, adjusted his cuirass, and swung himself back in the saddle, long thighs gripping at the powerful horse. With a quick nod in their direction, he trotted off to where his men were waiting, prisoners on foot.

"What were you doing?" Matthew's voice was soft but very cold, a mere half-inch from her ear.

"Doing? I wasn't doing anything. Well, apart from falling off a horse and scraping my knee pretty badly." She raised her skirt and looked down at the flowering bloodstain on one stocking. "God damn that horse!"

"You know very well what I mean," Matthew insisted, still as soft, still as cold. "You allowed that man to look you up and down as if you were for sale, and you didn't even attempt to order your dress!"

"I was talking to him."

"You were offering yourself to him," Matthew said, and Alex considered slapping him. Instead, she turned her back on him, and limped over to where her sons had decided it was time for food. His hand came down like a clamp on her arm, and she was forced round to face him, his hazel eyes very close to hers. "My wife doesn't allow a man to walk

111

every inch of her body with his eyes."

"You're overreacting. I was fully dressed. And what should I have done? Kicked his shin?"

"You could have started by not pushing your chest forward." He mimicked her stance: how she had placed her hands on her hips and lifted her breasts that much higher. Heat flew up her face, all the way to the tips of her ears. She had liked the way John's eyes rested on her, making her feel attractive.

"I wasn't doing that to flaunt myself," she lied. "I was doing that because I was mad at him. And now I have to get some food into our sons."

"Hmm," Matthew said, and it was clear this was not over and done with.

After dinner, their sons were told by their father to remain where they were and keep an eye on the hobbled horses. He then took Alex by the hand and led her up the hill, up among the crags and down into a little hollow in the heather.

"Mine," he said, undoing her cap, unpinning her hair to spill down her back. Her shawl was thrown to the side, her bodice was unlaced, his hands closing on her breasts.

"Ah!" she said when he squeezed a bit too hard. Her skirts and petticoats landed on the ground, her stays were undone, and moments later, her shift joined her other clothes.

"Mine," he breathed when he laid her down in the springy heather.

"Yours," she said, vulnerable in her nakedness while he was fully dressed. He undid the lacings on his breeches, no more, and took her on the warm hillside, all surging power and bright, bright eyes that stared down at her, demanding her submission. Only once she was twisting and bucking below him did he drive himself to a finish, his head thrown back as he came.

"If you do such again, I'll belt you," Matthew said when they made their way back to their sons.

"What?" Alex stopped. There was no doubt at all in her mind that he meant it.

"You heard," he said. She tried to pull her hand free from his, but he just tightened his hold on her fingers, dragging her along in his wake.

"Do what exactly?" Alex asked.

"You know." He came to a standstill and wheeled to face her. "Or are you saying you don't?" His eyes bored into hers, and to her huge irritation, Alex shook her head, feeling like a chastised child. "Never again," Matthew said. He was enjoying this, the bastard, mouth twitching ever so slightly. He kissed her. "Mine."

"Yours," she confirmed and walked calf-legged beside him.

They rode most of the afternoon in silence, now with Alex perched before Matthew. They made camp, and their sons were amazed that it should be so light so late, looking up at a sky gone violet with the approaching short summer night. On the eastern horizon, Venus winked weakly, and when they looked towards the west, the skies were still aflame with the slowly setting sun.

The evening was surprisingly chilly, and Alex wrapped herself in her cloak and stared for a long time to the west. May they all be safe, she prayed. Dear Lord, keep my children safe.

"Ruth's baby will be born by now," she said when Matthew joined her.

"Aye." He nodded. "Let us hope Julian isn't too disappointed if the wean is a lass."

"Yeah, and that the poor child takes after its mother," Alex said.

Matthew chuckled and draped an arm around her. "It would be unfortunate for a lass to resemble Julian."

"It's unfortunate enough for Edward. It's a most unbecoming colour of hair." Alex smiled at the image of their little grandson, thin sandy strands floating round his head: a fragile child in comparison with his sturdier Graham cousins, but sweet and mild-tempered for all that he was spoiled rotten by his minister father. Alex gnawed at her lip and watched the sun drop out of sight, leaving bands of green and yellow in its wake.

"They might be dead. Any one of them might have been injured or contracted the smallpox, or been savaged by a catamount, and we won't know until it's too late."

"They're not," Matthew tried. "Of course they're not."

"How do you know?" she said and tore herself out of his hold.

Chapter 14

Lanark came as a relief after Edinburgh, the boys eyeing the small town with appreciation rather than apprehension. Matthew stabled their animals at the inn, and then he and Alex went off to the graveyard.

It was market day, and the little town bubbled with excitement at the news of the baby prince. Not a general rejoicing by any means, Alex commented to Matthew when he steadied her up the three worn steps to the graveyard.

"Would you expect there to be? Here, where so many men have died and been buried solely for their non-papist beliefs?"

"No," Alex said, "but the baby's a Stuart, a Scottish line of kings that extends into a misty past."

"It used to be the Stuarts were staunch supporters of the Kirk. James VI was no papist, and his son, for all that he was an oath breaker, was none either."

"He married a Catholic wife, so maybe Charles the first was Catholic – in his heart."

"Mayhap – but I think not." Matthew walked down a long line of tilting headstones, stopping here and there to read an inscription. "The Stuarts turned their back on us. Since the Restoration, we, the Scots, have been hounded by the officers of the King, chased down like beasts in the woods, hanged, fined and deported. And you wonder that there is no rejoicing at yet another wee Stuart?" He stood for a moment in silence, looking over to where a stand of trees shaded one corner of the graveyard. "Orange William won't have problems finding supporters here, while King James and the wee laddie…" He shrugged expressively and resumed his reading of the stones.

It took them well over an hour, but there they were: Rob Gordon and his four girls – Ellen, Mary, Morna and Janet.

"I wonder if she buried the cat here as well," Alex said, kneeling down to place the posy she'd picked on the grass.

"The cat?"

"They all died. First her man, then one by one the girls, and finally the cat, a ginger tom her husband had given her. Sad, isn't it?" She busied herself rubbing lichen and moss off the stones until all the names stood stark against the weathered granite. She traced the dates of Rob Gordon and shook her head. "He wasn't even forty, and now it's more than forty years since he died, and she still, God help her, misses him every time she opens her eyes to a new day."

"You think?" Matthew knelt down beside her.

Alex nodded, her mind swimming with images of Mrs Parson in her constant dark clothes, her old-fashioned cap and collars, together with just as old-fashioned starched cuffs.

"She hasn't changed her appearance. I bet you she still dresses her hair as she used to do, first braiding it and then coiling it below her cap." Alex tugged at the grass. "It's so that he'll recognise her," she went on almost inaudibly. "So that her Rob will know her for who she is when he finds her in heaven." She got off her knees, brushing at her skirts. "Do you think they will?" Will we? she meant. Will you find me once I'm dead?

"Will what?" Matthew took her hand in his, fingers braiding with hers.

"Know each other."

"Aye," Matthew said in a thick voice, "aye, lass, I think they will."

"That's good." Alex nodded, and after one last caressing motion over the silent headstones, followed him towards the gate. "Mind you, things might get a bit complicated if Mr Parson shows up as well."

Matthew laughed softly. "Wasn't he a widower?"

"Oh my God, talk about an interesting reunion scene!" She had liked Mrs Parson's latest husband: tall and thin with white hair and kind eyes. From what little she had gleaned through the years, an exact opposite to Mr Gordon who had been fiery in colouring and temper, short and stout, with a loud voice and a capacity to laugh at anything. "Let's hope she doesn't complicate it further."

"You cannot think she is seriously considering to wed Thomas Leslie," Matthew said.

"Oh, I think the thought has crossed her mind – repeatedly. It's not as if she enjoys living in mortal sin."

"Mortal sin? She's nigh on eighty, and he, well, he's…" Matthew furrowed his brow, "…sixty-nine. Old, aye?"

"I'm sure they manage." She knew they managed, having come upon a far too intimate little scene some months back.

Matthew slapped his hat against his thigh and muttered something about voracious women.

"You think Thomas minds?" Alex chortled.

"Nay, of course not, but I can't have an immoral woman living under my roof, can I? No matter that she is old as the hills."

Alex made an unimpressed sound, and then they were back among the market stalls where they predictably found their sons buying hot pasties.

All next day, Matthew rode in a fever of anticipation. He took in landmark after familiar landmark, told his family small anecdotes of things that had happened here or there, pointed out a spectacular crag, the flight of a buzzard, but all the while he was counting down to the moment when he would see his birthplace once again.

And then they were at Lugar Water, nearly home, and Matthew had to stop and piss, his knees buckling when he dropped off the horse. So close, so very close. Matthew let his hand caress the smooth bark of a rowan sapling, and all around him was oak and alder, stands of hazel, and here and there an odd elm tree.

He was back on the horse, the boys falling back to let him ride first, and in Matthew's hand, the reins began to slide, slick with sweat. He felt Alex tighten her hold around his waist, in reassurance, he supposed. Just as the afternoon began to shift into purple twilight, they rode up the last incline. He held the horse in at the top, and below lay his farm, his Hillview.

It was like having a fist drive into your gut. Matthew's

knuckles whitened with the effort to remain quiet. He cleared his throat in an attempt to dislodge a disappointment so tangible it threatened to choke him. Was this it? The horse dipped its head, and he could feel Alex shift her weight to peek round his side.

Matthew looked down into the small, snug dale, and was filled with an urge to laugh at himself. This was a pitiful place, nowhere close to the burnished images he had so carefully nurtured over the years. He looked towards the water meadows, and all he could see was his yard in Maryland with the huge white oak to one side, the two-storey house he'd built himself, and the flowing fields that dropped from the house all the way to the distant river. So much bigger, so much better than this paltry little manor that lay before him.

Angrily, he banished these disloyal images from his head, swallowed down on the lump in his throat, and concentrated on the buildings below. An old man came out of the barn and halted abruptly at the sight of them.

"Robbie?" Alex gasped.

"Aye, I suppose," Matthew said, studying the barn. Still the same solid structure it had always been, and there were the stables, essentially unchanged, and Matthew's breathing eased, his stomach unclenched. Cows on the water meadows, a horse, some sheep…His shoulders relaxed. Still his place, for all that it had shrunk with the years. A dog barked, and Matthew nudged the horse down the lane, turning his eyes on the grey stone house where he had been born.

He had to halt the horse again, his throat working to overcome the conflicting emotions that surged through him. So small? But still, his house, and the casement windows stood open to the evening air, the kitchen door was propped ajar, and someone was cooking cabbage. A sense of deep peace stole through him when he took in the stone lintel over the door and the wooden window frames that he'd helped his da join and set in place. Further up the slope, he could make out the solitary rowan standing sentinel over the family graveyard, and his blood sang at being home, here, where his roots were.

Alex was silent behind him, and he had no idea what

she might be thinking. He couldn't let her see his own ambivalence, so he straightened his spine, called out something in a loud and falsely cheerful voice to his sons, and clapped his heels into the horse, causing the animal to snort and cover the remaining yards in a burst of speed.

He helped Alex off the horse, the kitchen door opened, and there were Rosie and several unknown people. But, look, wasn't that Gavin? And now Robbie had crossed the yard to greet the returning master, and Matthew allowed himself to be surrounded by his people, using the effusive greetings to hide himself from Alex's far too discerning eyes.

Alex took a step back to where her sons had dismounted.

"We'd best get the horses seen to," Alex said, not wanting to intrude on Matthew's homecoming. She led her sons over to the meadows, helped them unsaddle and unload, and remained there for a while, her elbows resting on the fencing as she took in the pastoral view before her.

If she strained her ears, she could hear the soft murmur of water from where the stream meandered on its way to join Lugar Water. The air was heavy with summer, rich with the scent of growing crops and clover, and from the dovecot came the muttering of the doves.

They hadn't moved the dovecot – as far as she could see it was the same dovecot as always – and the privy seemed to be more or less where it always had been, even if the structure looked rather new. She looked over to where the rowan tree rustled, and pushed off, making for the graveyard and Rachel's grave.

Someone had taken good care of it. Alex smiled through her tears. The rose she had planted grew huge but tamed, weeping white petals all over the little stone. Rachel Anne Graham, four years old at the time of her death.

"Hi," Alex whispered, bending down to let her fingers graze her daughter's name. "It's me, Mama." In her head, she could hear the joyous peals of laughter that accompanied Rachel throughout her days, and in her mind's eye, her little scamp danced, a lively bolt of mercury with hazel eyes and curling, dark hair that always escaped her braids. Tagging her came Jacob, a sturdy two or three, long fair hair falling like a curtain over his face as he called and called for Rachel to wait for him.

"I hope you've found him," she said to the stone. "I hope you and Jacob are taking good care of each other up there." In reply, she heard childish voices, and out of the corner of her eye, she saw two shadowy shapes appear and disappear behind the rowan, their breathless giggles lingering in the air.

She sighed: her Rachel and her Jacob, one dead as a child, the other as a young man. Hesitantly, she had told Luke the whole sorry tale, not because she wanted to, but because Luke had, despite all his faults, loved Jacob, and so deserved to know how her golden, sun-kissed boy met his death. A musket ball through the chest, and all that promise, all that bubbling life was cut short. Both her children dead in the defence of others, Jacob roaring in anger when he leaped to free his sister Sarah from her abductors, Rachel screeching in rage when the officer brought the flat of his sword down on her father's head, rushing to her da's defence only to have her head crushed by the hooves of the officer's horse.

Her eyes misted, her breath grew ragged, and around the rowan, her ghost children danced, one an imp, the other a tall, beautiful young man.

"Jesus," she muttered and closed her eyes, willing the shades back out of sight. She counted breaths: thirty-eight, thirty-nine, forty, and opened her eyes again. She found the little plaque Matthew had set by the rowan tree in memory of Isaac's visit to them.

"*Always present, never forgotten,*" she said out loud, and smiled ruefully. Not at all that present, but definitely not forgotten. "Be safe," she said, seeing Isaac as he surely was right now, busy in his painter's studio. "And you," she added, directing herself to Rachel. "You be safe as well, little angel child of mine."

Her hand slid down the rowan tree's stem, and for an instant, she could pretend it was the solidness of Jacob that she touched. An instant no more, and then she was crouched by the tree, her heart cracking apart with grief.

Chapter 15

"So what you're saying is that you think she's damned," Isaac said, striding at a pace he knew was uncomfortable for Carlos. They'd been discussing the story of Mercedes' life intermittently over the last few weeks. Today, Isaac was spoiling for a fight. He'd woken up with toothache, and on top of that, his latest attempts at painting a way back home had failed – dismally.

He had been here well over three months now, and just the other day, the abbot had politely if pointedly inquired how much longer Isaac aimed to stay. Isaac had no idea. Every now and then, he ventured out into Seville proper, but the heat and the general filth did not exactly endear the city to him, and now he was considering how to get to Scotland and Hillview – after all, Alex was his mother, and had no choice but to take him in.

"I don't think, Isaac. I'm attempting to explain that in the eyes of the Church, she's a witch, and thereby forever excluded from heaven."

Isaac sighed, and wished he'd been wearing jeans so as to shove his hands in the pockets. Now, he clasped them behind his back instead.

"Bloody unbelievable," he muttered, throwing Carlos a sidelong glance.

"Absolutely," Carlos said. His lips twitched, and a bubble of laughter burst away from him.

"What? You think this is funny?" Isaac glared.

"No, no," Carlos said, but there it was again, that bubble of incredulous laughter.

Isaac opened his mouth, but swallowed back his intended reply when Carlos froze at his side, a sibilant exhalation escaping his nose. Isaac followed the general direction of

Carlos' eyes to where three men were studying his mural, walking back and forth before it. The abbot's spine curved obsequiously whenever the black-clad man at his side said something, while Don Raúl walked a step or two behind them, now and then interjecting a comment, no more.

"What?" Isaac asked.

Carlos had a hand on his sleeve, was urging them backwards, back into the protective shadows of the walkway.

"That's Fray José." Carlos gulped. "He's a member of the Archbishop's administration, and a driving force in the Holy Inquisition."

"Oh," Isaac said, working hard to keep his hands open and relaxed.

They had been seen, and with a little wave, the abbot motioned them forward. Don Raúl was looking tense while Fray José turned a bland face their way, light eyes under bushy eyebrows studying Isaac intently.

"The artist," he said with a little nod.

"Yes." Isaac threw a look at his painted Madonna who seemed to smile specifically at him.

"Ah," the Inquisitor said, taking a little stroll round Isaac. "A most tantalizing mural."

"Thank you," Isaac said.

"It was not meant as a compliment," the man barked. "Rather the reverse."

Isaac looked at his mural, bathing in the morning sun, and made a deprecating gesture. "A painter cannot hope to please all."

"That is not what I mean," Fray José said. "I am rather referring to the disquieting aspects of this work."

"Disquieting?" The abbot shook his head. "It's precious, Fray José. It fills our brothers with peace and joy, not disquiet."

"The devil comes to us in different guises," Fray José growled, "and look at her. For all that she's dressed, she stands denuded before us."

"I would assume that depends on the viewer's imagination, not the work itself," Isaac bit back.

"Hmm," Fray José said. "And you're from where exactly?" The change of tack threw Isaac somewhat.

"From the colonies," Carlos said.

"I wasn't asking you, I was asking him." Fray José jerked his head in the direction of Isaac.

"It's as Carlos says, I'm from the colonies."

"Ah yes, but the colonies are vast, so from where exactly?" Don Raúl seemed as interested as the Inquisitor, raising himself up on his toes to properly see Isaac over Fray José's shoulder.

Isaac's brain scrambled for a reply. "My father was born in Veracruz," he came up with, grateful for all the time he'd spent studying the map of the New World, "but I was raised in Maryland." He sifted through everything Carlos had told him about his years in Maryland, about Alex and Matthew. "My parents have a farm there."

"Your parents? A Spanish colonist in Maryland? I think not."

"My stepfather," Isaac said.

"Ah. And is he Catholic?"

"Umm," Isaac said – a most dissatisfactory answer, he could see.

Fray José kept his eyes on him for some while longer, and then turned abruptly to the abbot. "Has he been properly interrogated?"

"Interrogated? Whatever for? The man was in need of shelter, and Carlos vouched for him."

"So you deem him a good Catholic?"

The abbot's brow creased together. "*Sí.*"

"Well, we'll see about that," Fray José said. "I'll be back in some days to conduct some investigations of my own. Until then, this young man is confined to the monastery – I will be sure to inform the gatekeeper on my way out." He gestured for the abbot to accompany him, and left them with no more than a cursory nod.

"Bloody hell," Isaac said in English.

"*¿Qué?*" Don Raúl wiped at his brow with his sleeve

"You brought him here, didn't you?" Isaac said.

"But not for this! He asked me to show him the mural he'd heard so much about." Once again, Raúl's arm swept over his face. "It'll not be too bad. After all, you have nothing to hide, do you?"

Carlos laughed. Isaac laughed.

Don Raúl looked from one to the other. "What?"

"It will take him less than a minute to realise I'm not a Catholic," Isaac said.

"You're not? ¡*Dios mío*!" Raúl had gone quite grey.

"It isn't my fault, is it? I was raised to believe only in science."

"Science?" Don Raúl made the sign of the cross – twice. "An atheist? Sweetest Mother of God have mercy on you, because Fray José most certainly won't." He backed away. "It will be best if you recant quickly, boy. If you plead for forgiveness, because if not—"

"It's much, much worse than that, dear uncle," Isaac said, ignoring Carlos' strangled warning. He regarded his relative for some minutes, weighing up his alternatives. "You see, if the Inquisition starts interrogating me, I will tell them things that will forever throw the illustrious Muñoz family onto the scrap heap. Unless we burn, of course – all of us."

Don Raúl gaped. "Us?" he squeaked. "Why us?"

"Same blood," Isaac said with a crooked little smile. He took a deep breath. "I'm not your nephew, Don Raúl. I'm your great grandson ten times removed or so."

"My what?" With a whoosh, Don Raúl collapsed to sit on one of the stone benches. He stared at Isaac, at Carlos. "That's impossible. You're lying, admit it!"

Isaac shook his head. With a despairing look, Raúl turned to Carlos, who did the same.

"How?"

In reply, Isaac nodded in the direction of the mural. "Sometimes, when I paint, windows open in time – unfortunately." He gave Raúl a long, hard look. "I will, of course, tell the officers of the Inquisition that this is an inherited talent, that all of my family have the ability to paint magic portals."

"But that isn't true!" Don Raúl bleated.

"Prove it," Isaac said. At Raúl's silence, he nodded. "So, dear uncle, how do we get out of this little conundrum?"

"I don't know," Raúl sighed, shoulders hunching together. For an instant, he looked old – very old even. He looked at Isaac. "Truly? You come from the future?"

"Truly." Isaac sat down beside him, and gave him a brief and not entirely complete version of events. On purpose, he did not say anything about Mercedes. "And just in case you're planning on throwing me to the wolves and denying any kind of relationship to me, I'd best tell you that I can add further detail to my story – details that will be most compromising for you and your family."

"I would never—" Don Raúl blustered, but Isaac wasn't too sure. His ancestor was eyeing him as one would a repugnant insect, something best squashed flat.

"Well, that's good. But just in case, I'll leave something in writing as well."

"Don't be absurd!" Don Raúl exclaimed. "That would be like handing someone a loaded pistol and offering your chest at close range for them to shoot at."

"Not my chest." Isaac shrugged.

"He's right," Carlos said once Raúl had left them. "Should you write something down, you could potentially damn all of us."

"I know, and I won't – for your sake. But why tell him that?"

Carlos gave him a weak smile. "He might call your bluff."

"Or he might save my arse. At present, I'm hoping for the latter."

Two days later, the abbot opened the door to their little room sometime just after Prime.

"There you are!" he said to Carlos.

"Father." Carlos bowed deeply in the direction of the small man accompanying the abbot. "Excellency."

Isaac followed suit, even if he had no idea who this peacock of a man might be. For all that he was entirely in black, he preened, his clothes decorated with inlays of gold and silver, crimson ribbons and a matching lining to his full-length cloak. What seemed like yards of lace hung from his cuffs, gold chains dripped down his front, his hands were crammed with rings, and the hat, held now in his hand, was decorated by a lavish arrangement of silk ribbons and feathers.

"His Excellency has need of your services," the abbot said.

"Oh?" Carlos asked.

"To England," the little man said. "You are to go to England and carry despatches for me." He smiled without baring his teeth, and gestured for Carlos to come with him, brusquely turning his back on Isaac.

"Who's he?" Isaac asked the abbot, his fingers twitching with the need to commit this rotund, self-inflated little man to paper.

"That is His Excellency Diego de Guzmán," the abbot said. "Not only a good friend of your uncle but also former ambassador to various courts in Europe—"

Isaac wanted to whoop out loud. This was Don Raúl's doing, and soon they'd be on their way to England, as royal envoys no less.

"…but since many years recalled to work directly for the Queen Mother," the abbot finished.

"The Queen Mother? Is the King a child?"

The abbot shook his head sadly. "A child? No, the King is of an age with you – twenty-seven come November."

"So what's wrong with him?" Isaac asked.

"Everything," the abbot replied, and left.

Brother Mauricio was more forthcoming when Isaac ran into him in the courtyard, explaining that the present King, Carlos Segundo, was, to all intents, an idiot, and severely afflicted by all kinds of disease. Over the next hour, he detailed all the intricacies of the Hapsburg dynasty to Isaac.

"His father married his niece?" Isaac made a grimace.

Brother Mauricio nodded. "To keep the blood pure. That's why they marry cousins or nieces."

"But that's incestuous!"

Brother Mauricio raised an irritated eyebrow. "The Pope has given dispensation."

"Oh well then," Isaac nodded, "and look how healthy all the children are."

"They're not," Brother Mauricio said.

"My point exactly," Isaac said. "So what will happen if this present king doesn't leave an heir?"

"Then, my friend, we become French." The monk shuddered, and it was obvious this was a fate worse than death.

"Ah." Isaac got to his feet. Carlos had been gone for quite some time now, and it was beginning to worry him. Halfway back to the little room, he was met by the abbot. "Where's Carlos?"

"Carlos? Well, I'd assume he's well on his way by now."

"What?" Isaac steadied himself against the wall. "He left without me?"

"Of course he did. You're not allowed to leave." The abbot frowned. "They'll be coming for you tomorrow."

"Coming for me?" It took an enormous effort to remain standing.

"Fray José has decided to conduct the interrogation in his own…ah…premises." The abbot patted Isaac's shoulder. "Pray, my son."

"Pray? And how the fuck will that help?"

The abbot took a step back, looking quite shocked. "What else is there to do? You must pray for fortitude. Fray José is an exacting interrogator."

Isaac swallowed, he swallowed again, and it didn't help. His windpipe was so tight it hurt to breathe.

"*Dios manda*," the abbot said gently. "God decides all our fates. Now, I have sent Brother Mauricio to pack your belongings."

"Pack?"

"Yes, the Inquisition have requested that all your drawings and your notes be sent to them." He gave Isaac a small smile. "It's out of my hands, Isaac Lind. I can only hope and pray that God will see you through this."

Isaac watched the abbot out of sight, wheeled on his

toes, and made for the gate. No way did he intend to stay here! He approached the entryway cautiously, cursing when he saw that there were four guards loitering in the entrance. He drew back, doing a mental walkabout of the monastery. There were two other entrances, one directly into the kitchens — and he knew from experience that there were always very many people in the kitchens — and the narrow door that led to the enclosed pasture that housed the abbot's two mules. From there, he could climb the wall and make his way into the city.

Isaac slid off, moving as silently as possible through the dark passages. His pulse whooshed through his head, there was an unfamiliar tightening of his throat, and he was overwhelmed by an urge to run and hide. Why, oh why had he painted that accursed courtyard? And where the fuck was Carlos? How could he do this to him? Cut and run, and leave Isaac to face whatever horrors lay in store for him alone. Isaac rubbed at his wrists. They'd put him on the rack, and his imagination was vivid enough to make him swallow repeatedly at the thought. Dislocated arms, torn ligaments and tendons... He drew a shallow breath. It wouldn't come to that, he thought bitterly, because he'd admit to anything they told him to before that.

The door was half-hidden from view by a messy tangle of vines. Isaac crouched down in a patch of shade and studied the area carefully. Nothing. No monks, no guards, just a couple of sparrows and some flies. He darted across the small patio, slipped in behind the vines, and tugged at the handle. It gave easily. Isaac expelled his breath. Almost there. He opened the door just enough to allow him to glide through, and stepped with caution into the small pasture beyond. Crickets chirped, flies buzzed, thistles and dandelions covered the ground. And just by the wall stood a guard.

"Let me go!" Isaac struggled against the hands hauling him along. "You have no right to—"

"We have every right," the abbot said from behind him. "Fray José has commanded us to keep you here, and so we will." He regarded Isaac and shook his head. "I must say that having you attempt to escape will only confirm his suspicions." He opened the door to Carlos' little cell. "Put him in here." Isaac was shoved inside, hard enough to have him fall to his knees. Behind him, he heard a key grate in the lock.

Isaac didn't sleep much that night. He drew and drew, he covered every blank space in Carlos' precious books with twisting funnels, willing each and every one of them to somehow come to life, but of course none of them did.

Oh God, they'd burn him, like they'd burned Mercedes. He rocked back and forth on the narrow bed, hating Carlos for abandoning him, Don Raúl for somehow setting this up, leaving Isaac all alone. No doubt his damned relative was presently whispering in all the right ears, ensuring anything Isaac might have to say was discarded as lies. Well, he had a trump card, and once they found Mercedes' painting in Don Raúl's little chest, it might all become a bit too hot for comfort, even for his dear uncle.

"If I burn so does he," he muttered, but it didn't help – not one whit did it help. Just before dawn, he finally fell asleep, and he was in the midst of a dream about Veronica when rough hands shook him awake.

It was still dark outside. Isaac was boosted up on a mule, his hands tied to the pommel, and surrounded by four grim men on horses they set off. Isaac had tried to protest when they tied his hands, but the responding cuff had made his eyes water, leaving a throbbing cheekbone in its wake.

"Dad," he whispered, "Veronica, Isabelle."

The city was eerily silent, a collection of shadows in different hues of black. Isaac's brain darted from one ludicrous suggestion to the other, anything to save him from what he was sure would be a terrible and painful experience. But his escort rode too close, the mule was on a leading rein, and there was nothing he could do.

They were well beyond the Royal Alcázar, on an empty stretch of road, when they were attacked. Several men rose out of the darkness, steel screeched against steel, and one of Isaac's guards screamed out a warning. "¡*Bandidos*! ¡*Moros*!"

Moors? Here? Isaac was helpless on his mule while, all around, men were fighting. One by one, the guards went down, were tied and gagged.

"Five slaves," someone said. "Won't that make our captain happy, hey?"

Slaves? Isaac tore at his bindings, clapped frantic heels into the flanks of the mule. Something hit him in the head. Again. The last thing Isaac registered was someone laughing.

Chapter 16

A whole summer gone in the blink of an eye, Alex thought towards the beginning of August. After a couple of strained weeks to begin with, she'd found herself adapting back to Hillview, rediscovering old haunts and walks up and down the hillsides that surrounded the little manor, but where this once had been paradise on earth, their little slice of heaven, it no longer was – at least not to her. No matter that she didn't voice it out loud, Alex was already counting days in her head, and she suspected Matthew knew she did, even if he never raised the subject.

Instead, Matthew was busy with his own rediscovery, bounding up slopes with the dogs at his heels, laughing and arguing with his tenants as he threw himself wholeheartedly into reclaiming what once had been his. His loud enthusiasm didn't fool Alex. She had chosen not to comment on his obvious disillusion when they arrived, worried that her genuine concern might be taken for a snide I-told-you-so, and so she stood on the sidelines and watched him grapple with this on his own, wishing he would talk to her about it instead of maintaining this enervating cheery façade – as much for his own sake as for hers, she suspected.

At Matthew's heels trudged their sons, and Alex sometimes felt very alone, longing for her daughters – including Naomi and Betty – Mrs Parson and even Agnes. No matter how she tried, she couldn't recapture the old ease with Rosie, and the two girls employed as maids in the big house, Ellen and Marjorie, were far too young and shy for her to even attempt a conversation.

She got to her feet, and inspected the kitchen garden with mild satisfaction. Given the state of it when they arrived, she was proud of what she'd achieved, but the growing season was soon over, and this would not go far in keeping them in vegetables over the winter. Alex rubbed at her protesting knee, and made a mental note to tell Matthew to buy a couple of bushels of onions and cabbage when he next went to market.

"No one's died of an overconsumption of onion soup," she told herself, and went to inspect the apple orchard, admiring the slowly ripening fruit. The hay was already in, and these last few weeks she'd been even more alone, with the boys and her man out on the fields from dawn to well after dusk while she and the maids were expected to cope with all the other chores.

She saw Rosie, and raised her hand in a sketchy wave, and Rosie waved back as well as she could, hoisting a bawling baby higher against her shoulder. Alex lengthened her stride. She liked babies, and Rosie had a bevy of grandchildren she proudly showed off. Snot-nosed, not all that clean, but loved the lot of them, even if Alex suspected this youngest had the rickets, having cautiously suggested that they give the child fish to eat.

Rosie herself looked old – scarily old given that she was eight years Alex's junior – and, as she walked toward Rosie, Alex straightened her spine and raised her chin, anything to avoid the constant hunch with which Rosie nowadays faced the world.

"Good year for apples," Alex said once she was within hearing distance.

Rosie squinted at the trees and nodded. "Plenty of cider, and Robbie says how the harvest looks right good as well."

"Knock on wood," Alex said, touching one of the gnarled stems.

Rosie gave her a strange look, but shrugged. "Wee Robin says you have visitors," she said, nodding in the direction of the yard.

"Visitors?" Alex shaded her eyes with her hand, and made out one very flashy horse.

"The brother," Rosie hissed. "The cheek of him."

"Luke?"

"Aye, the same," Rosie said.

Alex asked her to send Robin out to fetch Matthew, and went to greet their guest.

Luke was standing in the parlour, and on a stool by his side sat Nan. Sullen and unkempt, Nan made no move to rise when Alex entered the room, keeping her eyes on the scrubbed floor.

"She's with child," Luke said without preamble, and Alex could smell the anger leaking through every pore of his body. "Not Charlie's, not unless he was bedding her on the *Diane*, and he adamantly insists he wasn't."

"Every night," Nan said, making Alex throw her a cool look.

"He wasn't," Alex said. "But it could still be his."

In response, Luke yanked Nan up to stand, and indicated her rounded belly.

"Consistent with not quite two months?"

Not very consistent with three months either – rather four or five. Alex eyed her brother-in-law suspiciously. "Why have you brought her here?"

"I can't throw her out on the streets, can I? Not until the divorce comes through. And, until then, I thought she could stay here."

"Why?" Alex wasn't sure she wanted this petite femme fatale in her home. There was something enticing about Nan, and she had three young sons – and a virile husband.

"I don't want her disappearing until she has signed the decree, and in Edinburgh, she'll slip away like mist in the morn and return some years from now to claim support for herself and inheritance for the child."

Alex nodded. A child born in wedlock was always assumed to be legitimate. "And you don't think she'll do a disappearing act here?"

"She can't ride." There was another obvious advantage, he added. Here Nan would be conspicuous, and should Matthew put the word about that she was to be returned to Hillview, no matter where she was found, well, so she would be.

"Probably." Alex took a step back at the look of pure dislike Nan threw her way. "I take it you're not too thrilled." Both Luke and Nan looked at her in confusion. "You're not happy about it."

"He married me," Nan said.

"Under false pretences, it would seem." Alex turned to Luke. "And Charlie? How's he?"

Luke shrugged. In his opinion, it was more about bruised pride than anything else. For now, Charlie remained in Amsterdam, and Luke was to act his proxy in this whole sorry affair.

Luke sat back after an excellent dinner, and undid his belt a notch. The chicken had been delicious, cooked to tenderness before being fried, and with it Alex had served something she called coleslaw, and that consisted mostly of raw cabbage. Luke was not partial to cabbage. It reminded him too much of his mother, and of the pained look in her eyes when she'd told him she never wanted to see him again – ever – not after what he'd done to his brother. Luke shifted on his seat, and turned his attention to the pie.

Repeatedly, his eyes drifted in Alex's direction. If he looked at her through his lashes, he could pretend she was Margaret, albeit a louder, rounder version of his beloved wife. He looked at Matthew, and was stabbed by jealousy. His brother might sit in an old and mended shirt, with breeches the worse for wear, he might have less than a tenth of Luke's worldly goods, but damn it if his brother wasn't the better off. All those sons, and on top of that this woman who now served them all a cup of herbal tea, settling herself beside Matthew.

It wasn't fair. It wasn't right that his Margaret should be dead while Alex, this paler copy of his beautiful wife, was still alive. He hated it that his brother should still have his woman, he hated seeing how close she sat to him, how her eyes flashed to meet Matthew's, how her hand touched his hair, his shoulder. It made him feel gutted, because since the night Margaret died, no woman had touched him like that. Luke felt very alone and quite old – an unfamiliar and unwelcome sensation.

Every now and then, Alex would throw a look out of the window to where Nan was sitting on a bench with David in attendance while wee Samuel – the earless one – maintained a rigid distance from the little trollop. Luke noted Alex's frown whenever her eyes rested on Nan, a frown accompanied by a smoothing of her clothes, an instinctive fiddling with her hair. His sister-in-law clearly felt threatened by Nan, all blue eyes and fair hair that fell uncovered and unbound down her back. Not that Luke could comprehend why: since their arrival, Matthew had at most glanced at the lass. He sipped at his tea, and decided to shift the conversation from farming to politics.

"…so, it's already set in motion," Luke finished.

"What is?" Alex asked, tearing her eyes away from Nan.

"Dutch William has been offered the crown," Matthew said. "There remains but the technicality of wresting it from James that is."

"Who's offered it to him?" Alex said.

"The Pope," Luke jested, but went on to explain that there was a group of disgruntled Protestant grandees that had been most unhappy at the birth of a male heir.

"Too bad it wasn't a girl," Alex said. "Now, whatever happens, there will always be a pretender."

Luke bowed in approval at her insight. "Aye, unless someone assassinates the lad, but that I don't hold possible."

"I hope not!" Alex set down her mug. "It isn't his fault, is it?"

"Lads grow into men, and then what?" Matthew finished his tea and suggested they repair to the parlour instead. "James is a proven soldier," he said over his shoulder, busy lighting the candles with the taper in his hand.

"Aye, but William of Orange is no mean soldier himself." Luke sat down in one of the two armchairs, and accepted the proffered whisky. He couldn't recall the last time he'd sat at his ease in this room. It must have been before he was thrown out on his ear, so somewhere before his sixteenth birthday. "I'm not sure I'm doing the right thing," he said with a sigh. "James is an anointed king, my liege, and now there's a lad as well. And whatever the more bigoted among us may say, James isn't planning on forcing a return to popery. All he wishes is for Catholics to have the same rights as Protestants."

"Religion," Alex said. "Always this damned religion!"

"Aye," Luke agreed, somewhat taken aback, "it's a veritable bone of contention."

"Bone of contention? How many have died in this century alone due to Catholics and Protestants bashing each other up? Add a handful of Puritans and Presbyterians, and we have quite the soup." Alex shook her head. "And now, due to religion, a boy will be disinherited, and some will abide by it while others will not, and so even more people will die – many more over many, many years."

A small shiver walked up Luke's spine. It sounded like a prophecy.

Matthew took Alex's hand, drawing her close. "We don't know," he said, sounding admonishing.

With interest, Luke noted how Alex flushed, eyes darting his way for an instant.

"No," she said, "no, of course we don't. Pure speculation, that's all – after all, how would I know?"

Hmm. Luke was quite intrigued by her discomfiture.

"A month," Alex told Luke next morning.

"A month." He leaned down from his saddle and, for an instant, his gloved hand touched her cheek. "He's a fortunate man."

"And I'm a fortunate woman." She looked over to where Nan had emerged from the privy and brought her brows down in a heavy frown. "She isn't."

Luke followed her gaze. "She's a whore."

"You don't know that," Alex said.

"Aye, I do. Born in the stews of London and plying her trade well before her fourteenth birthday, according to the rolls."

"The rolls?" Alex asked.

"Even whores pay taxes." He looked at his daughter-in-law again. "It's in her best interest to sign the decree," he said ominously.

"Or else?" Alex asked.

"Or else? Accidents happen so easily." He smirked at the look that flew over her face. She was a bad dissimulator, was Alex Graham, and in her face he could read just how much she still distrusted him.

Chapter 17

Isaac woke, and it was dark. Very dark. He was being jolted up and down, and only after a few minutes did he realise he was lying over the back of a horse or something, his face banging regularly into the warm side of the animal. He groaned, tried to move, but he seemed to be wrapped in cloth, and his arms were strapped to his sides. It made him nauseous, this constant jolting, and, for a few brief moments, he was convinced he was about to throw up and drown in his own vomit, but then thankfully the beast came to a halt, and he was unloaded. He tried to say something, desisted. Too much effort, and his tongue was paper-dry, stuck like a stamp to the roof of his mouth.

Someone grunted; he was lifted off the ground. Something creaked. He could smell the sea, hot tar, and sun-warmed wood. A boat? With a thump, he landed on what he assumed to be the deck. A sawing sound, uncomfortably close to his eyes, and Isaac squished them shut. His wrappings gave way, a voice he recognised told him he was safe, and carefully Isaac peeked. Carlos smiled down at him.

"Where am I?" Isaac said.

"Cadiz. Quite the ride."

"I wouldn't know, would I?" Isaac tried to sit up. "Most of it, I've spent rolled into a cloak or something." His arms gave way. Pins and needles in all his limbs, a horrible headache, and on top of it, he'd pissed himself, the crotch of his breeches damp against his skin. But his leather satchel containing his drawings and diary were there, and Carlos was there. His Rolex, however, was not. "I've been robbed."

"Uncle Raúl wanted it," Carlos said, "and I was not in a position to stop him. A memento, he called it."

"He planned this?" Isaac spat to clear his mouth of the fusty taste of mouldy wool.

"All of it, even if it's true that I have letters to deliver in England."

"Oh." He glared at Carlos. "How could you just leave me like that?"

"What was I to do? Refuse the ambassador?" Carlos scratched at his peg – he did that quite often. "And once I was aboard, Uncle Raúl explained his little plan, so I knew you'd be safe."

"Oh, you did, did you? Well, I sure didn't! And, anyway, how could he be certain it would work out?"

"He told Fray José it was best to pick you up sooner rather than later, and preferably before dawn." Carlos stood, supported Isaac onto his feet. "He asked me to warn you never to come back. If you do, he'll have you killed, future relative or not."

"Well, how sweet of him," Isaac said.

"He means it. That, or he'll sell you to the infidel, as he's planning to do with the guards."

Isaac just nodded. He had no desire to revisit Seville, not in this time or his own. "And you?"

"Me? Well, he can't very well forbid me to come back, can he? The ambassador would be quite distressed, as would the abbot."

The first few days aboard, Isaac was mostly confused. Carlos and he were allotted a hammock each, they ate with the sailors, were expected to help when needed, but were otherwise left to their own devices. The captain was a surly Basque who told them he'd be delivering them to Calais as agreed, and from there they'd have to find another vessel to take them to Edinburgh. The crew were friendlier, a polyglot group of men from all around Spain and France with the odd Scotsman and even a Swede. When they discovered Isaac could draw, they queued up before him, asking that he commit their features to precious scraps of paper that they would then send home to sweethearts, wives or mothers. Even the captain thawed somewhat, demanding that Isaac do an imposing full-length sketch of him, one hand on the cannon, the other on his sword.

Surrounded by so much water, Isaac felt confident that here, at last, he'd be able to paint a time portal. He drew the cresting waves, and his belly flipped. He drew the ship, its masts, and the sails on paper billowed, the rigging vibrated. Yes! Isaac knotted his hand round his stump of coal, and decided it was time for brushes and oils.

Over the coming days, he committed the ship to canvas, and the crew would flock around him, commenting on this and that. He added humans to the riggings, the captain on the poop deck, and if he placed his ear close to the canvas, he heard his painted ship creak into life. The sails, the fluttering flag, even the miniature men that clambered like monkeys up and down the rigging, all of them moved. And then, finally, it was time for the sea.

"Red? Yellow?" Carlos looked from the blob of paint to Isaac. "Water is blue."

"You think? Look closely, cousin."

Carlos stumped over to the railings, stood there for a while. "Blue. No reds, no yellows. Maybe some green."

"You'll see," Isaac shrugged.

"You didn't tell me you'd be depicting a sunset," Carlos said a few days later. On canvas, the sea shifted from darkest blue through aquamarine and green, and a setting sun threw reflexes of red and orange, pink and white to dance on the waves. It heaved, it flowed, it sang.

"*Madre de Dios*," Carlos muttered, rearing back so abruptly he banged into Isaac. "There are things that move in the sea!"

"Of course, fishes and mermaids." Isaac smiled down at a waving tailfin, a flash of silver that flew by his painted ship before it sank into the depths. He held the canvas between his trembling hands and smiled. At last.

But no matter how much magic and talent Isaac poured into his painting, no matter how desperately he knelt before it, allowing his eyes to sink deeper and deeper into his depicted sea, nothing happened. The painting jeered, it beckoned, it teased, and sometimes he would see the waters begin to swirl, and all of him would tense with expectation, only to see it all return to normal. Isaac was drained of energy and hope. He lay down in his hammock, turned his face to the boards above him, and neither ate nor spoke.

...I'm stuck here. There's no way back, none at all, and, damn, I don't want to be here! And now I even have lice, a nice little extra included in the cruise. I have no idea what to do about lice – Carlos says you douse them in vinegar or shave off your hair – all your hair. So now I'm bald like an egg, and still all of me itches, and Carlos just shrugs and says that's the way it is. Most men have lice or fleas or something living off them. Shit, Dad, what do I do? And why the fuck am I writing this anyway? It isn't as if you'll ever read it, is it?

Chapter 18

"Get on." Matthew leaned over to offer his hand to Nan.

The lass stuck her tongue out and remained where she was, sitting on a stone. She raised her chest provocatively in his direction. "Why don't you join me down here instead?"

"I don't want to," he said.

Nan laughed, undid her bodice, the neckline of her shift. "No?" she purred. "It must be dreary for a man as handsome and healthy as you to bed the same old wife year after year. I dare say her tits sag more than these, do they not?" She exposed herself, pink nipples dark against the milky white of her skin.

"Cover yourself," Matthew said. "Get on the horse now or I'll tie you to it and drag you back."

A half-hour later, they rode down the lane with Nan sitting in front. She had not bothered overmuch with rearranging her clothing, and Matthew saw Alex's eyes lock on the unlaced bodice, on the breasts that bobbed up and down under the sheerness of the linen shift. With a hiss, she strode over to where Matthew was depositing Nan on the ground.

"Why are you half undressed?" Alex asked with a dangerous edge to her voice. "Did you meet up with a man that took your fancy?"

"It was him, he groped me, he did." Nan threw a disgusted look at Matthew who but looked back. This lass was in need of a belt, but damned if he intended to lower himself to beating a woman.

"The wee hussy unlaced herself," he said, dismounting.

Supper was delayed due to Nan's attempt at running away. The third time in a fortnight, and Matthew felt a flare of resentment that Luke should have left her here, and on top of it during harvest. Once they'd eaten, he was too tired to want anything but his bed, and when Alex had finished in the kitchen, they made their way upstairs, discussing Adam's future.

"But why?" Alex said. "Why send him all the way down there?" Every line of her body indicated how much she disliked the thought of sending Adam down to London to live with Luke.

"He can't very well go to school here, can he? And Luke offered. Seeing as the lad wishes to be a physician, it won't come amiss to have attended Westminster for some years."

"And just like that you've decided your brother will make him a good role model, have you?"

"No." It cost him to consider Luke an adequate guardian for their youngest son. "But I don't know anyone else in London, and Luke will see him on his way to Oxford. And he did right by Jacob, didn't he?" He sank down to sit on their bed, biting back on the pain that shot up through his lower back. He ungartered his stockings and rolled them off, sniffed at them, and threw them into an untidy pile by the door.

Another wasted day, he thought morosely. He had better things to do than chase a lass with child across the moss. His brow creased together when he recalled how Nan had brazenly unlaced herself, offering pert breasts for him to inspect and fondle. She was right eye-catching, she was, with that fair hair, those elfin features, and her big blue eyes. He slid a cautious look in the direction of Alex only to find her eyes nailed on him.

"So, did you?" she asked.

"Did I what?"

"Did you grope her? Fondle those little tits of hers that she so invitingly allowed to hang in open view."

"Alex!" Matthew gave her an affronted look. "Of course I didn't!"

"And did you want to?" she asked.

"Nay," he replied firmly. A chit of a lass, no more, and with the morals of a snake – no, not at all his type.

He pummelled the pillows into shape, and reclined against the headboard to watch her brush her hair and proceed with all her other evening rituals. If he closed his eyes, he could almost imagine it was twenty years ago, because here, in their bedchamber, very little had changed over the intervening years. The bed was still the one his da had made; the stools and the little table at which Alex was presently seated he himself had made. The candlesticks, however, were new, the old ones carried over the sea with them to Maryland, and the looking glass was new as well, a gift from him to her in Edinburgh.

She smiled at him through the mirror, uncorked yet another stone jar, and the room was filled with the scent of lavender and lemon balm. She greased hands, neck and face, looked about for yet another jar, and this time the room was suffused with peppermint. Happily, Matthew rolled over on his front, lifting his shirt out of the way to allow her to massage his sore lower back.

"It's even our old sheets," Alex said later, nodding at his comment about how time had seemingly stood still here, in their private space. "They've aged better than we have," she added, dragging a hand over the embroidered linen.

"They were made to last, while you and I, we walk the earth a short while only."

"But still several years left, right?" Alex said, curling up against him.

"Oh, aye, many, many more. I aim to live until you're crowned in white, all of your hair a beautiful white."

"Good to know," Alex laughed, "and next time I'm at the apothecary, I'll be sure to ask him about herbs to dye my hair."

"Dye this?" Matthew combed his fingers through the thick curly hair, noting how some hairs were white, others a silvered grey, but most of them were brown, a brown that shifted through chestnut and bronze to the deeper shades of hazelnuts. "That would be a shame, to kill all these colours."

"I won't." Alex yawned. "At least, not yet." She twisted round to lie on her back, and looked up at the ceiling, her brow furrowed in concentration. "I don't like having her here."

"It's not for that much longer," Matthew said, pillowing his head on her chest.

"I sincerely hope not, and next time she attempts to run away, I'm tempted to use a switch on her."

"You? You don't hold with corporal punishment."

"There's always an exception," Alex replied.

Despite being so tired his eyes ached, Matthew enjoyed lying this close to his wife. The evening shifted to deepest night, and still they talked – of the letter Alex had written to Ian and Mark, of how Samuel was settling in surprisingly well, even if he at times would escape for hours to walk on the moors, making Alex imagine all kinds of horrible deaths, chief amongst them being impaled on a thicket of gorse. That made Matthew laugh, long and hard.

Alex skirted the subject of Adam again, but Matthew inflected his voice in such a way as to convey that this subject was closed, he'd made up his mind, and that was that. So they moved on to discuss David, and would he enjoy Glasgow, or find it too cold, too grey, too full of stone?

"Cold, aye, but as to the rest…well, he's a young lad. He won't spend overmuch time perusing his surroundings."

"No, he'll have his nose in a book," Alex snorted, and they chuckled, knowing their son to be bright and curious and with a developing eye for the lasses.

Alex slipped a hand inside his unlaced shirt and tugged at his chest hair, making him grunt and attempt to shift away, half asleep as he was.

"Have you met them yet?" she asked. "All those old friends of yours?"

"Aye," Matthew replied shortly, not wanting to discuss this. It tore at him that men he had previously considered his friends had not as much as ridden by to bid him welcome back.

"And?"

Matthew exhaled, muttered something about it being late and him being tired.

Alex was not that easily dissuaded. "And?" she repeated.

"It's difficult." Matthew propped himself up on an elbow to see her better in the dim light. "They've lived through years of fear and persecution, have seen loved ones die on account of their faith, and here I come, returning unscathed and relatively prosperous, bringing with me three healthy lads and my equally healthy, bonny wife." He smiled slightly when he said that.

"They don't think you belong," Alex said, and Matthew collapsed back down with a little sigh.

"Nay, I'm an outsider. And it isn't only the other farmers, it's the tenants as well. It'll be a struggle to regain their confidence." He found a tendril of her hair and wound it round his finger. "I didn't expect it. I thought it would all be like before."

His wife didn't say anything. She just hugged him close.

With dawn, self-confidence returned to him, and he made it clear he had no intention of resuming their nightly conversation – at least not now. He was in a hurry to get outside, could hear his two eldest lads thumping their way down the stairs, and he kissed Alex on her cheek, making for the door. Halfway there, he suddenly remembered and turned back, his hand already groping in the pocket she had sewn into his breeches.

"For you," he said. "Happy birthday."

"It was yesterday," she said, extending her cupped hands to receive yet another addition to her collection of his small woodworkings. This time, he had captured her asleep, curled on her side with one arm stretched out before her, and the shift rucked up high, baring one buttock.

"Yesterday?" Matthew counted in his head, and then looked down at her. "Aye, so it was." No great matter, not really, he reflected, kissed her once again just in case she shouldn't agree with him on this, and bounded out of the room.

"It always ends the same way," Alex said an hour or so later. "I start frying pancakes and suddenly the whole kitchen is full of hungry men, and by the time I've fed all of them, there's almost no batter left for me." From where she sat, Nan actually laughed. Alex gave her a mock worried look. "Are you ill?"

"No." Nan sounded confused.

"Seeing as you laughed, a huge improvement on your constant sulking." Alex brought her plate over to the table, dribbled honey over her pancakes, and with a blissful little 'ah' began to eat.

"I'm kept here against my will," Nan said.

"Mmhmm," Alex agreed through her full mouth. "But it could be worse," she added once she had swallowed. "Luke could have turned you out to fend for yourself in Amsterdam."

Nan just shrugged and went back to her knitting.

"How could you do this to Charlie?" Alex asked, spearing the last of her pancakes. "Anyone with half an eye could see he was in love with you, poor devil."

"Which is why I wed him," Nan said.

"Oh, out of the goodness of your heart? You could have told him beforehand."

Nan snorted. "I wasn't sure myself."

Alex raised her brows. "It's not your first pregnancy, is it?" Most whores got pregnant now and then, no matter how careful they were.

"No," Nan sulkily admitted.

"And the father?"

"The father? How am I to know?" Nan tugged at the wool, her needles flying.

"Ah," Alex said. "And what will you do now?"

"Do?" Nan looked down at her stomach. "I imagine I'll give birth in due course, and then I'll return to London – with a sizeable amount of money, for all that it's not a full marriage portion. And once there, I'll go back to my trade. I'm very good at it," she said with pride.

"Oh, I'm sure," Alex nodded ironically.

"I can entice any man!"

"Yeah, I saw that yesterday," Alex laughed. "It seemed you failed dismally."

"How do you know? He might have had me before he took me back."

147

"Not my man," Alex said complacently.

"Any man," Nan repeated, a challenging look in her eyes. "Even yours."

Alex just laughed. "Do your best."

It was right odd: wherever he went, Nan would appear, always with those big eyes of hers fixed on him. It made him itch, to be the recipient of this much admiration, and he took to going roundabout ways so as to avoid her, to no avail. The lass must have the instincts of a hound, because, sure enough, if he was in the stables or in the fields, she'd suddenly be there as well, dainty like a poppet.

Matthew dragged a hand through his hair when he saw her loitering by the kitchen door, took a few long strides in the direction of the house, and there she was, stumbling over the threshold to land breathless and squealing in his arms. And she was soft and young, firm breasts pushing against his surprised hands. He righted her, gave her a dark look, and continued inside.

"What happened to you?" Alex asked.

"Nan," he muttered, "she fell into me, like."

"Oh, she did, did she?" Alex looked him up and down, and then over to where Nan had disappeared into the privy.

Next morning, Matthew climbed the ladder to the hayloft, and there was Nan, sitting with her lap full of kittens. Rounded with child, she looked right adorable, small and delicate with all that fair hair standing like a halo round her head. She smiled up at him and lowered her lashes.

"Pretty," she murmured, and her fingers moved in slow movements over the back of one of the cats. Up and down her hand went, and Matthew cleared his throat and moved over to inspect the hay.

Out of the corner of his eye, he saw her stand, shaking her skirts free of mewling kittens. She had to pass close by him to get to the ladder, and she giggled when her belly as if by chance brushed against him. She leaned into him, long enough that he should feel the shape of her.

"Get away with you," he said, stepping out of range.

Nan laughed, a sound like soft bells that faded as she disappeared down the ladder.

Over the coming days, Nan became his permanent shadow. At times, he saw Alex look first at Nan, then at him, something dark lurking at the bottom of her eyes. It irked him. His wife should know better than to think him anything but flustered by this constant, fawning attention. But she was right bonny, the lassie, and it was him, not one of the younger men she had fixated on. At times, it made him preen, extending his legs to walk that wee bit faster, straighter.

Nan trailed after the men and the lads to the fields, sat down in the shade of the trees, and studied him avidly, and Matthew pulled in his stomach, swung the scythe faster, and all the time those limpid blue eyes hung off him, wide and adoring. When she stumbled on the way back, he stretched out his arm to help her, and she smiled, holding on a bit longer than necessary, her hand sliding down his bare forearm.

"If you ever touch her that way again, I'll scratch your eyes out," Alex told him over supper, having caught him steadying Nan with a hand on the small of her back.

"I was but stopping her from falling," Matthew protested.

"Right," Alex said, and when he extended his hand to her, she just brushed by him, skirts swinging round her legs.

He was mildly irritated by her behaviour. It wasn't as if he had done anything, was it?

"What happened to your back?" Nan asked next day, walking beside Matthew.

"My back?" Matthew had forgotten she was there and taken off his shirt, baring his scarred skin to the sun.

"I saw…" Nan shook her head sadly. "It must have hurt." A small hand danced down his spine, lingered for some seconds.

"Aye," Matthew replied, and increased his pace to catch up with his sons.

"A right pity on such a beautiful back," Nan said from behind him, and Matthew pretended he hadn't heard, but his carriage straightened all the same.

"Why does she always have to come with us?" Samuel muttered a few days later.

"Mmm?" Matthew looked at him.

"Her, Nan. I don't like her, or the way she looks at you."

"At me?" Matthew laughed.

"Aye, she does." Samuel fixed eyes gone a muddy green on him.

"Fancies, lad. If anything, she gawks at you or David."

Samuel shook his head. "She's flaunting herself, Da – for you, not us. And at times it seems to me you like it."

Matthew wasn't quite sure what to say, muttered something about not being able to help if a lass threw cow's eyes at him.

"Mama—" Samuel began.

"Stop, we will not discuss this ridiculous subject further."

"…will not like it," Samuel finished. When Nan chose this precise moment to come up to them, he made a disgusted sound and hurried away.

"What?" Nan asked, turning those innocent saucers of blue on Matthew.

"Nothing," Matthew said, and strode after his son.

The tail end of the harvest, and Alex was run off her feet coping with all those things that had to be done by someone else than the men now that the barley and the rye screamed for attention. She rose at dawn to cook huge breakfasts; she spent the early morning in the kitchen garden, had food and beer and cider carried over to the fields. She checked stables and barns, fed the pigs and the hens and chided her men to wash and eat and clean their teeth. In all that, she didn't really have time to worry unduly about Nan, or the young woman's enervating habit of hovering round Matthew, a permanent laughing female appendage to her husband – until the day she decided to carry the food basket herself up to the field.

She heard them first, the voices of her boys, the low rumble of Matthew saying something, and Nan's high laughter. They were sitting in the shade, with Nan propped up against a tree while two of her sons – not Samuel – and her man lounged around her. She watched, mesmerised, when Nan slid one bare foot towards Matthew. Suddenly, those long toes brushed her husband's arm, and he didn't move it away. She willed him to. She stood on the path and waited for him to shift himself away from this invasive and unwanted intimacy, but Matthew continued with what he was saying, and the toes slid that much nearer, caressing the underside of his arm.

Alex crashed through the shrubs, and the scene before her shattered, as if she had lobbed a stone into a still pool of water.

"Alex!" Matthew leapt to his feet with a strained smile.

"Matthew." She set the basket down in slow motion, and then she raised her foot and kicked it, sending it flying into the air as stone bottles of beer, carefully wrapped pies, and the rose she had placed at the bottom fell to land around them. Without a further word, she left, half running in her haste to get away from them – from her, the little bitch, but even more from him, her husband.

David and Adam gaped, looking from the scattered foodstuffs and the bottles to Matthew.

Nan laughed. "Oh dear. What got into her?"

Matthew was tempted to shake her until her teeth rattled. Instead he attempted a shrug, said something deprecating to his sons about fickle women, but his eyes were stuck on the rose: a red, red rose, newly plucked and shorn of thorns.

Chapter 19

By the time Matthew got his wits back and rushed after Alex, she was long gone. She was being ridiculous, he told himself, to kick the basket like that and run off, for all the world like an irresponsible bairn, and for what? It was the lass making advances, not him, never him!

He couldn't find her, no matter that he looked everywhere for her. He hastened towards the house, threw a look at the empty kitchen, and flew up the stairs to their bedchamber. His box, the one where she kept all his birthday gifts, had been brutally thrown against the opposing wall, scattering carvings all over their bed. Carvings of Alex at all ages, laughing, crying, thinking, and on none of those carved faces was an expression close to the one he had seen on her face today: one of utter and absolute disappointment.

For an instant, he sank down on the bed, attempting to collect his thoughts, but all he could think of was the rose, her secret gift to him on this their thirtieth wedding anniversary, and he, oaf that he was, allowing a chit of a lass to pay court to him, flattered by the admiration he saw in those pale blue eyes.

He was outside again, calling her name as he ran from one outhouse to the other. She wasn't in the stables or the barn. Not in her precious kitchen garden, not on the wooded slopes, and when he reached the hilltop, convinced that here at least he would find her, she wasn't there. He had to sit for a while, find his breath, and then off he went, skirting the millpond on his way back down to the yard.

No one had seen her. Rosie gave him a helpless look, saying that last she saw the mistress she was packing the basket. Samuel appeared from the water meadows and shook his head, saying Mama had been nowhere close to him.

"What happened?" he asked.

"Nothing." Matthew averted his face to avoid Samuel's eyes.

"Nan," Samuel stated, sounding as if he wanted to spit on the lass. "Mama caught you making eyes at her, didn't she?"

"I have never made eyes at Nan! If anything, she has been making eyes at me."

"Aye, but you haven't told her not to, have you?" Samuel turned slightly, frowning as he inspected the yard. "Where can she be?"

"I don't know." Matthew sank down to sit, feeling tired. His amputated toe hurt – it always hurt, despite not being there, when he ran.

"Best find her," Samuel said, moving away.

"If you go looking along the stream, then I—"

"She doesn't want me to come looking, does she?" Samuel interrupted.

Matthew sighed and rose to his feet. The lad was right: it had to be him that came looking, him that found her. He pursed his mouth, trying to think where she might be, but came up with an absolute blank. Well, she was nowhere on the manor, so he set off at a trot up the lane, away from Hillview.

Half an hour on, and he was beginning to become seriously worried. Had she mayhap set off for Cumnock on her own, on foot? He recalled a night very many years ago when she had threatened to leave him, and something like an aching pit opened in his stomach. Surely, she wouldn't do something so foolish, not over something as inconsequential as a lass and her naked toes? He flushed. He should have yelled at the wee trollop, told her to keep her hands and her toes, her blue eyes and soft words to herself. But he hadn't, and now his Alex was running away from him, hurt to the quick because he had acted the fool. The rose… He groaned, promised himself he would make it up to her, and hastened on in his search for his wife.

Moments later, he crossed the dirt track to Cumnock, sank to his thighs in the bristling gorse on the other side, because now he could see where she'd gone. She'd left a blazing trail through the vegetation, and he wondered where on earth she was going, and what he could say to her once he caught up with her.

Mayhap he should return home. He came to a hesitant halt. Aye, it would be the sane thing to do: leave her time to soothe those ruffled feathers of hers, compose herself, and realise that there was nothing to be upset about – not truly. The lass was throwing herself at him, everywhere he went she was, a delectable female presence that begged for him to touch her, caress her, aye, even take her.

Matthew scrubbed at his face. He'd be lying if he claimed to be unperturbed, but better not tell Alex that. No, better to appear affronted and hurt by her lack of faith in him. And he hadn't actually done anything, he reminded himself yet again, nor would he ever have done so – of course not, not even if the lass had turned up naked in his bed. With an exhalation, he began walking again. To not go after Alex would be to compound the damage.

It was her foot. Had he not seen it, he'd have walked by her little hiding place but as it was, the worn but polished shoe leather caught the sun and sent a reflection his way. The slope was steep, riddled with stones, and he was sweating by the time he reached the top. Her foot was still there, unmoving. His heart did a double somersault. Had she fallen to break her neck in her haste to get away from him?

He swallowed and swallowed, trying to lubricate a throat gone tinder-dry, and those last few yards were the longest yards he had ever traversed in his life. The toe of his boot knocked against a stone, and the foot disappeared. She was on her feet when he rounded the standing rock, her back pressed against the stone behind her, her eyes a dangerous dark blue.

Matthew came to a standstill, only feet from her, arms hanging by his side. He took a step towards her, and Alex shrank back, making him stop. There were tear tracks on her face, and she must have wiped both eyes and nose with a dirty hand, leaving smudges all over her skin.

"Just leave me alone, okay?" she said, avoiding looking in his direction. Her right hand twisted her wedding band round and round, the sapphire glinting whenever the sun caught it.

He took another step in her direction, a slow, hesitant movement that brought him close enough to touch her should he dare to. "Alex, please."

She ignored him, shifting so that she was turned away from him, so that he couldn't quite reach her. She cleared her throat. "Arsehole." With that, she walked off.

"Nothing has ever happened," Matthew said once he caught up with her.

"Nothing has ever happened? Well, that's a relief, isn't it? And what was it I saw today, when her toes more or less dug into your armpit? What was that, Matthew Graham? Was that nothing?"

"Aye." Of course it was.

"So where do you draw the line? Is it nothing if her hand rests on your forearm? If you place your hand here?" She indicated her own waist. "Or here?" Her hand moved up to chest level, fingers cupping one round and shapely breast.

"It was nothing," he repeated, backing away from her angry eyes.

"I'll remember that, shall I? Next time I run into John Graham, or any other attractive man for that matter, I'll not only allow him to look, I'll encourage him to touch, to lay his hand on me, to draw his finger down my arm. After all, it's nothing – you just said so." She stood balanced on the balls of her feet, and Matthew kept a close watch on her, knowing just how effortlessly she could pivot on her toes and slam her free foot into him.

"That isn't the same, and I've never touched her like that."

"No. You've just enjoyed it when she has inadvertently touched you, haven't you? Your male ego has basked in her attention, and I bet it's made your cock twitch."

He didn't reply, because what was he to say?

"Fuck off, just go, will you?"

"Alex," he pleaded. "Come back with me."

"No," she said icily. "I'll just celebrate my wedding anniversary on my own, thank you very much."

"Alex." He tried to take her hand, but was brutally shoved away.

"Don't you lay as much as a finger on me!" she spat, retreating like a cornered cat. She found another boulder behind her and slid down to sit. "Go away. Why not ask Nan to do some more toe fondling – see if I care." With that, she crossed her arms over her chest, and he had no idea what to do. Finally, he opted for sitting down where he stood, extending his legs before him.

"I told you to go," she said. "I'm old enough to find my own way back, okay?"

"But I won't, not without you. If you intend to celebrate our wedding day out here, then I must be here too. I was there that first day, wasn't I?"

She gave him a cold look. "Seeing as it was you I married, of course you were."

He moved closer, and he could see a glint of blue from below her lashes as she peeked at him.

"You can't truly think I have any affection for her."

"No? So why didn't you tell her to keep her toes to herself? In fact, why didn't you make sure she understood just how irritated you were by her continued flirting?"

"I—"

"I'll tell you why! Because you enjoyed it!"

"Alex, please."

"Please what? Forgive you?"

"I haven't done anything," he protested, but from the way she regarded him, that was not the right thing to say. "I haven't," he repeated. "I would never do anything to dishonour you – you know that." She looked anything but impressed. "God's truth, woman! You know I love you – only you!" That made her mouth soften somewhat.

She sighed loudly. "Of course, I know you love me – and, no, I don't think you've fondled the little bitch. If I did,

I wouldn't be here. I'd be packing to leave you – for good."

His breath hitched at the thought, seeing an ice-cold Alex riding away from him.

"I had hoped to surprise you. I even went to the trouble of making your favourite pie."

He winced. He had forgotten, focused on his harvest. He extended his leg and nudged at her foot. "Come here. Come to me, my heart."

"No way," she said, retracting her foot from his touch.

He shifted closer to her, she scooted away, he came after, now close enough to take her hand. She let him, her hand lying limp and passive in his hold. He tugged a bit, patting at his chest, and she shook her head, pulling back.

He tugged again, she resisted, he drew her towards him, and then she was there, lying with her head on his chest. Matthew dragged his knuckles up and down her back in a soothing, steady rhythm that had her relaxing against him. There was a stone sinking into his shoulder, but he wasn't about to move, not now. The sun was warm, the air hummed with flies and bees, an occasional butterfly fluttered by, and his hand rested on her head, one finger rubbing small circles over the back of her skull.

"I forgot," he said.

"Typical male," she said.

"That's not fair. Over the years, I've remembered as often as you have."

"Huh," she snorted, but seeing as he was right, she couldn't very well say anything, could she? They lay quiet, she with her head pillowed over his heart, he with his fingers tracing her skull, her ears.

"You know, don't you?" he murmured. "I don't want anyone but you, and even if I may be old enough to be flattered by the attentions of a lass, that is nothing for you to bother unduly about. That is only me being a daftie. I love you, Alexandra Ruth. I want you and need you – only you. That's the way it's been since the day I first met you."

"You would say that – particularly in the present situation."

"Are you calling me a liar?" His hand slid down to grip

her round her nape. "Are you?" he demanded when she didn't reply. He rose on his elbow, flipped them over so that it was her staring up at him.

A pink tongue flitted out to wet her lips. "No," she said.

His hand cupped her face, his thumb running back and forth over her mouth until she opened it and bit him, softly.

"That's good. I would have had to call you out to fight otherwise. I can't have my wife impugning my honour." She laughed, and he dropped a kiss on her brow, came back up on his knees. "Now, lass, will you walk back with me and serve me dinner before I expire of starvation?"

"In your dreams, Mr Graham. I already made you dinner once today." But at least she allowed him to help her up.

They were coming down the lane when Samuel, David and Adam came in from the fields, trailed by the tenants and Nan. Alex came to a halt, uncertain as to what she was supposed to do. Rush over and slap the little slut? Haughtily ignore her, or perhaps smile blandly at her? She knew what she wanted to do alright, and that wasn't pretty, not pretty at all. She's pregnant, Alex reminded herself, and even if she'd fit through the privy hole, you don't push expectant women to wallow in shit.

Matthew looked down at her, swept his eyes over his sons, and raised Alex on her toes and kissed her, there in open view. Kissed her until her cap fell off, until her hair came undone, and their sons began to groan and tell them to stop, it was right disgusting, it was. When he let her go, she was breathless and warm, her hands already busy with her hair.

"Wow," she said in an undertone.

"Dynamite," he whispered back, and Alex burst out laughing at his anachronistic expression, making him look very pleased. When she straightened up, Nan was nowhere to be seen.

Chapter 20

Luke came riding down the lane to Hillview on a blustery September day, carrying the deed that annulled his son's marriage in one of his satchels. At his back rode two grooms, and he was carrying both sword and pistols – over the last few weeks, the political situation had further deteriorated, here and there igniting sparks of violence. Ah well, first things first, and foremost in his mind was to dispatch Nan back to where she belonged: the Southwark stews.

"I might still refuse to set my sign on it," Nan said, sniffing haughtily.

Luke raised his brows, no more. The silly lass deflated. He placed the deed before her, watching as a hawk while she inked a laborious N followed by some illegible squiggles. Once that business was concluded, Luke handed her a leather pouch, informed her the man outside would accompany her to Cumnock and ensure she found transport down south, and so, less than an hour after Luke rode in, Nan rode out, sitting pillion behind Luke's manservant.

"Good riddance," Alex said.

"Aye." Luke threw one last look at his former daughter-in-law and then wiped all thoughts of Nan from his mind, turning instead to his brother to suggest a wee walk.

"He has declared his intent to claim the throne," Luke said to Matthew as they made their way up the hill, in unspoken consent avoiding the millpond where their father drowned.

"On behalf of himself or his wife?"

Luke hitched his shoulders. William of Orange was a nephew in his own right to King James, married to his first cousin, Princess Mary. "He's too canny to claim it on his own behalf, but the crown has been offered to him – to him and her conjunctly."

"Do you reckon she loses sleep over it?" Matthew said.

"Aye, I'm sure she does. James may have many faults, but he was – is – a devoted father." He thought back to a recent encounter with the King, an elated father of a newborn son, who couldn't understand how his eldest daughter should be so cruel as to question the boy's legitimacy.

Luke was at present not proud of himself. More and more, it preyed on him that he was aiding and abetting in the disinheritance of a child. Even more, the King was no fool, and knew that his kingdom was shifting restlessly under his feet.

"He doesn't know who to trust, and, in truth, it seems to me he is paralysed, torn between his son and his firstborn daughter." Luke shook his head. "Nor does it help him much, this calumny that the prince is a changeling, smuggled into the royal apartments in a warming pan to replace a stillborn child."

James Stuart had been unfortunate in fatherhood. With his first wife, he had eight children of which only two daughters survived, and now with his second wife there had been nine – ten? – bairns that had been stillborn or died in infancy before the birth of the wee lad.

"So what will you do?"

"Do?" Luke hitched his shoulders. "Too late, brother. It is all set in motion, and I can't go back on my word – I'm far too compromised. As is my son."

"Well, at least he's unwed again," Matthew said.

Luke sighed. "Aye, well. As far as we know."

On the way back down, Luke swerved to the left, leading the way to the millpond.

"I didn't intend him to die," Luke said, "or maybe I did. I don't know, not anymore." He picked up a stone and sent it flying in the direction of the waterwheel, and inhaled loudly. "I hated him, for throwing me out like a flea-bitten dog, for closing the doors of my home in my face, and me not sixteen. You don't do that to your son, do you? Not for that, Matthew, not for loving and bedding a lass."

"Nay, that was wrong of him. But to kill him—"

"It wasn't quite like that." Luke frowned down at the clear waters by his feet. Well, aye, it was. He had lured his father up here, had appeared before him so suddenly old Malcolm had stumbled backwards in shock. The fool had smiled, had said he was glad to see him, and look what a man he had become, with a sword at his side and a pistol in his belt. Luke had taken a step towards him. Malcolm had said that Luke was welcome back, that all of them would be so glad to see him, even wee Margaret for all that she was now Matthew's wife. That was how he sealed his fate. Luke hadn't known until then, but when Da told him Margaret was lost to him, lost to the brother who already had it all…

Luke cleared his throat and spat into the pond before turning to face his brother. "It happened, aye? And then it was too late." A lengthy struggle, one final well directed push, and Malcolm had flown into the water, his eyes wide with fear. And Luke had been left holding the ring that his father carried on a chain round his neck, watching as his father drowned in the ice-cold December waters.

He glanced at Matthew, so solid by his side. Even now, there were days when he hated the fact that his brother remained alive. He should have hanged, and Hillview should have come to me all those years ago, Luke thought, surprising himself with his vehemence. He coughed, sidestepped Matthew, and strode over to duck out of sight among the trees.

"He can't," Alex said. "You'll have to keep Hugin in a cage while you're at school."

"He's never been in a cage!" Adam looked about to weep, for all that he was twelve.

"I don't see any alternative, unless you leave him here, with us." The bird would probably cry its eyes out, she reflected, and as to Adam… Adam stroked the black plumage of his bird, and Hugin muttered something affectionate, pecking at Adam's chest.

"I can wait," he said. "I don't have to go this year, and so I can teach him to sit in a cage."

"Adam! He's a bloody bird! However intelligent, however amusing, he's just a bird, and, no, you can't wait! You'll be riding down south with your uncle in four days."

"He isn't just a bloody bird! He's my friend, my only friend!" Adam's eyes shifted to a deep dark green and, after yet another hurt look at his mother, he barged up the hill.

"Great, just what I need." Alex turned back to where Rosie was overseeing the laundry. Too much linen, too few female hands, and for all that they'd been at it most of the morning, the piles of unwashed laundry remained disturbingly high. Alex missed the efficiency of Graham's Garden, where everyone knew exactly what their task was, from Agnes, who stirred and lifted, to Hannah and Maggie, who rushed back and forth with the hampers full of clean wet linen to hang and spread to dry.

A soft rustle in her pocket made her smile, her hand coming down to stroke the letter through the cloth. She had only rushed through it yet, to make sure no one had died, and later she was going to read it slowly, savouring every single word of Ian's penmanship.

Alex looked up the hill to where she could still glimpse Adam, looked back at the laundry, and took a quick decision that adolescent boys had to come first.

"I'll be right back," she said to Rosie, smiling briefly at Ellen and Marjorie.

"Back?" Rosie eyed the heaped sheets accusingly.

"You go ahead," Alex instructed, ignoring Rosie's displeased expression. "I just have to..." A smile and she was halfway across the yard, aiming for the sprawling briar rose behind which Adam had just disappeared.

She took her time, walking through trees that were beginning to shift into autumn blaze. Not at all as spectacular as the maple woods back home. She caught herself with a sad little smile. Home... Alex shrugged, drew her shawl tighter around her shoulders and concentrated on the here and now instead, on the rowan fronds that were going a bright yellow, the oaks in their paling greens and duns, and here and there the startling deep red of a blushing alder sprig.

She picked leaves as she went, filling her apron with her finds, and as she walked she hummed, no longer in any hurry to find Adam. She found a stand of hazels, the ground below littered with ripe nuts, made a mental note to come back for them some other day, and then she was in a clearing she remembered, and a shiver of fear flew up her spine when Luke broke through on the opposite side, dishevelled and somehow upset, with those bright eyes of his locked on her. This was the place where he had accosted her, nearly thirty years ago, and there, just beside the gnarled oak, Matthew had knocked Luke to the ground and cut off his nose.

Luke stretched his lips in an attempted smile, but his eyes were flat and cold, and Alex retreated, just as she'd done that long gone day, only to find her back against the smooth bark of a rowan tree. The same tree? She didn't know, and now Luke was too close and in his eyes she could read a slight amusement at her obvious fear.

She tried to say something, normalise the situation by dropping a comment about the weather, the hazelnuts she had found – anything. But there was no air, and suddenly his mouth was on hers, a soft, warm mouth that was scarily reminiscent of Matthew's. She twisted her head away, blood surged through her cheeks, and she was herself again, a strong woman who raised her hand and slapped him, hard. She pushed by him, the contents of her apron spilled to the ground, and without a backward look left the clearing at a run.

"You touch her again and I'll kill you."

Luke wheeled at the sound of Matthew's voice, hands raised in a placatory gesture. "I wasn't kissing her, your wife. I was kissing the memory of mine." With that, he melted into the woods.

"Hi." Alex sat down beside Adam. Her heart was still thudding too fast in her chest, and she wasn't sure what to do, whether to tell Matthew or not. Adam wasn't at all mollified by her appearance, and shifted away from her while Hugin flapped over to inspect Alex's hair.

"Hugin!" Adam hissed, but the bird ignored him.

"You still want to become a physician, don't you?"

Adam nodded warily, muttering that ever since he was a wean, as far as he could remember, he'd wanted to heal and cure.

"It didn't work very well with all those trampled snails you brought home," Alex said, "and the frog...ugh!"

Adam peeked at her, his mouth curving.

"If that's your dream, then it's time to face up to the fact that it won't be easy, right?"

Adam made a small dejected sound. First, some years in London, surrounded by lads he didn't know, and then several years at university, either in England or here, in Scotland, and after that, long years of apprenticeship, and by the time he was done with all that, he'd be some years past twenty, more or less dead.

"Not quite." Alex laughed softly. "But it's a long time, son. A very long time, far away from us."

Adam sighed, and Hugin landed on his shoulder with an inquiring gleam in his eyes.

"And Hugin?"

"I don't know, honey. Ravens can become very, very old. So maybe you should leave him behind, and we'll take care of him for you."

"But he'll forget me!"

"Forget you? I don't think so. And maybe he'd be happier here than in a cage." She collected her gangly boy to her, hugging him close. This her lastborn had a special place in her heart, soft-spoken and gentle as he was. "And if we have Hugin, then I know you'll come back," she whispered to his hair, and Adam wound his arms hard around her waist and hid his face against her shawl.

Some moments later, Adam was back to his normal, cheerful self, to a large extent due to the sudden appearance of Matthew, who pointed out a sparrowhawk to him, making Adam fly to his feet, his mother forgotten.

"I just hate it," Alex sighed, watching Adam leap down the slope to where Samuel stood waiting for him. "I hate that they grow up and leave, and suddenly they're all over the place, and how on earth am I ever to keep up with them all? A bloody letter takes two months to cross the sea, and that means that every single word, each syllable on this piece of paper is old news." She shook Ian's precious letter at him.

"But news nonetheless," Matthew said.

Alex nodded half-heartedly. She took a big breath. "Luke kissed me."

"I saw." Matthew nodded.

"I didn't like it, and I slapped him."

"I saw," Matthew repeated. "I don't think he was kissing you. He was kissing a ghost."

"Huh," Alex said, not at all convinced, and shivered again. "Will you kill him for it?" she added as an attempted joke after a moment of silence.

"Do you want me to?"

"No." Alex settled back against his chest, and looked down the hill to where the yard now was full of flapping white linen. "But if he ever does it again…"

"He won't touch you, not like that," Matthew said, his arms coming round her. "Now, will you read me that letter?"

It was a long letter, filled with anecdotes and everyday tasks: Agnes, their scatterbrained maid, had managed to burn the maple syrup; Lettie, wee scamp that she was, had released the pigs to 'run free in the forest' – and had not been able to sit properly for days afterwards; Betty had found a beehive and moved it into the kitchen garden, leaving her covered in stings but, according to Ian, inordinately proud of herself.

Wee Edward now had a sister, and here Betty had taken the quill to write a long and detailed description of the baby, ending with the laconic comment that, so far, the child fortunately showed no signs of resembling its father. Ian was back, his rounded script flowing over the page.

"You don't have to read it as slowly as he writes it," Matthew teased, and both of them smiled at the image of Ian sitting for hours at the little writing desk.

There was unrest in the colony, Ian wrote, with the

Protestant majority vociferous in their demands that Maryland be purged of Catholics. And at the belated news that the Queen was pregnant, vigils had been held throughout Providence that the child be a daughter, not a son.

"Didn't work," Alex said.

"Unfortunately. Had it been a lass, the English people would have grumbled and heaved, but wouldn't consider relieving the King of his crown. And so the succession would have been peaceful." He nudged at her to continue with the letter, and once she was done, she folded it and held it for a moment to her cheek.

"Safe, all of them," she said.

Matthew had a deep crease between his brows. "I worry for Sarah. To be a Catholic now…"

Alex snuck a hand in his. "Michael will take care of her." She liked Sarah's husband – despite his unsavoury, if dead, uncles – and had great faith in his protective capabilities.

Matthew nodded. "But where do they go, if the Catholic rule in Maryland is overthrown?"

"They come home, of course," Alex said. "There's room enough for them." Home. She looked to the west. God, how she wanted to go home!

Luke apologised to Alex later that same afternoon, saying he had no idea what had come over him.

"Just don't do it again," Alex said, giving him a chilly look.

"Oh, I won't," Luke assured her.

He couldn't keep his eyes off her. Shapely and vibrant, Alex carried herself as a much younger woman would, her back erect, her hips swaying as she walked back and forth in the kitchen, fetching bread and cheese, rabbit stew and onions. She crossed her legs when she sat down, and Luke could imagine just how it would feel to run his hands over the muscles in her thighs and buttocks. She inclined her head in the direction of Matthew, and for an instant Luke saw her bared nape, so white in contrast with her dark hair. Rounder than his Margaret ever was, but the more he watched Alex, the more he saw the likeness with his wife, and the more it twitched in him to hold her, take her, because surely it would be like loving Margaret. Impossible: he was here on probation, his newfound relationship with Matthew a fragile thing, and Luke had no intention of risking what little he had in the way of family.

Throughout the evening, Matthew was most demonstrative towards Alex, a repeated message to Luke that this woman was his, only his. Luke's mouth stretched into a mirthless smile. How unfortunate that his brother and he should have a preference for the same type of woman! He looked over to where Alex sat close to the fire, head bent over her mending, and sighed. Remarkable that two women should be so alike. Unfortunate that his wife should be dead while his eldest brother still had his wife by his side. It made him gag. Unfair, all of it was unfair.

Chapter 21

Sarah Connor, born Graham, actively disliked Minister Macpherson. She wasn't too fond of Minister Allerton either – ever since that day more than two years back when he had belted her, Sarah's relationship with her brother-in-law was a complicated matter. So it was with some misgiving she saw the ministers converging on her, wishing she could somehow make herself invisible and disappear before their eyes.

She knew beforehand what the topic of their discussion would be. Discussion? Sarah snorted softly while adjusting her new coif. Minister Macpherson harangued, and when it came to the subject of Sarah's recent conversion to Catholicism, Julian Allerton had a tendency to do the same, both men regarding her with avid interest as they explained over and over again that it was not too late: she could still admit to her errors and be welcomed back in the Presbyterian congregation – assuming, of course, that she subjected herself to a public and humiliating penance.

Sarah had no intention of doing so. Her husband would be most displeased, and just the thought of Michael made Sarah smile, eyes darting up and down Providence's main street in search of him. There was no point in looking up the slope – Michael had no business in the kirk's meeting house – so instead, she attempted to find him among the people presently thronging on the market square, down by the main wharf. It was impossible to pick out one man among the many that had come to town for the Michaelmas market, and Sarah's attention was distracted by the spectacle of Reverend Wilson's geese, yet again escaped from their pen and waddling speedily up the hill with the Anglican minister in hot pursuit.

"Sarah." Minister Macpherson stood before her, forcing

her to focus on him rather than the entertaining scene in front of her.

"Mrs Connor," she corrected, quite satisfied with how the fat minister flushed in response.

"Mrs Connor, then. What brings you here?"

Beside him, Minister Allerton – Julian, not her minister, not anymore – winced, eyeing his minister colleague with some exasperation.

"I am accompanying my husband," Sarah replied calmly. "And visiting family." They were staying with Ruth and Julian, and even if Julian was stiff round his Catholic bother-in-law, Ruth went out of her way to make the Connors feel welcome, wanting nothing more than to normalise her strained relationship with her sister. Sarah did little to make it easy for Ruth, thinking it was only fair that her sister squirm. After all, Ruth had helped Julian hold Sarah when he belted her some years back, and that was something Sarah still found hard to forgive.

"We don't want you here," Minister Macpherson said.

"Gregor!" Julian hissed.

"What?" Macpherson turned to Julian. "She and her husband are papists. The good people of Providence don't want them here."

"The good people?" Sarah snorted. "Well, that wouldn't include you, would it?"

"Watch your tongue!" Minister Macpherson loomed over her. "You should show some respect for your elders, no matter how depraved you are."

"Not my elders, not anymore." Sarah was on the verge of saying something far more scathing, along the lines that some of the elders – and especially a certain minister – had nothing but earwax in their head, but bit back, reminding herself that Da would not be pleased if she antagonised the elders of his kirk. She twisted inside, as she always did when she thought about Da and his reaction to her conversion. So, for Da's sake, she found it in her to curtsey to the ministers and paste a false smile on her face. "We do no harm, Minister Macpherson."

"You do harm by existing," the minister snapped. "Well,"

he added in a more conciliatory tone, "you can't help it, what with you being nothing but a weak woman. What you need is someone to help you find your way back to the light."

"And my husband?"

"Hmm." The minister wet his lips. "A lost case, I fear."

"Well, where he goes, so do I," Sarah said with a little smile. "I am his wife, and must do as he bids." She bobbed the minister yet another curtsey and tried to sidle off.

The big man blocked her with his bulk. "There is no welcome here for papists," he said harshly. "If you insist on holding to your conversion, best stay away."

"In this colony, Lord Calvert rules," Sarah snapped. "And in his colony, people are allowed to move freely, no matter their faith."

Minister Macpherson laughed. "Tell that to the two papists we roasted some weeks back." With that, he was off, moving ponderously up the street.

"Roasted?" Sarah felt ill. "You burnt two people?"

Julian rolled his eyes. "Gregor has a tendency to exaggerate. The poor unfortunates got caught in a barn that was on fire."

"Caught in a barn?" Sarah gave her brother-in-law a long look. "How can you be caught in a barn?"

Julian shifted on his feet, looking uncomfortable. "They chose not to come out."

"Ah. Why not?" When he didn't reply, she repeated her question.

"Because our militia was waiting for them," Julian muttered. "But they wouldn't have killed them – they just wanted to drive them off their farm."

"Ah." Sarah nodded. "A good Christian approach to things."

Julian gave her an exasperated look. "Sometimes you sound far too much like your mother."

"Thank you. You couldn't have given me a better compliment."

To his credit, Julian smiled – if briefly – before growing sombre again. "He is right, you know."

"Macpherson?"

"Minister Macpherson to you, Sarah. But, yes, he's right. To visit Providence while openly being papists is not wise, not in the present climate." He pursed his lips. "And it isn't easy for me – or for Ruth – to have you staying with us."

"We will move out immediately," Sarah said, a chill in her voice.

"I didn't mean it like that," Julian protested. "Of course, you're welcome to stay. But—"

Sarah sighed. "Mama is right, isn't she? All this religious strife is nothing but a bother."

"Hmm." Julian produced a handkerchief and fastidiously wiped his nose, his mouth. "It's going to go up in flames," he said, sounding sad.

"Like the two poor innocents that died in the fire?"

Julian patted her on the arm. "Best be careful, Sarah. I – and many with me – do our best to advocate compassion and restraint. Others argue that all papists should be thrown into the sea."

"People like Minister Macpherson," Sarah said.

They set off down the main street, making for the harbour and Julian's house beyond, she holding her basket in front of her, he clasping his hands behind his back.

"Yes. Gregor is not the most tolerant of men."

"And yet you made him your son-in-law?" Poor Patience, married to a boor such as Gregor Macpherson. No one deserved such an evil fate, and especially not Julian's mild-mannered daughter.

Julian's mouth all but disappeared into a thin, disapproving line. "My daughter is fortunate. Her husband does right by her."

"He hits her," Sarah told him. "Haven't you seen the bruises?"

"A man may discipline his wife," Julian said stiffly, but she could see he was discomfited. "How do you know?" he asked after a while.

"Know what?"

"That he hits her. Has she said anything?"

"Patience? She wouldn't dare to. But she was never a clumsy lass, and now she is constantly bruised, saying that she's tripped or fallen." Sarah took three hasty steps to the right, making a face at the dead rat in the gutter.

"Maybe she has."

Sarah could hear the hope in his voice. "Maybe. But I find it strange that the bruises on her arms look like they've been made by fingers sinking into her flesh. Or that she has managed to bruise the back of her neck."

"I—" Julian interrupted himself when Ruth came into view, near on running towards them. She was clutching something in her hand, a wide grin on her face. A letter from Da! Sarah danced towards her, Patience forgotten. At her heels came Julian, peering down at the folded and sealed letter Ruth was holding.

"It's addressed to me," Julian pointed out mildly, holding out his hand to his wife.

"It's Da's handwriting," Ruth said, "so it's really for me – for us."

"To me," Julian repeated, and Ruth made a little face but handed over the letter. Sarah suppressed a little grin. From the look Ruth gave Julian, he would pay in the privacy of their bedroom for robbing her of the pleasure of opening Da's letter. Serve him right, because the exasperating man was making as if to stuff the letter away into his pocket, unread.

He didn't, of course, and despite Julian grumbling some things one should not do in public, Ruth and Sarzah stood close together, eyes flying over Da's familiar handwriting.

"Safe and back at Hillview," Ruth concluded some minutes later. A shadow crossed her face. "Do you think they'll stay there?" she asked, directing herself to Sarah.

"No. They belong here, with us." Sarah crossed her fingers. Mama definitely did, but Da had walked around in a glowing haze, so happy to be returning to Scotland. It made her frown. She'd been born here, in Maryland, and this was home – to her, to her siblings, to Mama, but not, apparently, to Da. Her throat itched at the thought of them staying forever on the other side of the sea, and she gave herself a little hug. Of course they'd come back. Mama would make sure they did.

They were halfway to Julian's house when Michael appeared from one of the smaller alleys. Sarah had but to glance at him to know something was wrong. His hand was on the hilt of his pistol, and he was moving so fast his dark chestnut curls were dancing in the wind. His hat was gone, his cravat was torn, and, from what she could see, two of the buttons on his coat were missing.

"We're leaving. Now," he said when he came within earshot.

"Now?" Sarah's hands flew over him, ascertaining he was whole, despite a bloody nose and a bruised face.

"Now." He wiped his mouth with his sleeve and spat to the side, a globule of bloodied phlegm.

"What happened?" Julian asked.

"Why not ask Macpherson that?" Michael fixed light eyes on Julian, a lock of hair tumbling forward over his face. A shiver flew through Sarah, because there were moments when her husband was eerily reminiscent of his dead uncle, Philip Burley, the man who had abused her and come close to killing Da. Not Philip, she reminded herself. This was Michael, her husband, father to her son, wee Joshua. She hadn't known Michael was Philip's nephew when she met him – if she had, she'd have run screaming from him. Da still had days when he regarded Michael with caution, his large frame tensing when something Michael said or did brought Philip Burley to life. Come to think of it, there were days Sarah suspected that Da had bigger problems forgiving her for wedding Burley kin than for converting to Catholicism.

Michael's hand on her arm brought her back to the here and now, to the grim conversation between Michael and Julian. "They hit you?"

"More shoves than punches." Michael gave her a brief smile, squeezing her arm gently. "The minister didn't like it when I gave as good as I got, causing him to overbalance and land on his fat bottom."

"Gregor?" Julian shook his head. "He won't forgive such an affront."

"What was I to do? Allow the four of them to mistreat me?"

"No, of course not." Julian threw a hasty look down the street. "Best we get home."

"Aye." Ruth tugged at Sarah. "Come along."

They were nearly at Julian's door when Minister Macpherson came trotting round the corner, accompanied by a group of five men. "There he is! Take him," he yelled, pointing at Michael. Julian shoved Michael towards the door, and planted himself before him.

"What is this?" he demanded, looking at his fellow minister. "Why do you come running with a rabble at your heels?"

"The papist!" Minister Macpherson's face flamed into a purplish hue. "He raised his hand to me."

"In self-defence," Michael called out. "You were four and I was one, and you were doing quite some raising of your hands yourself, Mr Macpherson."

"Is this true?" Julian asked.

"And what if it is? A papist roaming our fair town – we can't have that. Now, hand him over, so that we—"

"No." Julian crossed his arms over his chest, and in that moment, Sarah forgave him everything. Her slight brother-in-law stared at Macpherson, at that lout Isaiah Farrell. He let his eyes travel over each and every one of the young men, and at his silent staring, some of them shuffled and ducked their heads.

"Move," Macpherson said.

"No. And may I remind you, dear son-in-law, that you owe me obedience, not only as my daughter's husband but also as a junior minister in this congregation." Julian stood on his toes and approached Macpherson, looking like an angry cockerel facing a bull. "I will not have louts roaming our streets and threatening other men – be they papist or not. And I will not tolerate a minister behaving thus – neither will Minister Walker. So, Gregor, I suggest you take your friends with you and leave. Now." His eyes swept the assembled men. "I will be talking to each of these young men's fathers later tonight, and I am of a mind to have them all in the stocks for some hours, just to teach them a lesson." Two of the men paled and started sidling off. Macpherson glared at Julian who calmly looked back.

"I—" Macpherson blustered.

"Yes," Julian cut in, "you have behaved despicably. For which, of course, you will apologise."

Sarah bit back on a violent urge to giggle. Minister Macpherson's huge fists were clenched so tight they looked white, and from the look he threw Julian, it was obvious he wished Minister Allerton a most hasty and unpleasant death. But he couldn't do anything, not when faced with Providence's second most senior minister, and after several minutes when all one could hear were Macpherson's ragged breaths, he inclined his head in the direction of Michael and mumbled an apology. Julian jerked his head, and Macpherson and his companions walked off, several of them throwing angry looks at Michael over their shoulder.

"Oh dear," Ruth whispered to Sarah, clutching at her arm. "He'll go home and vent his rage on poor Patience."

"Aye," Sarah sighed. She eyed her sister. "Haven't you told Julian Gregor uses his fists on his wife?"

"I've tried. I dare say he will be more inclined to believe me after today." Ruth guided Sarah inside. "You'd best leave."

An hour later, Sarah and Michael were well on their way due south. Little Joshua was squirming in his shawl, Michael's saddlebags were bulging with their hastily stuffed belongings, and both Sarah and Michael had their pistols at hand.

Julian drew his horse to a halt. "I'll not ride further with you. Will you be alright?"

"Aye." Sarah rode close enough to take hold of Julian's hand. "Thank you."

"Not all of us are intolerant bigots," Julian said with a little smile. "And Alex would never forgive me if something had happened to you – or your husband." He touched his hat with his fingers. "May God see you safe – and stay well away from Gregor. That man knows how to carry a grudge, be he minister or not." With that, he was gone, urging his horse to a trot back the way they had come.

Chapter 22

Market day at Cumnock was generally an unexciting affair, involving quite a lot of bartering and very little real money. Today was no exception, and after having ensured Matthew did in fact procure both garlic and onions, Alex grabbed her basket and strolled off to the draper's, mentally doing her sums.

The little market town had remained remarkably unchanged over the last twenty years, and here and there she saw faces she recognised, but when she smiled and nodded a greeting, she was met with a blank stare, or at most a slight inclination. Alex had no idea what she'd done to be so cold-shouldered, and even in the shops, she was treated with deference but no warmth, her attempts at conversation stonewalled by a steady stream of monosyllabic 'aye's or 'nay's.

She was returning to the main square, her basket packed with her purchases, when a troop of soldiers clattered down the street towards her, and Alex stepped back, pressing herself against the door to the apothecary. Once she recognised the man riding at the front, she straightened up, pulled in her stomach to be as flat as it could, and smiled.

"Why, if it isn't the charming and handsome Mrs Graham!" John Graham held in his horse and swept his hat off before dismounting, landing lightly a foot or so away from her. He was standing close, far too close, and Alex could feel disapproving stares sinking like shards of glass into her back. Well, they could stuff it, and so she remained where she was, skirts brushing at his boots.

"Mr Graham." Alex nodded, glancing at Matthew who was a fair distance away, deep in discussion with an unfamiliar minister. She looked John Graham up and down with open admiration, taking in the thigh-high boots, the sumptuous velvet in a hue she'd never seen before, somewhere between dark green and clearest blue, the flattering cut of his coat, and his breastplate.

"Most dashing," she said, "although perhaps the breastplate is a trifle excessive in a sleepy little market town like Cumnock?"

"I think not. This is, after all, the home town of John Brown." It came out with a bitter tinge. He obviously resented his local nickname of Bluidy Clavers, and seeing him straight and tall, open-faced and with eyes disarmingly wide, Alex had problems believing him a man who would lower himself to mindless and cruel killing.

The door to the apothecary swung open, shoving Alex and causing her to more or less fall against John.

"Oops," she said, righting herself with a shaky little smile. John retained a hold of her arm, to the casual observer a supporting gesture as she regained her balance. But Alex could feel his fingers caressing her arm, was flustered by the light in his eyes, so close to her own.

"May I say just how lovely you look today," he murmured, lips almost at her ear. His warm breath sent tingles through her.

"Probably because, for once, I'm not crawling on the ground when we meet," she said, making him laugh out loud. But she was glad that she'd worn her best bodice to town, that the shawl around her shoulders was the new one, and that her hair was recently washed – no matter that most of it was covered by her cap.

The horse snorted, yanking at the reins held firmly in John's hands.

Alex took a half step back and smiled teasingly at John. "And look, my favourite horse in the world."

Caesar rolled his eyes, stamped his hooves, bared his teeth, and lunged at Alex. She swiped him over the nose with her glove, backing away when the huge roan shied and reared, flailing with its forelegs.

"I don't think he likes me," she said. "That's the second time he has tried to bite me."

John swore and hung on when the stallion danced over the slippery cobbles, all heaving flanks and widened nostrils. By the time John had the horse back under control, he was sweating, calling the horse a long string of names, none of them particularly flattering.

"I'm still of the opinion that he's more of a horse than you can handle." Alex grinned.

"And you, foolish woman, you should learn not to strike a horse over his nose!" The sharpness of the reprimand was belied by the twinkle in his eyes, by the pressure of his thigh against hers. She shifted that much closer, enjoying the way his proximity unsettled her.

"Teach him not to bite then," Alex said.

John laughed and, without knowing how it all came about, Alex had suddenly invited him to dine with them, should he be passing by. When he made his farewells, John bent forward and kissed her – on the mouth. Soft, warm lips, a slight wetness that had Alex half opening her lips in response before she collected herself and pulled back with a little gasp. John Graham grinned and swung himself astride his horse. Moments later, he was gone, and on the other side of the street stood Matthew, eyes uncomfortably bright as he made his way towards her.

"He kissed you!" he hissed. Alex patted at her hair.

"He did." She locked eyes with him. "It was nothing."

For several heartbeats, they stared at each other. His chest was heaving. She licked her mouth, unnerved by his silence but quite pleased by how hurt he looked.

At long last, he cleared his throat. "Punishment, is it?"

"Punishment? More an opportunity to make you feel what I felt when you were cavorting with Nan."

"I wasn't cavorting! And I most definitely didn't kiss her."

"I didn't kiss him either – he kissed me. You know, just like you didn't do anything with Nan – it was her touching and simpering, never you." She glared at him, surprised by the anger that bubbled through her at the thought of that day when she'd brought him lunch and the carefully chosen rose.

Matthew sighed. "I never meant to hurt you, lass."

"Well, you did." More than she'd understood until this very minute, when the soft impression of John's lips still lingered on her mouth.

He looked away and nodded, extending his hand to her. She took it, their fingers braiding together. He squeezed, none too gently.

"I may have deserved that kiss, but you do it again and I'll belt you – as I've promised. And as for the man who kisses you…" He dragged a finger over his throat, and Alex's face heated at the possessive look he gave her.

They were back at their horses when she informed him she'd invited John to dinner.

"You did what?" Matthew blew out loudly through his nose.

"Why not? I like him."

"Well, I don't, and even less after today." Matthew locked eyes with her, and to Alex's irritation she felt herself blushing. "Besides, he isn't welcome in Ayrshire," Matthew continued, "He and his dragoons are regarded with dislike – nay, even hatred – and now you've invited the man to Hillview. It's difficult enough as it is to blend back into the fabric of everyday life, and having Claverhouse a guest at Hillview will not make it easier."

Alex lifted one shoulder and let it fall. She wasn't planning on staying here anyway. She could see how her gesture cut him, his eyes darkening, but he didn't comment, helping her up on her mare.

John Graham took Alex at her word, appearing that self-same afternoon at Hillview. It was a strained visit. Matthew made it abundantly clear he was uncomfortable with John's presence. Alex sent flaming looks at her husband, but he ignored her, settling himself for a political discussion at the table.

"That William!" John said. "For a prince, a competent general and leader of men to so callously grasp for another man's crown. And, damn it, once I served under him, even liked him! Outrageous, isn't it? Well, don't you agree?" he demanded, staring at Luke. If Matthew was uncomfortable, Luke was three times worse, very far removed from his witty, normal self. Every time John turned in his direction, Luke shifted on his seat.

"Not everyone does," Matthew said when it became apparent Luke had no intention of answering. "The whole kingdom is skidding this way and that, what with old loyalties dissolving and new ones being wrought."

"Men of honour don't change their loyalties like they do their shirts," John said coldly.

"Mayhap not. I myself have never changed my convictions," Matthew replied with a shrug.

"Some cider?" Alex placed a mug before John, and when she offered bread and cheese, he accepted that as well.

"Back to Edinburgh?" Matthew asked, cutting himself a thick slice of cheese.

"For some days, no more. Then it's to London with Douglas." John stretched out his legs. His spurs scraped against the floor, and he swatted at his boots. "Let the Dutchman come, and the Scots army will teach him a lesson or two!"

"And your wife?" Alex asked.

"My wife?" John gave her a confused look.

"Is she going with you?" Alex said.

"No," he said, "she's not much taken with London."

"Not much taken with anything English, and in particular not with a popish king," Luke muttered from his corner.

John looked as if he was considering ramming his mug down Luke's throat.

"Better she stay at home then," Matthew said.

John nodded. "Aye. Safer as well."

"So what does she think?" Alex asked

"Think?" John poured himself some more cider.

"About all this mess," Alex said. "You know, the King, Dutch William, religion—"

"We don't discuss religion – or politics." John sounded curt.

"Oh no, of course," Alex snorted. "You mainly discourse about the weather, right?"

"We talk about many things," John said, "but what we say is none of your concern."

To Alex's irritation, Matthew grinned at this elegant put-down.

"No, well, I suppose it isn't," Alex managed to say, and for the rest of the short visit sat quiet.

"Poor man," Alex said to Matthew as they watched John Graham ride off.

"Why?"

"He loves the King," Alex sighed, "and soon—"

"Shh," Matthew said, and Alex fell silent as Luke joined them.

"I wonder if he loves his wife," she mused out loud, making both men look at her in surprise.

"His wife?" Luke echoed.

"Well, yes, it's customary to love your wife."

"It is? What makes you say such nonsense?" Luke pointed in the direction of where John had crested the hill and dropped out of sight. "John Graham is a wealthy lord, a leader of a clan. He doesn't marry for love. He marries for power and connections. Surely, that is the way the ruling classes do things in Sweden as well?"

"I wouldn't know. It's ages since I've been there."

"Jean Cochrane comes well connected," Luke said, "and I don't doubt but there is some affection between them. He had other choices, after all, and to marry a Covenanter given his own convictions... Well, you know what they say – opposites attract."

"Is she pretty?" Alex asked.

Luke mulled this over. "No, not pretty, but pleasant in her own way, and somehow quite appealing."

"Oh, well then," Alex said, "that's just what he needs, a man like that. Somewhere to feel safe and welcomed."

Luke made a derisive sound. "A man like that needs a woman who gives him living sons, and that she hasn't succeeded in doing." He swivelled on his toes and walked off, and Matthew moved closer to Alex.

"I have both," he said in a satisfied tone of voice. "A welcoming wife and a fertile one."

Alex grinned. "You were probably a very good little boy, and so God decided to reward you – with me."

On the day of his intended departure, Luke woke with a racking cough, and after a quick inspection, Alex told him he wouldn't be going anywhere anytime soon.

"But Adam," he croaked. "His school! We're late already, what with all this Nan business."

"I'm sure you'll be able to sort that out once you're back." Alex was secretly very glad of this reprieve. So was Adam, his face lighting up when he realised he was to have at least one more week here, with them all. The only one not at all pleased with this development was Matthew.

"I don't like it," he said to Alex, "leaving you here with Luke while I ride off to Glasgow with David." He scowled at Luke who had shuffled outside wrapped in a blanket to see them off.

"He's ill," Alex told him with an amused smile.

"Hmph! He gawks at you." He fingered his dagger, mouth pursed in thought.

"Matthew…" Alex gave him a quick hug. "You said so yourself. How it is Margaret he suddenly sees, not me." That didn't help. If anything, it made Matthew even more unwilling to leave her. "If he tries anything, I'll kick him, okay?" Kick him? She'd send him flying, courtesy of those martial arts skills she still retained and worked so hard to uphold.

"I'll be back in five days at the most," Matthew said, kissing her before swinging up in the saddle.

"I'll bolt my bedroom door," Alex promised, but the intended joke fell flat to the ground.

Two days later, Matthew rode into Glasgow with a saddle sore and quiet David in his wake. The lad was suffering severe heartache, had wept for most of the first morning, however silently, and at Matthew's gentle prodding had admitted it was leaving Samuel that so distressed him.

"But you knew beforehand he wasn't coming with you."

"Aye," David sighed, "but I didn't feel it, did I? Not until I had to leave him behind."

Matthew smiled. His sons were all close, brothers of the heart as well as of blood. Not at all like it was with him and Luke: a cautious reserve that, at times, threatened to crack open and spill burning rage to flow between them.

Glasgow was a bustling town, laid out along the Clyde. David took one look at it and fell in love, despite it being grey and much smaller than Edinburgh. They toured the quays, and Matthew stood for a moment looking off to the west – not that he saw much more than the broad band of the river and the surrounding land – before recalling he had letters to send, therefore hurrying off in search of the harbourmaster with his son in tow.

Just before he left the port area, he stopped for an instant and threw a last look towards the west. May they all be safe, he prayed. May the Lord look to their needs and keep them whole. With a slight shrug and a rueful smile in the direction of his perceptive son, he led the way into the city proper, commenting repeatedly on how it all had changed since he was here last.

"More than twenty years ago." David grimaced, clearly bored by the continuous reminiscences.

They walked up the High Street in the direction of the cathedral, and suddenly the university loomed before them, and both stopped, awestruck.

"It's big," David said in a hushed voice. It rose before them in smooth, golden stone, roofed in grey slate, and with a soaring clock tower placed between the two courtyards.

"It is." Matthew was choking on his pride: his son, to study here and become a gentleman of sorts. He studied David somewhat sceptically. The lad would make a fine lawyer, but a gentleman...no, not quite. "Best see you settled," he said, and together they walked into the coolness of the entrance hall.

★

"...took to it at once, he did," Matthew told Alex once he was home. For two days straight it had rained, and he'd arrived back at Hillview chattering with cold. Now, he was lying on his front on the kitchen table, blissfully warm after a crammed session in the old hip bath, while Alex massaged his back. "Met one of the lads he'll be sharing quarters with. Likeable enough."

He shifted under her hands. Strong and small, warm and competent, they forced blood into tensed muscles, rubbed the scented oil deeper and deeper into his skin.

"I met others as well," he said in an entirely different tone, and Alex paused for an instant. "The Scots army is moving south, and the whole Ayr garrison is on the move, captained by John Graham, no less."

"Oh." Alex sounded only vaguely interested.

"He sent his regards."

His wife didn't reply and continued with what she was doing.

Matthew pillowed his head in his arms and sighed. They couldn't stay, not in a country torn asunder by internal strife. They wouldn't stay anyway, but he'd hoped to have two or three years before Alex claimed on his promise, and now it all seemed to be coming to a head much too fast.

He caressed the worn, thick planks of the table beneath him, and in the flickering light from the fire, he could see it all again: Mam, Da, himself and his brothers and sister, and they were sitting at this same table, supping while Da told them of their Graham ancestors, of how Hillview came to be theirs to begin with – bequeathed to them by the Bruce himself, and since then there had always been a Graham on this land. Always, you hear?

Matthew stroked the dark wood. Soon, there wouldn't be. Soon, he'd leave his home for good. Again. His stomach shrank together at the thought, leaving him breathless and dizzy. He clenched at the tabletop, a futile anchoring to a place already lost to him – because she, the woman presently working on his back, would never acquiesce to staying.

"What?" Alex dropped a kiss on his nape.

"Nothing."

Alex made a disbelieving sound, but didn't push, moving down his body to check on his foot instead.

"As good as new," she pronounced once she was done. "Bed?"

"You go. I'll be right up."

Alex pursed her mouth but nodded, blew out the few candles and left him alone. In the hearth, the fire collapsed upon itself, glowing a muted red, and on the table, Matthew Graham pressed his cheek against the soft grain of the wood, suffused by a heavy sense of loss.

Chapter 23

The day Isaac rode down the lane, Alex thought she would expire on the spot, gaping stupidly at the two Carloses on horseback. But one of them had both his legs, and there was something very familiar about his tentative smile, and Alex wasn't sure whether to cry or laugh, so she did both.

Beside her, Matthew drew in a ragged breath, and on her other side stood Luke, his silver nose twitching with curiosity.

"Isaac? Isn't he dead?" Luke sneezed, dug into his sleeve for his handkerchief, and dabbed at the snot leaking out from under his false nose.

"He doesn't look it to me." Alex walked over to greet Carlos and Isaac, glad to have Matthew's hand on her back.

She had no idea how to approach Isaac. With Carlos, it was so easy. She just swept him into a warm embrace, but with Isaac... She wanted to touch him, to run a hand over his shaved scalp, but something held her back, a combination of shyness and guilt.

The man before her was a stranger, shaped by other influences than hers, and his dark eyes gave nothing away, regarding her with what she assumed to be curiosity coupled with resentment. Alex gave him a wobbly smile, and extended her hand, fingers splayed. Isaac did the same, and when their fingertips met, they simultaneously released pent-up air, a long exhalation.

"Hi," she said, torn in two between joy at seeing him and anger at him for obviously having sailed too close to the edge. He breathed a 'hi' of his own, and when she held out her free arm to him, he sort of folded together and fell into her embrace. Alex staggered back, felt Matthew's arm come round her waist, and then he was holding Isaac too.

Some hours later, she was sitting in the kitchen with Carlos, drinking hot milk and honey. Upstairs, Isaac was fast asleep, Matthew had taken Luke and their sons and propelled them outside, and Ellen and Marjorie were busy in the small dairy shed. Carlos had brought Alex up to date, and was presently describing Isaac's painting of the sea, with Alex listening intently.

"…and I saw it, Alex: how, for an instant, the waters came alive and began to churn. Not enough, apparently." He crossed himself, took a sip of his hot drink, and propped his chin in his hands, looking tired. "Since then, he has retreated far within himself, and he has refused to paint, even draw."

Alex watched with detachment how her hand trembled as it lay on the table. If Isaac were to be stuck here…God! She wasn't sure she'd cope with that responsibility.

"And the picture?"

"I burnt it," Carlos said. "It was awful, a desecration almost, but I didn't dare to leave it undamaged, not with the way it crawled with life. Anyone who studied the painting in detail wouldn't miss it. How doors swayed, sails unfurled, a hand moved." Yet again, he crossed himself. "It was the right thing to do, even if it shrieked as if in pain when I set fire to it."

"Yes, it probably was," Alex croaked, her hands clenching round her mug. A witch – her son was a witch, just as her mother had been.

"And you?" she asked, leaning over to clasp his hand. "Are you alright?"

Carlos shrugged, his narrow fingers smoothing at his sleeve. Not in a cassock, which Alex considered a smart move: to ride through Scotland in priestly garb would be like waving a red flag at a bull.

"I'm content, even if now and then I wonder what could have been." He made an expressive face.

"Nothing could have been," Alex said. "You had nothing to offer her, did you? And how long before you began to blame her for your broken vows and your lost soul?"

"I love her," Carlos rasped, and Alex smiled sadly at the present tense.

"You love the image you've created for yourself. You love the victimised Sarah, the raped and damaged girl who turned to you, only to you. You don't love the strong, self-sufficient woman she truly is – and she would have grown to despise the qualities in you she used to admire."

"Why?" Carlos challenged. "In what way wouldn't I have been enough?"

"In every way," Alex said as gently as she could. "Starting with how would you support her?" When the priest made as if to rise, she held on to his hand, refusing to let go until he settled back down.

"She's married and happy. But even today, there are moments when she thinks of you – like every time she touches the rosary beads you gave her."

"She still has them?" Carlos asked.

"She uses them daily. She's a Catholic now. And that, I think, is more because of you than because of her husband."

Carlos leaned back in his chair, stunned. And then he smiled – a brilliant smile.

Isaac woke in the late afternoon to a sensation of total disorientation. He recognised the room, had slept here before, and for a hopeful second, he was certain he was back where he belonged, before noticing all the small things that were missing: no embedded screen, no traffic sounds, no constant whirring as the electrical appliances that were the backbone of his life went into active mode.

He strangled back a frustrated groan and rolled over, only to meet the blue eyes of his mother, sitting on a stool beside the bed. They didn't say anything. He looked at her as she looked at him, drinking in detail after detail.

She should be fifty-six or thereabouts, he concluded after a quick calculation, eyes lingering on her hair, hair that was collected in a heavy bun and showed a multitude of colours, not the carefully maintained youthful chestnut of his stepmother's, Diane's, hair. Skin that was lined around the eyes, a creased brow, lines of laughter bracketing the mouth, but otherwise smooth, white and seemingly soft. The hands, left open and relaxed on her lap, showed sign of continuous work, nowhere close to Diane's neatly manicured hands.

Alex stretched and smiled at him, and he could hear the creak of her stays, wondering if beneath them her body was flabby or taut. Mentally, he compared Diane, in her tight jeans and silk shirts, with this modestly attired woman, and Diane won, hands down. His inspection had been a bit too frank, and Alex frowned down at him, dark eyebrows very like his own pulled together in a demanding 'V'.

"What? I don't compare?"

"You look too different to compare," Isaac said, high-fiving himself for this elegant answer.

"Well, we would. Diane's had all the benefits of living in a cushy, modern world while I live in a physically demanding time." Alex stood up, and he saw that her waist was still trim, although who knew? That might be the corsets or stays or whatever they were called.

"Supper is in some minutes, down in the kitchen. You remember where it is, right?"

"It isn't exactly a major challenge to find it even if I didn't. All I have to do is follow my nose. Not exactly a palace you're living in, is it?"

"I'm sorry to disappoint you," she said, slamming the door behind her.

When Isaac entered the kitchen, the entire household was already seated. Introductions were made, and he slid in to sit opposite an older man with tired red hair and an intriguing silver nose.

"I'm Luke Graham," the man offered.

"Luke? Ian's father?" Isaac asked, and the mood plunged dismally around him, with Carlos gaping at the tall red-haired man.

"I'm Ian's father," Matthew told Isaac.

Isaac was confused. He had met Ian a couple of times twenty-odd years ago, last time he decided to drop through time for an impromptu visit, and at the time Ian had clearly said he was Luke's son.

"I'll explain later," Alex promised in an undertone, and set down a steaming pot on the table before fetching bread and butter to go with the soup.

Isaac was suddenly ravenously hungry, and his stomach growled in agreement, making the younger of the two boys facing him grin. Isaac smiled back. A Matthew clone, as was his brother, with dark, unruly hair shifting between brown and chestnut, hazel eyes and a long mouth.

Isaac eyed his half-brothers with conflicting emotions. Alex had chosen to be here for them instead of trying to return to him. As far as he was aware, he hadn't really felt the loss of her, content in his life with his adoptive father John and Diane, their daughters – his sisters – and, lately, Veronica and Isabelle. But now, seeing her with part of the family she had so obviously preferred to him and John…and what was it with her and Carlos? One could almost think she was his mother too, fussing about to ensure he ate and drank.

Despite still being hungry, he shook his head at a second helping, ignoring the rich, mouth-watering scent. He wanted a salad, a nice, medium rare steak, and for afters a helping of Diane's apple crumble, the one with the crushed cardamom seeds. He rested his shoulders against the wall and studied his family in silence.

Luke was doing some studying of his own. He vaguely recalled that the boy called Isaac had been here at Hillview back in 1663 or so, and then he had just disappeared.

Dead, Margaret had assumed, referring to a new headstone in the graveyard. Not at all dead, because this young man looked in prime health, if somewhat low-spirited. A painter, Matthew had said, and that in itself was enough to make Luke curious. He was an avid collector of art, had a fondness for the Dutch painters and their clear, simple pictures, and he wondered in what style Isaac might paint.

"Umm," Isaac said, when Luke asked him, his left hand coming up to tug at his earlobe. Luke studied the gesture in silence. "I just paint. City scenes, buildings and people." Isaac met Alex's eyes with a challenging light in his own. "And I'm fond of painting water, small paintings of a lively sea. Mostly in blues and greens."

"The sea? Just the sea and nothing else?" Luke asked in a casual tone, noting out of the corner of his eye how still Alex had gone.

"Just the sea," Isaac nodded, holding up his hands in approximation of the size.

"Ah." Luke nodded, and now it was him attempting to catch Alex's eyes.

He'd seen a painting like that, a small oblong square of swirling blues and greens, and he had also seen what could happen if you looked too deeply into it. It had been one of the more terrifying experiences in his life, that evening when he and Jacob had experimented with the painting, watching with horror as the kitchen lad began to disintegrate before their eyes, disappearing bit by bit into the wee square of blue and green paint.

Luckily, Jacob had grabbed at the seat of the lad's breeches and pulled him back before he had dissolved into nothingness. Even more disconcerting, Alex had known what the picture could do: she'd been the one who warned him not to allow himself or anyone else to sink into the beckoning little picture. He looked from mother to son and across the table Matthew's eyes met his, a silent, warning golden green.

Luke spent the rest of the evening examining Isaac, drawn like a moth to a candle by his evasive answers and his general air of strangeness. Even the priest, for all that he was Catholic and Spanish to boot, fitted in better than Isaac did. He noted mannerisms that were oddly familiar: that unconscious tugging at the left ear, the way Isaac's hand would drift up to finger his mouth repeatedly while he was thinking, or how he sat, with crossed legs and one foot bobbing up and down, up and down. It was with a jolt that he made the connection. Margaret used to do all that! Luke increased the intensity of his scrutiny.

"Explain," Luke said to Matthew and Alex, once they were alone in the little parlour. So bare, Luke reflected. A couple of new armchairs, bearing the signature of Matthew's competent hands, the table Malcolm Graham had made before either Matthew or Luke had been born, a few shelves, a small chest, and not much more. None of the comfortable opulence of his own home, and that pleased Luke.

"Explain what?" Matthew said.

Luke exhaled loudly, and had he been a horse, he would have stamped his hooves.

"Isaac, the wee painting..." He turned penetrating eyes on Alex. "How could you sit, on the other side of the ocean, and know immediately what type of painting Jacob was describing in his letter? And how could you possibly know what that wee scrap of paint could do – unless you'd seen it used?" Even now, so many years later, Luke shivered at the recollection, and Alex had gone a sickly pale, her hand gripping Matthew's hard. "And now Isaac shows up after a quarter-century and speaks of painting in blues and greens – just like that bitty piece of black magic!"

"He said how he painted the sea," Matthew said.

"Did you burn it?" Alex cut in. "Did you do as I told you and destroy it?"

Luke nodded that of course he had, turning guileless eyes on her.

"You lie," Alex said. "You lie, you bastard, and what you did nearly cost me my life."

"I didn't—"

"Oh, stop that! We both know you sent the fucking painting as a kind-hearted gift to Simon."

Luke sat back, shocked by her language, even more discomfited by the rage in her voice.

"He's a murderer, wee Simon," he said, and noted that none of them even flinched. They knew, then, of the man Simon had killed in one of the closes behind St Giles. "But you digress," he continued. "I want you to explain how you would know so much about a picture left to Margaret by her long dead mother."

"And I don't feel like telling you," Alex said, and left the room, followed a few moments later by a stone-faced Matthew.

Next morning, Luke caught up with Alex halfway up the hill, and this time he wasn't about to let her evade him again, so he grabbed her by the arms and pulled her to a halt. Dear God! The same height as Margaret, more or less the same build, and those flashing eyes throwing bolts of ice at him as she struggled to free herself.

"Tell me the truth," he said. "Tell me now!" He winced when her stout shoe connected with his unprotected shin, but held on.

"Take your hands off me!" Alex spat, and when he didn't comply, she struck him over his forearm, making him gasp, grabbed at one of his hands and, with a twisting motion, sent him through the air to land in an undignified welter of arms and legs.

Luke slowly got to his feet, probing his legs, his arms. His eyes flamed in her direction, his hand fumbled for his knife – never had he been this humiliated by a woman, and to add insult to injury, the damned woman was grinning.

"I have to know," he managed to say. "I must know!" He took a step towards Alex who retreated.

"Sisters," Alex said. "We were sisters, okay?"

Luke stared at her. "Sisters? But how?"

"I have no idea. Ask our mother – should you find her."

Luke's brain was working furiously. Alex was Swedish, was she not? And Margaret was from Glasgow. The family had lived there for some time before it all collapsed around her. First, the mother disappeared, propitiously, given the murmurings about black arts, and then the father hanged – for theft. The mother... He swayed where he stood.

"And your mother?" Luke whispered. "What was she?"

"Once again, ask her."

"Ask her? She's gone, dead by now, if not before."

"Mercedes Gutiérrez Sánchez was a witch." Carlos'

voice dripped with condemnation, making Luke whirl towards him. The priest hobbled out from beneath the trees. "Not, perhaps, an evil witch, but a witch all the same." With a stiff bow, he left them, striving up the hillside.

"A witch?" Luke turned to stare at Alex. "Was she?"

"Surely you don't believe in superstitious nonsense?" she retorted, but her hands twisted at her apron, and she refused to meet his eyes.

"Answer me!" he yelled. "Please," he added in a more controlled voice.

Alex tugged at her shawl, tightening it around her shoulders and bosom. "I'm not sure," she mumbled. "But I had one of those paintings too. It screamed when I burnt it," she added before rushing off.

All in all, Alex was not happy at having Adam ride off with Luke an hour or so later, but if Matthew shared her concerns, he didn't voice them, insisting that the lad had need of good schooling to make the best of himself, and had not Luke already contracted a tutor to help Adam with Latin and astronomy?

Luke had come down from the hill his normal calm, unruffled self, and had taken Alex aside to assure her the boy would do well with him, nephew on both sides as he was – this last said with a crooked smile.

She could see all the questions jumping in his eyes, but he seemed to sense he would get no further answers, at least not now, and with a slight bow, he proceeded to oversee the preparation of the horses and his packing.

It was Luke that decided that Hugin would go with them, throwing a concerned look at the blanched face of his twelve-year-old charge.

"While you're in school, he'll sit in a cage, and maybe he won't like it much, but at least you'll have him with you the rest of the time."

Alex and Matthew walked them up the lane with Samuel trailing behind, and right at the top, Adam scrambled off his horse to rush at them both. Alex smoothed the ruffled hair off his brow and kissed him, her heart a heavy lodestone in her chest. It would be ages before she saw him again: at the earliest, next summer.

Long after Adam had disappeared round the closest bend, she remained standing at the top of the lane, the shawl pulled tight around her shoulders. This is what he wants to do, she reminded herself, but what boy of twelve truly knows that? Samuel gave her a hug, rested his head against hers, and she tried to smile, but the tears spilled over, making her swipe at her eyes with the fringe of her shawl. "I hate it that you grow up."

Samuel gave her a serious look. "Better than the alternative."

"Well, of course, it is, you idiot! I just meant—"

"I know what you meant," Samuel interrupted with a slight smile. They walked down together, a few steps behind Matthew.

"Will you mind awfully? Here, all alone with only us?" Alex asked.

"No," Samuel said, "and I have neither the head nor the hankering for schooling myself."

"So what do you hanker for?"

"Home," Samuel breathed. "I miss it. My home, the forests, all my wee nephews and nieces. I dream about it a lot, about Ian and Mark and…"

…Qaachow and Thistledown, Little Bear and all his other Indian friends, Alex filled in silently. She squeezed his hand.

"So do I," Alex said. "So do I."

Chapter 24

"You look like a thistle gone to seed." Matthew smiled, propping himself up on one elbow.

Alex threw a look at her reflection and could but agree. Her hair stood like a fuzzy cloud around her head. "That's because I slept with it unbraided," she said, "and yet I distinctly recall having braided it before I got into bed."

Matthew hunted about and produced the dark green ribbon he'd pulled off last night.

"Dastardly man," she muttered, and moved over to the chamber pot. He liked undoing her hair when they made love, and last night had been no exception. She tugged at her shift, still unlaced, and threw him a quick look. He smiled back, a slow smile that lit his eyes from within.

He remained in bed, watching while she did her standard set of morning exercises, and she put extra effort into them, liking the admiring sheen in his eyes when she counted off her push-ups. But he laughed when she groaned with the effort of putting her palms on the floor while keeping her legs straight, saying he could not think of one single situation in which this particular position might become useful.

"Let me," he said when she began to do battle with her hair, and so they sat in silence for some minutes while he teased the comb through the tangles and curls.

"He knows," Alex said. "Carlos knows it all." She pulled her knees up to clasp them to her chest. "I don't like that he does, and he looks at me differently now, doesn't he?"

"Not to wonder at, is it? It makes for quite a disconcerting story."

"Well, at least he doesn't think I'm a witch." She fiddled with one bare toe, frowning down at the too long nail. "He thinks Isaac is one, though."

"Mmhmm." Matthew nodded, thereby voicing his agreement with Carlos.

"What on earth do we do with him?" Alex sighed.

"What can we do? He's here."

"And so unhappy it's unbearable to watch," Alex said.

"We can't help him with that, lass. We can but help him cope."

Which was bloody difficult, when a full-grown man regressed into adolescent behaviour, complete with tantrums, scathing remarks, and a constant flow of denigrating comments about this life, this place, these people. Alex made allowances for him: she turned a deaf ear on his complaining and tried instead to encourage him to paint, even if any suggestions along those lines were brusquely rebuffed.

"And if it fails?" Carlos asked when she raised the issue of Isaac's painting – or rather his non-painting – with him. "What then?"

"Unless he tries, we won't know if he fails, will we? It's like hoping to win the lottery without buying a lottery ticket."

"*Quizás*," Carlos agreed, "but he's playing for a much higher stake than a mere lottery win."

"Yes," Alex said, "he's playing for his life."

Carlos rolled his eyes. Isaac was alive and well, there were no imminent threats to his life, and maybe he just had to adapt.

"I don't think he can," Alex told him. "I think he's left his heart in his own time."

"And you didn't?"

For a long time, Alex sat silent, and then she looked to where Matthew was exiting the barn, pitchfork in hand and Samuel at his side.

"No," she said, "I found it here."

That made Carlos smile. He leaned across the table and covered Alex's hand with his own. "Fortunately – for him and for you."

★

"I have to leave on the morrow," Carlos said to Isaac one morning, closing his breviary.

"You do?" Isaac looked up at his distant cousin with consternation. His shoulders fell, and he nodded morosely. "Of course, you do. You're going home."

"I have obligations to discharge first, and coming with you has already delayed me three weeks or more. His Excellency will be most displeased if his precious letters do not reach their recipients soon."

"Sorry for being a nuisance," Isaac muttered, but was immediately ashamed of himself.

"You could…" Carlos was busy with his single stocking, his face to the floor. "…If you want to, you could come with me."

"And go where?" Isaac asked. "I can't go back to Seville, remember? Raúl will have me killed. So where? A monastery in Toledo? Madrid? Perhaps take holy orders?"

"There are worse lives," Carlos said.

"I'm sure there are, but I… No, Carlos, I still have to try, you know? And going back with you would indicate I've given up."

"You have," Carlos said. "You sit and mope, you're insupportable to all around you, and not once since we got here have you even tried to paint."

"It's not that easy! I can't just flip a switch and have inspiration flow through me."

Carlos made a face at him. "You used to try all the time. But since painting the sea, you're too afraid, aren't you?"

Isaac stomped out of the room.

Samuel and Matthew decided to ride with Carlos to Edinburgh and see him safely aboard a ship to London.

"I can't have him setting off on his own," Matthew said. "It isn't safe, what with the general state of things, and him undoubtedly a foreigner." When Isaac was asked if he wished to come as well, he shook his head. Whatever for?

"Carlos might appreciate it," Alex said.

"Why? I'll still have to tell him goodbye. Better here than there," Isaac muttered, eyeing the scraps of paper he had laid out on the table as a challenge to himself.

He could feel his palms break out in a sweat at the thought of picking up the coal to draw but grudgingly he recognised Carlos was right. He had lost his nerve, and unless he got it back ASAP he never would, and then what?

"Suit yourself," Alex said.

Just after dawn the next morning, Carlos wrapped his cloak around him and stepped outside. Matthew and Samuel were already mounted, waiting with badly concealed impatience for Carlos to make his final farewells. Isaac stood to the side, and watched Alex take a long and intense farewell of the Spanish priest before coming over to say his own goodbyes.

"I'll pray for you," Carlos said.

Isaac gave him a wavering smile. "Thanks, I'm sure it will help." He didn't want Carlos to leave him. It was like having an umbilical cord severed, leaving him floating untethered in space. But he couldn't very well say that so instead, he clasped the priest's hand hard, very hard, his Adam's apple bobbing up and down painfully with the effort not to cry. "It's been a pleasure to know you."

"A pleasure you could have done without," Carlos said.

"Honestly? Yes. But things being as they were, I was lucky to land where I did, right?" Isaac cleared his throat. "I'll never forget you."

"Nor I you. *Que Dios te proteja.*" Carlos made a swift sign of the cross on Isaac's brow, and mounted his horse.

"Don't forget!" Alex called after him.

"I know, I know." Carlos waved back. "Every week, Alex, both stump and peg."

Isaac spent the morning of Carlos' departure doodling. Nothing, no surges of inspiration, no churning waters. He sighed, shoved the papers together, and sat for some minutes listening to the sounds of the house around him.

Wood shifted and creaked, somewhere an unfastened shutter banged in a sudden flurry of wind, and from the grate came the constant crackling of the fire, intermingled with a hiss when a larger piece of wood disintegrated into ashes.

A high-pitched squeal, his mother's − Alex's − voice raised in hasty instruction, and then a shriek filled the air, a sound of pure and absolute agony, cut abruptly short. Isaac jumped at the sound but sat back down, recalling that today was the day they were killing the pigs.

Yet another agonised shriek, a second of total silence, and then Alex must have said something, because he heard Robbie and Gavin laugh out loud. With an exhalation, Isaac pulled the paper towards him again, and drew one thick line straight across. He drew a few more, the coal began to fly, and there on the paper, flowered a woman, sitting with her back towards him.

"Veronica," he breathed, and for an instant, he hoped that something would happen, but nothing did. He fisted the paper together and threw it into the hearth before standing up to go in search of live human beings.

They were all in the yard, dismembering the two pigs. Alex was a repulsive sight: bloody all over, her hair covered with a kerchief, and with smudges of substances he didn't want to think about up her arms and even on her cheek.

"You can help, you know." She used her head to indicate the huge ham recently scalded and debristled.

"I'm not sure I want to. It's all very messy, isn't it?" He felt positively ill when Ellen heaped coil after coil of cleaned intestines into the basket beside her, muttered something about barbaric, and made as if to leave.

"Hey!" Alex's voice brought him up short, and reluctantly he turned towards her. "If you want to eat, you'd better start helping." She nodded to where the barrow stood, heaped with offal. "You can begin with that. Dig it down deep enough that the dogs don't get at it." She didn't even bother to check if he did as she said. She just turned back to her work.

Isaac's cheeks heated with her reprimand, but damned if he intended to do anything about the stinking heap in the wheelbarrow. Without a word, he returned inside.

"You're almost thirty-three, for God's sake, not a child of six! Will you please start behaving like an adult?" Alex glared at Isaac, arms akimbo, and he glared back from where he was sitting by the kitchen table. "I asked you to help, but, no, the hoity-toity artist won't lower himself to getting his hands dirty, will he?"

"It made me sick just to look at it," Isaac said.

"Right, so instead old Robbie did it, despite having been up since dawn to do all his other normal chores." She threw him yet another angry look. "It might help to stop wallowing in self-pity."

"Self-pity?" Isaac spluttered. "How dare you accuse me of being self-pitying – this is all your fault to begin with!"

"My fault? How the bloody hell can it be my fault that you, Isaac Lind, were stupid enough to paint what you knew – oh yes, you did! Don't look at me like that. You knew alright what you were playing with – what you knew was tempting fate."

"If you hadn't abandoned me in the first place, then—"

"I had no choice! I didn't set out to end up here, and you know that."

"But, once here, you've never wanted to come back. Not to me, not to John. All you wanted was to stay with your oh so precious Matthew!"

"And you pined, did you? Did you go around and miss me, long for me? Did you?"

"No," Isaac said. "Actually, I never thought about you," he added cruelly. "After all, I had Diane."

"Well, bully for you," Alex said, crossing her arms tight over her chest.

"At least she was there," he threw at her as he left the kitchen.

Alex was somewhat distracted from her chafing concern for Isaac by the arrival early next morning of a small delegation. She recognised one of the men as being a nephew to the martyred John Brown, another as being a cousin to Matthew.

The minister heading the little group was a stranger to

her, and unfortunately for him, the man reminded her of Richard Campbell. This man, however, introduced himself as Mr Donaldson, and Alex nodded in greeting, which made the minister pull his brows together. Alex wasn't about to curtsey to a man several years her junior, and instead waited for them to state their business.

"Is the master not at home, then?" the minister finally asked, seeing as Alex made no sign of inviting them in.

"No."

"Ah. And he'll be back shortly, I assume?"

"No doubt."

"And the priest?" the man who was Matthew's cousin asked.

"The priest?" Alex tried to remember the cousin's name, and decided this was yet another John.

"Don't try that on with us, mistress." The minister gave her a sour look. "We know you're harbouring a papist priest."

"We most certainly aren't," Alex said.

Isaac chose this moment to appear at the door, and the minister used his head to indicate this dark, swarthy man, so obviously not a true-blooded Scot of the Kirk. "And him?"

"Him? Oh, that's my son." Alex ignored the surprised look from Matthew's cousin. "I can assure you he isn't a priest – or a papist." Or a Presbyterian, or anything much when it came to religion.

"We know, mistress, that you've had a priest here," John said, leaning forward over the neck of his horse. "You had two men riding in some days past."

"He's gone, and he was foremost a friend, not a priest seeking refuge." She could have bitten her tongue off. She could see how the faces of the men before her shuttered at the thought of Matthew Graham being on friendly terms with a papist. "My friend," she added, and that made them look at her as if she were a whore.

Isaac joined her, nodded at the men. "Everything okay?" he asked.

"Yes," she said.

The minister looked Isaac up and down. "I haven't seen you in kirk, nor you, Mistress Graham, not more than the once."

"Well, it's a bit of a ride," Alex said.

"Not far enough to excuse you from attending. I'll expect you come Sunday. All of you." With that, the minister wheeled his horse and left, followed by his acolytes.

"Shit," Alex said succinctly, and beside her Isaac smothered a laugh. "I don't see why you're laughing. You're coming too, remember?"

"Shit," Isaac voiced, looked at her, and for the first time since he had arrived, they laughed, together.

Chapter 25

"I had forgotten just how much it rains here," Alex said with a sigh to Samuel, staring out at the wet day. Not that she gave a rat's arse about the weather at present. She threw a worried look up the lane. Matthew should have been back by now. He had ridden out just after dawn, promising to hurry back from the meeting in Cumnock. He hadn't wanted to go, muttering that he was getting tired of the minister and his peremptory demands that Matthew attend this meeting or that.

"Not only kirk every other Sunday," he'd muttered. "Now, it's nigh on weekly he expects me to ride all the way to Cumnock."

"Where is he?" she muttered, her fingers drumming against the windowsill. There. Her shoulders dropped several inches when she saw Matthew walk his horse down the lane, hunched against the November rain. Once at the stable, he dismounted clumsily before disappearing inside, leading the horse. Alex frowned. Something was wrong.

"Stay here," she told Samuel when he made to follow her, stuck her feet into her clogs, and hastened across the cobbled yard.

He'd left the door open, and for a moment she stood in the doorway, peering into the gloom inside. She heard him first, his dark voice talking to the horse while he unsaddled it. In the weak light, the man before her was ageless, a solid permanence that moved with fluid ease around the horse. Or not. He was limping and she hurried down the central aisle to where he was rubbing the horse dry.

"Are you hurt?"

"Nothing serious," he replied through his teeth, and when she placed a hand on his drenched back, she realised he was shaking with contained rage. He threw the bulging leather satchel to lie in the aisle, took several deep breaths, and turned to face her. "We won't be staying here longer than necessary." Before she could say anything, he was clambering up the ladder to the hayloft.

She followed him up, rung by careful rung, and stood to the side as he hefted a couple of pitchforks of hay to land below. "What's the matter?"

Matthew dug the pitchfork into the hay at random, angry jabbing movements. "William of Orange has landed on English soil, and here in Cumnock, there is general rejoicing that the end of the Stuarts is nigh." He threw the pitchfork to stand quivering in the hay, and sank down to sit, scrubbing at his hair. "Papists are to be hounded out of the shire, and men with doubtful loyalties, well…"

"Oh." Alex came over to sit beside him. She placed a hand on his thigh, and he winced at her touch. "And you're a man with doubtful loyalties, I take it."

"They ambushed me as I rode out. They ran alongside and pelted me with stones and eggs, and one of them went for the horse's head, to hold him like, and I swear, Alex, had I carried my sword…" He mimed a slashing motion. "They don't want me here. I don't much wish to be here. Not anymore." He smiled crookedly at her. "Aye, I supposed it would make you pleased."

"Not if it hurts you."

Matthew regarded his boots in silence. "I'm man enough to be able to tell the difference between dreams and reality," he said, squaring his shoulders. "We'll leave sooner than later." Without even looking at her, he dropped back down to the waiting horse, and Alex remained sitting in the hay, trying to contain the whooping joy that built inside of her.

She tiptoed around him the coming days, struggling hard not to let it show just how happy his decision had made her. She tried to anticipate his needs, generally fussing over him like a mother hen until he exploded, told her he didn't need to be coddled like a wee bairn, and he wouldn't be back for dinner. He jerked his head at Samuel, picked up his musket, and said something about going out on the moor for some hours.

The door reverberated behind him, and Alex felt foolish and diminished, pasting a false smile on her face before turning back to meet the curious eyes of Ellen and Rosie.

"Men," she said, and escaped into the parlour where she found a moody and depressed Isaac, glaring at his latest effort. "Yet another man," she sighed, retrieved her sewing basket, and decided the rest of the day would be best spent on her own, in their bedchamber.

She had just settled herself by the small casement window, comfortable in the weak beam of sunlight, when a strangled yelp had her out of her chair. She heard feet flying from the kitchen, Ellen exclaimed, and Rosie muttered something that, even from here, Alex could make out as a prayer. She was already halfway down the stairs.

"What?" she asked, shoving Rosie aside. "Oh my God! And now what have you done, you stupid, stupid man!"

"It was an accident!" Isaac gasped, holding his bleeding hand to his chest. "I forgot I was holding the knife."

"An accident?" Alex eyed the well-honed blade of the small palette knife, and frowned at the quantity of blood seeping through the cloth he had wound around his hand. His right hand. He met her eyes over Ellen's dark head, and she could read the terror in them.

"...so I hope it'll heal," Alex said to Matthew later, "even if he cut himself pretty badly."

Isaac hadn't handled pain well, and to judge from his creative cursing, it had hurt like hell when she first cleaned then sewed the deep gash between the second and the third finger.

"I don't think he sliced through any tendons, but he won't be painting or drawing with that hand for quite some time." She shook her head. How Isaac was to while away his days was something of a mystery to her. "Sometimes, I don't think he'll ever make it back, but how on earth do I tell him that?"

Matthew hitched his shoulders. "Fool, to tamper with

time, and now that he's here, he had best adapt. The lad's good-looking, has his health and an obvious talent. He could make himself a comfortable life here – rich men are always willing to pay to have their unprepossessing features committed to canvas."

"I don't think he even wants to try," Alex said.

She sat staring into the fire, feeling tired. All these needy men, and none of them seemed to spare a thought for her. Sometimes, she considered retreating to bed for a couple of days, pulling the covers over her head, and leaving them to sort out their respective issues best they could. As if he could read her mind, Matthew came to stand behind her, kneading at her shoulders, her nape.

"Will he be alright?" She kept her eyes on the embers.

"Isaac? I'm sure you did a right good job, lass."

"Not Isaac. Adam. He's down there, where the armies are." She slipped her hand into her petticoat pocket to touch Adam's latest letter, surprisingly long and well written for someone that young. He sounded content, going on and on about London, Luke's impressive home, and his cousin Joan.

"He's in London, and Luke will see him safe." And, anyway, he added, from the few reports that were making their way up north, the King was unwilling to confront the usurper in the field, playing an elaborate game of hide-and-seek over the countryside.

Next time Matthew had to go to Cumnock, Alex insisted on coming along, reciting a long list of things she had to acquire.

"I can buy it for you," he said, but Alex just shook her head. No way. He was going nowhere without her. This time, Matthew drew his belt through the scabbard of his sword, and tucked into his belt was a pistol, wads and balls conveniently at hand in his coat pocket.

Isaac watched these preparations with a raised brow. "Are you expecting trouble?" he asked.

"It doesn't hurt to go armed when the country is in uproar," Matthew replied in a relaxed tone.

Absolutely not, Alex agreed, sliding her hand in through the slit in her skirts to close on the worn handle of her little knife.

"Oh." Isaac looked at his bandaged hand.

"Why don't you ask Samuel to teach you to shoot?" Alex said.

"With this?" Isaac waved his hand at her.

"You can move the finger. You don't need more than that." Matthew clapped Isaac on the back. "You surely have the eye for it." He helped Alex up onto her horse, swung up into the saddle, and with a little wave they were off.

The day was fine – as fine as a late November day could be – with a crispness to the air that brought roses to your cheeks, reddened your nose, and chilled whatever side of you that was presently exposed to the biting wind.

By the time they got to Cumnock, Alex was stiff with cold, and very relieved to be off the horse. She stamped some blood into her feet, pulled the hood of the cloak up high around her head, and set off to do her errands.

She heard them but ignored them, the soft jeering whispers that followed her when she crossed the square and went about her purchases.

"Papist lover," they whispered. "Stuart whore," they added, making her cheeks flame. "Closet Catholic," some said. "Traitor," others hissed. By the time she met up with Matthew again, her fingers were clenched so hard round her basket she could barely disengage them.

"Are you alright?" he asked in a concerned voice.

"Are you?" she asked back, noting that, if anything, he was just as tense as she was.

"Nay," he said, his eyes narrowing as he studied some of the men around them.

"Me neither, and I'm not sure whether I'm mostly angry or mostly afraid." She leaned closer to him, close enough that the breath coming in visible puffs from them both mingled into one exhalation. "Small-minded, uneducated bigots, the lot of them, and now that they begin to see that things may go their way, they're already honing their blades to take revenge for these last years of persecution."

"Aye," Matthew said, sounding sad.

They were well on their way home when Matthew drew his horse to an abrupt halt. The bushes to their right seemed to have come alive, and they were surrounded by a gang of youths. Matthew cursed loudly.

"Get back," he said to Alex, which was a totally useless instruction given the three boys behind her. This time, it wasn't eggs and rocks. This time, it was cudgels and knives, and when Matthew drew his sword, the attackers fell back, wary of the obvious ease with which he handled it.

"Papist!" one of them shouted, and sent a rock to hit Matthew's horse squarely on its rump. The horse shied, neighing loudly.

"I'm no papist, you piece of shite!" Matthew roared back.

"You've had a Catholic priest staying with you," one of them jeered. "A friend, no less, of your wife."

"He is, and a far better man than any of you lot." Alex had at last found her knife and pulled it free.

"Man?" One of the youths came close enough to grab at her leg, falling back with a surprised yelp when she sank the tip of her dagger into his forearm. "How would you know he's a man?"

"Generally, all it takes is a peek under a man's shirt but in your case, I dare say the balls may be there, but the manhood is not," Alex spat back, struggling hard to keep herself astride her skittish horse.

Some of them actually laughed, but remembered themselves and went back to circling them.

"Not only papists, but traitors," one of them called out. "You sup with Bluidy Clavers."

"A murderer," another of them hissed. "A man who slays godly men for naught but reading their Bibles, and you sit at ease with him." A clod of earth landed on Alex's cloak, followed by another.

"Go," Matthew threatened, spurred his horse into a tight circle, and brought the flat of his sword down across the face of one of them. "Go before I do you harm!" In response, four or five of them launched themselves at his horse, and Matthew used the hilt on one of them, slashed at another, and would probably have had them all on the run if Alex hadn't called out when one of the louts grabbed at her leg and pulled her off. Matthew roared her name, wheeling his horse towards her.

Four of them threw themselves at Matthew, a rock struck him in the head, and the bastards cheered when blood ran down Matthew's face. Two of them grabbed hold of Matthew's boot and pulled. There was a scream, a boy staggered back holding an arm sliced open from elbow to hand, but more youths took his place, like a pack of hyenas circling a wounded wildebeest. Alex tried to sit. Someone shoved at her, trying to pin her down. In your dreams. Her knife flashed in the sun, and the thug's cheek split open like a ripe peach.

She heard Matthew grunt. Well, maybe she didn't hear him, but she saw him jerk, saw the blade that ripped through his coat. Up, get up. More hands, very many hands, but Alex used her voice and her hands, shrieking boys in the ear, twisting hair and ears, jabbing at legs and arms with her knife.

The two young men hanging on to Matthew's boot tugged, and this time they dislodged him, sending him flying through the air to land with a dull crack.

Alex regained her feet, and when the youth closest lunged, she kicked him straight in the stomach, making him double up in pain. Out of the corner of her eye, she saw Matthew, immobile, and with a shout, she took a leap towards him, throwing herself at the apprentice trying to prise Matthew's sword loose from his hand. One well directed kick sent him flying to land on his rump.

Instinctively, she sank down, balancing on her feet, arms raised in a defensive stance. "If he dies, I'll kill you, you hear?"

Someone grabbed at her, and she whirled, slamming her elbow hard into an unprotected face. Another, and her hand chopped at an arm, her eyes never leaving the apprentice she'd kicked to the ground. He scrambled back to his feet, but Alex was blinded with fear and rage, and she kicked him, and kicked him again, and she might have killed him had not Matthew's voice broken through.

"Alex!" he gasped. "Let him be, lass. Come to me."

Oh God, she thought, he's dying, and instead of trying to save him or at least hold his hand, I'm kicking an idiot to pulp. Her knees wobbled. She tensed her thighs to stop her legs from shaking, ignoring her body's loud protests that it was far too old for this kind of activity. Her elbow throbbed, her fingers ached, but no way was she going to show this pack of scavengers just how close she was to tears. Instead, she advanced on them.

"Go!" she yelled. "Go and take your sorry friend with you. But remember, I'll find each and every one of you if he dies." She must have looked a fright, because they backed away, dragging their moaning companion with them.

Alex staggered towards the horses and her man. She hiccupped, loudly, and her hand found his, and it was warm and dry, his pulse a steady, strong beat that flowed into her.

"I won't die," he said. "At least, I don't think so."

"And how would you know?" she snivelled. She folded back his coat, found the cut from which he was bleeding, and sat back on her heels and cried. He was right. This wouldn't kill him.

"I don't think they'll jump you again," Alex said, once she'd calmed down. She tried to lever him up to sit. There was blood in his hair, on his face, an ugly contusion where one of the rock-wielding apprentices had gotten a blow in, but all in all, the damage was less severe than Alex had feared. But then she saw how gingerly he was holding his leg, and wasn't so sure. "Your leg?"

"Aye, it broke," Matthew said, and she noticed how pale he'd gone.

"It broke?"

He smiled weakly. When he was thrown off the horse, he said.

How on earth was she to get him home? She couldn't expect him to ride with an unset leg. Resolutely, she stood, walked over to a stand of hazels, cutting four stout lengths. Just as resolutely, she sawed through the leather of his boot and eased it off, closing her ears to his muffled gasps of pain, and then she studied the break as well as she could.

"It snapped clean off," Matthew told her, attempting to study his own leg.

"It did? And how do you know? Can you see inside the leg?"

"I heard it," he said, pointing to the misalignment halfway up his calf.

"I hate doing this," Alex muttered, just as she always did when she had to hurt anyone in her own family, "I really, really hate it." But set bones she had done before, albeit under Mrs Parson's eagle eye, so with a quick look at his face to ensure he wasn't about to faint, she flexed her hands, grabbed hold of his foot and pulled – hard.

He did faint, slumping back against the ground, and Alex made the most of it, swiftly setting and splinting the leg using her petticoat, torn into strips, to bandage it. He came round just as a group of men came riding towards them, and groped for his sword, insisting that Alex had to get him up to stand.

"Here," he said, shoving his pistol into her hands.

"It's unloaded," she said.

"They don't know, do they?" he wheezed.

"Master Graham." The minister broke a lengthy and icy silence.

"Donaldson," Matthew said, withholding his title.

The minister flushed, an unbecoming hue of pink flying across his pock-marked face, all the way from his throat to his receding hairline. Matthew locked eyes with his cousin, and John averted his face.

"It would seem you've met with misfortune," the minister said.

"Well, well, bloody Sherlock Holmes in person," Alex said in an undertone. "And you, of course, had nothing to

212

do with it," she went on in a more normal tone.

"Really, Mrs Graham, what do you think of me?" The minister sounded affronted.

Alex wasn't impressed. In her experience, men of the cloth made glib liars.

"Somewhat coincidental, they run off, you ride in," Matthew said, "and they accused us of papist sympathies."

The minister looked away, murmuring something about overzealous youths.

Alex just raised her brows. "Overzealous and very fired up. One could almost imagine someone had been preaching to them."

She threw Matthew a look. From the way he'd gone grey around his mouth and nose, she could see he was in pain. He breathed in short breaths, staring straight ahead. His coat was dark with blood from the long cut, and Alex had no time to stand about exchanging inane comments with Mr Donaldson. She had to get Matthew home and into a warm bed.

"It would calm things down if you were to declare yourself openly for William and the advent of a Protestant reign," the minister said.

"Mayhap, but as I'm in two minds, I can't very well do that. I don't like the thought of a daughter ousting her father, of a wee lad being disinherited."

"He's a papist!" the minister said. "And you know well how papists do with us!"

"Yet King James hasn't done that, has he?" Matthew replied. "Has he not advocated tolerance? Is it not because of his Indulgences that you've been able to return openly to your ministry?"

Alex could see him begin to totter, and pretended to stagger against him, allowing him for a moment to rest his weight against her. When the minister opened his mouth to say something more, Alex decided enough was enough. "Not now. In case you haven't noticed, your band of brigands have caused my husband damage. So I'm going to get him home. You will punish the perpetrators..." She waited until the minister nodded. "…and then we can resume this political discussion at a later date."

"Can you ride?" she whispered to Matthew as he limped towards the horses.

"I don't know." He was shivering, sweat dewing his forehead. They both started when his cousin appeared beside them, his arm coming out to support Matthew.

"I'll see you home," John said. "I won't have it said of me that I stood by and saw a kinsman badly hurt and did nothing to help him."

"Thank you." Alex swallowed back on the recriminations she wanted to throw in his face.

Chapter 26

David came home the day before Christmas. With him, he brought a dumpling of a lad, with red corkscrews and an engaging grin. Over his dark breeches with matching coat he had wrapped a tartan plaid, a brown bonnet perched on his curls, and from his belt hung a basket-hilted sword. The young man dismounted and swept Alex a deep and dignified bow.

"Coll MacGregor, at your service, ma'am," he said in a deep, dark voice. It made Matthew smile, the contrast between his size and his voice. "Sir," the lad added, turning towards Matthew.

"Master MacGregor," Matthew replied, inclining his head.

The stout lad smiled before replacing his bonnet on his head and sauntering over to where David was greeting Samuel.

"Rob Roy in person," Alex said. "Lucky you don't have all that many cows for him to steal."

"My cows?" Matthew didn't understand.

"Never mind." She smiled. "I'm not even sure Rob Roy exists as yet. Besides, he was huge."

After supper, Alex converted the kitchen into a bath-house, supervising with a beady eye as a reluctant Coll submerged himself in the tub, saying this excessive exposure to water would probably kill him. Once Coll was adequately scrubbed, Alex had Samuel and Matthew empty the tub. Then she refilled it, and motioned for David to get in. Matthew bit back a grin at the obvious pleasure with which David sank down as well as he could in the small tub; even more when that look converted to grimaces as Alex attacked David's skin and hair with pot soap and brush.

"We've become fast friends," David said some time later in response to Alex's question. "He's a younger nephew to a Highland chief, and his uncle decided law might be a good career – for Coll and for the clan."

"Ah." Matthew was not overly pleased. Befriending a Highlander – however civilised – could be something of a liability in the present intolerant climate: papists, the lot of them.

"Sit still." Alex pressed down on David's shoulders, and went on with her hairdressing activities, cutting back David's long hair to a more practical length. "And he didn't go home for Christmas because…?"

David shrugged. "It's a long ride to Glengyle and beyond. I suggested he come with me instead. I couldn't leave him to sit through Hogmanay on his own, could I?"

"Nay, of course not," Matthew said, sharing a small smile with his wife. For her it was Christmas, while for him and his bairns it was Hogmanay.

Alex concluded her work by hugging David and kissing the top of his head. "I'm glad to have you back."

David squirmed, and changed the subject to how Isaac came to be here – he'd always thought Isaac was dead – and why Da was hobbling around on crutches. Matthew chose to concentrate on replying to the last of those questions, and by the time he was done, it was time for bed.

"Comfortable?" Alex asked, smoothing back a stray strand of hair from Matthew's brow.

"Well enough," he said, shifting his leg against the sheets. It didn't hurt much, and Alex had him doing long sets of exercises to keep his thigh muscles in relative shape. But it irked him, nonetheless, and every day he nagged at her, asking if today might be the day she'd release him from his splints.

"A week after New Year," she'd promised earlier in the day, and Matthew had groaned theatrically, but now he lay back with good grace, enjoying her touch. The slash down his side had healed, leaving a new addition to the scars that covered his body. His whole life was documented on his skin. The old, barely visible scars of his youth when he had fought in the Civil War, the faint lines that walked up and down his back after repeated floggings, the scars on his thigh after axe and sword, and then his left foot, permanently maimed after a May day soon four years in the past when that bastard Philip Burley cut off his fourth toe, leaving an unsightly gap and a tendency to chafe.

He raised his head to look down his body to his bare foot. "Do you find me disfigured?"

In reply, Alex's hand floated over his body, tantalisingly close, but not yet touching. His body hair stood straight up, heat flying up his skin like a shadow under her hand.

"To me, you are perfect." Her warm hands settled gently on his arms, his shoulders. They travelled down his chest, stroked his belly, and Matthew stretched like a purring cat beneath her touch. A fleeting touch on his member – enough to make his balls tighten – and her hands continued down to his legs, caressing his whole leg all the way down to his foot until she turned her attention to unwinding the bandage that held his splints in place. They were silent, his hand resting on her back as she rubbed blood into his calf, leaving a scent of crushed mustard seeds and mint in her wake. She reset the splints and with a small sound subsided to lie by his side.

"God, I'm tired," she said, pillowing her head on his shoulder. She would be: the whole house smelled of her efforts. From here, he could make out the scents of saffron bread and baked ham, of pies and cider sauce.

Matthew, however, wasn't – not now, when his body stirred with inner heat, when her proximity made his cock swell. His hand did circles over her shoulder blades, his fingers dug into her nape, massaged her scalp.

He tickled her, insistently, until she raised her face and kissed him. He chuckled. She had tasted her own produce, and she had made treacle cake as well. Alex smiled down at him, undid the ties of her shift and shoved it off her shoulders, over the slope of her chest, releasing her breasts to fall into his waiting hands. He weighed them, running thumbs over her nipples. He rose on his elbow, pressed her down on her back, his fingers already touching and teasing, sliding into the warm moisture of her cleft.

"Oh," she said, her fingers burning into his skin as she slid her hand down to fondle him. Her thighs were wide, her hands urgent on his waist, his hips. He was clumsy in his movements, hampered by his leg, but he ignored the fleeting sense of discomfort and came into her. He barely moved, and she wriggled below him until he was so deep inside of her he was sure he was nudging at her heart. Slowly, they rocked, welded together from pubic bone to chest, and his eyes never left hers, wide open and unblinking in the weak light of the bedside candle.

"Happy Christmas," he whispered afterwards.

"And to you," she whispered back.

It was a good Christmas, Matthew reflected some days later, sitting in the kitchen with a laden breakfast plate before him. Good, but lonely, he amended, because ever since that November day when Alex and he had been attacked, there had not been one single visit.

Not even his accursed cousin had been polite enough to drop by to enquire about his health, and even if he had sent messages to most of his old friends and neighbours, he was already reconciled to the fact that none of them would come to the Hogmanay dance. And yet every time he went outside, his eyes leapt up the lane, hoping to see someone riding down towards him.

He suppressed a sigh, downed the last of his food, and after giving Alex a pat on her arse, told the lads to come with him. He had a job for them.

"And you?" David asked, throwing the ram a long look.

"Me? Well, I can't do much, can I?" Matthew said, using his cane to tap the splinted leg. "Besides, it isn't much of a challenge for three lads to catch one wee ram."

"Wee?" Coll looked at the ram.

"Smaller than you at any rate." Matthew smiled, although should Coll drop down on hands and knees, it would be touch and go.

He stood to the side and cheered them on as they attempted to separate the ram from the ewes. Not very successfully, not at first, but the lads did not seem to mind, laughing as they nimbly leaped out of the way when the irate ram charged them.

Ellen drifted over to watch, stood to the side, and giggled with her hand over her mouth as Samuel made a grab for the ram but missed, landing heavily in the by now muddy ground.

"Your mama will not like it," Matthew warned, laughing as well. "She'll scrub you with lye if you get any dirtier."

With a triumphant whoop, Coll succeeded in grabbing hold of the ram's right horn. The beast set off, dragging Coll in its wake. Matthew was laughing so hard his sides were aching, Samuel and David rushed to help, and together the three of them manhandled the ram to where Matthew was standing with the rope in his hands.

The ram was finally standing still, sides heaving, neck straining against the rope. The lads were all gulping air, somewhat the worse for wear after their recent struggle with the beast.

"Good lad." Matthew ruffled Coll's bright hair. "Now, it's but a matter of cutting him. There." Matthew pointed with his cane.

"Are you sure it's a boil and not an extra ball?" Coll asked.

"A boil," Matthew replied. "It wasn't there a month ago, and I don't think you grow extra balls, no matter you're a beast or a man."

"He won't like it, that you cut him there," David said. They stood in silent commiseration and regarded the animal.

Like one, they turned when Isaac approached. A knowing look flew among the four of them, and when Isaac reached them, Matthew handed him the knife.

"You cut." He nodded at the rear end of the ram.

"Me?" Isaac looked doubtful, hand closing experimentally around the handle. Just out of his bandage, Isaac was careful with his hand – too careful, according to Alex, who had confided to Matthew that she suspected her son had lost his nerve, sitting for hours staring at his coals without as much as touching them.

"Just be quick with it," Coll encouraged. "One swift cut."

"Cut how?" Isaac squinted at the growth. Matthew made a slashing motion, using the cane to indicate where he should cut. The ram attempted to sit, bleating warningly to tell whoever it was that was poking at his rear end that he was going to kick if they tried anything underhand. Isaac closed his right hand around the knife.

"Aye," Matthew said, "a tight grip is best."

Isaac opened his hand, stared at his fingers, and closed his fist. "Tight." A small smile appeared on his face. "I can do tight." He grabbed the ram's tail with his left hand and sliced through the boil in one decisive movement.

The ram bellowed, kicked straight out with both hind legs, Isaac leaped away, David lost his grip on one of the horns, and suddenly the ram was free, rushing towards his waiting flock, while Coll hung on grimly to the rope, with Samuel bounding after, the steaming tar brush in his hand.

They were still laughing when the dogs began to bark, and Coll was on his feet in an instant, hand on the hilt of his dirk. Matthew watched his reaction thoughtfully, but followed suit, loosening his dagger in its scabbard. David and Samuel were at his side, Isaac hovered only a foot or so away, and in the doorway, Alex appeared, musket in hand.

Matthew muttered under his breath when he recognised the lead horse. Alex retreated into the house, probably to return the musket to its keeping place, but a few minutes later, she reappeared, coming over to greet their guests.

She looked suspiciously rosy, his wife, as if she'd pinched her cheeks a couple of times. Matthew's gaze wandered over her. Small curls danced most enticingly around the cap, the shawl had been rearranged to highlight rather than cover her chest, and she had to be walking on her toes, how else to account for her carriage, breasts held high and round, back ramrod straight. When John Graham dismounted, she smiled, far wider than was strictly necessary or appropriate.

Matthew limped towards her, followed by their sons. "John." His hand closed on Alex's arm, squeezing just that little bit too much, enough to make her draw in a surprised breath.

"Matthew," John replied wearily, and Matthew turned to study him instead, taking in the lines of total exhaustion and dejection in the man before him.

"The King—" John swayed drunkenly on his feet. He gave Matthew a rueful smile. "I'm sorry to importune you, but I've been riding hard for nigh on five days, and I…well, I—"

"Come inside, man," Matthew interrupted. "My lads will see to your horses, and your men can bed down in the hay."

John nodded, and a few minutes later he was fast asleep, head pillowed on the kitchen table.

"Let him be," Matthew told Alex when she made as if to wake him. "He sleeps well enough there."

"He should be in bed," Alex said, her hand almost touching the unkempt hair that presently decorated the table. Matthew cleared his throat. Alex retracted her hand as if burnt.

"David can take him upstairs later, but leave him a few minutes first." He had already ascertained that the man was unharmed – filthy and exhausted, but essentially whole.

He eyed his wife, saying nothing when she flushed and smoothed the hair back to lie neat beneath her cap, no wayward curls bouncing round her face. He looked again, and the shawl was tightened into place, effectively covering her entire chest. He beckoned her towards him, leaned forward until his mouth was level with her ear.

"I told you never to do so again." He straightened up, let a finger run back and forth along his belt, and nodded seriously before calling for David to help their guest to bed.

A few hours later, and John was at the table, eating as if he hadn't seen food in days.

"We would have been victorious!" John tore at the warm

bread and dipped a chunk into the rich stew set before him. When Matthew offered him some more beer, he nodded eagerly. "He's a fine general, the King is, and we were the greater army in the field, but would he stand and fight?" He brought his hand down hard on the table, making all of them jump. "No! He wouldn't, saying how it would not be him who loosened the spectre of civil war again on his people." John made a loud, derisive sound, conveying just how weak he considered that argument to be. "So, instead, for well over a month, we played a complicated game of peekaboo, and with every mile he allowed William to cover, the Dutchman got closer to London and his supporters." He wiped his bowl clean and held it out for refill, beckoning for Samuel to hand him some more bread. "Very good," he said through his full mouth. "Most delicious, Mrs Graham."

"And then what?" Coll was sitting on his hands, hair sprouting around his head like startled vipers.

John gulped down his beer, wiped his mouth on his sleeve, and sighed. "Well, then he was captured." A hiss went through the room, one of combined shock and relief, because if the King was a prisoner then the war was already over, and so life would not be further disrupted.

John nodded dourly. It had been a terrible setback, he said, and men previously proclaiming their loyalty to the King began to melt away, leaving but a small core of loyal followers to fight for their liege. "But he escaped," he added with perfect timing, and his audience gasped.

"Escaped?" Matthew asked. "Escaped where?"

"To France. Where else? His royal cousin will welcome him warmly, and by spring he'll be back, with money and troops, and then we'll see who is truly the King of England."

"James is," Coll said stoutly, "and our king as well, is he not? A man of our blood, a man of our people."

Matthew was hard put not to laugh. He doubted James considered himself other than royal and English. Just like his brother, he'd proclaim his Scottish blood when it suited him, and forget all about those ancient roots of his when it didn't.

"Right you are, laddie." John Graham beamed at Coll. "And we won't forget it, will we? Up here, in the north, we'll hold true."

David and Coll nodded eagerly, and Alex frowned.

"It depends what you mean by the north," she cut in. "Most of this part of Scotland won't come out for the King, will it?"

"Probably not," John said, a certain caution in his eyes. He stood, surprising them all into standing with him. "I'd best be gone. I have it in my heart to be home for Hogmanay." His mouth curved into a smile.

"Now?" Alex asked. "But it will soon be dark."

John was adamant: they'd had their hours of rest, had been well fed, and a night more or less on the moors wouldn't bother them unduly.

"I wish to apprise my wife of my new title," he added. "Viscount Dundee, no less."

Isaac's head snapped up, dark eyes studying John with far more interest than before. Matthew pursed his mouth, studying his guest who was now pulling his boots back on.

"What will you do?" David asked, handing John his bonnet.

"Do? I will fight for my king. Until I die, or he is victorious, I will fight and hold my lands in his name."

David looked impressed, as did Coll.

"All men will be welcome," John said. "All men willing to fight for their king will find a place by my side."

Matthew supposed John didn't notice the black look Alex sent him, and if he had, he would probably not care.

Matthew hobbled after their guest out into the dusk, and stood to one side while John called men and horses together. Girths were tightened, leather creaked in protest, men sat up in their saddles, and in less than a quarter of an hour, John had his men ready to go. He pulled his blue bonnet down tight over his ears, and smiled down at his host from Caesar's restless height.

"Thank you for your hospitality," he said, "and may there be a day when we can sit and drink together to the health of our king and prince."

"Amen to that," Matthew said, not because it would ever happen, but because he felt this gallant man might need to hear it. He pointed John and his men up the hill towards the moor and raised his hand in farewell.

"He'll be dead shortly," Isaac stated, coming to stand beside Matthew.

"He will?"

Isaac nodded. "That is Bonnie Dundee, and of him men will sing for generations – of him and his bonnet." He made a disparaging sound. "Men generally don't become heroes before they're dead."

Matthew agreed, looked again at the point where John Graham had disappeared, and went to find his wife – he had matters to discuss with her.

Alex Graham wasn't about to let anyone, not even her husband, lay a finger on her without a fight. Matthew found her very beautiful, backed defensively into a corner with her eyes wide and dark. He took his time, unbuckling his belt to let it swing back and forth, and Alex licked her lips and tightened her hold on her hairbrush. With his free hand, he gestured for her to approach, attempting to look stern.

"No way," she said.

"You did it again."

"Did what? And look who's talking, anyway."

Matthew ignored her comment. "You preened for him!"

"And you let other women fondle you!"

He stood looking at her for some seconds more, and then threw the belt into a corner.

"Come here." He extended his hands, empty and wide towards her. The moment she was within reach, he grabbed her, twisted the brush out of her hand, and smacked her, hard, on her rump. He was laughing as he did it, laughing at how she squealed, at how she struggled.

"You…" she spluttered. "You bloody oaf of a man!" She tore herself loose, snatched her brush back, and brandished it threateningly. "If it weren't because you're injured…" she said, miming a kick at him. Matthew retreated, the bed caught him behind the legs, and he fell heavily into it. She came after, brush still in hand, and now it was him defending himself, until he pinned her arms to her side and gathered her to his chest.

"Kiss me," he demanded.

"In your dreams," she snorted, but her lips were soft and curved. He rolled them over, tickled her mercilessly until she surrendered between bouts of laughter, and kissed him over and over again.

"Isaac says how he will die," Matthew said later. He had spooned himself around her as well as he could with his splinted leg, eyes stuck on the small square of night sky visible through the small window.

"Everyone dies."

"Soon."

"Soon? How soon?" Alex shifted in bed.

"He doesn't rightly know, but if you're both right and James is to be king no more, then it can't be long. As long as yon Claverhouse draws breath, he will be a cocklebur up the Dutchman's arse."

He stared out at the black night, recalling the look of open admiration on David's face as he sat opposite John Graham. Thank the Lord the lad was safely settled at the university. He yawned and slipped his hand into place around one of Alex's breasts.

Chapter 27

It was not quite daybreak when the men from Cumnock galloped into their yard the day after, demanding that Bluidy Clavers be turned over to them, now.

"How do they know—?" Alex began, but then her eyes found Robin, one of Rosie's sons, and she had her answer.

Rosie gave her a belligerent look as if saying that she wasn't about to aid a man responsible for so much death and sorrow, a man who slaughtered Covenanters right, left and centre without any compunction whatsoever.

"He isn't here," Matthew told the men, and they bristled and shouted, but when first Samuel, then Isaac appeared with their rifle-bored flintlocks, when Coll stepped into the yard with a swagger and an evident familiarity with the sword in his hand, they muttered and fell away. "He won't be coming back," Matthew said, and that met a murmur of grudging approval, and one by one the men rode off.

For a long time, Matthew regarded Robbie. The old, shrunken man twisted under the master's evaluating gaze, sending angry looks at his wife and his son.

"You'd best pack up your things," Matthew said. Rosie gasped, her hands clutching at her dirty apron. "I won't be betrayed by my own people." A swift lunge, and Robin was whimpering in his grip.

"Your people? And where were you, master, during the killing years?" Rosie challenged. "What help were you to us when Bluidy Clavers and his men roamed the land?"

"You know where I was, and you know why. I didn't leave out of free choice, did I?" He stared at her until Rosie lowered her eyes and shook her head. Matthew turned back to Robbie. "This time you may stay, but this son of yours isn't welcome on my land." He released Robin to land on his knees in the mud. Robbie muttered a heartfelt thank you, grabbed his wife hard by the arm, and dragged her off.

As a consequence, it was a depressing Hogmanay, for all that Alex had cooked and Matthew opened casks of beer and cider. The tenants came, ate and drank, drank some more, but no matter how the fiddler tried, the dancing was half-hearted at best, and Alex could see Matthew was far too aware of the people who were missing: his cousins, his friends of old, his closest neighbours…

Well before midnight, he disappeared out into the night, and an hour or so later, Alex found him where she'd known he'd be, up on the hill. At least he'd been wise enough to use his crutches rather than his cane, but it must have been a struggle to get all the way up here on his own.

The night was bitterly cold, the stars strewn like shards of crushed glass on a velvet background. Matthew was sitting at the point from where one could see all of Hillview – in the night mostly darker shapes against a dark background, but from the barn light still spilled, and strands of music drifted up through the air. She could smell the whisky on him, had seen him methodically drink his way through a sizeable quantity of beer throughout the evening, and the practical part of her was already considering how to best get him to his bed, half drunk and on crutches.

"I want to go home," he slurred, breaking the silence. "Now." He laughed softly and swigged some more from his flask. She sat down beside him, tucking her skirts in tight around her legs. He offered her the flask. She drank, letting the whisky lie first in her mouth before swallowing it down to burn its way down her gullet.

"But you are home," she ventured.

Matthew shook his head vehemently. This had been home, he said, and the land still called to him: the rocks and the fells, the stream through the meadows – all that was home, but the people… He dropped the flask to the ground and cradled his head in his hands.

He didn't understand, he mumbled, wasn't sure what he felt or wanted, not anymore. He missed his bairns, he wanted to laugh at Lettie's latest escapade, admire the new calves, take his musket and spend a day out hunting, with only himself for company. He missed the taste of the water in Graham's Garden, the bench under the oak, and his friends. Aye, that was it: there he had friends, he was a man well-liked and respected, while here he was become a stranger, a man to regard with suspicion.

Alex took hold of his arm and gave him a little shake. "What did you expect?"

He shrugged. He'd assumed that it would all be as it used to be. Instead, he was resented for not having been here during the last two decades, and besides…

"I've changed. It's no longer black and white with me, but here it still is, and they find me lacking in backbone and faith." He looked at her, groped for the flask, and upended the last of the whisky into his throat. "Was I like that? Was I so convinced I had the right of it?"

"It narrows a man, to live under constant persecution, and had we stayed, then yes, you would've been like them." Or dead, she reminded herself, most probably dead.

Matthew scuffed at the dry winter grass. "I can't condemn a king for the sole sin of being a papist, and I fear that I'm very alone in that here in Ayrshire. I keep thinking of the lad, born to be king, and now it has been stolen away from him."

Down below, the barn was plunged in darkness when the candles were extinguished, a solitary lantern making its way across the yard.

"I thought it would all be the same," he said.

"That's the way it is, isn't it?" Alex rested her head against his shoulder. "You no longer belong here. You'll never fully belong there. The eternal curse of the emigrants – they yearn for what they left behind and paint it in colours so bright they start to forget why they left. And so, some return, only to come face to face with the unappetising fact that the memories they've carried with them have little to do with reality."

"Quite the philosopher," he said somewhat snidely. "It's

easier for you. You have no ties to this place, not like me. I'm rooted here, fettered almost by the knowledge that from here springs my family, one generation after the other."

Alex made an exasperated sound. She'd heard it all before, and remained as unimpressed now as then. "So, now they'll spring forth from the ground of Maryland. And frankly, the home you've built for us there is much, much better than this."

"You think? Aye, mayhap it is." She could hear it, the pride in his voice. There was not a building at Graham's Garden that he hadn't built, not a single piece of furniture he hadn't crafted himself, and every square foot of the fields that now flowed from the big house to the river, he had cleared, together with his sons. Close to a hundred acres under the plough, and more than twenty times as much in wooded pastures and virginal forest – all of Hillview would fit easily within the fields closest to the house.

"Anyway," she said when she helped him up to stand, "we're going back there soon, right? So what do you care of the opinions of the men left behind here?" Just the thought of going back made the blood fizz through her veins, a childish impulse to jump up and down building inside her.

Alex handed him the crutches, and together they began the slow descent, making for the solitary candle burning in the kitchen window.

"It's okay to miss it," she said once they were back down. "All of this. Of course you'll miss it and love it from afar." She grabbed at him when the left crutch slipped on the cobbles, holding them both upright while he struggled to regain his balance.

"Aye," he said, and threw a last look at the starry skies before hobbling inside.

"Too much whisky?" Alex teased next morning, setting a bowl of porridge before Isaac.

"Too much everything," Isaac groaned, "but at least I'm up and about while your other sons are still drunk as skunks in their bed."

229

Alex frowned, irritated with herself for not being more attentive last night.

Isaac laughed softly. "And as for Coll, well, if he moves before tomorrow morning that will be a miracle."

"Seeing as they ride back tomorrow, let's hope he shows some sign of life during the day." Impulsively, she reached out to ruffle Isaac's messy hair, and he froze.

Alex retook her hand, and went over to serve herself some breakfast. There was a huge barrier between them, with Isaac evading any physical contact beyond the necessary, and Alex not daring to push. She studied him from below her lashes. He looked so alone, abandoned somehow, and with a silent 'what the hell' ringing in her head, she strode over to him and hugged him.

Isaac's initial reaction was to wrest himself free, but she wouldn't let go, and suddenly he relaxed against her, arms coming round her waist to press himself closer against her.

Alex kissed the top of his head, straightened up, and asked if he wanted some of her precious real tea, and he nodded that, yes, he did, and there in the kitchen, while the rest of the house slept around them, he told her of the painting he'd seen at Raúl's, and the blood ties between Mercedes and the proud family Muñoz de Hojeda.

"I already know," Alex said with a crooked little smile. Briefly, she told him of her encounter with Carlos' cousin, the unlikeable Ángel, and what she had found sewn into his breviary – several brittle pages covered in Mercedes' distinctive scrawl describing the last years of her life. "Weird, isn't it?"

"Very." Isaac grimaced. "Poor Mercedes."

"Yeah." Alex gave herself a little hug, as uncomfortable as always when discussing Mercedes' life. "At least she had all those years with Magnus." She smiled slightly, recalling instance after embarrassing instance when her parents couldn't keep their hands to themselves.

Isaac sat back and regarded his hands, turning them this way and that. "Mercedes' blood – it comes into me from both father and mother." He glanced at Alex. "If you knew, shouldn't you have told Carlos?"

"I had no idea how to explain," Alex muttered. "So what did he think about all this?"

"What do you think?" Isaac snorted, loudly. "It's one thing to live down a rumour of a witch Jewess ancestress up your family tree. It's an entirely different thing to know it to be true."

Alex stood and, with a shaking hand, refilled her cup. "It's strange, how we keep on running into the Muñoz family."

"Strange?" Isaac laughed, that high-pitched laugh of his that made her ears shrivel in protest. "Blood calling to blood, you think? The witch reuniting her own?"

"Don't be ridiculous!"

"You never ask me anything about them," Isaac said accusingly once they'd left the subject of Mercedes behind. "Not one question about Dad, or Veronica or Diane."

"I've been under the impression that you don't want to tell me."

"I don't," he agreed.

"There you are, then," she said, and they both laughed. "But once you do, I'll be very glad to listen." Isaac nodded, ducking his head to hide his face. Alex watched him with some concern, but chose not to say anything.

Later that day, she brought down her precious box to the parlour, and set it on the table before him. Isaac smiled, fingering the corner that had recently been repaired by Matthew.

"What?" Alex asked.

"I have it in my studio," Isaac said. "I found it in an antiques shop in Annapolis fifteen or so years ago, when Offa left me to go to you."

"Annapolis?"

Isaac rolled his eyes. "The capital of Maryland."

"Oh," Alex said, very pleased with this augury that they would somehow make it back there. "How did you know to look there?"

"I just did." He gave her a sheepish look. "It came to me in a dream," he intoned in a deep voice, making her laugh.

"It did actually," he went on. "I kept on dreaming about sycamores and strange birds – orioles, I think." He lifted up a miniature Magnus and turned it this way and that. "He made it to you."

"He did." Alex smiled. "Stubborn idiot, to go time travelling with cancer."

Isaac listened as she told him about Magnus' final years, all the while cradling the carved depiction of his grandfather in his hands. Once she was done, he replaced it in the box. He touched the bottom, ran a palm over the smoothly sanded wood, fitting snugly into the little box, but lying loose.

"It's flat!"

"Of course, it is. Matthew made it, right? No shoddy finish allowed."

"But in my time it isn't," Isaac said, "and I've always thought that maybe I should try and lift it to see what's stuck beneath."

"Maybe it's the wood," Alex said. "It might have swollen over the years."

"Perhaps." Isaac sounded doubtful. He picked up a little figurine of Alex and grinned at her. "I have a gigantic insurance on them. They're valued at thousands and thousands of pounds." He handed the box back to Alex. "They're beautiful, each and every one of them a labour of love." He muttered something about doing some creating of his own, and hunted about for the leather satchel in which he kept his papers.

…Yesterday I picked up my coals, and for the first time since that stupid accident – was it an accident? I'm no longer sure – attempted to draw. And it was there, Dad! I was no longer thinking, I was just living the lines on the paper, and when I was done it was Veronica, a laughing Veronica that stretched her hand towards me, and I swear I could smell her, hear her. It's back, Dad, it's finally back!

Chapter 28

"So what do we do with Isaac?" Alex asked one early spring morning, plumping the pillows into inviting mounds before tweaking the sheets and quilts back into place.

"Do?" Matthew looked up from where he was tying his garters into place.

"Well, we can't very well leave him here, all alone, can we? And at present, he's refusing to go to Maryland, saying that he has to remain close to home."

"He's an adult. He'll have to make his own way. You can but offer him to come along, and if he won't come…" Matthew hitched his shoulders.

"But—" Alex began, only to have his finger placed firmly across her lips.

"No buts. We leave in September, as we've decided." Now that he'd made up his mind, he'd really wanted to go before, and it had taken a hell of a lot of convincing to have him agree to staying long enough for Alex to have her sons with her for one last summer. It would be years before they laid eyes on either of them again – if they ever did. Alex banished that very worrying thought to an indistinct area behind her ears, forcing her attention back to the issue of Isaac instead.

"All he has is me."

"He's a man. There's a place for him in our home, but if he doesn't want to come, he'll have to cope on his own."

Alex hugged herself. He was right, of course he was right, but to leave Isaac behind was to abandon him once again, and this time in a world where he was entirely alone. She was drowning in guilt at the thought – what mother would do that? Besides, she could see in Isaac's eyes that he felt he was but claiming his rights when he stated he wasn't going anywhere, and shouldn't she stay until he made it safely back? At least his painting seemed to be progressing in leaps and bounds. No time funnel, not yet, but Isaac seemed confident it was just a matter of time – the relevant question being just how much time.

She was still turning this infected subject round in her mind when a small group of men rode into their yard just before noon. Alex looked up from the chicken soup she was making with three stringy hens, the last of the parsnips and a few wilting leeks, and wondered what John Graham was doing back here.

"I thought you'd have taken ship, to join your king," Alex said, keeping at a respectful distance from Caesar, as skittish as ever. James Stuart had landed in Ireland just some weeks past, his expedition financed by the powerful French King, Louis XIV.

"The King wants me to remain here," John said, "and so I've been down to Ayr and beyond, collecting my dragoons."

"Your dragoons? Aren't they the King's dragoons?"

"Mine," John replied. "It's for me they fight." He nodded a greeting to Matthew, and explained they were on their way to Edinburgh where the Estates were to convene in April to discuss the present state of the monarchy.

"The English Parliament has found for William and that false daughter Mary, but the Irish Parliament stands firm by our king, and here in Scotland, we are as yet undecided." John twisted his mouth into what could have been a smile.

"Here they will find for the usurper, and you know that," Matthew said in an undertone.

"We'll see." John's eyes hardened.

He declined dinner, said he had but been passing, and must now hasten on to round up the rest of his men. There was a nerviness to him she'd never noticed before, hands fiddling constantly with the reins, his sword. He had lost weight, narrowing his face into a grim combination of cheekbones, nose and determined jaw. But he smiled at Alex, for an instant his eyes softened, and all she wanted to do was to hold him, whisper that things would be alright. A total lie, of course.

"Some beer at least?" Alex pressed. It was a warm, windless March day, dry after weeks of constant rain, and John accepted with alacrity – on behalf of himself and his men. Alex walked alone among the horses with her pitcher, aware that neither Rosie nor Ellen, not even Marjorie, had any intention of helping.

"They see you as an incarnation of Satan himself," Alex muttered to John, who swept his eyes over the household.

"Aye," he said, and held out his mug for some more. Just as Alex raised her pitcher, Caesar decided it was time to move, dancing sideways so that the beer sloshed over John's gloved hand and onto the ground.

"Damned horse!" Alex snapped. "It has a brain the size of a pea, if you ask me." In response, the stallion stamped and whipped his head round, making Alex retreat so abruptly she overbalanced, sitting down with a thump in the puddle of beer. She glared up at the horse. The bloody thing seemed to be grinning, and, as to its rider, John was struggling manfully to keep his face straight.

From behind her came the unmistakeable sound of Matthew converting a guffaw into a cough, and slowly Alex got to her feet, straightening up to stare the horse in its eyes.

"Hamburger," she threatened, "sausage and dog's food. I'll boil your hooves for glue, use your hide as a doormat, you hear?" Notably unimpressed, the horse shook its head, and Alex turned to John, indicating her muddied skirts. "That horse…" she began before swivelling on her toes to hobble towards the house. "That's the third time, John Graham," she called over her shoulder. "That stupid horse is mine now."

"I can do it myself!" Alex inspected her swollen ankle, and rooted about for something to bandage it with.

"Of course you can," Isaac said, "but let me at least help you with the bandage, okay? I took first aid in school, you know." Alex gave him a black look but extended her foot.

"It's not funny!" she told him.

Isaac just shook his head, his mouth twitching.

"And it hurts." A lot, actually, and she was convinced that

235

the dratted horse would ensure she went limping to her grave.

"You have but sprained it," Matthew said from the door. He came over to study Isaac's neat work. "You'll live, and if it hurts, I'll blow on it for you." He grinned, and stepped back outside, avoiding the wooden spoon Alex threw at him.

"Blow on it," Alex muttered. "I'll give you for blow on it." With a scowl in the direction of Isaac, she hoisted herself back on her feet, making for the door.

"You shouldn't—" Isaac began.

"I'm okay! And I have guests to bid farewell." And this particular guest she had an uncomfortable feeling she might be seeing for the last time.

John had dismounted, standing with his arm around his horse's neck as he caressed him over the long nose. He looked forlorn, somehow, when he extended the reins to Alex.

"Here," he said.

Alex sighed. "I don't want him, John. More importantly, I don't need him – but you do. How could I possibly take him away from you?" Their eyes met, and she saw anger and fear in his, so she stepped close enough to touch him, wanting to offer him silly reassurances that everything would end well.

John cleared his throat. "I must go." He swung himself astride.

"Be careful," Alex said, shading her face to be able to properly see John's eyes.

He shrugged, smiling down at her. "I should have met you years ago."

"Yeah, right, like when you were twelve and I was twenty-eight," she snorted, touched to the core.

"It wouldn't have mattered." He nodded to where Matthew was coming towards them. "Does he have any idea how fortunate he is?" He leaned forward, touched his fingers to her lips, and it was as intimate a gesture as if he had kissed her. "Even all covered in mud, you're delectable, Alex Graham, and I don't think I've ever said that to a woman before."

"I already told you, your eyesight is going." But she

236

stood on her toes and, for an instant, placed her hand on his thigh. "Go with God, John Graham. May He hold you in His hand and always keep you safe." Caesar stamped, restive under his rider. "Not that you're making it easy for Him, not with that horse." His hand closed over hers, clasped it hard. Bloody hell, her eyes prickled with tears, and he didn't need that, did he? So she smiled widely, retook her hand, and motioned up the hillside. "Go on, you have places to be, things to do, right?"

"That I do," he replied, and, with one last wave, spurred Caesar up the incline, his blue bonnet held like a flag over his head.

"Oh God," Alex said, "should I have told him?"

"Told him what?" Matthew asked, draping his arm over her shoulders.

"You know, that if he sticks with James Stuart he'll soon be dead."

"That would be meddling with fate. Besides, he already knows."

"He does?"

Matthew sighed and nodded. "John Graham is no fool. The odds are stacked against him and his king."

"Stupid, gallant man."

"All heroes are," Matthew said.

"Some actually win."

Matthew laughed, somewhat sadly. "Not the ones we remember. Not the ones we write songs about."

Late that same afternoon, Alex was in the kitchen garden, turning down the manure into the open beds. She was planning tomorrow's laundry when out of the corner of her eye she saw first Ellen, then Samuel, pass by.

Alex frowned. For weeks, she'd noticed how Samuel and Ellen gravitated towards each other, and now she decided to follow them, finding them behind the smoking shed, Ellen on her back and Samuel very much on top, albeit still in his breeches. She took a good hold of his hair and yanked.

"What are you doing?" she asked rhetorically – she could

see what he was doing, or at any rate planning on doing. Ellen had gone the colour of a boiled ham, smoothing down skirts and buttoning up her bodice at the same time.

"I like her," Samuel mumbled, tucking shirt back in place.

"You like her," Alex repeated. She eyed Ellen in silence. Small and fine-boned, with two overlarge grey eyes in a heart-shaped face, the girl was pretty, if rather thin. With a wave of her hand, Alex motioned for her to leave. She waited until Ellen had scurried off before wheeling back to face her son. "Like her well enough to marry her?"

Samuel cinched his belt and made an ambiguous gesture.

"Because you see, Samuel, if you bed her, you wed her. Your father won't allow you to dishonour her."

Samuel gave her a wary look. No, he mumbled, not enough to want to marry her.

Alex bit back a small sigh. In some ways, this was a harsh world for the young and horny.

"Will you tell Da?"

"Do I have to?" Alex replied.

Samuel didn't think so. It wasn't about to happen again.

"Good. Besides, you're too young," she told him. "Not quite fifteen."

At that, Samuel snorted loudly. "Not among my Indian brethren. There, I'm considered man enough to bed a lass."

"And have you?"

Samuel didn't reply, but she had her answer anyway, in the way his eyes went blank.

"Not yet fourteen, he was!" Alex said, upset to the point of stuttering. "A child, Matthew! What on earth was Qaachow thinking, to allow him to sleep with a girl?" She was tearing old garments into long strips, strips she would then tie together and use to weave a thick rag rug.

"Mayhap Qaachow didn't know," Matthew said.

She stopped halfway through a tearing movement and looked at him. "And what about her? What age was she?"

"I don't know," Matthew replied, "but if you want, I'll ask Samuel."

"Yes, you do that." She tore again, banged her forearm against the armrest and cursed. "And what are you grinning at?" she demanded, turning on Isaac.

"I wasn't!"

Alex gave him a narrow eye. "How old were you?"

"None of your business!" Isaac said. Alex went back to her tearing. To her huge irritation, both Matthew and Isaac were grinning.

For once, Alex was in bed before Matthew, both hands shoved under the pillow while she watched him undress, clean his teeth and wash. A candle was burning on the mule chest, the wick uncut and giving off a sooty, yellow flame. She looked at it in silence, watching the flame elongate and shrink, elongate again, become a timid flutter, and flare upwards in a surge of light.

"What is it?" Matthew asked, coming over to sit beside her.

Alex hitched her shoulder. "Nothing," she said, making him smile.

"Alex…" He leaned towards the chest and blew out the candle.

"It's just…I don't like it, that's all!"

"Like what?" Matthew slid in to curl himself around her, cupping her in the hollow of his longer body. She relaxed against his warmth.

"I don't like it that Samuel still to a part considers himself Indian."

"Mmm," Matthew said, blowing softly on her nape. "Mayhap he won't feel the same for them once we return."

She twisted to look at him. "He loves them." And now there was a girl in the picture as well. "Did you ask him? About the girl?"

"It's no more than an infatuation," Matthew said.

"Infatuation? A bit more than that. He's had sex with her!"

"Hrmph. Aye, he has." Matthew sounded disapproving. "And not only once, but several times to hear him tell it."

"What?" Alex sat up in bed. "And she's how old?"

"The lad didn't tell me much. He squirmed like a worm on a hook, but I gather she's older than him."

"Cradle-snatcher," Alex muttered.

Matthew laughed, pulled her back down. "I dare say he was willing – most willing." She stroked his cheek. He hadn't shaved the last few days, and the stubble was long enough to be soft, not prickly. "He's no but a lad, Alex. It'll pass, aye?"

"Not among the Indians, he's not. There he's a man, as he told me earlier today."

"Even among the Indians. You can't think Qaachow considers Samuel a full-grown man."

Alex gave him a long look. "Yes, he does. Old enough to go on raids, at least." And Samuel had been not quite thirteen at the time.

"Well, he won't be doing that again, will he?"

Alex just nodded. No, her Samuel was crippled, would never be an Indian brave. "But he would want to," she whispered to herself, and decided it was better to talk of other things instead.

Chapter 29

Sarah Connor was not an easy woman to intimidate. But, right now, her lungs filling with smoke, her son bawling in her arms, and her dazed and bleeding husband leaning most of his weight against her, she was definitely afraid. The huge mountain of a man refused to budge from where he was blocking their way out of this death trap.

"Please," she repeated.

"You and the bairn, aye. The papist dies." Minister Macpherson swayed on his feet, regarding Michael as if he might suddenly sprout horns.

"Da will not like it," Sarah said. "He'll kill you if you harm us."

"Matthew Graham isn't here, is he?" The minister burped, staggered to the side. "And, truly, I am doing him a favour, am I not? The papist must die, eternally damned for having enticed you away from your faith. And then…" Minister Macpherson grinned. "…well, then we'll wed you to a good, upright man."

"Get out of my way!" The whole house was ablaze, and the inner roof behind her collapsed, bringing the flames that much closer to her and her family.

The minister stood his ground, small piggy eyes gleaming red with the reflections of the fire. "He stays."

"He's my husband!" Sarah said. "Do you expect me to abandon him?"

Minister Macpherson shrugged.

"Sarah," Michael mumbled, and slid to lie on the floor. Sarah set Joshua down, patted him on his back, and told him to run into the yard and wait for her there. She had to help his father. Minister Macpherson moved aside for her son, but when Sarah dragged Michael towards the threshold, he stood to block her.

"The papists must die, all of them. Coode has the right of it. We must cleanse our colony of these vermin, and I will – nay, must – do my part."

"Your part? And that includes bringing a plank down on my husband's head, does it? Pushing him inside a house set on fire to roast to death with his wee son and wife?"

The minister shuffled on his feet. "I did not see you and the bairn at first, and you are free to go. Your laddie's calling for you." He nodded in the direction of the yard from where came Joshua's high, wailing voice calling for his mam. He took a step towards Sarah as if to grab her by the arm and hoist her outside. His pudgy fingers closed around her arm, and Sarah did what she had to, fervently thanking Mama for having taught her how.

Rising on her toes, she twisted, slammed her body into his, saw his eyes grow round with surprise, and then Minister Macpherson was flying, a heavy, breathing projectile that struck the floor a few feet away. Sarah took hold of Michael, straining and heaving to move him, to get him outside. She screamed when the wall between the kitchen and the parlour burst into fire, she could see the wooden ceiling begin to give, and she dragged and dragged, and at last she was out in the yard, her shoulders near dislocated by Michael's unconscious weight.

She didn't stop. Yelling for Joshua to come, she dragged Michael all the way to the small privy, crouching behind the hydrangea while her home folded itself neatly into a pyre.

Her lungs ached with heat and soot, Michael lay like the dead at her feet, and Joshua pressed his face against her side. Sarah stared at the burning house. All their worldly belongings – all but the horse and Michael's share in the printing press. Something moved. Sarah watched in terror as the overweight minister sat up, burning like a guy. His hair, his coat, his arms, even his face seemed to be on fire, and the mouth opened into a black hole, the eyes gone. There was a horrible exploding sound, the air filled with the stench of roasted meat, and the minister fell back. Over him toppled the chimney, bringing the remnants of the house down with it.

"Shh!" she said sharply to Joshua, holding him in her arms as a band of men swarmed into the yard. For a moment, they seemed taken aback by the damage they'd done, but then one of them laughed and said it served him right, the papist, that he burn to death. The others joined in, young men most of them, and from where she sat, Sarah could even recognise two of them.

Joshua squirmed, but she whispered that he had to be quiet, very quiet, or the bad men would kill them all, and Joshua slumped against her. For a moment, she feared he'd begin to cry, and at her feet Michael moaned, feebly moving an arm. She tried to stroke him over the head, but her hand came away sticky with his blood.

In the yard, the men had decided there was nothing more to see. One of them called for Minister Macpherson. Another – Isaiah Farrell – voiced that the minister was probably by now wetting his throat down at one of the taprooms, and they should all follow suit, celebrate their grandiose overthrow of the papist hegemony in this the Colony of Maryland.

She waited, she listened, she waited some more before setting Joshua down.

"Alright then?" she whispered, trying to sound her normal self. Joshua nodded and stuck his thumb into his mouth, grey eyes black in the April night.

Sarah touched Michael. She had to do something about his head, and then…then? She stared at the devastation around her. In Michael's pocket, she found his pouch, a light, inconsequential weight. She looked again at the house, at her son, and she knew there was only one person she could go to for help.

William Nuthead wasn't pleased to see Sarah Connor, and he made no effort to pretend otherwise. "Here? Are you out of your mind? What if they follow you? They might set the whole printing shop alight, and then what?" He glared at her. "Most irresponsible, Mrs Connor!"

"Where was I to go? Should I just have left Michael to bleed to death by our privy?" She was of a height with him, and in her terrified and singed state, her clothes smeared with blood and soot, she looked quite the avenging angel, her thick blond hair standing on end around a face so pale the bright blue eyes looked like sapphires in a silver setting.

"No," he sighed, defeated. "I suppose you couldn't." He stood aside to allow her entry, grudgingly admiring her for having transported her husband all this way on her own – and with her young son clinging to her skirts.

Next morning, William Nuthead found her kneeling by her husband, whispering to him that he had to wake up. She had cropped Michael's hair, and managed to wash and clean the nasty gash where a nail had sunk into his scalp. Half of his face was a huge bruise, his right arm was just as mangled, and in only a shirt, he looked oddly vulnerable, very removed from the self-contained and confident young man with whom William normally spent his days.

"I aim to go about and inform myself of things," he said. Sarah nodded, muffling a bout of coughing against her dirty shawl. While William did have a shirt to lend Michael, he had no female garments at all in his house – not with his wife away visiting her kin – and accordingly Mrs Connor looked most dishevelled, skirts and bodice stained with soot and blood, what he could see of her linen shift streaked with dirt.

"I'll see what I can find for you," he said, and Sarah mumbled a thank you before going back to her insistent prodding.

Michael opened one redshot eye. "Leave me be," he croaked. "Let me sleep." Well, it would seem his partner would live after all. William Nuthead was in two minds whether this was good news or not.

The town was in uproar, and shrouded in a pall of smoke. Some of the Protestant militia had amused themselves by setting fires – most of them quickly brought under control, but some, like the one that had engulfed the Connors' home, spreading to other buildings as well. The state house was under Protestant control, and from what William could glean, the Catholic government had surrendered rather than risk loss of life and property. The victorious Protestants roamed the streets, and after witnessing the third violent altercation between the youthful louts that went for Protestant militia and the good, if Catholic, tradesmen of St Mary's, William Nuthead cut his shopping expedition short and returned home with a little frown. Only an ungodly man would turn the Connors out at present, so it would seem he was stuck with his unwelcome houseguests. A week, he decided, he would give them a week. That should be sufficient for Connor to heal, and then they could go elsewhere.

Three days later, William Nuthead returned in something of a panic, setting down the purchases he had made with a dull thud. "A murder!" he exclaimed. "They say there has been a murder!"

"Several, I would think," Sarah said. "Didn't quite a few men lose their lives that night?"

"Those are but victims of war, my dear, expected casualties, no less. But this is a minister, and the leaders of the militia are leaving no stone unturned in their search for him."

"Search? He isn't found?" Michael said.

William shook his head. "No, not so far. But they will, mark my words, even if they have to dredge the harbour." He shook himself and looked at both of them. "Who would do such a dastardly deed? Kill a man of God?"

"If they haven't found him, he might not be dead," Michael pointed out.

"And where would he be? He's a big man, so how come no one has seen him? His comrades seem convinced he's been the victim of foul play."

"He may have brought it on himself," Sarah said. "Maybe he provoked by ungodly behaviour."

William Nuthead regarded her for some time. "That will not help the perpetrator, once they catch him. He will hang, Mrs Connor, mark my words." He gave Michael a long look. The man had been badly bruised and bleeding when they came in search of shelter.

That afternoon, Sarah snuck back to their old home, and spent an hour walking through the uncomfortably warm ruins. She kicked at collapsed rafters, she pretended to sift through the ashes for valuables and belongings, but all the while her feet pulverised anything remotely resembling bone. So brittle, she reflected, swallowing back on nausea when she stamped down on what she thought might be the skull. Something glinted dully, her hand closed on a deformed ring, and she pocketed it discreetly. She found a twisted piece of burnt leather that she took for a boot and threw into the neighbour's privy pit, there was a blob – no several blobs – of pewter that she scattered here and there.

"Mrs Connor?"

Sarah leapt at the sound of the reedy voice, and blinked at her elderly neighbour, standing on what had once been a thriving street.

"There's nothing there for you to find," the old lady said gently. "It's all destroyed."

"I thought…" Sarah wiped at her face with her hand, smudging herself with ashes. "I hoped…my silver candlesticks, at least."

The old woman shook her head. "Gone, Mrs Connor. It burnt for a night and a day and some more. Nothing survives such heat."

Teeth do. They grinned up at her from between her feet, even now resisting her discreet attempts at trampling them to pieces. Mrs Mitchell regarded her shuffling with worried interest.

"Hot," Sarah mumbled. She sighed exaggeratedly, and swept a hand over what used to be her kitchen. "I have to try. We are left paupers by this."

Mrs Mitchell nodded, lifted her basket higher on her arm, and hurried off to her own damaged but serviceable home.

The teeth plopped like pebbles into the water. Let

them dredge the harbour, they'll never find him there. She dragged her hands up and down her skirts and still they felt dirty, filmed with grease, so she knelt and dipped them in the water, scrubbing hard.

When she got back, Michael studied her shoes and skirts in silence. A layer of ash clung to her hem, and when she crossed the floor, she left an imprint on the wooden floor.

"You killed him," he said.

"I didn't mean to. He wouldn't let you out, he wanted to see you burn, and I couldn't let him do that, could I?"

Michael's eyes darkened into the dark grey of lead. He stretched out his hand, and brushed her gently over the cheek. "Mr Nuthead is right. They won't listen to your reasons. He's a minister and he's dead on account of you."

She shivered at his words, folded her arms across her chest. "I was but defending me and mine. He wouldn't let me pass, so I knocked him out of the way." Michael found a rag, bent and wiped the floor, had her lift her shoes so that he could clean them too.

He straightened up and kissed her on her brow. "I love you."

If anything, that made her shiver all the more, because Michael rarely vocalised his feelings, and for him to do so indicated just how concerned he was. Sarah rested against him, the slight bulge that was their unborn child pressed close to him. What were they to do now?

Yet another two days, and Mr Nuthead came back white around the mouth, his eyes staring at Sarah, at Michael.

"It's said around town how Minister Macpherson was last seen before your house," he said. "His companions say he left them to go round the back."

"Oh," Sarah said, "I never saw him there."

"They want to talk to you," Mr Nuthead continued. "They're asking for you throughout the town." He gave her a wild look. "It will only be a matter of days before they come here, and then what?" He whirled, making for the door. "I'll go and tell the officers that you are here, with me. I can't be hiding fugitives." Before they could say anything, he was gone.

★

When the printer returned with the constable in tow, his little house was empty. His musket was gone, his best winter cloak as well.

"Well, well," the constable said, rubbing his hands together, "a clear admission of guilt." He turned to frown at the printer. "Any idea where they might have gone?"

William Nuthead hitched his shoulders. "He's from Virginia somewhere, and she's from beyond Providence, from a place called Graham's Garden."

"Hmm." The constable pursed his mouth. "We'll find them," he assured Mr Nuthead, and strode out of the room.

Chapter 30

...Today, I found a drowned kitten in a bucket behind the stable. It hung a few inches below the surface of the water, and its fur floated like a halo round the small body. One of its paws was raised in what looked like a wave, the pads a startling pink in all that dark water. And I knew, Dad. The moment I saw it, I knew this was it: this was what I was going to paint to find a passage back – the water sloshing over the edge, the circles speeding over the surface when I touched it with my finger. Poor cat.

It was still too cold to go swimming, but the May day was agreeably warm, and after a long walk through the woods and up on the moor, Alex was relieved to sink down to sit in the shade by the eddy pool. She laid the bouquet of bluebells carefully to the side before taking off shoes and stockings to dip her feet into the iciness of the water.

Today had been a wonderful day, from the moment they woke to the sound of a lark, through the hours spent walking, to now, when they sat together with only the sounds of the water around them: water and birds, because in the shrubs surrounding them hopped wrens and robins, blackbirds and thrushes, and when she craned her head back she could see the lark like a microscopic dot against the pale blue sky.

"John Graham has been branded a rebel," Matthew said out of the blue. "He was requested to lay down arms and present himself in Edinburgh, but refused to do so, and now he has taken to the hills, in keeping with the successful strategies of his kinsman Montrose."

Alex sighed and splashed her foot in the water, causing a curious wagtail to hop away.

"He has a son," Matthew added, "and he has commended

his wife and the wean in the keeping of his father-in-law." He picked up a stone and sent it skipping over the water of the pond. "The lad will never know his father."

"What a waste." So sad. John should have been allowed to celebrate the birth of his son, not ride hell for leather through glens and hills. She fingered her lip, mentally blowing John Graham a kiss. Beside her, Matthew fidgeted, and she turned to meet two intense eyes, so close she went cross-eyed.

"What are you thinking?" he asked.

"John." She hitched her shoulders. "He deserved some more years of life, the opportunity to watch his son grow into a man."

Matthew grunted an agreement, sat back, and extracted the latest letter from Ian – a very efficient distracting manoeuvre, however transparent.

Alex listened, laughing when Ian commented that Mrs Parson would no doubt live to be well over a hundred, this after watching her chase Lettie into a corner after that wild child had taken it upon herself to add a couple of rows of her own haphazard knitting to Mrs Parson's progressing work. Agnes was with child; Mark had constructed a right canny water conduit from the spring behind the house to the laundry shed and beyond to the stables; and he, Ian, had shot a bear. And Malcolm, the wee daftie, had fallen off the stable roof.

"Fool," Matthew said with some pride. "A lad not yet fifteen to attempt a roof repair all on his own."

"Mmm," Alex said, smiling at the thought of their eldest grandson, Ian's firstborn. "He was lucky in that it was his arm, not his head, that was broken."

Matthew nodded, and went back to the letter. The maples were in full colour, Ian wrote. The shores of the river were edged with frosts, and soon it would be winter. In his last paragraph, he told them that every night they lit a candle and set it in the kitchen window. A beacon, if they willed, a shard of light to keep them safe and guide them home.

Alex wiped her eyes and smiled at Matthew. "Quite the poet at times."

"Manipulative," Matthew snorted before helping her to her feet.

They strolled back towards the house, hand in hand.

"I'm going to Cumnock a week Thursday," he said, and Alex came to a surprised halt. Ever since it became common knowledge – thanks to Rosie – that Matthew Graham was not intending to stay, they'd been left well alone, even by the minister. Matthew had been to Cumnock a couple of times, the last time with Alex and Isaac accompanying him, but the chilly reception in shops and inns reduced what could have been a pleasant outing to a shopping expedition, no more.

"Why?" Alex asked.

Matthew braided his fingers round hers and didn't reply.

"Why?" she repeated.

"I have an oath to swear, yet another oath of abjuration, yet another pledge of loyalty that I must make."

Alex made a face. Last time, in 1665, he had been one among hundreds unwilling to take the oath. This time, he would be one of the few not falling over their feet in their haste to abjure the king that was.

"I'll stay the night," he continued. "There's an execution to be witnessed the day after."

"Do you want me to come?"

Matthew shook his head. "I'll take Samuel with me, him and his musket."

Alex relaxed. Their son was an awesome shot – and despite his youth, quite intimidating when he wanted to be.

As if on cue, Samuel came walking down the hill towards them, with Isaac at his side. Both carried muskets, and from the way Isaac was moving his free hand, it was apparent they were deep in discussion about something or other. She smiled at her sons, thinking that it was a relief that Isaac had somehow managed to punch a hole through his self-imposed isolation. It all had to do with the fact that he was back to painting again, hours spent in the small bedroom at the bottom of the landing. Now, in shirt and breeches, he looked as at home here as did Samuel. She said as much to Matthew, which only made him shake his head.

"But he doesn't belong, and more importantly, he doesn't wish to stay."

"No," she sighed. "Let's hope he manages to make his way home."

They shared a wry smile. Both of them preferred not to discuss the magical properties of Isaac's paintings. Heck, most of the time Alex tried to avoid even thinking about it.

Matthew was uncomfortable leaving her behind when he set out for Cumnock. Bands of soldiers had been seen the last few weeks, a consequence of a general call to arms to ride north with the army of the new King.

"Don't worry, I'm not about to join up, am I? Besides," she added, inspecting herself critically, "I don't think they'd want me."

"They should," he said, a smile hovering in the corner of his mouth. He smoothed back a strand of escaped hair from her brow, kissed her, and walked over to his horse with her trailing him.

"It's just words." She shaded her face as she squinted up at him, already in the saddle.

"Just words," he repeated, but she could see how he hated having to do this.

She took hold of his boot and gave it a small shake. "Think of me," she said, and batted her eyes at him.

"I always do." He rested his hand for an instant against her cheek before riding off.

She waited until he had dropped out of sight before going to find Isaac. The day was too glorious for him to remain stuck before his easel, and, besides, she needed his help in the garden.

"It's a nice day," Alex said some time later, smiling at the antics of a couple of lapwings that flapped and wheeled only feet from the ground.

Isaac grunted from where he was digging through yet another bed in her kitchen garden, but straightened up to regard their surroundings. "It helps that it isn't raining, and it definitely helps that the stink after the pig shit has faded."

Alex laughed. "Good manure."

"Everything is good manure according to you. Even the privy pit."

"At least it's all natural. I'd probably earn a fortune back in your time selling my ecologically produced vegetables."

"Probably — until they caught on it had all grown in shit."

Alex went back to her weeding, working her way up and down the rows.

"Will you miss us at all?" she asked, keeping her face to the small cabbage plants.

"Yes," Isaac answered, "more than I did before all this."

She made an amused sound. "Duh."

"Duh," he agreed, laughing softly.

Once he was done with the digging, he dropped a kiss on her head, and muttered something about getting back to his painting. She smiled and waved him off.

Isaac was immersed in his work. He had finished the outline, the bucket standing three-dimensional on his canvas. He was doing this very slowly, his heart thumping when he began painting the water. Today, he'd heard a drop plop against the floor as he painted, and knew he was finally on his way.

His hand shook. A couple of steadying breaths, a long time spent mixing pigments and oils into just the right shades of grey and white, blue and brown, some more time spent dithering over what brush to use. He hummed a *Kyrie Eleison* as he worked, a monotone repetition of holy words in a language he didn't understand, and a couple of hours later, he stood back to look at his creation.

The water was flowing over the edges of the bucket, spilling in transparent curtains down its sides, and where the kitten floated, a small maelstrom had formed, without any conscious decision on his part.

He trembled with anticipation, and in his head burst images of Veronica, so close, so tantalisingly close. He dabbed at a blob of olive green, and raised his brush. His hand jerked at an angry shout from outside, and suddenly he was aware of many sounds, chief amongst them his mother's voice. Isaac wandered over to the window, irritated by this disturbance to his concentration. He frowned down at the scene in the yard: Alex surrounded by mounted men, remonstrating with one of them who had a firm grip on the arm of the youngest farm lad, a boy he recalled was named Tom. He sighed, wiped his hands on the towel that hung from his belt, and resigned himself to going downstairs to support his mother.

When Isaac came out of the kitchen door, Alex's throat narrowed into a chute. Tall in comparison with most of the men around her, well fed and obviously healthy, Isaac immediately attracted the attention of the officer, and before Alex could open her mouth to warn him, the officer had urged his horse forward, cornering Isaac against the wall.

"A son?" he asked over his shoulder.

"A guest," Alex said.

"A son of the house. No guest!" Rosie cut in, her hands grasping at her Tom. "And healthy. Not racked by cough like my wee Tom." She glared challengingly at Alex, a dull red suffusing her cheeks. Isaac had by now extricated himself from behind the horse, walking stiffly towards Alex.

"Are you alright?" he asked, sliding his hand with evident familiarity down the barrel of the musket he had grabbed coming out.

"They're looking for recruits." She tried to place herself between her son and the approaching soldiers.

"Oh well, none to find here." Isaac turned to face the officer, backing away when he found the officer on his feet, just behind him.

"But there is." The officer gave Isaac an appraising look.

"No, there isn't," Isaac said. "I have no intention of riding off to war. I have other matters to attend to."

"Matters you'll have to postpone, for surely the safety of the realm comes first."

"The safety of the realm?" Alex put in. "No major threat, is there?"

The officer's face clouded, reminding her curtly that the erstwhile king was still at large in Ireland, and here in the north, that damned Dundee had raised his banner in the name of James Stuart, and from what they heard, men were flocking in their hundreds to him.

"Each household is to offer up one recruit," he said.

"Not my son," Alex pleaded. "He doesn't know how to fight. He's a painter, an artist."

Pointedly, the officer looked at how Isaac held the musket. "All able-bodied men can fight, mistress. Your son will be no exception."

"No! I have no intention of riding with you, you hear?" Isaac strode off back towards the house. The officer jerked his head at two of his men, and Isaac was summarily grabbed and pulled towards the horses. The unhanded musket landed on the cobbles. "No!" He swiped at them, was cuffed roughly on his head "Help me, Mama!" he screamed, and Alex stumbled towards him, only to be restrained by the officer.

"You help him more by packing some things together for him," he said.

"Let go of me!" Alex pulled herself free and ran to help her struggling son. The officer's hands came down on her arms, yanking her to a halt. Once again, she wrested herself free and threw herself in Isaac's direction. Yet again, the officer grabbed hold of her, and Alex could only watch as her son was heaved onto a horse, still ranting, still insisting he wasn't going anywhere.

His feet were tied to the horse, his hands to the pommel, and he shrieked for her to come and help him. Alex twisted, stamped down on a booted foot. A brutal chop to one of the restraining arms, and the officer howled – but he didn't let go. Instead, he shoved her, with such force she landed on her hands and knees. Ellen came out of the house, a hastily packed bundle in her arms.

"Here," she said to the officer, who took it and motioned for his men to move out.

"Mama!" Isaac screamed. "Mama, please!" And he was

no longer thirty-three. He was a boy of two, a child abandoned by his mother, and Alex's heart cracked at his panicked eyes, at the way he desperately leaned towards her. She began to run.

"Isaac!" Alex was almost at his horse, tears coursing down her cheeks. She tried to find some kind of action plan, something she could do to keep him here, but what would that be?

With a sharp command, the officer set his troop to trot, and Alex ran alongside, calling for her son, telling him it would be alright, she'd come and find him, of course she would. She had her hand on his thigh, her fingers clutched at the cloth of his breeches, for a moment she had hold of the rope that tied him in place, and then she had to let go, felt him slip out of her grasp.

"Isaac!" She stopped, out of breath, at the top of the lane. The horses were already well ahead of her, raising a cloud of dust behind them. In the air still hung Isaac's last desperate cry for her, for his mama.

Chapter 31

"Nothing," Matthew said, dropping off his horse. "I've ridden as far as Lanark, but there's no trace of him, and the people I ask can't tell one soldier from the other." He scrubbed at his hair, trying to avoid the begging look in Alex's eyes. She drew in a shuddering breath and wound her arms tight around her midriff, for all the world as if she were stopping herself from splitting wide open to spill her innards to the ground.

For the last three weeks, Matthew had ridden out repeatedly, even if he knew it was futile – an empty gesture, no more. He placed a hand on her shoulder, intending to gather her close, but she stepped away, as she had done consistently since the day her son was dragged off.

Matthew sighed, watching as she darted away. Alex wallowed in self-recriminations, from the moment she opened her eyes to the second she closed them, repeating over and over that she had to do something – they had to do something – because it wasn't right, that Isaac be carried away to fight in a war that ended three centuries before he was born.

Any attempts from his side to exonerate her from blame for Isaac's situation were met with silence and dejected shrugs, and this uncharacteristic behaviour served to underline just how deep was her despair, a mute agony that dulled her eyes and pinched her face.

Samuel came over to take the horse, and nodded in the direction of where his mother had ducked behind a flowering stand of elders.

"She spends her days up there," he said, a long finger pointing at the hilltop, "staring towards the north." He threw a baleful look at Rosie and turned to Matthew.

"It was her fault. Meddlesome witch. Had she but kept her mouth shut, they wouldn't have taken Isaac."

Matthew sighed. The lad was right – to a point. He looked at Rosie, reduced to an apologetic ghost over the last few weeks, and grimaced. He should evict them, but Robbie was old and they had no other home but the little cottage down by the water meadows. "Nay," Matthew said, "they would have taken her son instead." Besides, he added, he wasn't that sure it had made all that much of a difference – guest or son, Isaac was the best grown man on the farm barring his own two lads, and they, thank heavens, were both safe – Samuel on account of his arm, David behind his books in Glasgow.

Samuel made a non-committal sound and hurried off with the horse, leaving Matthew to frown at his back.

First things first. Matthew strode off in the general direction of the moor. His head was buzzing with the news he had gleaned through this his latest ride, of how Dundee and his men were leading General Mackay and his troops quite the merry dance over the Scottish Highlands. Over three thousand men on his tail, and Dundee had vanished into thin air.

According to the minister in Lanark, Dundee had joined forces with the clans headed by Cameron, and now sweet William had a Highland war on his hands. Not that the minister had seemed unduly worried, scathingly referring to the Highlanders' documented tendency to melt away into the hills when faced by superior numbers.

With each day, Mackay's forces swelled. Many of the new recruits were pressed into service, like Isaac, but many more wore the orange sash with pride, seeing this as an opportunity to turn blades and muskets on the Highlands, as the Lowlands had been scoured for two decades by the Highlanders.

Matthew ducked under the lower branches of an oak, shooed a foraging pig out of the way, and walked up the bare slope. Should James Stuart choose to come to Scotland from Ireland and set himself at the head of the spontaneous army gathering in his name then William would have something to worry about. But he wouldn't, and so gallant men like Dundee and Cameron took the field for a cause already lost. He assumed that in itself was good news for Isaac, safely with the winning side.

"People die on both sides," Alex said when he tried to convey this glimmer of hope. She was perched on a rock, dissecting elderflower corymbs to cover her skirts in drifting white blossoms.

"He'll survive," Matthew tried, sitting down beside her on the stone.

"Or not."

"We must put our trust in God." Matthew draped an arm round her shoulder and drew her close.

"Yes." She exhaled loudly. "I'm drowning in guilt. Guilt that I failed him, guilt that I didn't try hard enough." She kept her eyes firmly on her hands. "He's my firstborn," she said in a thread of a voice, "and yet...had it been any of our sons they had tried to cart off, I'd have died before I let them take them." She gave him a rueful smile and went back to dismembering the clusters of flowers in her lap. "I don't love him enough."

"Aye, you do, of course, you do."

"Not like I love ours. Never like I love ours."

"Is that so strange?" he asked. "You haven't had the raising of him. You don't know him as you know our bairns. Or Ian."

"Ian is ours," Alex said, blue eyes frowning into his.

"Ours," he agreed, chastised.

She held his eyes for a moment before nodding. "I feel that I owe Isaac — and so does he."

"For what? For being propelled through time against your will?"

"No," Alex replied, "for choosing to stay with you, and for finding that such an easy choice."

He slid down to sit on the grass, resting back against her legs. "Was it? Easy?"

"Idiot." She bent over to kiss the top of his head. "You

259

know there wasn't a choice – not once I'd met you."

His hand came up to her nape as he kissed her upside down.

"It wasn't much of a choice for me either," he said, once he released her mouth.

"Of course not. Veritable guy magnet, I was."

"Still are," he said, and Alex laughed against his hair.

"Will he be alright?" she asked a while later, brushing the flowers off her lap to float upwards in the sudden breeze.

Matthew considered her question for some time, debating how to reply. For a man unused to battle to be in the midst of it was a terrible thing. The noise, the general confusion, the horses bearing down on you...men rushing back and forth, and if you lost sight of your banners or your officer then how did you know where to go and who was friend and who was foe? And to fight the Highlanders in their mountains – well, that had to be a very frightening experience.

"I don't know," he said. Alex crossed the ends of her shawl tight around her, and rose to stand. He followed suit. Before them, the moor was an explosion of colour, late gorse a bright yellow against the fresh green of grasses, complemented by purple moss campion and the bright blue of the occasional harebell. Here and there were dots of white, sheep let out to graze on the fell, and in the sky wheeled a kite. Alex slipped her hand into his, and he closed his fingers comfortingly over hers.

Once down, Matthew retained his hold on Alex, and went in search of their son. The horse had been released to graze in the meadow, the tack had been greased and returned to its place, and Matthew's saddlebags had been left just inside the kitchen door, as had his musket.

"Samuel?" Matthew asked Marjorie.

"Out," the lass replied before going back to scrubbing the floor. "I think he went fishing," she threw over her shoulder.

They found Samuel down by the stream, fast asleep in the shade of the alders. He woke with a start at their approach, eyes shifting from drowsiness to full awareness so fast it was disconcerting.

"Any luck?" Matthew used his toe to prod at the long pole.

"I haven't started. I was just stretching out for a wee bit, like." Samuel yawned.

"Good spot for that." Alex sat down beside him. Samuel hitched his left shoulder. In his experience, any spot was good if you were tired enough.

"But it's easier to sleep outdoors in the summer," he went on, throwing a worried look at his mother. "No hardship at all, as long as you have a cloak to wrap yourself in." And Isaac had a cloak, he hastened to say. Ellen had assured him she had not only packed an extra shirt, his pouch and his wee scraps of paper, but also stockings and his cloak. Alex hid her face in her hands and moaned.

Matthew looked down at his son. The lad was avoiding his eyes, and Matthew had been a father for far too long not to smell a rat where there was one.

"Have you heard from David recently?" he asked, eyes never leaving Samuel's face.

"Recently? How recently?"

"Samuel," Matthew warned.

Samuel widened his eyes. "He's busy with his studies."

"Aye, safe from strife and battle."

"Oh aye," Samuel eagerly agreed.

"And he hasn't even considered joining Dundee, has he?" Matthew asked.

"Dundee? What are you talking about?" Alex straightened up, eyes boring into Samuel. "Has he said anything, Samuel?"

Samuel twisted under their combined looks. "Umm..."

"What?" Matthew barked, hoisting Samuel to his feet.

"It's Coll," Samuel said.

"Coll?" Alex sounded confused.

Matthew gave her an exasperated look. "He's a Highlander, Alex, a clansman."

"The clans are gathering," Samuel said, "and Coll was called home by his uncle."

"And…" Matthew prompted, a snaking feeling in his belly.

"And David rides with him," Samuel said in a small voice.

"Oh, Jesus," Alex whispered. "One son in either camp."

Dearest Lord. Matthew drew in a lungful of air. The moment he got hold of David, he was going to belt him – if he got hold of him in time, before… Nay, he refused to conclude the thought.

"But what about his studies?" Alex asked, and Matthew wanted to yell that this was the least of the lad's problems, but chose not to at the blank look on her face. Samuel hastened to assure her this was not an issue, seeing as David had falsified a letter requesting his presence at the bedside of his ailing mother.

"How quaint," Alex said, "and whose name did he sign on this missive?"

"Da's."

Matthew speared Samuel with his eyes. "How long have you known?"

Samuel mumbled about not being sure. A lad had ridden by several days ago and handed him a message.

Matthew held out his hand, and Samuel dug his hand into his breeches and extracted a letter. Matthew scanned it, crumpled it together, and slapped his son. "With what right did you decide we shouldn't be told?"

"David…" Samuel said, holding a hand to his bright red cheek.

"David! And if he dies, if he's pierced by a sword on a northern hillside?"

Samuel blanched. "Dundee will win, he has the clans behind him, and men flock daily to his banners."

"Dundee may well die," Matthew told him harshly. "The clans will melt away into the hills, and then what?"

Alex made a strangled sound, struggled to her feet, and began to run towards the house.

"And her, Samuel, didn't you spare a thought for her? She has one son already on his way to war, and now one more!"

"It wasn't me, Da," Samuel said. "It isn't me that rides to join the clans."

Matthew gave him a searing look. "No, and I'll have you swear to me right now that you won't even consider it."

From the way his lad squirmed, he knew Samuel had more than considered it, conveniently ignoring that with his damaged right arm he was of little use on a battlefield.

"We've lived the loss of you once, lad. We won't survive living through it twice."

Samuel half closed his eyes and nodded. He wouldn't leave, he promised.

For the second time that day, Matthew went in search of his wife, and this time he found her in the small room Isaac had used as his own. She had spread out half-finished sketches on the floor around her, sketches occasionally of Alex and their sons, but mostly of unknown Veronica, of a wee lassie he assumed to be Isabelle, and of a man his age, eyes rimmed by glasses, a slight paunch straining against the buttons of his shirt. Alex smiled down at the depicted man.

"Look," she said, "that's John." Matthew gave the sketch but a cursory glance, uncomfortable with the way she smiled at it. "And Veronica," she indicated, but Matthew already knew that.

"And that?" He placed a finger on a sketch lying very much to the side.

"That's Diane."

"Ah," Matthew replied, amused by her obvious dislike. The woman looked remarkably well preserved, hair short and gleaming, body taut and fit. He peeked at his wife only to find her blue eyes locked on him as she attempted to analyse his reaction.

"He didn't think I compared," she said.

Matthew smiled and rested the back of his hand against her cheek.

"He wouldn't know. He hasn't seen you thus undressed."

"Undressed? She's fully clothed!"

"And all of her is visible," Matthew said, "from the

shape of her crotch to the swell of her bosom." He studied the revealing fit of the shirt. "Small breasts, and you have far better legs."

Her lips stretched into a smile, her hands busy ordering the sketches.

"His ticket home." She pointed at the canvas that stood backside out on the easel. Even from a few feet away, Matthew could see how the down on her arms stood straight up. "Not done," she went on sadly. "Well, obviously not, because then he'd be gone." She inhaled a couple of times. Huge eyes met his. "What do we do about David?"

"I don't know, God help me, lass, but I don't know." He'd have to set out after him, but at times he felt his age, and to spend days, nay, weeks in a fruitless chase over unfamiliar moors was not an appetising concept. He held out his arms to her, and, with a muffled sob, she hid herself against his shirt.

Chapter 32

He had ridden off at dawn well over a week ago, and for the last few days, Alex had done very little but wait. He came riding back over the moss, just as she'd known he would, and Alex stood at the edge, waiting for him as she'd done yesterday and the day before yesterday, and the day before that, willing him to hurry home. It was late evening. The setting sun hung like a ball of fire on the western horizon, and before him came huge, disjointed shadows. She could only make out the shape of him, but she recognised every line of that familiar body, from the way he raised his hand in a greeting at the sight of her, to how his thighs clenched round the horse below him. She took a faltering step in his direction, she took one more, and then she just picked up her skirts and ran.

She yanked off her cap, letting her hair fall in a cascade round her face. He sat on his horse, eternally young in the forgiving haziness of sunset. She stopped, several yards away, and tried to slow her loud, heavy breathing. He slid off his horse and came towards her. She dropped her shawl to the ground, standing in her chemise and stays. Her breasts rose and fell, pressing against the sheerness of the worn linen. Her skin was prickly with heat, all the way from her chest and up to her cheeks. She undid the ties on her skirts and her petticoats, and now he was there, just before her, his fingers grazing her skin through her shift.

"Hi," she whispered, twisting so that he could reach the laces on her stays.

"Hi, yourself," he breathed back. A shimmering light clung to his hair, his face, as if he'd been dipped in gold. The shift rustled over her hips, whispered its way down her legs. Gently, he laid her down on a bed of discarded clothes, of crushed bracken and heather.

He sat back on his heels, looking at her. She twisted demandingly. She needed him, had felt the lack of him for days, had no patience to wait while he took his time. He was here, with her, and the dreams that had plagued her in which he too had been conscripted and carried off were just that: nightmares. His breeches, his garters, his stockings… His shirt flapped wide around him before floating to land by her side. His hands on her legs, on her thighs, and then his mouth, and oh God!

Her hands on his head, trying to find something to hold on to, her eyes on a sky that was infinitely blue. He moved, his whole length was on her, he kissed her, and she tasted herself on his lips and, as always, it made her ridiculously shy, this total intimacy between them. She exhaled, lifted her hips to take him inside.

For an instant, they froze, a moment in which she savoured the size of him, the surging strength inside of her. Her heart was loud in her chest, a strong, steady thudding that reverberated through her blood and into her head. From her fingertips to his back, from her mouth into his, her pulse flowed into him, and she no longer heard her own heart, she heard his, and that was as it should be: all of her invaded by him, every single cell taken over by him.

Afterwards, he kissed the hollow of her throat. "Will it be like this always?"

"I hope so," she said, arms refusing to let him shift his weight off her just yet, "although I think over time we'll need more in the way of mattresses."

He laughed, nuzzled her, and bit her ear. "I'm well mattressed, nice and soft this my bed is."

"I'm glad you like it." She waved a hand at a small cloud of gnats, and jiggled her hips to indicate he should move. They dressed, he waited while she braided and coiled her hair, and then they walked the hundred yards to the hill hand in hand, with the horse trailing them. All around them stood the pungent scents of early summer, of grasses and flowering shrubs, and above them the sky was a shimmering mass of pinks and violets, while the colours on the ground were slowly shifting into purple greys. It rose from below, dusk did; like a hovering mist, it fell not from the sky but grew out of the ground, and everything was for an instant held in perfect harmony, light and dark equally balanced before day finally succumbed to night.

No sooner had they reached the manor but Matthew decided to do the rounds, inspecting his beasts and buildings. He cursed when he saw his storage sheds.

"What was I to do? Quarrel like a fishmonger's wife over every item?" Alex asked.

Minister Donaldson had appeared some days ago with several men in tow, demanding that Hillview contribute to the war effort in kind.

"I wonder if they've been quite as rapacious elsewhere," Matthew grumbled.

"Probably not. After all, you're the rich overseas bloke, right?"

Matthew snorted with irritation. Him, rich? Aye, he owned land, a lot of land even, in Maryland, but as a disposable asset it left a lot to wish for, didn't it?

"It's not for sale." Alex stuck her hand into the crook of his arm and, after showing him the thriving piglets, she asked him to tell her about Glasgow and David.

"Daftie!" he said succinctly.

"Fantastic. A one-word summary that makes me not one whit the wiser. Besides, I already knew he's an idiot." She sighed, her hand tightening on his arm as her composure cracked. "How will he manage? And what does he think this is? A Sunday jaunt complete with picnic hampers?"

Matthew smiled slightly. As far as he could make out, the lads had set off near three weeks hence, he told her. Some further asking about, a long ride up to Stirling and back, and he had gathered that the clansmen were moving into Perthshire. But the further north he came, the more askance were the looks he received, and Matthew had decided it would be unwise to push on further.

"Good decision. So, now what?"

Matthew swept with his hand over his lands and fields.

"I have work to do. Some days, at least, and then…" He shrugged.

"I can go with you."

"No," he replied, in a voice that stated this was not up for discussion – at all.

"Why not? How can this be worse than other places we've gone?"

"You haven't seen a battlefield, and I won't expose you to it – you or any other woman under my care." And if something should happen to him, he added, how would she survive the combined perils of being far from home and all alone?

Alex just looked at him.

"If something should happen to you," she echoed. "And if it does, Matthew? Who'll take care of you? And how will I ever know?" He opened his mouth to say something but she just shook her head. "I can't let you go without me. It would kill me, and you know it."

"I can't let you come," he said. "It would kill me should something happen to you."

They had not advanced any further beyond this impasse when Luke and Charlie rode into Hillview halfway through July, with an ecstatic Adam in tow. He was off his horse before it came to a stop, flying over the yard to where Alex stood dumbstruck.

"Oouf!" Alex exclaimed when he barrelled into her, and for a moment they were precariously close to overbalancing on the dirty cobbles. She clutched at him, noting with laughing asperity that now she was definitely the shortest in the family, wasn't she? He still smelled of himself, despite being very changed from last she saw him.

She released him, shoved him in the direction of his father, and stood gawking at this elegant young man, entirely transformed from the farm boy he'd been less than a year ago. In well-cut breeches of dark serge, stockings and shoes far finer than any Alex owned, he looked quite the gentleman, and the coat he was wearing was of excellent make, and what was that round his neck? A cravat?

"A certain standard is upheld at his school," Luke mumbled, giving Adam a proud look.

"I can see that," Alex replied, feeling the proverbial country bumpkin in comparison with her son. Out of the corner of her eye, she saw Samuel, standing so still as to be almost invisible, his eyes never leaving his younger brother. Alex wasn't sure what she saw in that dark hazel gaze – admiration or envy? Samuel looked down at his bare feet, brushed at a stain on his worn breeches, and her heart went out to him, that he should somehow feel diminished in the presence of Adam. She caught his eyes and smiled, mouthed a silent 'I love you', and Samuel blushed before coming over to join them.

At least Adam was still a couple of inches shorter than Samuel, and where Samuel was already filling out into the man he would be, Adam was an asparagus, all legs and arms and very little bulk. He was overjoyed to see his brother, and after a quick initial wrestling match, the boys rushed off together, Adam now as barefoot and coatless as Samuel was.

"Boys." Alex sighed, and picked up the carelessly discarded coat and cravat from the ground. "Men," she corrected when Charlie draped his own coat haphazardly over an upended wheelbarrow. Charlie laughed and swept her into a hug, crushing her against a broad, strong chest. She took a step back to properly see him. In the year since she'd seen him last, he'd changed, the last vestiges of the boy forever gone, and instead here was a man, quite an impressive man, for all that he resembled Luke too much for Alex's liking.

"How's your Dutch?" she teased.

"Thriving, but the King prefers us to speak to him in English that he may quickly become entirely fluent." He fussed with his long, dark red hair, using a ribbon to tie it off his face.

"Oh, and you speak a lot to him, do you?" Alex asked.

Charlie shrugged self-consciously. "At times, although not so much since arriving in England. New places, new men, and, chief among them, John Churchill." Charlie looked as if he had bitten into a lemon, and Alex changed the subject.

"And now you're here because…" she prompted.

Charlie stretched to his full six feet three and smiled down at her. "I'm to join Hugh Mackay, a commissioned captain, no less." He obviously expected some type of congratulations, so Alex murmured something along the lines of 'well done', while keeping an eye on Luke. Not a happy man, Luke Graham, not at all, and from the looks that flew between father and son, it was evident this was a sore subject between the two of them.

"I would have thought he'd had his fill of battlefield glory." Luke sounded morose. "He's lived first-hand what it's like to be on the side of the defeated."

"And perhaps that is why he wishes to do this," Matthew said. "To openly stand against a king who punished him so harshly."

Luke sighed. "The fool has no concept of how fragile life is. No matter that he near lost his own four years back, it seems he has forgotten." He sat back and regarded his brother. "What is this about Isaac?"

"As if that was all," Alex muttered, stirring the soup forcefully.

"Not all?" Charlie said from the kitchen door. "How not all?"

"Umm." Alex prevaricated. She wasn't sure it would be wise to tell Charlie one of his cousins was off to join the Highlanders, so instead she launched herself into a description of how Isaac had been carried off against his will, frowning at Charlie as if all of this was his fault.

Charlie squirmed, said that the King didn't approve of men being pressed into service, and maybe this had been a stray occurrence.

"He can't fight!" Alex said.

Luke raised a sceptical brow. "All men can fight. Being faced with an enemy charge has the tendency to concentrate the mind, and even an artist can wield a club."

"A club?" Alex asked.

"Well, once you've fired your musket, that is all it's good for. For all that they have these newfangled bayonets, I don't think there'll be time to fix them into place, not during an ongoing skirmish." Luke patted Alex on the thigh, his hand resting that infinitesimal moment too long. "He'll be alright, and Charlie here will do his best to find him."

"Of course," Charlie hastened to assure her. "But it would help if I had a likeness."

"He looks just like Carlos," Alex said, drawing a blank.

"Carlos, the wee priest aboard the *Althea,*" Matthew explained. "You remember, when we brought you home from the Indies."

"Isaac has a peg leg?" Charlie asked, sounding astounded.

"No," Alex told him. "He most certainly doesn't – unfortunately, in this case. But in all other aspects, they're incredibly alike." She disappeared for some minutes, and on her return handed him a sketch Isaac had made of Carlos: dark eyes, dark hair, very little of Alex, and absolutely nothing of Matthew.

Charlie gave Alex a curious look. "And he's your son?"

"Yes." She wasn't about to elucidate. Instead, she served them soup and bread for supper.

"So what else?" Luke asked, once they were alone again.

Matthew shrugged, looking uncomfortable. "It's David. The lad's ridden off to join Dundee."

"What?" Luke sat up straight, his eyes a vivid green.

"You heard," Matthew said. "It runs in the family for laddies not yet properly out of smocks to ride to war. I did it – cost me four years in Cromwell's army, it did. You did it, living the life of Highland raids as a fervent supporter of Charlie Stuart, and Charlie was not quite nineteen when he joined the Monmouth Rebellion."

"You must bring him home," Luke said. "Find him before he gets himself killed."

"How?" Matthew snapped. "How do I find my lad in the Highland wastes? I don't know the place or the people."

"We must find him, then." Luke looked as if he intended to set off that very minute.

"We?" Alex said.

"I know the hills and the people." Luke gave them both an appraising look. "I'll help you find him, and, in exchange, you'll tell me the truth about Margaret and yourself." He inclined his head slightly in the direction of Alex.

"That's blackmail," Alex said, "and so we'll manage without your help."

"We can't." Matthew raised his shoulders in a helpless gesture and took her hand. "I can't find him on my own."

"I don't like it, not at all do I like it," Alex whispered to him, trying to ignore how Luke's eyes glued themselves to her face.

"No choice, Alex. At least you'll have time to think through your story," Matthew murmured back.

"Great comfort that is," Alex muttered.

"Will you be alright?" Matthew asked the next morning.

"No," Alex replied, "and you know I won't."

"Alex," he sighed, and Alex gave him a hug.

"I'll be fine," she said. "It's just that I hate it when we're apart."

"I've been gone from you before." He tweaked at a curl, smiling down at her.

"And I've missed you every time," she admitted to his chest.

"That's as it should be," he said.

"Huh, and how would you like it if it were me traipsing off to find our idiot son in the midst of a brewing war?" She scrubbed her cheek against the worn linen of his shirt. "Go on," she said, letting him go. "Hurry back, okay?"

"I will. And you be a good lass and stay here, aye?"

"Well, it's not as I'm planning any last-minute trip down to some hot Mediterranean location." She followed him over to the horse, unwilling to relinquish his hand. "Find him, please find them both."

Chapter 33

"Mr Connor!"

Michael woke immediately and leapt to his feet.

"What?" He was already shaking Sarah awake, hunting about for his shoes.

"The militia," the old woman said. "They're a mile or so away, but you must make haste." By now, Sarah was up as well, hastily bundling up their few blankets.

Joshua whined when Michael lifted him out of his warm bed, but at a whispered hush from Michael, the little boy subsided against his shoulder, thumb plugged into his mouth. Joshua rarely spoke, their previously so cheerful son converted into a wary little ghost, constantly clutching at either his mother or father.

"Here." A small canvas sack was pressed into Sarah's hands, and they followed the woman across the yard and into the woods.

"Go with God," the old lady said, "and keep off the roads for some days."

Michael nodded, listened to the whispered directions to the closest Catholic home, and led his family deeper into the forest.

They didn't talk as they walked. Michael carried Joshua on his back and held the loaded musket in his hands while Sarah lugged their few bundles and the precious package of food. Occasionally, they stopped, short breathers before they continued, walking mostly in single file. All through the morning, they pushed on, holding a steady course towards the north. Sarah coughed, she coughed again, and slapped herself hard in the chest.

"It's nothing," she said when Michael suggested they stop. Nothing? His wife wheezed as she walked, but she insisted they had to push on, they couldn't rest here, in the midst of a natural meadow. Grasses brushed against his thighs as he set course towards the trees and the safety of moving shadows.

Recently, the militia had been too close, and this morning's hasty departure was becoming something of a norm. Three days ago, they'd nearly been cornered in a barn, and only the fact that Sarah had woken in time had allowed them to slip away. He shuddered. Sarah's skirts had gotten caught in the planking, her eyes as blank with panic as those of a cornered doe, and only at the last moment had he succeeded in tearing her free. He held out his hand to her, and a long-fingered, dirty hand snuck into his, warm skin against warm skin.

A flash of colour to his far left made Michael drop down on his haunches, pulling Sarah down with him.

"Militia," he whispered, jerking with his head. Sarah pressed closer, drew her shawl over her head to hide her hair. They huddled together, hidden behind an inadequate screen of saplings and brambles. Five horses, loud men that laughed and talked as they rode by. Bright orange in their sashes, the creak of harnesses, the odd jangle of a spur, and then they were gone. Michael peered in the direction they'd taken, promising himself that should they get out of this safe and sound, he would never have as much as a scrap of orange in his house.

The birds resumed their chatter, the wind rustled through the trees, and Sarah began to cry. Michael soothed her as best as he could, holding her while he told her quietly to shush, things would be alright, somehow things would work out. After some time, she dashed at her eyes, settled their son in her lap, and gave him a heel of bread to gnaw on.

It was dusk by the time they finally dared to move, and it was night before they stopped, deep in the forest. Michael had been carrying Joshua for the last few hours, a boneless weight in his arms. His son's open mouth was warm and moist against his neck, every exhalation tickling him.

Sarah sank down, turning a pale, exhausted face his way.

"We have to eat." She rooted around in the sack she'd been carrying and found cheese and ham, hard-boiled eggs and dark rye bread. Mostly, they were met with kindness, people sharing food and even clothes with them, but reluctant to offer them a roof over their head, even for a night. To harbour fugitives in the present upheaval could come at a very dear price.

Sarah nudged Joshua awake, coaxing him to eat by offering him eggs and the end bit of a sausage. Joshua bolted it down, protested when Sarah decided to wash him, giggled in surprise when she tickled him on his bare stomach, and for a short while they all pretended it was like before, the moonlit little clearing filled with shrieks and laughter as Joshua and his parents played.

Michael shifted against the trunk, pulled the blanket higher up around Sarah's shoulders, and ensured that the musket was within reach. His wife muttered in her sleep, snuggled even closer to him, and began to snore. He craned his head back, saw an owl outlined against the paler sky, and all around him the woods breathed and rustled, full of life.

These last few months were beginning to tell – on all of them. He noticed how often Sarah had to stop, an arm protectively cupping her belly. He ached inside at how tired she looked, constant purple hollows round her eyes, a pinched look to her mouth. And Joshua... His eyes drifted over to rest on his son. This was no life for a little boy, and repeatedly he'd argued with Sarah that they should leave him with one of the multiple families they'd stayed with, but she refused. Only with her own kin, she'd vowed, turning a deaf ear when Michael tried to explain that if there was one place they couldn't go, it was to Graham's Garden. Sarah just shrugged. If so, their son stayed with them. He was far too precious to entrust to anyone else.

"Da will come, once he hears of all this. He'll come, and he'll know what to do."

"Come?" Michael had exploded. "He's on the other side of the ocean! It might take him months to get back."

"He'll come," she repeated. "He won't leave me to face

this on my own." But in her eyes he could see how afraid she was that Matthew might come too late.

"I'm here," he'd reminded her, feeling diminished by her faith in Matthew. "It is I that see you safe, not your father."

"You and him," she'd replied. "But it is you I can't do without – ever."

He toyed with his sleeping wife's hair. The normally so bright, fair mane was lank and greasy, hanging in an unkempt braid down her back. Her clothes were torn and dirty, she'd lost her shoes a few weeks back when they crossed the swamp, and she'd been limping today, waving away his concern with an irritated gesture. If only he'd had Pegasus! But the horse was too conspicuous, and so they were now on foot, moving in a vague half circle towards her home.

His hand left her hair, stroked her over her cheek, and, with a humming sound, Sarah rubbed her head against him. Three months since that fateful night, almost as long since they'd slept in a bed, except for the odd night here and there, and Michael couldn't quite recall when last he'd loved her. A hasty coupling some nights back, a highly unsatisfactory and urgent affair, but before that…

His hand dropped lower, resting on her abdomen. The babe heaved and danced inside, unconcerned and unaware of the troubles its parents were suffering. Michael exhaled, a stifled sound of utmost dejection. What was he to do? No worldly goods, no home, one child of two and a new one on its way. And what if they were caught? His wife – they'd hang her, scream that she was a papist murderess, and then what?

"It'll be alright," Sarah said, and he looked down to find her eyes open. She took his hand and gave it a comforting squeeze. "Somehow, it'll be alright." She yawned and just like that dropped back into sleep. Michael sat with his woman pillowed on his lap, his son a curled ball at his feet, and wasn't sure he believed her.

Chapter 34

...What have I done? What have I become? I...hell, just to try and write it down... We were all tired and scared, one of us had died in an ambush earlier that morning, and the bloody hills stood dark around us. They sneak up on us, like fucking guerrillas they suddenly appear, loosen a shot or an arrow, and then melt back into the trees and the shrubs, and it's impossible to catch them, and sometimes we hear them laughing, and Captain Murphy we buried a week ago, so now we trudge behind Lieutenant Hill. It's supposed to be summer, but not so you'd notice – except for the fucking midges that bite us all to death. All of us scratch, and for the last weeks it has rained constantly, so we've slept damp and cold, making all of us cranky and sleep deprived. Excuses, excuses. Oh my God!

Isaac stepped back from the girl, drank from the offered bottle of whisky and helped hold her down when the next man took his turn. It was her own fault, he rationalised blearily, hers and the other two women, for firing on them in the first place and killing Andrew the second. Poor Andrew, eyes round with astonishment as his life bled from between his fingers.

He staggered over to where two of his companions were busy with the oldest of the women and stood waiting his turn. He was drunk. They were all drunk and scared and angry, and it was a long time since any of them had had a woman, and these three, well, they had it coming, shooting at them when all they wanted was somewhere to sleep out of the rain. The woman shrieked – in pain? in anger? – and Andrew the first laughed and slapped her. Someone jeered, the air stank of dirty, damp men, of sex and fear, and Isaac shoved himself inside yet another unwilling cunt, his eyes on anything but the face belonging to it.

The third woman fought. She struggled and hit wildly, and Isaac laughed at the futility of it, because how was she ever to win? She raked her nails across his face. Isaac slapped her, flipped her over, and took her from behind. He was nothing but a giant cock, punishing these women for everything that had happened to him since he fell through time to land in this hellhole. He panted and gasped, stumbled back with his breeches halfway down his legs, and for an instant the veil of anger and fear lifted from his brain, showing him just what it was he participating in. Oh God!

The women were no longer attempting to protest or fight. They lay silent and broken as the men took their turns, and Isaac mumbled something about needing to piss and escaped outside to throw up. He remained outside, closing his ears to the sounds that repeated themselves throughout the night. Come morning, his companions joined him, dragging the women with them.

Isaac wanted to crawl away and die with shame. In the faint daylight, the women looked mauled, a collection of bruises and gashes, and they stank of semen and blood and sweat. The lieutenant barked an order, and Isaac nodded, went inside to kick life into the fire, chased the children outside before setting the croft alight. He stood with his brothers in arms and cheered weakly when the little building burnt, a glorious victory over the accursed rebels.

The euphoria among the men lasted through the morning, but by noon it was back to the customary silent plodding, eyes flying from one collection of rocks to the other, and now they were even more afraid than before, because reasonably those women had male relatives, and they all knew the Highlanders believed in vengeance.

It was with relief they reached Mackay's main camp in the late afternoon, safe in the sheer numbers of men around them. Isaac was cold and hungry, but those were constants in his life, as was being dirty and unkempt. Two months, more or less, since he was dragged screaming from Hillview. Fifteen months, six days and twenty hours, give

278

or take, since that evening in his studio.

He regarded his feet. The shoes were worn down to a series of holes up and down the soles, and to keep out the damp, he had resorted to wrapping strips of cloth around them, giving him the impression of walking with both feet in casts. He jingled discreetly at his little money pouch. Having gold was no use at all when you were never in the vicinity of any shops, and so his breeches had tears, his shirts were mostly dirty, and his stockings were worn paper thin across the heel.

The first few weeks he'd kept an eye out for the first opportunity to escape, but after seeing first one then another of his companions summarily strung up and left to rot for attempted desertion, he had given up on that idea. How was he to find his way back anyway, through miles of barren moor, and him with absolutely no sense of direction?

Morosely, he regarded his surroundings. He had no clear idea of where they were, except that they were somewhere in Perthshire, and tomorrow they were to march towards Blair Castle. Well, he knew where that was, having visited with his grandfather, and vaguely he recalled that Magnus had explained how the castle had been of strategic importance in the various wars fought on Scottish soil. Why, Isaac had no idea.

He found somewhere to sit, and produced his primitive little notebook, flagellating himself by writing down the events of last night. He was a beast, a gangbanger, and even worse, he had liked it – at least at first. A rapist, a soldier, however involuntarily. He inspected his hands: dirty and full of scabs. Fighting in this day and age was uncomfortably intimate. It was fingers tearing at your face, muskets fired at close range, swords flashing only inches from your body. He had become adept at firing and reloading, at swinging the musket around to become a deadly club, and by now he was decorated with quite the patchwork of shallow, half-healed scars from where blades had nicked at him. So far only nicked, but he was painfully aware of the fact that such luck wouldn't hold for ever.

He scratched at his crotch and stood up. "Come on, let's find ourselves some food."

Andrew the first lurched to his feet, and fell into step beside him. If they were lucky, they might even find some meat. They didn't talk much during the evening, sitting together as the last of the July light disappeared.

By dawn, they were on the move, a long, straggling line that walked steadily due north-west. Isaac and his companions kept their eyes on the ground, a ragged band of men that went under the epithet of volunteers, even if most of them had been forcibly dragged off. The regular soldiers laughed at them, sneering at their lack of equipment and weapons, and two or three had been heard to comment that the ragamuffins were meant for the front line, cannon fodder like. It made Isaac's guts heave, but what was he to do? Turn tail and run? He'd not get up the incline on his right before someone blew a hole in him.

It was only by chance that Isaac had stopped to piss when a troop of cavalry rode by, harnesses glittering in the July sun. Their commanding officer was an uncommonly tall man, with hair that shone like burnished copper in the light. The officer twisted his head, looked Isaac full in the face, and almost fell off his horse.

"Isaac?" The unknown man regarded Isaac with open revulsion. Isaac tugged at his grimy cuffs and nodded warily. The officer kneed his horse towards him.

"Isaac Lind?" he repeated.

"Yes," Isaac said, aware of just how unsavoury a wreck he must look, a dark bristling beard covering his cheeks, his clothes decorated with stains, and all of him so dirty he could drag a finger over his skin and leave a visible lighter line.

"My God, Aunt Alex was right! You do look just like Carlos!" The officer grinned. "I'm Charlie Graham, a cousin of sorts, I believe."

Finally! Isaac grinned back. Someone to find him and carry him home to his half-finished painting.

"I promised Aunt Alex I'd keep an eye out for you," Charlie continued. "I'm with Belhaven's regiment. Come and find me later on."

Isaac nodded, and with a new spring in his step, he hurried to retake his position in the line. She hadn't forgotten him, hadn't abandoned him, and now it would soon all be over.

It was hot, at first a welcome change after far too many weeks of feeling chilled to the bone. After a few hours, though, the heat had become an issue, and when the command was called to halt, Isaac and his companions hurried to stand in the shade of some stunted trees. Isaac stared out across a veritable sea of men.

"How many, do you reckon?" he asked Andrew, who stood to attempt some kind of count.

"Twenty thousand?" Andrew ventured.

An officer riding by laughed. "Twenty thousand? I think not! But well around four thousand or so – enough to once and for all have Dundee biting the dust." He tipped his hat at them and rode on, up towards the narrow pass that led to Killiecrankie.

At noon, they began the ascent towards the pass, and the men began to murmur, not at all liking the look of this. Narrow and contained, with the River Garry to one side and what was nothing but a muddy, slippery path at its bottom, this was the perfect place for an ambush, and the men gripped their muskets, loosened swords in their scabbards, and kept their eyes on the slopes rising above them. Apart from the creaking of leather and the jingling of harness, it was eerily quiet, birds having fled at their advent, and the troops defiled in silence through the mile and more of narrow pass. Once the valley began to widen, to a man, they heaved a deep sigh of relief.

"Fools," Andrew commented. "They had their chance to stop us at the pass. Now it will be mayhem on the rebels, hey?" He offered Isaac an onion and a piece of bread, and they munched as they walked for a couple of hundred yards before being commanded to stop. From all around came hushed exclamations, whispered curses, and Isaac stared up the facing slope.

"The Lord have mercy on us," Andrew croaked, and Isaac made a sound of agreement.

Sun glinted on naked sword blades and the studs of the targes; the air was filled with the jeering calls of the Highlanders. So many men, so many banners flying in the wind, and even Isaac, novice as he was to the art of warfare, could see the rebels had the advantage of the higher ground, sitting well above them. And Mackay, God help him, had the Garry running at full spate behind him, effectively fencing him in. They should retreat, fall back, but from the pass came the crack of sniper fire, and what had seemed a certain victory now took on the shape of ignominious defeat.

An hour or so later, and nothing had happened, except that most of Mackay's troops had assembled below the Highlanders. Orders were barked, Isaac and his troop were ordered to the left of the centre, to stand with the Balfour regiment, the light cannon were deployed, and volleys of shots rang out, a steady recurring sound that had the ground shaking. Most ineffectual, Isaac concluded, a lot of noise and puffs of smoke, while the projectiles fell too short of the massed enemy before them.

"What are we waiting for?" Isaac asked. "Are we just to stand like this?"

The soldier beside him nodded in the direction of their general and his commanding officers, seemingly holding an impromptu war council there and then.

"It will come to nothing," the soldier said. "The rebels can see how many more we are. No doubt, the general is considering what terms to offer them."

Isaac privately thought the man an idiot. To be as many as they were was no advantage when faced with a steep incline and determined opposition. He snatched at vaguely remembered history lessons, trying to recall what battle this might be and who it was that won. He had his own tactics very clear: fire his musket, wait for the tumult, and then hare off to the river and swim across. He fiddled with the strap of his canvas bag, adjusting it to lie diagonally across his chest.

Just as the sun dropped below the hills, the Highlanders charged. Rooted to the spot, Isaac's head was blank of anything but terror as the air filled with war cries and the hillside before him became a tidal wave of men, men who bounded with the grace of deer towards them, entirely undaunted by their enemy's superiority in numbers.

"Shoot!" the soldier beside him squealed, and Isaac did, and then they were over him. He turned to run for the river, screaming out loud with fear, and his legs buckled when a blade drove straight through his side. Blood. Oh my God, he was bleeding, a dull throbbing pain forcing him into a crouch. Something hard whacked him over the head, spilling him face first onto the ground. Someone trod on him, his face was pressed into the wet grass, and it all went blissfully black.

He regained consciousness. All around him, people were screaming, and he wasn't sure where he was or what had happened to him. He tottered to his feet, ignoring the fire rushing up his side, and moved sluggishly towards the river. He had to get away. He coughed, surprised that his mouth should fill with blood. His vision was coming and going, and his legs gave way, causing him to fall to his knees and crawl instead.

All around him, men were moving, the air filled with the grating sound of steel clashing into steel. He managed to get up on his feet, driven by a burning urge to run. Isaac whimpered as a troop of Horse charged by, collapsed to the ground, and wrapped his arms around his head. Someone close by shrieked. A targe landed beside him. More screams, piteous wailing cries for mothers, for fathers.

"John!" Isaac sobbed. "Dad!" He squished his eyes shut, and for the first time in his life, Isaac truly prayed.

Some time later, he raised his head, relieved that the sounds of fighting seemed to have moved away. Everywhere, dead people, wounded people, men like him, moving feebly in an effort to retreat from these killing fields.

"Veronica," he moaned. No, he couldn't die, not here, not now. You weren't supposed to fucking die before you were born, were you? He laughed hysterically, and the pain made him weep. He heaved himself over a fallen body. He dragged himself across a boy thrown onto his back, arms wide, and eyes a sightless blue. His breath whistled in and out, he could taste his own blood in his mouth. An arm round his waist, and he was helped to stand.

He had no idea who this giant of a man might be, but whoever he was, he was eternally grateful, even if it hurt like hell when he was helped to lie across the horse. There was a shout, a shot, and the horse danced for a couple of paces, sending ripples of agony up Isaac's wounded flank. His saviour sat up, and off they went. Isaac was unaware of anything but a mauling pain, a steady throbbing up his side, and of the inhuman effort it was to breathe.

What seemed like an eternity later, the horse came to a halt. Isaac was carried into a smoky room and deposited on a table.

"Where?" he croaked.

"Dunkeld," someone said. "You're safe here, man."

Safe? Isaac wanted to laugh, but he couldn't quite remember how. Hands tore at his soiled and stinking clothes. Every breath bubbled. How strange. Was it supposed to do that? He was so cold, his hands clenched into permanent fists, and when the red-haired man – Charlie, yes, this was cousin Charlie – called for hot water and linen and began to wash him, it was at first wonderfully warm, but then the shivering increased, and he shook like a landed fish on the table. His heels scrabbled, trying to find some purchase, something to steady his jerking body against.

A shirt – a clean one – a bed, a pillow stuffed with feathers, and a warm, warm quilt. Someone rolled stockings up his legs, a hand brushed his inner thigh, busy with the garters, and he breathed and breathed, struggling for air. He could feel the blood oozing beneath the bandages, how it was first warm, then cooled and became sticky. He attempted to keep his eyes wide open, convinced that as long as he didn't sleep, he'd live, and he had to live, he must...his painting. Veronica.

A weight on his chest threatened to crush his ribs, but when he looked, there was nothing there, nothing but the quilt. A hand touched him, there was a cup and he drank, and it hurt like hell to swallow, so he coughed, and, Jesus, that hurt even more. He stared wildly, and that magnificent red hair was so close, eyes a deep green looking down at him.

A voice in his ear, suggesting that he try and rest, and Isaac managed a nod, grabbing at the offered hand. Sleep? How sleep, when his chest was a hole of burning pain, when every breath was a conscious effort? But he closed his eyes, inviting in the dark, and there, in his head, he saw Veronica, and she was smiling and crying at the same time, her violet eyes so very close.

"Veronica," he breathed, and struggled back to the surface, opening his eyes wide. "Veronica," he repeated, and let himself drop like a stone into the welcoming numbness of unconsciousness.

It was dark when he woke next time. A candle stood on the nearby table, a ridiculously weak beacon of light in all this damned dark. Charlie was still sitting beside him. A woman entered with some more quilts, and together she and Charlie covered Isaac with them.

"Dead before the morrow," the woman said. "Waste, really, to bed him down in my best bed. Mind you, I'll charge you for the mattresses if he soils them." With that, she left.

"I can't die," Isaac said, surprised to hear this reedy thing of a voice. I have to go home, he wanted to add, but couldn't.

"In God's hands," Charlie said, "and you're not dead yet, are you?"

No, not yet. Isaac drew in a long, unsteady breath, ignoring just how much it hurt.

"Veronica!" he gasped, struggling up on his elbows. "Veronica!"

Chapter 35

There is a certain sound to a battlefield after the event, Matthew reflected, halting his horse when he rode out of the pass. Torn banners fluttered in the wind, and the looters kept up a low steady mumbling as they went from body to body, stripping the poor dead bastards of everything of value. Every now and then, a protesting cry rang out, and the looters scurried away before the devastated rage of a father, a son, a brother.

And then there were the birds, the wheeling corbies and circling kites, the clumsily flapping crows. Loud and irreverent, they raucously discussed the quality of the table spread before them, hopping from one corpse to the other.

Beside Matthew, Luke cursed. "Carrion eaters, the birds and the men both."

"Aye," Matthew said, watching the birds rise in a disturbed cloud when a couple of looters approached.

One of the nearby bodies moaned, clearly not entirely dead, and Matthew's mouth filled with bile when one of the looters knelt and slit the throat of the lad.

"For the love of God, man!" Matthew exclaimed. "He was alive."

"He'd have died anyway," the looter said with a shrug. "Why leave him to die slowly?" He wiped his knife on his breeches before setting to work. In a matter of minutes, the lad was naked, a nameless man among hundreds of unknown men.

Matthew was shocked by the sight of so much death. All through the pass, they'd seen them: men hewn down in full flight, sprawled lifeless and cold along the path. In the shallows of the Garry bobbed drowned men desperate enough to attempt to leap across, despite not knowing how to swim. With the experienced eye of an old soldier, he took in the devastation, the field littered with government dead.

"Fools," he said, thinking of the commanding officers.

Luke nodded. "A neat trap. Dundee knows how to choose his ground." He dismounted, and Matthew followed suit, however reluctant he was to set foot on the bloodied, trampled ground.

He breathed through his mouth, not wanting to draw in the scent of putrid decay that was already tingeing the air. In the July heat, bodies bloated quickly, and dying men tended to shit and piss themselves.

Here and there, an orange sash still shone cockily against chests forever stilled. A horse hobbled by on three legs, and everywhere there were scavenging birds, bodies thrown in a haphazard jumble. So many young men, scythed down in their prime... Was his David mayhap here? Charlie? Matthew threaded his way over the field with Luke at his heels. With each body he passed, he relaxed. Nay, not my son, thank God, not this one either.

Occasionally, the men busy dragging the bodies into stacks gave them a look, but mostly they were left alone as they made their way over the battlefield, holding on to the reins of their nervous horses.

"What do you reckon?" Matthew said in a hushed voice. "How many lie here?"

"Thousands," Luke replied. And not all were dead, he added, pointing to where two men in plaid heaved a barely alive third to lie over the shoulders of one of them.

"He might be anywhere!" For all that David was well grown, how was Matthew to recognise him if he was lying somewhere in this overpopulated field? And Isaac? Everywhere lay men with dark hair and dark beards, looted men left naked and anonymous on the field.

"Or not." Luke stopped briefly at a red-headed corpse before exhaling and moving on.

"Or not," Matthew whispered, and it was a heartfelt prayer.

"That's Dundee's horse," Matthew said some moments

later, nodding in the direction of where a skittish Caesar was being brought under control by three men. The huge stallion's coat was dark with sweat, the saddle had slipped to sit askew, and even from here, they could see the whites of his eyes when he backed away from these strange men.

"And Dundee?" Luke asked. "Where is he, do you think?" He scanned the field around them.

"Not here, I hope," Matthew said, and then he saw his son, and all other thoughts vanished from his mind.

David was weeping, clutching at the body in his lap.

"David?" Matthew knelt beside him. Wee Coll was dying, no matter that David was rocking him back and forth, his hands moving rhythmically through all that wild hair while he repeated over and over that Coll would heal, of course he would. There would be no healing, not with a stomach pierced by a sword at close range, and from Coll's tight features and colourless lips, Matthew suspected he'd been dying for hours – a slow, protracted affair.

"Coll laddie, here." Matthew held his flask to the lad's lips, tipped it to send a swallow or two of whisky down Coll's gullet.

"It doesn't hurt much," Coll breathed. "That's good, isn't it?"

"Aye," David said, "'tis on account of you healing already."

Matthew shared a look with Luke. The lad was bleeding to death, would be dead in a matter of minutes, no more. He tipped some more whisky down Coll's throat, and the lad smacked weakly, tried a wee smile.

"So foggy," he murmured. "Warm but misty. Like a summer morn in the Highlands."

David moaned, hugged his friend even closer. Coll's hand rested for an instant on David's arm before slipping off to hang lifeless by his side.

"No!" David shook him.

"He's dead," a voice said, and David glared up at the speaker. A young man fell to his knees beside them, hair an even more vivid shade than Coll's. He made as if to take Coll, and David kicked at him.

"And you are?" Matthew asked, taking in broad shoulders and an impressive height, all of it accentuated by the bright red hair falling well down to his shoulders.

"I'm Rob MacGregor," the young man said. "Wee Coll is my kinsman." He held out his arms. "It is I that will carry him up to the kirk."

"He…" Unwillingly, David relinquished Coll.

"…is dead." Rob closed Coll's eyes. "Go home, laddie. This is not your war," he continued as he got to his feet with Coll cradled in his arms. The young man tipped his head in Matthew's direction and set off. Coll's head lolled back, mouth open. David stared down at his hand, streaked with Coll's blood.

"He's right," Matthew said, watching Rob's progress up the slope. "This is not your war."

David crawled into his arms like a wee bairn, and wept.

"Dundee is dead," David told them some time later. He closed his eyes, long, dark lashes shading cheeks that were pale despite the tan. "A musket ball under his breast plate, so he didn't die at once."

"Ah." Matthew looked at the corpses that surrounded them. Very few of the men on this field had died at once – only the truly fortunate had their life extinguished in one fell blow. The rest had died over hours of pain and fear.

"He won," David said in a tendril of a voice. "At least, he won."

"Aye, that he did." And Isaac had been on the losing side, probably standing in the frontline to act as a bulwark between the regular forces and the attacking Highlanders. Matthew swallowed, boosted his son up on the horse. "But it's a great loss that he's dead. With him dies all hope of a final victory."

Luke nodded. "A Pyrrhic victory this, and now William will unleash more men, more horses, more guns…"

"But he'll be remembered," David whispered.

"Oh aye." Matthew gave his son a sad smile. "Well after he is nothing but dust in the ground, his name will be recalled, and the shout for gallant Dundee and his bonnet will reverberate through the hills."

Luke insisted that they had to go up to the kirk and look for Charlie among the dead and the prisoners.

Matthew took hold of the reins and urged his horse into a walk. "And Isaac."

"Him as well." Luke led the way to where a huge bear of a man was standing some way off, surrounded by guards and banners.

"Well, well, if it isn't Luke Graham himself," the large man said once they'd reached him. He grinned, looked Luke up and down, and told him how little he'd changed since 1654.

"You flatter me, Ewen, and you haven't changed much yourself, have you?" Luke tweaked at the large man's belted kilt, baring hairy knees.

"Aye, I have." Ewen Cameron laughed. "Look, I'm all grey, and my face is no longer as fair as it was."

"Fair? You were never that. The lasses would take one look at you and run the other way."

"Not like you, then, that had the maids on your lap in droves."

They beamed at each other. Ewen's eyes snagged on Luke's silver nose, but went on to inspect the other parts of him instead. He greeted Matthew with some reticence and quite some curiosity, returned in full by Matthew, who couldn't quite tear his eyes away from this tower of a man. He estimated Ewen to be close to his own age, three score or so, but carrying it well – very well, for all that he was no beauty.

"Wine?" Ewen pressed a cup into his hand, offered one to Luke. "In celebration of our victory," Ewen said with a crooked smile, eyes darting off in the direction of the kirk where Dundee lay dead.

"Your victory," Luke echoed, raising the dented cup.

Ewen drank, closed his eyes, and sighed. "He hoped that the King would cross the water and come and fight with him, with us." The large grizzled head bent in contemplation over his wine goblet, broad shoulders rounding. "If he had, then there'd be someone for us to follow, even now when John is dead." He replenished their wine, gulped down his own, and for a moment sat very still. "What a waste. Scythed down in his prime. What is it the Holy Book says? *As for a man, his days are as grass: as a flower of the field he flourisheth.* Ah well, it must hearten us to collect that even a field flower scatters seeds, and yesterday Dundee seeded the hills of Scotland for years to come – until the King is reinstated and beyond." Cameron attempted a smile, but didn't seem to believe himself.

Ewen listened in silence, eyes hardening into ice when Luke explained that Charlie had been fighting for Mackay.

"And you?" he demanded. "Where do your loyalties lie?"

"Me? I helped return the Stuarts to the throne!" Luke scowled.

"Hmm." Cameron stroked his unshaven cheeks. "And yet you come looking for your traitorous son."

Luke sighed and scrubbed at his face. "I only have the one."

Ewen looked at him for a long time. "Over there," he finally said, gesturing towards a byre. "You may look for him, but should you find him, you ransom him – or else he stays."

Luke paled but nodded.

No Charlie, no Isaac. Two of the captured officers remembered seeing Charlie ride off, but Matthew's questions about Isaac were met with helpless shrugs. Matthew dragged a hand over his face, feeling just how tired he was after these last few days of enforced riding.

"Let's hope they come to their senses before it's too late," Matthew commented as they rode off.

Luke shook his head. "Not about to happen, is it? Valiant fools, the lot of them."

"How fools? They won," David said. "They did, Da!"

"This time they did, son, but a headlong charge like that... Had the field been somewhat wider, had the light cannon not shattered, had there been some more battalions of cavalry—"

"But there wasn't, and the ground was as it was. He chose, Dundee did!" Two bright spots of red appeared on David's cheeks, making him look substantially younger than his sixteen.

"That's the only way they know to fight," Luke said. "A wild charge or a silent ambush. Your da's right: in the long run, they won't prevail."

"Aye." Matthew shifted in his saddle. He knew it was a lost cause. James Stuart would never be King of England again, but his son and grandson would plunge Scotland twice into rebellions in their name – Alex and Isaac had told him so. But he wasn't about to tell his brother that.

It took them six days to ride back, and it was late on the evening of the second of August that they came over the moor to ride down by the millpond.

Alex was outside by the time they halted their horses in the yard, her eyes flying from son to man, man to son. She greeted Matthew first – she always did – and then David was crushed to her chest, kissed, slapped on the head, berated for being an inconsiderate fool, kissed again, slapped, and all the while tears spilled down Alex's cheeks.

"Dolt," she laughed, "idiot, you could have been dead!" She shoved him in the direction of the house, told him to get soap and towels – and his brothers while he was at it – and go and wash, thoroughly.

After greeting Luke, she turned to Matthew, chewing her cheek. "And Isaac?"

"I don't know." How was he to find one dead man among all those still and twisted bodies? But he had tried, God help him, he had tried.

"He might not be dead!" She glared at him, as if this was his fault.

"Let's hope so," Matthew said. "And if so, he'll shortly make his way back home." Or lie dying in agony – but that was not something he wanted to voice out loud.

They were all too tired for supper to be anything more than a hasty affair, a silent breaking of bread no more, before

Alex hustled Matthew outside to wash, accompanying him down to the eddy pool with wash cloths and soap. By the time she was done, his skin tingled, all the way from his insteps to his ears. Dressed in only shirt and shift respectively, they walked back to the house, enveloped in the soft darkness of the August evening, and after having locked his doors, Matthew followed Alex upstairs, longing for his bed and his wife.

She was sitting by her looking glass, working her way through her hair.

"John Graham's dead," Matthew said, taking over the brush.

"I know, David told me." She fiddled with her hairpins and sighed. "What a waste."

"Aye." He concentrated on her hair, spreading it down her back His cock hung half engorged, prodding at her, and she rested back against him, an invitation to stop all this brushing and instead explore and fondle. Matthew just smiled. He braided her hair, tying a ribbon deftly into place. Alex swivelled on her stool.

"It was bad, right?"

Matthew nodded, closing his eyes in a futile effort to eradicate the images of the Killiecrankie battlefield.

"Thousands of young men," he said, "no but lads, some of them."

She leaned her head against him, arms coming round his waist. "At least you saved our son." He heard it in her voice: the unspoken fear that Isaac might be beyond saving.

Matthew lowered himself to his knees, brushed his nose against hers. "He'll be alright," he said.

She smiled weakly. "Of course he will." Hands fluttered over his face, his ears, the faded scars that decorated his shoulders. She splayed her fingers over his chest, his heart, leaning forward to kiss the hollow of his throat. "My Matthew."

He smiled when she rubbed her face against him, that signature caress of hers. Her hands were back, stroking his arms, his chest. He took her hand, led it further down. She closed her hand round him, and his erection throbbed in her hold.

A kiss, a gentle probing that ended in hungry exploration, and he slid himself inside of her, congratulating himself yet again on the perfect height of the stool. He loved taking her like this, loved how implicitly she trusted him to hold her as she leaned back, anchored by his hands. Deeper, she urged wordlessly, crossing her legs behind him. Please, Matthew, please! He could feel his balls press against her, and still she tried to get him closer. He held her and loved her, held her as she came, cradled her as close as he could, and kissed her, still joined, still fused.

"Do you really think he's alright?" she asked against his neck.

"Aye," he lied, glad that she couldn't see his face, "of course I do, lass."

Three days later, Charlie rode in, and the horse he led behind him carried the unmistakeable bulge of a shrouded body.

"I'm sorry," Charlie stuttered, trying to avoid Alex's eyes. "I did what I could."

Alex couldn't reply, her tongue oversized in her mouth. He shouldn't even be here, and now he was dead. She reached out to touch her son's dead body: a slab of meat, cold and inert under her touch.

"How?" she asked, and the men looked at her as if she were a witless fool.

"How?" Charlie echoed. "He was there, at Killiecrankie. On the wrong side, as it turned out." The poor man had struggled to stay alive for two days, he told her, had hissed and gurgled, breathlessly insisting that he couldn't die, not here, not now. At the end, it had all been Veronica, Veronica and Dad, and someone called Offa.

Alex listened in silence, not knowing what she felt at so obviously having been omitted from the people Isaac had called for. Wryly, she conceded to herself that it hurt, but what right did she have to expect anything else? It hadn't been her that had been there for him when he grew up.

Even worse, if she had to choose between David and Isaac – she shied away from even concluding that thought.

She stretched out her hand to touch Isaac again, folding back the shroud to look at the still, pale face, the jaw tied together by a strip of linen. His hair moved in the air, a lock of life in all that death. She traced his nose, his lips, she found his hands and stroked his fingers, uncurling them from the slight clench of rigor mortis – such beautiful hands, long, dexterous fingers. Too bad he hadn't been born without them, because then he would never have been here.

Her head was ringing with his name, crammed with images of him as a baby, as a small boy, as a desperately unhappy man. Her son – and now he was dead, and the people he loved would never know, his daughter would grow up without him, just as Isaac had grown up without Alex.

"Isaac," she breathed, smoothing back his thick, dark hair. "My son." She lifted his hand to her face, and placed the cold palm against her cheek. She kissed it, rocked back and forth with his hand clasped to her chest.

"We'll make him a coffin," Matthew said, placing a light hand on her shoulder, "and you can lay him out."

Alex nodded. Yes, lay him out, wash him one last time, and struggle with stiff limbs to dress him in his best. She couldn't swallow, her windpipe closing up alarmingly and for some moments she gulped air frantically before the sob that had gotten stuck halfway up escaped, tearing at the tender membranes of her throat.

"I'll help you," Rosie said, an arm coming round Alex's waist. "We will see him done right by, the two of us together, aye?"

Alex wanted to hit her. She wanted to rage at Rosie, tell her it was her fault that Isaac was dead. But it wasn't, not really. Her son had tampered with time – and paid the price for doing so.

"Isaac," she whispered, choking on his name. She gripped at Rosie, at Matthew.

"Isaac!" she yelled.

Chapter 36

"So," Luke said a couple of days after they'd buried Isaac. "The truth about you and Margaret." He regarded Alex quizzically, twirling the small pewter cup of whisky round and round.

Charlie had ridden back to join his regiment, the Graham sons were on their way to take a swim after a long day in the fields, and it was only Matthew, Luke and Alex sitting on the bench just outside the kitchen door, the evening too warm to be spent indoors.

"I don't know the truth." Well, she didn't, did she? She had no idea which of them had come first, if Mercedes had lived first here, then in the future, or the other way around. All she knew was that somehow her mother had managed to give birth to two girls with a 300-year gap, and that was something she'd decided she wasn't going to tell Luke – ever.

"You know something," Luke said, "and you must know if your mother was present during your childhood."

"She was – mostly," Alex replied, seeing an elegant way out. "There were a couple of years when she was gone," she lied, "and then, one day, she came back."

"Ah," Luke said.

"Those paintings…" She stopped, twisted her hands together. "Sometimes, people disappeared into them." This was definitely true, but she'd never seen something like that happen while she was a child. "And sometimes, Mercedes had to leave, on account of too many questions being asked."

"But why? Why paint those wee scraps? Did she set out on purpose to make people vanish?" Luke sounded unruffled, as if people being sucked into postcard-size pictures was very much the norm. But his left hand was shaped into the sign against the evil eye, two fingers raised like horns. Not entirely unperturbed, her dear brother-in-law – rather the reverse.

"No," Alex said, "she was, I think, trying to find her way home."

"Her way home?" Luke's voice squeaked. Alex studied him carefully, assessing his reaction. She had to give him something, and to tell him Mercedes was a time traveller was a great deal safer than to tell him she was as well.

"The pictures she made, they, well…" She licked her lips and took a big breath. "They led to other times."

"Other times?" Luke echoed. "How other times?"

"She was born in the fifteenth century." Alex watched with a mixture of amusement and trepidation as Luke's face first blanched, then assumed an expression of absolute incredulity, to be followed by a tightening of his mouth and eyes.

"You lie, such is not possible."

"I couldn't agree more," she said, "but, unfortunately, it is – at least in Mercedes' case."

She hesitated, uncertain as to how much to tell him, but decided to give him at least some background. Luke leaned back against the wall, submerging his entire face in shadow while she told him of Mercedes and Hector Olivares.

"So each one of those paintings was an attempt to get back, but I think sometimes they didn't work – not on her – and so she painted more and more." She was so angry with her mother for not having destroyed them, all those dangerous bits and pieces.

"And you?" Luke asked. "Have you fallen through one of them?"

"No," Alex replied – quite truthfully. "But they make me very ill."

Luke nodded. "It was the same for Margaret. She never looked at the painting, saying it made her break out in a sweat." He looked at Alex. "But you know of people who have."

"Huh?"

"Fallen through one of the witch's paintings."

"Oh yes," she said coldly. "Our niece, for one."

"Our niece? Wee deaf Lucy?" Luke stuttered.

"Well, you sent her father the picture, didn't you?" She hitched her shoulders. "It killed Joan."

Luke squirmed. "She was already ailing, had been ill for years."

"But seeing Lucy fade away didn't help," Matthew said.

"I didn't know what it could do," Luke tried.

Matthew hawked and spat at Luke's feet. "Oh aye, you did. Alex had told you the picture had to be destroyed before an unsuspecting soul fell through it. But you chose not to, hoping to cause serious mischief – which you did, heartless bastard that you are at times."

"Heartless? And who just rode with you to save your fool of a son?" Luke demanded.

"The least you could do after I saved Charlie. Despite what you had done to me, I might add."

"Despite?" Luke's voice rose. "And what about what you did to me? To Margaret?"

There it was again: all those years of bitterness and hatred, like bubbling lava under a thin crust of soil. The brothers leaned towards each other; eyes flashed and challenged. Under Alex's restraining hand, Matthew's muscles bunched and hardened, and then he sat back, drained the last of his whisky, and poured some more. He waved the flask in the direction of Luke who nodded, holding out his cup with an unsteady hand.

Next morning, Alex decided to do what she'd been putting off for days. With a small sigh, she entered Isaac's room and stood for a moment by the door: his paints and brushes, the sketches, his primitive easel with the half-finished picture still facing inwards. Just by the threshold, Matthew had placed the little canvas bag containing the sad collection of belongings Charlie had brought back, and hesitantly, Alex pulled the bag towards her. A pair of stockings, his pouch, a sharpened piece of coal, and a crudely stitched sketchbook, except that this one was full of writing. Most of it in quill, but right at the back the last entries had been made with coal, smudged slightly but still fully legible. A diary of sorts, a cry of despair at finding himself here, so far from those he loved.

Alex began to read, uncomfortably aware that none of this was intended for her eyes, and halfway through she closed it, not certain if this was out of a belated decision to respect his privacy or because she just couldn't bear it. She placed it on the bed together with the sketches, and systematically began to clean the room of Isaac. His few items of clothing had too much wear left in them to throw away, but the carefully folded boxer shorts and jeans she found hidden under his pigments she was going to burn. For a moment, she held the jeans, her thumbs stroking a fabric she vividly recalled despite not having worn it in more than three decades. Oh God, Isaac was meant to go back, to wear these again, not die of a pierced lung. Alex closed her eyes against the rush of grief, and threw the jeans away from her.

She was nearly done. One thing left to do, and she didn't want to, her body hair bristling with apprehension. She flipped the painting right side up, backing away so fast she slammed into the wall. Even from here, she could hear it whisper, a soft, enticing murmur that made her knees begin to fold. No more than that, just a general sense of disquiet, of time being slightly out of joint.

"What's that?"

Luke's voice made her jump, and before she could stop him, he strode over to the easel and lifted the painting into his hands. For some moments, he stood staring down at the brimming bucket, at the drowned kitten, the white tipped tail waving softly back and forth.

"Isaac did this?" he asked, looking queasy.

Alex shrugged. No point in denying it.

"He had it from his grandmother," she said, "the capacity to paint like that."

Luke flashed her a suspicious look. "Why would he paint like her?"

"He doesn't paint like her," she replied, her voice catching on the wrong verb tense. "He's a far better painter than she ever was."

Luke was still absorbed in the bucket, in the water that flowed over the edge and down the sides. "Aye, a wee masterpiece, this is, however unfinished."

Alex tried to look unaffected, walked over to him, and retook the painting. It scalded her, and for an instant her vision splintered, and simultaneously she saw thousands of lives, her head invaded by a cacophony of sounds.

"It burns," she said, and darted out of the room.

She set fire to it behind the woodshed. A thin plume of smoke, a muted roar when the oil in the paints caught fire, and it was gone. Alex sat on her knees and regarded the pathetic little heap of ashes. Her son... She poked at the pile, and it scattered, some flakes drifting up towards the skies.

"Go with God, be at peace." She laughed hollowly. If anything, Isaac was pissed off with God, not at all in a conciliatory mood. It almost made her smile to imagine him filling in a bright yellow Claims & Complaints document, loudly insisting he had been short-changed and should be sent back down – to his right time. And St Peter would wring his hands, mutter something about this being most unusual, yes, very unusual indeed, and might Isaac want a cup of tea while they looked into it? Slowly, she rose, stamped on the smoking ashes, braved the waist-high stand of nettles that bordered the water meadows, and made for the hillside beyond.

She was hot by the time she reached the millpond, and it was a relief to sit down, take off shoes and stockings, and paddle her bare feet in the cool water. She tugged at her neckline, undid a couple of buttons in her bodice, and kicked at the water, sending sprays of water high into the air. The miller called out a greeting, and she waved back, and then he was gone, leading a horse behind him.

She cupped water in her hands, splashed her face and neck, and rivulets of water rushed over her heated skin. Again, cold water trickling between her breasts, dampening shift and stays. Again, slippery coolness sliding along her nape, under her collar and onwards down her spine. She undid her hair and shook it out, letting what little wind there was lift it. A shadow fell over her, and she reared back, having to squint against the sun to see who it was.

"Oh, it's you." She shifted away when Luke sat down beside her, not at all comfortable with having him this close to her.

"You think I might push you?" he said.

"It wouldn't much avail you. I happen to know how to swim."

"You do?"

"Unlike your father," she said, unable to help herself. Luke's face clouded. "Was it fun?" she asked. "Did you enjoy watching him drown?"

The green eyes boring into her acquired an impenetrable iciness.

"Aye," he answered, and his tone made her guts contract, even if she tried to hide it.

"There's no statute of limitation on murder, is there?" she said to get her own back, and his eyes narrowed into slits.

He didn't reply, and when she made to stand up, his hand closed round her wrist.

"Let me go!" she hissed.

"I think not," he replied, holding her easily when she tugged at her hand.

"Stop this." She yanked. In response, Luke lunged, flattening her to the ground.

"A kiss for your brother-in-law?" he taunted.

"Fuck off," Alex spat, shoving at him. "Luke! No!"

She squirmed like an eel in her efforts to dislodge him. His fingers were a painful manacle around her wrist. She fought and struggled, told him to stop, please stop, but Luke didn't seem to hear.

"It's so unfair," he said, dragging a hand through her hair. "So unfair that you should still be here when my Margaret is dead."

"Not my fault!" She hit at his shoulder.

301

"Why should he have what I do not?" He imprisoned her with his weight, so heavy she had problems breathing.

"…eh…" she wheezed.

He looked down at her, smiling crookedly. "Just like her, my Margaret. So soft, so round…"

"I'm not your Margaret!" She tried to dislodge him.

"He took her," Luke murmured, and his eyes had gone blank, staring straight through her. "My accursed brother made free with her, forced her to wed him. My Margaret! Mine!" He moaned. "Margaret," he whispered, and then he kissed her. It made her gag. He kissed her again, and she whipped her head back and forth but Luke's mouth, his tongue… She screamed into his mouth. She wasn't getting any air, she spat, and slapped at him with her free hand.

"Aye," he panted, "you know I like it rough."

Alex set her free hand to his chest and heaved. Like attempting to budge a boulder. He was big, as big as Matthew, and just as strong. A leg between hers, his hand pushing her skirts out of the way, and Alex bucked. Oh God! His hand, there! His mouth on hers, swallowing her protesting screams. Alex knocked his nose askew, and that made him raise his head. With an ear-splitting shriek, she dug her nails into his cheek.

"Get off me, you son of a bitch!" she screamed. "Let me go, you bastard!"

Luke blinked. His pupils shrank back to normal. He flung himself away from her.

She sat up, wiping at her mouth. He had somehow managed to paw her bodice down, and one of her breasts was straining against the rumpled fabric of her shift. Her thighs…so white, and Alex smoothed down her skirts with a trembling hand.

"I," Luke said, "Alex, I—" He inhaled loudly, held his breath for an instant before releasing it in a sibilant rush. "I don't know what happened. I never intended to dishonour or hurt you." He raised a hand to his bleeding cheek, a confused look in his eyes.

"But you did." Alex was on her feet, her knees shaking

so violently it was an effort to put a few yards between them.

"I did." He didn't attempt to explain or excuse himself.

Alex wheeled and crashed straight through the closest shrubs in her haste to get away from him.

She walked for hours. Repeatedly, she smoothed her hair; just as often, she adjusted her shift and her bodice. She found tart, unripe blackberries and ate them just to rid her mouth of the taste of him, and then she recalled she'd left her shoes and stockings by the pond.

When she snuck back, he was still there, sitting with his head bowed, every line of him breathing dejection. He stiffened at the sound of her approach. An involuntary whimper squeezed its way over her sore lips, and she turned and ran. The shoes and stockings could wait.

Matthew. What was she to tell him? Alex came to a standstill. The truth, of course, she admonished herself, she had to tell him the truth. Then what? Alex clapped her hands over her face, and sank down to sit. He'd kill Luke. And then they'd come and fetch him and hang him for murder. She splayed her fingers, and regarded her lap through the created lattice effect. No. Not tell Matthew – at least not now, perhaps not ever.

Once she had recovered sufficient composure, Alex made for the house and the reassuring presence of her husband. He was sitting on an overturned bucket by the stable door, and Alex raised her hand in a wave but got no response whatsoever. As she got closer, she slowed her speed. He was staring straight ahead, slack-mouthed, eyes a dull, strange colour in a face gone ash-grey. At first, Alex thought he might be having a heart attack, and with a racing pulse, she rushed the last few yards towards him. Then she saw the paper he was fisting, and she faltered, coming to a swaying halt before him.

"What?" she croaked, all her recent experiences forgotten. Ian! Or maybe Mark or Lettie.

"Sarah."

She could barely make out his voice.

"Sarah?" Alex imagined all kinds of things, a cavalcade

of one possible death after the other flashing across her brain.

He held out the letter to her, but there was nothing left to read: he had shredded it.

"There were riots in St Mary's City," he said hollowly. "Protestant men demanding that the colony recognise William and Mary as rightful monarchs, that the papist governor be deposed and replaced by one of their own." He fell quiet. "In April, it was," he added, as if this was of any importance. "That damned John Coode being inflammatory again," he muttered, and Alex wanted to take him by the shoulders and shake him.

"Sarah?" she demanded instead.

"Gone. Julian rode with the militia, and Ruth begged him to make sure Sarah was safe, but they weren't there. Their house…" He swallowed, looking at her, at their sons, at Luke, who had materialised out of nowhere, three parallel scratches down his cheek. "It was burnt to the ground."

"But not them," Alex pleaded. "Not our Sarah and Michael and little Joshua."

"No, not them," Matthew replied.

"We have to…" Alex began and then broke off. Had to do what? Before they were home, it would be October.

"Ian and Mark are looking for her. Julian writes how they are scouring the country for our lass." Matthew held out his hand to her, clasped her fingers hard. There was something more, she could see it in his eyes.

"What else?"

"She's wanted for murder," he whispered. "Minister Macpherson, no less."

Alex gaped. Her Sarah? No, they had to be wrong! Matthew raised a shoulder, met her eyes. She could, he silently told her. If she felt sufficiently threatened, she would. Yes, Sarah definitely could – Alex had taught her well.

"They haven't found him," he said, "and without a body it's difficult to prove a murder. So for now we pray."

"Pray! And what good does that do?"

"What else can we do?" He straightened up. "Her brothers are looking for her, for our lass. They'll find her and keep her safe, of course they will." He sounded as if he was trying very hard to convince himself.

Alex tried to nod and smile, all the while seeing her daughter swinging back and forth from a hangman's noose.

"You'll want to leave as soon as possible," Luke said.

Alex threw him a hasty glance before averting her heating face from him.

Matthew looked from one to the other, his eyes lingering on Luke's cheek. "What happened?" he asked.

Luke made a wry face, said something about even small kittens having claws, and threw a meaningful look at one of the tenant's wives who propitiously appeared from behind the smoking shed.

Matthew frowned, clearly not taken in. Well, who would be? Alice was primmer than prim, and not much to look at either – not Luke's type, not at all. Matthew's frown deepened. He stood and Luke ambled out of reach, mumbling something about needing a drink.

"Tell me," Matthew said in her ear.

"What?"

"Tell me," he repeated, jerking his head to where Luke was already entering the house.

"Tell you? Oh, about that!" She waved her hand dismissively. "He got upset when I asked him if he'd enjoyed watching his father drown." She shrugged expressively.

"Hmm," Matthew said. But he dropped the subject, returning to the far more urgent matters they had to consider.

Chapter 37

It had been just as heart-wrenching as Alex had suspected it would be to say farewell to Adam. Her baby, just thirteen, and next time she saw him, he'd be a full-grown man – if she saw him. But she'd had a long conversation with him in the hayloft, just the two of them, and for all that he was terrified, Adam insisted that this was what he wanted to do.

"I can't go back now," he explained through a mouthful of purloined cake. "And it isn't as if I'll be entirely alone. David's here."

"Well, it's not exactly next door, is it? Glasgow and London."

"Closer than Maryland, and then there's Uncle Luke and my cousins as well."

"But you'll come back to us," she said. "You will, won't you?"

Adam had grinned at her, his face golden in a ray of sun. "Aye, I will, me and Hugin both." On cue, the bird had flown in through the loading hatch and landed on Alex's head.

And so they stood on a wet, surly August day and waved Adam out of their lives – at least for the coming seven or eight years – and Adam twisted repeatedly in his saddle, Hugin flapped back and forth, and Luke didn't look back once. Well, he wouldn't, would he? Ever since that incident by the pond, they'd circled at a careful distance from each other, both of them aware of the speculating look in Matthew's eyes. Only once had Luke spoken directly to her, and that was to assure her Adam would be safe with him. Alex had just nodded. She already knew that, and it was obvious Adam was very fond of his uncle.

"Do you mind?" she asked, turning to face Matthew.

"Aye." He threw one last look after his brother.

"Ridiculous as it may seem, I don't like it that Hillview now is his."

"He loves it too." Plus he had offered a generous price when Matthew announced his intention to sell.

Matthew nodded. "Charlie doesn't."

"Nor do our sons," Alex said. "They are rooted elsewhere."

For the following two days, Alex kept a worried eye on Matthew, noting just how often he escaped to say farewell to his land alone. From a distance, she watched as he walked through pastures and groves, sat for hours by the millpond, and just as long on the little graveyard bench, his hunched frame dappled by the moving shade of the rowan tree. But when she asked, he shrugged, admitting that his mind was already elsewhere, leaping anxiously across the sea and through the forests of America, chasing after his lost daughter, his wee lass.

"That makes two of us," she said, and they stood side by side staring out over the moor towards the west.

Like tourists, Alex reflected on the day of their departure. That's what we've been for this last year – at least I have. Always, always counting days until they would leave, all the while knowing she'd never stay. She adjusted her stirrups, looked for one last time at the solid, grey house, and found Rosie, a few yards away.

"Take care of my children," she said, jerking her head in the direction of the graveyard. Rosie nodded, saying that wee Rachel she'd been caring for since last time they left, and Isaac, well, it could have been her Tom that lay there. She swallowed and ducked her head, muttering yet another of her endless apologies.

Alex looked away. Poor Isaac, constantly abandoned by her. As a small child, as a man dragged off to fight, and now even as a corpse. She clapped her heels into her mount, it took a startled leap, gripped the bit between its teeth, and careened up the slope.

By the time they reached the top of the lane, Samuel and David were already well ahead. Alex and Matthew stopped to look back. Matthew rode some feet to the side and sat very alone, his cloak fluttering in the wind. The morning sun threw long shadows in the apple orchard and glinted off their bedroom window, the land rose and folded, rose, rose some more, and there was the distant moss, at this distance a hazy purple.

Matthew exhaled, shoulders falling together. Below in the yard, Robbie took a step forward, raised his hand and bowed, a silent farewell to his master. Matthew returned the gesture, wheeled his horse and spurred it away, his clenched jaw signalling that for now he didn't want to talk.

Two days later, they arrived in Glasgow. They saw David installed in his lodgings, spent days scanning the docks for a ship, and then, finally, there was one: a ship captained by an American, eager to get back home to Virginia as soon as possible. Three days before they sailed, and suddenly there was too little time for all the things Alex wanted to say to David. He listened patiently, but she could see the amusement lurking in his eyes, and knew that everything she said was flying unrecorded through his brain, discarded as being irrelevant to him. Still, she persevered, her hands touching him constantly in a feeble attempt to memorise him.

Three, two, one, and then it was the morning of their departure, and David's face was set with the effort of not crying when he hugged Matthew and Alex farewell. And then it was Samuel, and for a long time, the brothers clung like limpets to each other, both of them weeping. At last, Samuel took a step back, wiped his face with his sleeve, and attempted a smile.

"I'll be waiting for you," he said, "when you come home."

David cleared his throat. "When I come home."

And there, in the grey of the August dawn, Alex was swept with the premonition that maybe he never would. She pressed herself hard against Matthew, who gave her a surprised look but wrapped his arm round her shoulders. One last, lingering embrace, her signature swift caress – running the back of her hand down her son's face – and she was in the long boat, eyes locked on David who stood so forlorn on the quay. Once on the ship, she stumbled over to the railing, and for as long as she could see him, as long as there was a dot that could be him, she waved.

Alex spent a miserable couple of days throwing up, promised herself she would never, ever, do this again, and finally made it up on deck. Samuel gave her a weak smile before going back to scanning the horizon.

"What are you looking for?" Alex asked after a while.

"Something, anything – I don't like this emptiness." He regarded the sea around them with open dislike. "So much water."

"That's why it's called an ocean."

He smiled and wiggled his toes. "He's so far away – David, I mean."

"So's Adam," she said, looking back along the ship's wake.

"Aye, so is Adam," Samuel nodded, "but it's David that I miss so it hurts."

She gripped his hand and held it hard.

"Here," Matthew said the next day, handing Alex a new little work of art. "Happy birthday, lass."

"Oh!" she exclaimed, turning the little wooden baby round and round. "Like the first one you gave me, you know, on the moor."

He smiled down at her. "For the same reason, I think. That you may touch this one and think of them, imagine they're thinking of you – both Adam and David." Alex drew a finger down the curve of the carved infant's back.

"And Isaac, and Jacob, and Rachel."

"And them." Matthew brushed at her cheek.

She rested her weight against him, nestled her ear close to his chest, searching for the reassuring thump of his heartbeat. "Thank you."

"So," he said after a while, "what was it that happened with Luke? The day you came down so drawn, with your clothes damp, and your hair tight against your scalp?"

"Umm," Alex replied, attempting to look confused.

Matthew laid his hand on her arm and squeezed – hard

enough that she should know not to lie.

"He kissed me," she mumbled, and his fingers sank into her flesh, making her yelp. "It was nothing, really."

"Alex…" Matthew looked about for somewhere to sit, propelled her before him to the closed hatch. He sat her down, kneeled before her, eyes on a level with hers. Alex swallowed, attempted to look away. "You're a bad liar, lass."

Alex nodded. Yes, she was. She took a deep breath, surprised that she should be crying, a steady flow of tears running down her cheeks.

"Ah, lass," Matthew said, and bit by bit, he winkled the whole sorry story out of her, from the moment she'd found herself on her back with Luke on top, to when she'd knocked his nose off.

"I clawed him in the face, and he just threw himself away from me," she finished, twisting her fingers through her shawl.

At first, Matthew sat mute. Then he rose, his face mottled, his throat working. "Why didn't you tell me?"

Alex stood, tried to take his hand. "And if I'd told you, what then? You'd have killed him!"

"Mayhap." He crossed his arms, tucking his hands into his armpits. "And now our son resides with him," he spat.

"Well, at least he isn't into boys, is he?" she retorted. "And, anyway, we both know Adam's happy with him. It shows, how much he likes his uncle." Besides, there'd been no time to find alternative arrangements. Matthew looked at her as if he considered throwing her overboard, before stalking off to stand as far away from her as he could. She followed after.

Alex slipped her arms around his waist, ignoring how he tensed. "I couldn't risk you doing something stupid and getting hanged, could I?"

"Mmph!" he snorted, conveying just how weak an excuse that was.

Slowly, she rubbed her face up and down between his shoulder blades. "I can't live without you, honey. Besides, I'm not sure if he was truly aware of what he was doing –

for an instant, he confused me with Margaret."

"You think? His wife is dead, and you make a mightily solid ghost."

"You know what I mean. We were very alike, and he's frightfully lonely without her." She rested her head against his back, closed her eyes. "I love you," she whispered after a while.

"Mmph," Matthew repeated, relaxing against her. When she took his hand, he let her, following her towards their cabin.

Later that evening, Alex sat with her carved box in her lap, and around her she had ranged his yearly gifts. Each and every one of them, she touched and held, inspecting them minutely, and now she was back to holding the latest addition in her hand. She looked at all the versions of herself and rolled her eyes.

"A veritable Barbie," she muttered. "All I need is to sew up some different wardrobes."

She smiled sadly when she remembered Isaac's proud expression when he told her this very box was in his studio. There had been something wrong with the inner bottom, she recalled him saying, as if something was hidden beneath it. She ran her fingers over the smooth wood, and, on impulse, lifted the loose bottom out. Something hidden beneath it, he'd said. She withdrew Isaac's diary from where she kept it, stowed away in one of her satchels. After smoothing at the pages, she placed it in the box, before refitting the bottom. She had to struggle a bit to get it back in place, the wood caught and screeched to a halt, and Alex frowned at how it all now tilted. She returned her carvings and closed the lid. But the baby she kept in her petticoat pocket – just in case.

★   ★   ★

It was a terrible thing to have to do. John sighed, sitting down to survey the emptied studio. A whole life dismantled, most of it packed away in the black bin liners that stood by the door. He had a pretty clear idea of what had happened to Isaac, had slashed the damned painting to shreds as he loudly cursed God, his son, and life in general for doing this to him again.

For the first few weeks, he'd clung to hope: that Isaac had gone AWOL, that he'd had an accident and woken up with memory loss. Days spent with a distraught Veronica, endless hours of listening to her silent weeping. Excruciating periods of time sitting with Isabelle, trying to smile and sound reassuring when she asked where her dad was – and then, one day, she simply stopped asking... John wasn't sure which was worse: to constantly talk about Isaac, hope he'd soon be back, or to stop speaking of him, reconstructing their lives without him.

Now, sixteen months later, he had given up on Isaac ever coming home. He was stuck somewhere in the past, perhaps even dead, and all John could do was hope that it had been quick and easy. He got to his feet, making for the last row of cupboards.

He recognised the box immediately, recalling how Isaac had found it in Maryland all those years ago. A box full of little Alexes, a collection of exquisite statues depicting the woman he had once loved in a parade of three-dimensional snapshots. He lifted them out one by one, lining them up on the large worktable. And then the box was empty, and John frowned down at the uneven bottom. The vagaries of time, making the wood swell so that a perfect fit no longer was. He pressed against the wood, and it gave in some places, not in others. He pushed harder. There was something there, something secreted and preserved beneath the thin layer of wood. John found a screwdriver and tried to open the bottom. It wouldn't give. Not until John brutally splintered the wood.

Papers, stitched together into a primitive note book. Old paper, so brittle the edges crumbled. John stared down at the familiar handwriting, and for an instant he considered throwing it away, unread. But he couldn't, of course he couldn't. With a racing pulse, he touched the first page.

God, Dad, what have I done? And how the fuck do I get back home?

John tightened his hold on the fragile paper and wept.

Chapter 38

They were all cold and hungry. No matter how often Sarah wiped his face, Joshua had two strings of yellow snot hanging from his nose, and since a couple of weeks back, Michael kept up a constant coughing. But right now he was smiling, looking from Sarah to the dead deer.

"Well done," he said in a gravelly voice.

"Bang," Joshua said, miming aiming a musket. "It went bang."

Pure chance that they had come upon the little herd. Sarah hadn't stopped to think, grabbing the loaded flintlock. The shot had been loud in the stillness of the October woods, it seemed to Sarah that it still reverberated in the air. A foolish thing to do, she chided herself, but the thought of hot roasted meat made her salivate, one hand coming up to caress the wean inside of her. They all needed sustenance. Weeks of nuts and berries complemented by the occasional gift of food from people they met had left Sarah with a gnawing, permanent hunger, an ache in the pit of her stomach.

Michael finished dressing the small doe, and wiped the knife against the fading grass. Off one knee, off the other, and he was back on his feet, grabbing at a nearby sapling.

"What?" Sarah's hands flew over him. He'd been ill for weeks, since the few days they'd spent with the kind but ailing Polish couple, but over the last few days, her husband's condition had deteriorated visibly. Strangely enough, as Michael's health and strength failed him, Sarah seemed to regain hers – or maybe it was just a matter of survival.

He hitched his shoulders and coughed. "No matter." He looked at their son, sitting some feet away in a patch of weak sun. "Mayhap we can stay here for some days."

Days? Sarah opened her mouth, shut it again. Pointless, his tone told her. All this wandering was getting them nowhere. For the last few weeks, they had walked in circles, Sarah's attempts to approach her home, or the Chisholm farm, hindered by horsed militiamen. It made Sarah's innards cramp. What were they to do if they didn't find shelter before the winter?

At times, she considered whether it would be best to turn herself in, but the single time she'd voiced this to Michael he had been so distraught she had promised never to mention it again. But she thought about it on a daily basis, and what with their present state of health, she was quickly running out of options. She stroked her neck, swallowed repeatedly.

"No." Michael stood before her, covered her hand with his own. "You'll not hang. I'll not allow it."

"We can't go on like this," she said. So far, the autumn had been mild, but the nights were becoming colder, and their clothes were worn too thin after months on the run. She tried out a weak smile. "They can't prove a thing. There's nothing left of him."

"Hounds baying for a fox aren't interested in proof." Michael frowned, clear eyes shrinking to slits. "We should make for Providence. This time, maybe I can evade the militia and sneak into town to find Simon." They'd tried that before, but all the same Sarah's belly filled with hopeful flutters. Maybe this time they'd succeed, and Uncle Simon was a renowned lawyer, a man skilled in words and law. Aye, this was their best option.

"Tomorrow. We start out tomorrow." She gave her husband a concerned look. Assuming he was in a fit state to walk, of course. She suspected he was running a fever, and when he wasn't coughing, he was wheezing, every breath a constricted effort.

"Why don't you rest?" she suggested, pointing in the direction of a large hemlock. It was indicative of Michael's present state that he didn't argue. He nodded and walked off.

Sarah was busy by the fire when the two men came into the clearing. Thin slices of venison were cooking on a flat stone, accompanied by some mushrooms and a slice or two of old bread. A twig broke, Sarah got to her feet, ungainly due to her big belly. Like a silent ghost, Joshua glided through the grasses to stand beside her, small hands knotted in her skirts.

"Well, well," one of the men said, "just in time for dinner, it would seem." Sarah looked about for the musket before recalling their single weapon was with Michael. She shoved Joshua to stand behind her.

"What do you want?" she challenged, gripping a stout branch in her hand. Renegades, the both of them, with avaricious eyes and nervous, snatching hands. One of them had a beaver cap on his head, they were both in buckskins, and from the smaller man's braid sprouted several decorative feathers.

"The meat." The man with the braid used his booted foot to nudge at the remains of the doe.

"And you, of course." The beaver cap man bared his teeth in a leer.

"Me?" She shook her head. No man would ever lay a hand on her against her will – that was a promise she'd made herself four years ago. Her right hand closed on the handle of her dirk.

"You're the murderess," the braided man said, "and whoever brings you in stands to get a right fat purse."

"Murderess?" Sarah tried to laugh. "Me?" She used the dirk to nudge the bread off the stone before it burnt to cinders, making sure they saw just how long and sharp the blade was. The man with the beaver cap looked at the knife, snickered, and dug about in a capacious pouch, producing a deed of sorts that he unrolled.

"You." He held it up. Sarah looked at her likeness. Damn Nuthead! The original sketch had been made a year or so ago, and Nuthead had presented Sarah with this image of herself, saying proudly that it was him that had done the etching.

"Not me," she shrugged. "I am but the wife of a poor woodcutter." She tightened her hold on the dirk.

The smaller man laughed. "I think not, Mistress Connor." He produced a rope, nodded at his companion to grab her.

The shot struck the taller of the two in the small of his back. He made a whooshing sound, clutched at his belly, and fell to his knees. Blood leaked through his fingers, it tinted his lips a bright red. From Joshua came a single whimper. Sarah backed away, dragging Joshua with her. The wounded man coughed, spraying his clothes and the grass around him with fine droplets of blood.

We can't let his companion live, she thought with surprising clarity. The thought seemed to have struck the braided man as well because, instead of attempting to aid his companion, he was retreating, stumbling backwards with his musket levelled at Sarah.

From somewhere came a hoarse yell, and the fleeing man swivelled towards the sound. Sarah didn't stop to think. Three clumsy leaps, a hand in his hair, and the blade slit his throat wide open. He gargled and toppled over, his head hitting the ground with a dull thud. A quick death, not the crawling agony the other man was living.

From under the hemlock, Michael appeared, an unsteady shadow of his normal self. But the musket was held firmly in his hands, and somehow he made it across the clearing to where Sarah was standing.

She couldn't quite collect how to move her limbs, or how to coordinate lips and tongue sufficiently to speak. Blood on her hands, on her skirts, blood on her dirk. But when the dying man clutched at her skirts, she screamed and kicked herself free. Joshua howled. She pressed her son's face to her thighs, hushing him as she repeated that things were fine. Her man staggered to a stop some feet away. Sarah wanted her da.

Much later, they'd left the clearing well behind. Due north, Sarah insisted, because to return to Providence no longer seemed much of a plan – not with prize hunters and militia scouring the woods for her. She slid her husband a look. Michael was walking in grim silence, every step an obvious effort. He coughed, all the time he coughed, and it made Sarah want to scream at him to shush, because how were they otherwise to avoid capture. She licked her lips. Two men, and Michael hadn't as much as batted an eyelid as he watched the first one die.

"So where to?" Michael said, his voice hoarse.

Sarah adjusted the shawl in which she was carrying Joshua before replying. "We go to visit my brother's Indian kin."

"And do you know how to find them?"

"No." She took his hand, steadying him as he stumbled. "But they'll find me."

Chapter 39

Matthew thanked the captain of the little sloop that had transported them from Jamestown to Providence, and helped his wife off the boat. Already October and surprisingly warm, at least in comparison to what it would have been like in Scotland. He turned to look back at the huge estuary, bordered by stands of brown and golden reeds and grasses, the waters the dull grey of lead under an equally dark sky.

A bit further out from land lay one of the slavers belonging to Mr Farrell, but from the way she rode the waves, she was empty of cargo. The stench was there though: a pervading smell of blood and shit and sheer despair that made most men wrinkle their noses. The wind shifted, and a waft of that same smell came their way, but this time from the slave pens on the further side of the harbour. Mr Farrell came bustling towards them, a small rotund person that looked most benign in his grey clothes, a huge hairpiece falling in arranged curls to halfway down his back.

"Back again?" Mr Farrell said. "Said so, didn't I? Foolishness, Brother Matthew, to return home — whatever for?" His pudgy countenance rearranged itself into a mask of severity. "I dare say you've heard, how this colony now is ruled by upright men such as ourselves. The papists have been ousted, praise the Lord, and Lord Calvert can squeal as much as he wishes, but we won't return the reins of government to him or any other papist."

"Aye, we heard, just as we heard how the brave militia set the houses of innocents alight – a right godly behaviour."

Mr Farrell flushed and muttered something about incensed young men and the lack of strong officers.

"Goaded further by men such as Coode," Alex said, and Matthew suppressed a little smile at the irritated look Mr

Farrell sent her way. In the trader's opinion, women should at most be seen, never heard.

Pointedly, Mr Farrell directed his following comment to Matthew. "And then, Brother Matthew, there's the sorry matter of our dear Minister Macpherson." His sharp eyes bored into Matthew's.

"Disappeared." Matthew nodded.

"Murdered, mark my words," Mr Farrell corrected, "and we fear by your daughter." He shook his head in mock sympathy. "Well, what can you expect? The girl's a papist."

"Oh, so now all Catholics are murderers?" Alex put in. Mr Farrell looked flustered. "Besides," Alex went on, "there's no body, is there? So how can it be murder?"

Mr Farrell gave her an irritated look. "Men burn as well as wood if the heat is sufficient."

Alex looked him up and down. "The minister was there? He took part in setting the fires?"

Mr Farrell admitted that this was the case. "A forceful man, Minister Macpherson, not given to being a bystander."

"Nay, I think not," Matthew muttered, thinking that Gregor Macpherson was one of those ministers that was more of a liability than an asset. Small-minded, prone to hasty judgements, enamoured of his own dignity and learning, he grabbed at any opportunity to showcase himself, be it apprehending runaway slaves or voicing accusations of witchery. To think him dead and gone was not a bad thing, however uncharitable the thought.

It took them some time to traverse the small town as, repeatedly, they were stopped and greeted, men clapping Matthew on the back, women smiling at Alex. It warmed his heart, these effusive welcomes, and even more so when he saw Ruth come waddling towards them, preceded by a belly the size of a beer cask. Beside him, Alex inhaled, and Ruth came to a halt, a defensive hand on her swell.

"And now how do I reach around to hug you?" Alex jested, no doubt to compensate for her unguarded reaction at finding Ruth pregnant again.

"We'll manage." Ruth took the proffered olive twig and

crushed Alex to her, even if it did seem quite uncomfortable. "Da." His daughter hugged him as well before leading them up to her nearby home.

Wee Edward was as he'd expected to find him – taller, but still very much the same laddie as when they left. The wean, however, came as a huge surprise.

Alex stared at their little granddaughter. "She's so big!"

Ruth burst out laughing. "Not a babe in arms anymore. Faith has been walking for well over four months now."

Matthew crouched down to smile at the red-haired lass who regarded them out of eyes the colour of pewter. "She's bonny," he said.

Ruth fussed with her daughter's cap, adjusted the smock. "A biddable lass, quiet and obedient."

"Ah." Alex sounded as if these were dubious qualities in a bairn well short of two.

While his wife and Samuel remained with Ruth and the bairns, Matthew went off to find Julian, hungry for news – any news – about his Sarah. Julian was submerged in a huge tome, so concentrated on his reading that Matthew had to cough twice to catch his attention.

"Matthew!" Julian rose to his feet, beamed, and waved Matthew over to sit in the single armchair in the little study. He poured them both some whisky. "You look well."

Matthew just grunted. "Tell me."

Julian sighed, sat down, and spent some minutes arranging the skirts of his coat. Matthew regarded him with mounting irritation, wondering how much longer his minister good-son was planning on fiddling with his clothes.

"Gregor is gone," Julian began. "Not a trace of him since that April evening – nor of Sarah." That was not entirely correct, he added, however well put dramatically. Sarah and her husband had spent near on a week with Michael's partner before absconding.

"Absconding?" Matthew said.

Julian squirmed, muttered something about Isaiah Farrell insisting that Minister Macpherson had been with them when they set the Connor house alight – the minister had a grudge to settle with Michael Connor – and seeing how he had not been seen since, it was only to be expected that suspicions should be levelled at the Connors.

"But why Sarah? Why not Michael?" Neither of them had heard Alex entering, and Julian rose to greet her before replying to her question.

"Michael had been injured."

"He had? How?" Alex said.

"Minister Macpherson chose to smite him over the head with a plank before shoving him inside the house."

"Inside the house," Matthew echoed. "The house just set alight?"

Julian nodded, eyes on his shoes.

"To burn?" Alex croaked, "They wanted him to burn?"

Julian inclined his head again. Young Farrell and his friends had gone well beyond the norms of acceptable behaviour, he hastened to add, fuelled by an overconsumption of spirits.

"Aided and abetted by dear Gregor," Alex said, "your oh so beloved son-in-law."

"Not beloved." Julian sounded grim. "Not at all beloved."

The reason for that comment became apparent at noon, when Patience came to visit her father. As great-bellied as Ruth was, Patience had none of the glow of motherhood, her mouth pinched into a minute prune, her face pasty. When Matthew spoke to her, she flinched, shrinking together on her stool. Constantly, she smoothed at her apron, her oversized cap, and of the bright lass Matthew recalled from two years hence, there was nothing left.

"He hasn't been a kindly husband," Ruth said in an undertone. "Julian hates himself for having married her to that brute, has even threatened Minister Macpherson with divorce."

Matthew shared a look with his wife. Gregor Macpherson was incapable of even spelling words such as considerate and caring, let alone devoted and loving.

"Well, at least she doesn't seem to miss him, does she?" Alex said to Matthew as they made their way across town.

"Boor, to so intimidate his wife."

"Absolutely. No great loss to humanity." Alex nodded.

"Alex," Matthew reprimanded her half-heartedly before smiling at the sight of Kate Jones making her way towards them.

"Alex! How nice to see you!" Kate squished Alex to her bosom. "And you," Kate added, turning to Matthew. She pecked him on the cheek and stood back, beaming at them. "Happy to be back?" she asked, laughing at Alex's responding eye roll. "You too?" she demanded of Matthew.

"Aye, I am." And he was: setting foot in Maryland was much more of a homecoming than it had been to step onto the wharves in Leith.

"But worried," Alex broke in with a sigh.

"Mmm," Kate commiserated.

"We're on our way to Simon," Matthew said, "to discuss the matter with him."

"You are?" Kate laughed. "Well, I'm not." She lowered her voice. "It wouldn't do, would it, if Widow Jones were to visit Mr Melville at all times."

"Probably not," Alex said with a grin. "After all, what might the ministers say?"

"The ministers? Pfff!" With that, Kate was off, her plum-coloured skirts held high as she crossed the street.

"She's looking good," Alex commented, brushing at her russet bodice.

"Hmm?" Matthew retook his eyes from Kate's upright carriage and silvered hair, just visible under her hat.

"Don't even try," Alex snorted, but was mollified when he took her hand and drew her close enough to kiss her brow.

Two hours later, they were on their way home, Matthew and Alex sharing a horse. Julian had suggested they stay the night, but Matthew had declined, saying they were in a hurry to get home, a statement that had both Alex and Samuel nodding eagerly.

"So, in conclusion, there's no body, no witness, no

proof. Why did she run away, stupid girl?" Alex clutched at Matthew's waist when the horse took a sudden jump to the left.

"She took the right decision at the time," Matthew said. "I don't think the newly elected magistrates would have looked much further than an adequate scapegoat."

Alex sat silent for a while, arms round his waist.

"Do you think she…?" she whispered.

Matthew threw a look at their son, riding some yards away. "Aye," he whispered back, placing his hand over hers.

"Oh God," Alex mumbled.

"What choice did she have? Was she to burn alive?" Ever since Julian had told him that Minister Macpherson had last been seen ducking into the yard to stop the papist from coming out the back door, he'd known. He was ferociously proud of his daughter for saving her husband and son, wished he'd been here to help her sooner, to put himself between her and her accusers.

"And Simon? What does he say?"

"You were there," Matthew teased.

"I was otherwise occupied," Alex said.

Aye, with wee Duncan, all blue eyes and fair hair, at three and a half a winsome child, able to twist most adults round his little finger. Duncan, their grandson, adopted by Simon when Sarah refused to even look at him, shrieking that never, ever would she be able to look at the wean without seeing the face of her rapists.

"Bonny lad," Matthew chuckled.

"A handful. He must be running Simon ragged."

"Aye well, we did tell him he was too old." At sixty, Simon looked substantially younger, despite having the girth of a cow, and since Duncan's arrival, he was a happy man, however much he groaned about the hardships of fatherhood. Kate Jones had something to do with Simon's general air of contentment as well, but Matthew preferred not to think about that. It wasn't as if he wanted Kate – he had his Alex – but he found the thought of handsome Kate with his fat brother-in-law preposterous.

"He says how he will speak for her, should there ever be a need to," Matthew said, reverting to the original subject of their conversation. "Now that matters have cooled somewhat, he doesn't think anyone would find for murder." But, Simon had added, the fact that Macpherson was a minister was troublesome, as was the fact that the lass had gone missing and remained missing.

"It isn't as yon Gregor was much liked," Simon had continued. "It's enough to have eyes to see how unkindly he treated that young wife of his, and she both pretty and soft-spoken. But he's a man of the Kirk, and the ministers will close ranks around him – with the exception of Julian, I presume."

Alex sighed from where she sat behind Matthew. "Where can they be? Where can they go?"

Matthew exhaled just as unhappily. He didn't know. He had set in motion a discreet search while in Virginia, had even ridden over to York River to find Michael's brother only to be assured very rudely that Michael had not been seen, nor would he be welcomed should he choose to come. Here, in Maryland, there were several wealthy and powerful Catholic landowners still in place, and mayhap they had been taken in by one of them. But would a Catholic dare extend protection to a potential minister killer?

"Why not come home?" Alex asked.

"And you don't think that is where they would look first?"

"Ian and Mark wouldn't let anybody hurt them!"

"Ian and Mark can't take on the militia, Alex." Their conversation ground to a halt, and for the coming hour they rode in silence.

Ever since they set foot in Providence, Samuel had been like a quivering hound straining at his leash, and now that they were finally on their way, the lad looked happy enough to burst, commenting that wasn't it right fine, wonderful even, to be back home? Matthew couldn't but agree. Despite a recent spell of cold weather, the trees were still in leaf, and he smiled at the sight of bright yellow chestnut leaves, the odd deep red maple, and the carpet of colours at their feet. So much space, so much air...

Samuel urged his horse into a gallop, charged off down the path, and by the time Matthew and Alex caught up with him, he was already busy starting a fire, the horse hobbled to the side.

They'd just finished their supper when one of their horses nickered, and from the track came a responding neigh. Matthew and Samuel were on their feet, muskets in hand and eyes fixed on the path, when a group of men materialised from the surrounding dusk.

It was not an agreeable meeting: on one side, a troop of militia, tired, dirty men longing for home and feather beds, hot stews and welcoming wives; on the other, Matthew Graham, his wife and son.

"Ah, Matthew Graham himself," one of the horsed men said, shifting his eyes to rest with obvious dislike on Alex.

"Bloody hell, Richard Campbell in the flesh," Alex mumbled, looking at the minister as if she hoped to incinerate him with the weight of her gaze. Unfortunate that she hadn't, Matthew reflected some minutes later, after listening to a diatribe concerning the perfidy of Catholics in general and of minister-killing ones in particular.

"You were there, were you?" Alex said.

"No," Richard answered, "but I've heard all the relevant facts."

"Oh, like Gregor Macpherson bashing our son-in-law in the head with a plank and laughing as he pushed him inside the burning house?" Most of the men looked away, there was a lot of shifting in the saddles, here and there disapproving murmurs. "Brave of him," Alex added. "And how in line with the Scriptures. Tell me, Minister, what Bible verses might dear Gregor have based his actions on?"

"For shame!" the minister spat out. "He's dead!"

"He is? And where is his body?" Matthew asked, deciding to step in before Alex managed to ignite the very short fuse of this particular minister.

"Gone. Sunk into the sea, buried in a pit, burnt to cinders – by your daughter."

"Oh aye? And you have met many carrying women that can take on a man the size of Minister Macpherson?"

A suppressed gust of laughter ran through the men. What a ridiculous thought!

"Carrying?" Alex gasped. "Was Sarah pregnant?"

"Not now," Matthew said.

She snapped her mouth shut, and Richard Campbell smirked.

The men dismounted and began preparing their food. Matthew steered Alex to sit outside their circle, and motioned for Samuel to join them. They sat in a tight huddle, cloaks and blankets shared for warmth, and listened to Richard Campbell's never-ending sermon – now an explicit description of the sinful nature of women.

"I don't like him," Samuel said. "Too fond of the sound of his own voice."

"What did I ever see in him?" Matthew groaned, thinking back to a long gone summer when he'd invited Richard Campbell to his home, thereby causing one of the more serious rifts in his marriage with Alex.

"An opportunity for self-flagellation?" Alex suggested, and Matthew was glad she couldn't make out his face in the dark. She was right: it was all on account of a wet night down at Mrs Malone's – that and a light-fingered whore who almost enticed him to bed. Alex leaned back against him, tilted her head back to look him in the face. "Pregnant?"

"Aye." Matthew sighed. "Julian told me. The printer – Mr Nuthead – was sure she was two or three months gone." So now it wasn't only Michael and Sarah with wee Joshua. Now there was an unborn wean as well.

Chapter 40

Samuel rode several yards ahead of them. Repeatedly, he looked back at them, urging them wordlessly to hurry, not dawdle. Equally often, his dark brows pulled together in a frown when Matthew refused to urge his horse into anything more than a sedate trot.

"Oouff," Alex protested when he did, and so they fell back into a walk, and Samuel groaned out loud. Finally, their son couldn't stand it anymore, and, with one hasty wave, he set off, ignoring his father's shouted reprimand.

By the time Matthew and Alex reached the top of their lane, the welcoming committee was already there. Their grandchildren ran barefoot around them, calling loudly for them as they rode down to the yard. October sunshine gilded the damp cobbles, it shone on Betty's red-brown fuzz, glinted in surprising flashes of chestnuts in both Mark's and Ian's wavy, dark hair, and splintered like ice shards on the silver pin in Mrs Parson's collar.

Matthew handed Alex down, and she just stood there, overcome by emotions. They were all alive. Hastily, she counted the flock of children. Yes, all five of Ian's, all five of Mark's, and there was Agnes with little Judith and an unknown baby in her arms. Naomi was laughing and crying while Betty was just crying, and Mark had Alex in his arms, swept her round and round until her cap came loose.

Mark set her back down, and Alex's eyes flew to Ian, took in that he was using his cane, favouring his right side. What she wanted to do was to rush to his side, bully him inside, and check how his back was doing. What she did do was smile, eyes promising him she'd be by later to talk to him, alone.

"Nice pin," she said to Mrs Parson.

"It'll do." Mrs Parson nodded, peppercorn eyes as sharp as always.

Alex kissed her on the soft, wrinkled skin of her cheek. She sniffed, relaxing at the familiar scents of mints and wool, of pie crusts and beef stew.

"From Thomas?" she asked, poking at the pretty piece of jewellery.

Mrs Parson's eyes glittered mischievously. "I was definitely worth it."

"You, old woman, you're a veritable maneater, you are."

"Och aye, but they don't complain. It seems they like it, no?" Mrs Parson flicked at the end of her collar that had dared lift itself from its preordained position.

"Men are simple creatures." Alex winked, and they both laughed. Then Alex cried a bit, relieved to find Mrs Parson still here, still alive. "I've missed you," she said, now very serious.

"Every day, lass. Not one single evening without praying that you might come back to me." The black eyes misted with uncharacteristic emotion, and then Matthew was there, loudly demanding a hug from the old woman.

Alex just held him. For a long, long time, she held Ian, listening to the sounds he made: his breathing, his pulse, the slight creaking when he shifted his weight. Her hands roved over his arms, his chest. She fingered the buttons of his everyday coat; she brushed at a spot of mud on his sleeve; and finally, she allowed herself to finger-comb his hair, trace the lines of cheek and nose, his chin, his ears.

And Ian, well, he did the same, his hands flowing over her limbs, touching her hair, her face. His exhalations tickled her skin, and still she clung, the frozen weight that had lain deep inside her gut since the day she'd boarded the *Diane* at last beginning to thaw. Jesus, how she had missed them, each and every one of them, but Ian, her Ian, most of all. They shared a swift, wry smile, silently recognising the dependency between them.

"Your back," she said, and Ian made an irritated face.

It was all this riding, he explained. Since late spring, he and Mark had crossed the colony ten, nay twenty times, searching for their sister. Twice, they had almost caught up with them, once on an isolated little farm down on the eastern side, once on a dilapidated plantation north-west of St Mary's City. Both times, the militia had beat them to it, arriving a day or so before, enough that Sarah and her family had to flee, melting away into woods and marshland.

"Let me see," Alex said, and Ian stripped off coat and shirt, loosened his breeches, and lay down on the kitchen table. Betty joined them, and together they inspected Ian's back, with Alex digging in a knuckle here or there, occasionally making Ian yelp.

"We think they're attempting to make their way north, to here," Ian told her, before saying something very foul when her elbow was driven into the sore trigger points of his gluteus.

Matthew sat down on a stool by the table, rested his hand briefly on his son's shoulder, and nodded for him to continue.

"It makes sense for Sarah to come here when her own home was burnt to ashes," Ian said.

"Aye," Mark broke in, coming in through the door. "But the militia commanders are not complete fools, and so they've kept themselves very close, always on the lookout." He frowned, recounting in a few terse words a recent acrimonious encounter, further inflamed by the fact that the Chisholm brothers − papists as was their whole extended family − were riding with them. "They've been very helpful, the Chisholms, searching almost as much as we ourselves have. And Qaachow is looking too − he promised he would when we ran into him some weeks ago."

"She's with child." Ian sighed, and they were all quiet, contemplating how difficult it must be to be on the run with a growing child in your belly.

"They sold Pegasus," Mark went on. "We found him stabled just outside Providence some months ago. We bought him back." Not, from the expression on Mark's face, a voluntary sale, but at least Michael's flamboyant piebald stallion would be waiting for him when they came home – if they came home. Alex had finished with Ian's back, leaving it a glowing bright red.

"So they did make it some way north," she said, "seeing as you found the horse in Providence."

"Mmm." Ian nodded from under the folds of his shirt. "But, since then, we haven't heard anything of them." His head popped out through the collar. "Mayhap they're making for Virginia."

"Virginia? Are you daft?" Mrs Parson snorted loudly. "Anyone not Anglican receives a cold welcome there, and 'tis a very long walk, no?"

"Catholics are not much welcomed anywhere," Mark reminded her.

"That's as it should be," Mrs Parson said. "Popery cannot be condoned, what with its love of pomp and flair." Alex glared at her, making Mrs Parson shrug.

"You know I love the lass and her husband, just as I loved the wee priest. But that is despite of, aye?" She went back to the striped stockings she was knitting, her needles flying back and forth. "No great loss, though, yon fat minister, I mean." She calmly met Alex's eyes. "We all know that Sarah wouldn't hesitate if it came to defending her own." She shifted her eyes to Matthew for an instant, and then looked back at Alex. "Has it from her mother."

Ian and Mark broke out in a loud coughing fit while Matthew's long mouth curved into a proud smile.

Despite the chafing, constant worry for Sarah, it was wonderful to be home. Alex woke after that first night in their bedchamber, in their own bed, taking in every familiar aspect of the room: the row of pegs that held their clothes, the simple chest, the dressing table with its looking glass and, hanging over the mirror frame, her various garters and ribbons, surprisingly garish in a room otherwise very plain – well, with the exception of the window, of course.

She craned her head back to properly see it, the squares

of coloured panes inset as a border around the plain glass, and, as she watched, the sun rose, filling the room with red light, with shards of green. She shifted, and a cloud of dust motes swirled upwards to be trapped in all that colourful light, and Alex hugged herself with joy at being back.

Matthew rolled towards her, warm with sleep, and she nestled back against him. He made a series of interrogating noises, large hands stroking her shift higher and higher up her legs while he undulated against her. How many mornings in her life had started like this, she thought, beginning a half-hearted calculation. Many, many, she concluded, and pushed her arse closer to him, sighing contentedly when he slid himself in place, still half asleep behind her back.

Alex spent the morning rediscovering her home: the stables and the barn, the well-filled storage sheds, the smoking shed, the bunker-like root cellar where she spent a happy hour communing with her vegetables. She walked up to inspect the kitchen garden, chatting companionably with her three eldest girl grandchildren, Hannah, Maggie and Lettie, and, in less than half an hour, she was up to date on all the gossip in the neighbourhood, including a detailed description of Adam Leslie's wedding. Apparently, Thomas' son had acquired quite the drab little bride.

"Quite ugly," Hannah informed her.

"Very," Maggie agreed.

"But nice all the same," Lettie added, "and when she smiles, she sparkles, like."

The two elder girls agreed. The new Mrs Leslie might be short and round, with mousy hair and pudgy hands, but she did have a very nice smile. They sat together on the garden bench, sharing a few late raspberries, but Alex wasn't really listening, her eyes on Samuel who was moving down to the river. As if he'd felt her eyes on him, he turned and waved. She waved back, disconcerted to see him in buckskins and moccasins.

"Is he really half Indian?" Nine-year-old Maggie watched her uncle with awe.

"Of course not," Alex told her. "Does Grandda look Indian to you?"

Maggie considered this for some time. "No, but Samuel does."

Yes, he does, Alex agreed silently, and look how eager he is to be off, to find his foster family.

She was sitting in the little graveyard, speaking to Jacob, when Matthew came to find her. At first, she'd felt ridiculous, the habit of talking to her dead son broken by these long months away from him, but after a few minutes, it was like it always was, a long, detailed monologue of life down here so that Jacob should be properly informed.

"Hi," she said when she saw him, wiping at her wet cheeks.

"Hi, yourself." He settled her gently, but insistently, on his lap.

"He's gone," she said, tugging at the lacings of his shirt.

"Jacob?" He glanced at the headstone.

"Samuel," she clarified. "No sooner did we get here and he took off."

"I said he could," Matthew told her. "Is that why you've been crying?"

Alex hitched her shoulders. Partly. "I still sometimes forget that he's dead. I keep on hoping he'll pop up, that suddenly I'll hear his voice, his laughter on the wind."

"And don't you?" He did, he said: often he could swear he heard Jacob, or saw him, tall and fair, striding across the furthest fields.

"Yes, at times I do, and it makes me so happy – for like a microsecond, before I recall that he's dead."

"He isn't dead. He lives in our heads and our hearts."

"Not enough," Alex said dejectedly. "Not at all enough."

Samuel slunk in at dawn a week later, and it took but a look at his face to have both Matthew and Alex leaping out of bed.

"What?" Alex said.

"Sarah," Samuel explained thriftily.

"Sarah?" Alex quavered, and Samuel assured her his sister and her family were well enough but that they should make haste.

"On foot?" Matthew asked, already belting his breeches in place.

No, Samuel replied, they'd need horses.

Ian was already in the stables, seeing to the beasts. "I'll ride with you," he offered, helping Matthew saddle the horses.

"It's rough going," Samuel said.

Ian nodded angrily. "Aye, the resident cripple has to watch his every step."

Something flickered in Samuel's eyes, and he raised his right arm as high as it would go, which wasn't far.

Ian smiled ruefully. "Two cripples, then."

For two days straight, they rode. After a short night's rest, Samuel insisted they had to push on, and in the cold dawn, they set off, this time over ground so rough it made more sense to walk and lead the horses than actually ride. Alex had never seen a forest this thick. Impenetrable, it rose around them, all of it conifers that effectively shut out most of the daylight. Their footsteps were muffled by the deep carpet of pine needles. On occasion, they heard the far-off chattering of a bird, but mostly it was silent, a threatening, unwelcoming silence.

Abruptly, they stumbled back into the light, entering a small clearing in which stood an Indian village. From nowhere, Thistledown appeared, gesturing for Alex to come, to hurry. After a quick look at Matthew, Alex followed Thistledown into the closest longhouse.

She was unharmed, alive. Alex released a pent-up breath, bit her cheek to stop herself from bawling with relief. Her Sarah was fast asleep, thick blond hair plastered to her forehead. In a soiled chemise, with a newborn child in her arms, she looked a battered Virgin Mary, down to the straw bedding. Alex stroked her daughter's face, and eased the baby out of Sarah's protective hold. Blue eyes flew open, a hand groped for a knife, something to defend herself with.

"Sarah?" Alex made a series of soothing noises. "It's me, honey, it's Mama." With a strangled sound, Sarah hid her face in Alex's lap.

"A son," she croaked a bit later, lying with her eyes closed while Alex stroked her over her back.

"I know." Alex smiled. "I checked."

Sarah yawned. "His name is Matthew. Had it been a lass, it would have been an Alexandra."

"Poor child," Alex murmured, and Sarah laughed.

She grew serious, heaved herself up to sit. "Michael is ailing, and I don't know what to do."

Matthew watched Alex duck into the longhouse, and followed his son to where Samuel's foster father stood waiting.

"Qaachow." Matthew greeted the Indian chief cordially, receiving a slight smile in reply. "My daughter?" he asked, his eyes alighting on the wee white toddler standing forlornly to the side. The laddie was pale, there were hollows under his eyes, and snot hung from his nose, had crusted on his cheeks.

"Alive," Qaachow answered, "as is her husband and son." He indicated the bairn presently sucking its thumb.

"How?" Matthew asked.

Qaachow smiled again. The girl had walked straight out into the wilderness, calling loudly for Qaachow at regular intervals. He propelled Matthew in the direction of the little lad, who raised grey eyes to the stranger. Warily, the laddie backed away.

Matthew crouched down. "Joshua," he said, and the lad froze at his name. "Come here, come to me, aye?" Joshua regarded him from beneath a fringe of curling chestnut hair. When Matthew smiled and opened his arms, Joshua sidled towards him.

The lad had not said a word nor unplugged his thumb. But he softened in Matthew's embrace, sliding into a boneless sleep. Matthew didn't dare to move, despite his uncomfortable position, and so the short afternoon slid into dusk, and still Matthew sat outside, cradling his grandchild to his heart. Qaachow appeared and beckoned him inside, and after a few attempts, Matthew rose, carrying Joshua into the warm longhouse.

It was a relief to sit down by the fire, extend cramped legs to allow blood to surge through them.

"Da?" Samuel stopped a few yards away, and in his arms was a bairn. "My daughter, Karen-do-uah," Samuel presented, and in his eyes stood a naked need that Matthew somehow approve.

"Your daughter?" Matthew placed Joshua on the pelt beside him.

Samuel nodded, setting down the little lass so that she stood unsteadily on her own, albeit with a firm grip on Samuel's leggings.

Matthew studied the bairn. "Bonny." He made an effort to sound pleased.

"Like her mother," Samuel said.

Matthew groaned inside: his son, still a bairn himself, and now he was the father of an Indian lass.

"Have you told your mama?"

Samuel shook his head in a no. He'd wanted Da to be the first to know.

Matthew smiled at his touching pride. "And now what?" he asked gently.

Samuel's hazel eyes clouded over. "I don't know. I have no obvious place here, among my Indian brethren, not now that I'm no longer whole, but Chee-na-wan, my woman, she would die if we were to live at Graham's Garden."

"Ah." It would sort itself, Matthew decided. He had no energy to spend on this particular problem right now. To his surprise, when Alex joined them, she agreed. She inspected the robust lassie with far more enthusiasm than he had been able to muster, and told Samuel not to worry overmuch about the future.

"What can I say?" she said when Matthew pressed her on this. "The girl's there and by his own reckoning he's a man, and men have to take responsibility for their own lives, right?"

"And women don't?" he teased.

"Of course we do! My point was rather that he'll have to make his own way in the world, and we can but support him in his choices, not make them for him."

"Uh," Matthew grunted, and then went on to ask Alex about Sarah and this new namesake of his. Alex replied distractedly, and finally Matthew caught on to the fact that something was worrying her. "What?" he asked, taking her hand.

"I think Michael has pneumonia," Alex confided in an undertone.

"I stay," Samuel said two days later.

Alex nodded, far too concerned about Michael's state of health to care. She smiled at the Indian girl who was the mother of little Karen. So young, she sighed inside. If she was a day over sixteen, that was about it. Bloody Qaachow! She sent a flaming look in the chief's direction, was met by two calm, dark eyes in which she could read a silent joy at this turn of events. Samuel was now tied to his Indian tribe – forever.

"Make sure you're back for Christmas," she said, and went over to ensure her son-in-law was properly bedded down on the primitive stretcher.

"Will he be alright?" Sarah hovered like a huge, enervating fly around Alex.

"Of course he will," Alex assured her.

Michael coughed, a barking, sore sound that made Alex wince.

Chapter 41

"Measles?" Alex voice slid up an octave, ending in a painful squeak. Joshua had developed a fever a day or so after they'd returned home from the Indian village.

Mrs Parson inspected Joshua's throat yet again, and nodded. "I'm afraid so."

Alex drew in some badly needed air. "If he has it, then—" She half stood, sat back down, stood, and stared at Mrs Parson. "The children!" Over Joshua's bed, she met Matthew's eyes, saw her fears replicated in them. Oh God! None of them had had the measles.

"Poor laddie." Mrs Parson wiped Joshua's face. "He's in a bad state. The fever is burning him up, and to hear it his head hurts something frightful, no?"

Alex just nodded. Joshua kept up a constant crying whenever he was awake, which wasn't too often.

Alex sank down on a stool. "What have I done? I had no idea Michael might have the measles."

"Nor did he," Mrs Parson patted Alex on the arm. "And how were you to know? He was well past the measles when you brought him in." She frowned in the direction of the little room further down the hall from which a constant coughing emanated. "He's not mending much, is he?"

"No." Despite hourly infusions of liquorice root, aniseed and fennel, Michael's lungs remained congested. But at present, Alex was far more worried about Joshua than about his father. "We have to get word to Qaachow," she said to Matthew, "and to Samuel."

"I'll go myself." Matthew stood up. "I'll go immediately." She didn't want him to, but there was no one else to send, not with all the children potentially infected. Ian and Mark had to stay home, be there, should their children sicken. So all she did was nod, clasping his hand in a wordless farewell.

The coming days passed in a horrible blur. One by one, the children succumbed to the measles, and if Alex wasn't spooning honeyed water into one sore throat after the other, she was steeping willow tea, or washing clouts, or comforting the mothers.

Joshua was not getting better. In a matter of days, his baby cheeks melted away, the bright chestnut hair was constantly damp with sweat, and only rarely was he lucid enough to recognise the person sitting by his bed. Mostly, that person was Sarah, her son's hand held in hers as she whispered stories to him, or sang, or just sat beside him.

"He's dying, isn't he?" Alex asked Mrs Parson halfway through yet another night of vigil.

"Aye. Poor laddie, no?"

Poor mother, Alex thought, poor father.

It took Alex and Mark to separate Sarah from her dead boy. For hours, she'd screamed at them, telling them this was all a mistake – look at him, he was but sleeping. Finally, Alex forcibly unclenched Sarah's fingers from Joshua's nightshirt, and Mark dragged a keening Sarah out of the room, hushing her as they went. The silence in her wake was like balm to Alex's frayed nerves. For a long time, she sat by Joshua, staring unseeing at the dark of the night outside.

What with a household full of sick children, the trauma of Joshua's death and her own exhaustion, Alex hadn't really noticed Matthew's absence. Not until he appeared in the kitchen doorway did it strike her just how much she'd missed him, needed him, over the last few days. He looked as tired as she felt, his normally so bright eyes opaque under brows pulled together in a concerned frown.

"Joshua?" He kicked off his muddy boots. He must have ridden like the wind to make it to Qaachow's village and back in five days. Had he even slept?

"Dead." The calm Alex had worked so hard to uphold began to shatter. "Dear God," she groaned, sitting down with a thud on one of the kitchen benches. She looked across the table at Matthew. "Lettie and Rosie aren't that ill, and

I think Grace and Christopher will recover. But Timothy..."
And Joshua, already coffined and waiting to be buried.

Matthew took her hand. "You couldn't do more than you did."

Alex laughed hollowly. Do? All she'd done was sit beside the boy trying to soothe and comfort both him and a frantic Sarah. And now the baby was ill as well, but not too badly, and Alex was convinced he'd live, protected by the miracles of breast milk. She said as much, and Matthew closed his eyes, lips moving in soundless prayer.

"The Indians?" Alex asked, and Matthew exhaled, muttering it was in the hands of the Lord.

"Half of the village is ailing," he said, but hastened to reassure her that little Karen was already over the worst. He took her hand. "And Michael?"

Alex shrugged. She was filled with draining weariness at the thought of rising and going to check on him.

"Not much better," Mrs Parson said, "and it didn't help to hear that wee Joshua was dead."

Alex sighed. "I have to talk to Sarah. She hasn't been in to see Michael once these last few days." She rubbed her hands up and down her thighs a couple of times in preparation of making the effort to stand.

"Nay, lass, I'll go," Matthew said.

Sarah was sitting in bed, mechanically holding the wean to her breast while her head was populated by images of her Joshua.

"He's dead," she said when Da entered the room.

"He is." Da sat down beside her.

"Measles," Sarah went on dully. "His father gave him the measles, and then he died."

"Sarah." Da lifted the babe out of her rigid hold, placed him on the bed beside them, and took her by the hands. "Look at me, Sarah." Sarah stared straight through him, enclosed in a bubble of rage and grief. "Michael isn't to blame."

"Then who?" Sarah asked. "At whom do I rage for the death of my lad?"

339

"At God? At fate? But not at him, not at the man who wallows in guilt and thereby hovers uncomfortably close to death's door himself." Sarah moaned at that. She tried to twist her hands free, but Da wouldn't let go. "Your mama tells me you've refused to see him."

She'd been with Joshua, and then she hadn't wanted to, punishing him for the death of their son by her absence from his bedside.

"Don't you think you should?" Da pushed.

Sarah broke eye contact.

"And if he dies too, Sarah? What then? If he dies, and you haven't said a kind word to him, held his hand, how will you ever go on?"

"Will he die?" Sweetest Virgin! What was she doing?

"I don't know. Mayhap. He's right poorly."

Sarah reached for her infant, hid her face against the swaddled body. She attempted to stand, wanting nothing but to run and hide.

Da put a restraining hand on her arm. "Michael."

She nodded, clasped little Matt for protection, and followed him to the room in which Michael lay.

The first thing that struck her was how wasted he looked – she'd never noticed before how big his nose was. He coughed, a heavy, liquid sound that left him gasping for breath. He coughed again, and struggled to sit, mouth wide open as he drew in lungful after lungful of air. He saw her, his eyes filled for a moment with light and hope before dulling back to the colour of slate.

He sank down on the pillows, turning his face away from her as he wiped at his damp, sweaty hair. Sarah's guts twisted at the despondency in his gesture. She crossed the few feet to his bed and placed his baby son in his arms, realising with a start that so far he had never held the wean.

"Hold him while I fetch some hot water to wash you with." She bent down and brushed her lips against his feverish brow. "You don't die on me as well, you hear?" she said fiercely.

Michael smiled, for the first time in a very long time.

"I wouldn't dare." The smile wobbled, the corners of his mouth turned down, and he closed his eyes. "Joshua," he said in a thread of a voice, "our Joshua."

She didn't fetch water. Instead, she crawled into the bed, and they clung to each other, neither of them saying anything.

It was all Matthew could do to remain standing by Alex's side when Richard Campbell rode down his lane some days later, jutting jaw set in a grin. He was accompanied by a small troop of militiamen, most of whom had the grace to look discomfited at disrupting wee Joshua's burial. Not so Richard Campbell who after a cursory look at the small coffin, dismounted.

"We have come for her." Richard pointed at Sarah.

Matthew raised his brows at this blatant discourtesy. "And good day to you too, Minister Campbell," he said, having the satisfaction of seeing the wee man flush – not a pleasing sight, all in all, given his general colouring.

The minister mumbled a greeting and repeated that he was here to take Sarah with him.

"Aye well. She's a trifle busy at the moment – burying a child, no less." Only one, thank the Lord. The wean had recovered and was presently fast asleep in his mother's arms.

"Some God smites immediately." Richard nodded.

"Smites? For what? For having her home burnt to the ground by a rabid mob?" Alex sounded as if she wanted to kick Campbell. Out of sheer precaution, Matthew placed himself between them.

"You know well enough what I'm referring to," Richard said. "She killed a man."

Sarah shrank back, shaking her head so hard she dislodged one of her braids, a heavy rope of golden hair sliding down her neck before she got hold of it and shoved it back under her cap.

"She did? So where is your proof?" Matthew succeeded in keeping his voice calm.

"Proof? We all know she did it, and now she comes with us."

"I think not," Matthew said.

"She is to be tried for murder."

"And so you will tell me the date and place and I will bring her myself. But I won't entrust her to you."

"And how do we know you won't spirit her away?" Richard sneered.

"Are you casting aspersions on my honour?" Matthew said through his teeth. He used all of his six feet and some to loom over the wee man.

"No, no," Richard retreated, "of course not."

"Good. Get you gone then." Matthew crossed his arms over his chest, and watched them ride off.

"They can't prove anything," Thomas Leslie said that same evening, sucking at his pipe. "They already know that."

"Aye, and that in itself has me worried." Matthew made sure neither Alex nor Sarah were within earshot before continuing. "It makes me suspect that Richard Campbell has something up his sleeve."

"Simon eats men like Richard Campbell for breakfast," Thomas scoffed, "so it's nothing you need to be too concerned about."

Matthew nodded slowly. His brother-in-law was impressive in the courtroom. He shifted his shoulders and sat back, feeling somewhat reassured. Thomas moved the conversation to the sad state of affairs in England instead, with one former king still at large, and a new king firmly in place.

"The Jacobites were destroyed at Dunkeld," Thomas was saying when Alex joined them. "God knows how many dead, and since then the Highlanders have melted away into their hills. Ah well, at least that rebellion is truly crushed."

"You think?" Alex asked derisively. "You don't think France and Spain have an interest in upending that particular apple cart?"

Thomas blew a smoke ring at her. "Of course they do. And things are further complicated by the little boy, the former prince."

Alex nodded. "Ah yes. The Stuart heir."

"William and Mary may yet have a child of their own," Thomas said, "and if so, that child is just as much a Stuart."

Matthew threw his wife a cautionary look. As she told it, neither Mary nor her sister Anne would leave heirs of their body, thereby opening the field for the future Stuart Pretenders. But best not share that with Thomas, however close a friend he was. Alex caught his glance, stuck her tongue out, and moved closer to the light of the fire.

"Was it as you expected?" Thomas asked, accepting a refill to his brandy.

"Hmm?"

"Going back home," Thomas clarified.

Matthew looked over to where Alex was sitting, ostensibly focused on her sewing. He smiled to himself. He could swear the tips of her ears twitched in his direction.

"Yes and no. Aye, because the land was the same." He looked away, engulfed by memories of Hillview, his place. Softly, he sighed, keeping a wary look on Alex's back.

Thomas leaned forward, the emigrant's eternal longing for what he'd left behind written plainly on his face. "Was it not wonderful to stand again in the land of your birth?"

"Aye, that it was." Matthew sipped at his brandy, trying to find words to fit to his feelings. "But it was mine no longer, and while there, I yearned for here." His hand stroked the armrest on his chair, the smooth, well-worn oak soft as silk beneath his fingers. "And I missed you," he grinned, breaking the maudlin mood, "although you've been keeping yourself right busy elsewhere."

Alex snorted with laughter, and Thomas gave them both an aggrieved look before meeting Mrs Parson's eyes.

"Don't mind them," Mrs Parson told him. "They're just jealous." She stood, and with her rose that impressive chest, highlighted in white against the starkness of her dark bodice. Matthew watched, amused, when Thomas automatically rose.

"A slice of pie?" Mrs Parson suggested, batting her eyelashes.

"A slice would be nice." Thomas followed her like a lapdog out of the room.

"Pie, my arse." Alex did some adequate batting of her own. "Bath?" she purred.

"You planned this," Matthew said when he opened the door to the laundry shed. A fire had been laid and lit beneath the cauldron, there was a stack of towels on the bench, and the huge tub had been scrubbed, smelling of rosemary and mints.

"I thought we needed it," she said, her shoulders rounding.

"Aye, we do." What with Sarah and the baby, Joshua and the measles, there had been very little time for them.

Matthew filled the tub, stripped and got in, his breath hitching when the hot water made contact with his skin. With a grunt, he sat down and leaned back, watched through the vapours as she undressed, shaking out her garments before folding them together. She pinned her hair up on the top of her head, shimmied out of her shift, and poked a toe into the water.

"Shit! It's like being boiled alive!" But she slid down, inch by inch, and with a little sigh, reclined against the tub, all but her face submerged.

"Do you think you could drown like this?" she said drowsily a while later.

"I think you'd wake up." Matthew studied the way her breasts floated, the nipples like dark islands just breaking the surface. His member floated as well at first, but then it took on a life of its own, rising strong and taut from his loins. He cupped himself, caressed the stalk of his cock, its swollen head. It quivered, telling him loudly it didn't want his hand – it wanted her, her secret places, moist and welcoming.

Matthew stood, and the water sluiced down his body. Alex opened an eye, smiled at his arousal, and extended her hand.

"Help me up," she said. They made it over to the broad bench, Matthew piled discarded clothes, quilts and towels into some sort of bed, and turned to face her, only to be pushed to sit, with her kneeling before him. Dearest Lord! Matthew leaned back against his arms, and all over his lap her hair spilled, tickling him with the wet ends. He strained upwards, buttocks bunching. Her tongue, her fingers, and all that hair... Matthew was awash with sensations, his toes curled, his thighs hardened.

"No!" Matthew gasped. "Not yet." He tugged at her. She rose to kiss his mouth. When he gripped her arse, she straddled him, and she laughed at his attempts to pull her down to meet his eager cock. Slowly, she undulated, teasing him. He took a firm hold of her hips and guided her into place.

"Don't move," he whispered, brushing a long, damp tendril of hair off her face. "I just want to sit like this for a while." She did as he asked, remaining immobile as he stroked her back, her arms, the roundness of her buttocks. His woman, his heart.

Carefully, he rolled them over, and for an instant, they were both precariously balanced on the edge of the bench before he had her safely on her back, still with his cock inside. He moved, slowly, flexing his hips. She exhaled, lifted her hips to meet his thrusts. Slowly, so very slowly, each grinding movement accompanied by soft sighs, by whispered nothings. Her eyes never left his, her hands caressed his back, his arms. A wet mouth trailed kisses up his arm, she rose slightly to claim his mouth, and he bent to meet her. Such soft lips, such a warm, welcoming mouth. His Alex, now shifting restlessly below him, demanding with her body and her eyes that he ride her to completion. So he did, increasing pace and force until she gasped his name, head thrown back in abandon. His Alex, his woman... Aaah! With a rush, he came, burying his cock deep inside her.

Much later, they lay curled together in their bed, hair damp, bodies liberally oiled. The house was silent around them, populated by the ghosts of the missing just as much as by the living. They had spent the last hour talking about Adam and David, had discussed Samuel for a while, and had shared stories of Jacob and Rachel, small anecdotes they both knew by heart and that still, at each retelling, brought them back alive.

"At least we have stories to tell." Alex sighed against his shoulder.

"All parents have stories to tell of their bairns, no matter how brief their time on earth."

"I didn't even know Joshua," Alex said. "I met him three, no, four times, and now he's dead."

"A bonny, brave laddie," Matthew whispered to the air. "I hope Rachel won't bully him as she was wont to do with Jacob."

"Yes, she was quite a minx at times." Alex laughed. "Remember when she convinced him to crawl into the privy to look for her dropped doll?" She shook her finger at the ceiling. "Behave, honey," she said sternly.

Aye, lassie, Matthew smiled, be good to wee Joshua. In reply, he heard Rachel's tinkling, teasing laughter.

Well after midnight, and Matthew was asleep on his side. Alex slipped out of bed and went over to the window, struggling to get it open without making too much noise. It was a clear night, with star-studded skies that invited wolves to raise their snouts and howl at the glory of it all. A full winter moon hung just above the treeline, and the yard below lay bathed in its silver sheen. A night of magic, of elves and little folk – except, of course, that Mrs Parson firmly insisted they hadn't crossed the sea nor ever planned to, and so this brave new world might have Indians and spirits of its own, but elves and fairies, goblins and trolls, they had been forever left behind.

Alex rested her chin in her hand, and inhaled the cold, crisp air. A star shot from the firmament, left a wake of glittering fire, and was gone. Like a flash in the pan, like all human life – here today, gone tomorrow. Another falling star, and Alex splayed her hand and pretended she could catch it, hold it safe against her heart, and cup all that fragile, ephemeral life. A single tear trickled down her cheek, others followed, and she gripped the sill and wept quietly, the brilliance of the night sky blurry with her tears.

A sudden gust of wind cooled her face and, after a couple of steadying breaths, she wiped her eyes with her sleeve. The moon slid behind a screen of clouds, but she found the North Star, blew a kiss to her father and one more for Isaac. The image of her angry, hurting son rose before her, and he was screaming that it wasn't fair – he didn't want to die, not here, not now.

"Life isn't fair," she whispered to the night. Another star blazed a trail through the dark, and Alex closed her eyes and made a wish. For Isaac, for her firstborn, that he be at peace, safe in heaven with his Offa.

Something skittered over the ground, paused for a frozen instant, and turned goggled eyes to stare in her direction before leaping onto the smoking shed roof.

"Horrible pests," Alex muttered, but with no real heat. "You get at my ham and I'll blast you to pieces." The raccoon sat outlined against the moon, and for a moment Alex was convinced it was indeed an elf, a wood sprite from a distant, long-lost shore. A series of jumps, and the racoon melted into the silent forest. Alex closed the window. Matthew rolled towards her when she got back into bed, opening his arms to gather her to him. "Mmhmm?"

"Nothing." She patted him. "Let's sleep, okay?"

Chapter 42

The three Chisholm brothers rode in a fortnight before Christmas, complete with four mounted men and a jittery messenger.

"We found him some miles off," Robert Chisholm said, "so we suggested we ride together." He flashed a wicked grin at the Providence man. "I'm sure your eternal soul won't be permanently tarnished for having spent an hour in the company of papists."

The messenger seemed not to agree, drew himself up to his full, not so considerable, height, and produced a letter that he handed to Matthew.

"Summons for the murderess." He was still coughing a few minutes later. He scowled at Matthew and palpated his reddened throat, swallowing a couple of times. "That was uncalled for."

"No more than your name-calling," Matthew bit back, and then jerked his head to show the man it was best he left – now.

The Chisholms had dismounted during the altercation, and now moved forward.

"I'm sorry for your loss," Robert said in a stilted fashion, directing himself to Sarah.

She just nodded, her eyes stuck on one of the men accompanying the brothers. Alex followed her gaze, took in an unsavoury character that sat his mount like a sack of potatoes, had his whole face covered by a gigantic slouch hat, wore a cloak two or three sizes too big, and had a peg leg. A peg leg?

Robert's face broke out in a grin, as did his brothers'. Alex shared a swift look with Sarah, elbowed Matthew hard in the side, and then Sarah was running towards the mule, with Alex following at a more sedate pace.

"You must have a death wish!" Alex exclaimed when Carlos swept the hat off his head. "You're supposed to be in Spain, Carlos Muñoz, not here!" She kept her eyes on Sarah's face, attempting to analyse the expressions that she saw flying across it: surprise, quite a bit of joy, followed by belated awareness that she was now a married woman, and so must not be too effusive. The wide smile dimmed, but the eyes still glistened, and her cheeks shone pink in the December sun, and once Carlos had dismounted, she fell into step beside him, talking in a low, intense tone as they made for where Matthew was standing with the Chisholms.

"So that's the famous Carlos." Michael came to stand beside Alex. His grey eyes flitted from the priest to Sarah and back.

"Famous? More of a fool, if you ask me." Alex smiled affectionately in the direction of Carlos.

"Not to Sarah," Michael said.

"No, not to her." Alex slipped a hand in under Michael's arm, glad to feel the muscle under her touch. "He saved her sanity. When none of us could properly reach her, he could. Somehow, he helped her forgive herself for something that wasn't her fault to begin with." She was uncomfortable discussing this with Michael. It had been his uncles who had abducted Sarah and abused her so vilely, leaving her a pregnant wreck.

"Remind me to thank him properly," Michael said, and every word leaked jealousy, bright green, snarling jealousy. He coughed, hawked and spat, and Sarah wheeled nervously towards him.

"So why?" Alex demanded of Carlos later, switching automatically into Spanish. "*¿Por qué*, Carlos?" They were alone in the kitchen, where Alex had conducted a quick inspection of his stump after Carlos complained that it itched. Of course it did. He hadn't been using oils as he should.

"Someone has to. The Holy See can't leave whole

flocks without a pastor." Carlos watched Sarah through the window.

"Oh, and you volunteered, did you?" Alex nodded in the direction of Sarah.

His cheeks darkened, but he met her gaze calmly. "As a matter of fact, I did, and seeing as I'd already been here, the powers that be found it wise to send me here." He finished strapping the peg back in place, and slid off the table to sit on the bench.

"¡*Dios*!" she exclaimed, ignoring his displeased frown. "You're not only Catholic, you're Spanish! And Spain, as far as I know, refuses to recognise the new King of England—"

"And rightly so! A usurper, a purse-pinching Dutchman abetted by the faithless daughter of an abandoned father!"

"…and so every Spaniard is a spy," Alex finished. She regarded him in silence. The likeness to Isaac was painfully apparent, in everything from how he quirked his mouth to his straight, dark brows.

"He's dead." She hadn't mentioned Isaac to anyone since they got back – with the exception of Ian.

"I know, Matthew told me. Poor Isaac, he must have been so afraid."

Alex nodded, swallowing back on a wave of grief.

Carlos sighed, and leaned back against a non-existent back rest, almost toppling over before regaining his balance. "How serious are these accusations against Sarah?"

"Serious enough," Alex replied, "but I doubt it'll amount to much." December 29 in Providence, and then they'd see.

It was late afternoon before the Chisholms left, even later before Alex had the time to take her planned walk up to the graveyard, accompanied by Ian.

"The Chisholms aim to keep him with them," Ian told Alex, stopping for an instant to take the weight off his right side. He looked gaunt, all those long nights of vigil over his sick children stamped on his face.

"Who? Carlos?" Alex asked, stooping to pick a particularly beautiful sprig of dry leaves.

"Nay, the Pope." Ian used his knife to cut off a branch of hemlock for her, and followed her the last few yards to the graveyard.

Joshua's little mound was still mostly bare earth, but they should be grateful, Alex supposed, that they'd only lost one child. But she didn't voice this out loud, swamped by a superstitious fear that to do so would be to tempt fate, what with Timothy still so weak. Instead, she went about her decoration with brisk efficiency, sweeping away withered wreaths from Joshua's grave and replacing them with her carefully selected leaves, bound together by a faded ribbon. She patted Jacob's stone, hands lingering on his inscribed name. As a final touch, she set down the lantern she'd been carrying with a fat tallow candle in it.

"To light up the dark for them," she said to Ian, placing the light between Joshua and Jacob. And for the four unknown Indian children who had died of the measles. Samuel had come home stricken, telling of a village reeling with loss, and all because Qaachow had shown compassion and generosity towards their Sarah.

"Mmm." Ian nodded.

"Why?" Alex asked.

"Why what?" Ian helped her up, and, for a couple of steps, she limped, her knee protesting.

"Carlos, why keep him?"

"They don't want to do without the services of a priest." The Chisholm settlement was an impressive collection of farms, complete with its own small village containing a blacksmith, a cooper, a miller, and now also an undercover priest. "I dare say Sarah will be pleased," Ian ventured.

Not too much, Alex hoped. She turned to look back up the hill to where the little light twinkled and beckoned like an earthbound star in the winter dusk.

"She liked it that he christened the wean," Ian said, "and she looked very relieved after confession."

Yeah, while poor Carlos had been the colour of old parchment, his dark eyes filming with the effort to seem unconcerned.

"Michael won't be too thrilled." Every time Michael's eyes alighted on Carlos, Alex could see it flaring, a jealousy that ate at him.

"Then he's a fool. Anyone but a man completely blind, deaf and dumb can see how much she loves him."

"You can still be jealous," Alex said, thinking of the complex emotions she experienced whenever she saw Matthew and Kate together.

"How insulting to her and her sense of honour."

Alex smiled. "Or how flattering. Depends on how you see it."

In their little room, Michael lay gasping, with Sarah collapsed on top of him, her long hair veiling them both.

"Wanton," he murmured, and arched his chest against her swollen breasts.

"I just had to," she whispered, embarrassed by her own recent behaviour.

Tired of waiting for him to reclaim her now that Matt was over six weeks old, she had ambushed him on the landing. She sat up, aware of how thin he still was, and flopped over to lie beside him.

He shivered with the sudden cold, and Sarah pulled up quilts and sheets, patted them down around them, and nestled as close to him as she could, realising with a start that this was the first time since their house burnt that they'd lain naked together. He fiddled with her hair, drawing it through his fingers, his eyes lost in the bed hangings.

"I keep on looking for him," he said in a brittle voice. "Every day, I look for him."

Sarah didn't reply, she just kissed his naked shoulder. To her, Joshua was everywhere, a teasing shadow that ducked out of sight whenever she saw him out of the corner of her eye. She'd catch a glimpse of sun on chestnut curls, whirl, and there were only dust motes dancing in the sunlight. Or she'd see him on the far side of the yard, his smock trailing in the dirt as he hunched down over something, and she'd fly towards him, and when she was halfway there, the wind would lift the rag draped over a bucket, and she'd come to a stumbling, breathless stop.

Michael sighed, he half coughed, half sobbed, and Sarah pressed herself even closer.

"We have Matt, and there'll be more." Gently, she tugged at his chestnut hair, cut short during his recent illness. The same colour as Joshua's hair, she reflected.

"But not like him," Michael said.

"No, not like him."

From outside came the sound of bairns playing hide-and-seek in the dark, from below wafted scents of food and pudding, there was an odd burst of laughter, the low rumble of voices, and in their bed Sarah and Michael lay quiet and immobile, listening for the lad who was no longer there.

As they were getting dressed, Michael took hold of Sarah's arm, turning her to face him.

"Carlos." One word, no more, but loaded with insinuations.

"Father Carlos," she corrected with asperity. "He's a priest, Michael."

"More than that," he reproached, and Sarah could feel the heat fly up her cheeks, touch her ears.

"My friend. Do you mind?"

"Yes. I shouldn't, but I do." He finished buttoning his breeches, tightened his belt, and stood waiting while she rearranged her hair, pinned it up, and capped it. "You'll not see him on your own, except for confession, of course."

"I talk to him," she tried, but she knew it was a lost cause.

"You talk to me. Only with me do you share the secrets of your heart." It was a statement, not open for discussion, and Sarah bowed her head in acquiescence.

"He's right," Matthew said once Alex had given him a brief update. Sarah had whispered it to her over the dishes, how Michael would not allow her to speak alone to Carlos. Bright red roses on her cheeks, eyes that flashed kingfisher blue with passion, and Alex had smiled at her daughter, at her obvious pride in that her man should care enough to tell her no, at her equally apparent irritation that he should presume to do so.

"She's a grown woman, old enough to choose her own friends," Alex said.

"She's a wife – his wife – and as he bids her, she must do."

"Huh!" Alex sniffed.

Matthew smiled, made an elegant grab for her, and crushed her, squealing, to his chest. "You do."

"No, I don't, not unless I want to!"

"Fortunate then that you always want what I wish." He swallowed any further protests with his mouth.

"Seriously," he said later, scooping up some of her lotion and rubbing it into his hands, "it's best that she doesn't spend too much time with Carlos."

"Mmm." She set down her tooth twig and reached for her brush, but he beat her to it, drawing it through his own hair before settling down to work his way through hers. "A novel kind of hair shirt," Alex said, recalling the way Carlos' eyes hung on Sarah from the moment she entered a room to when she left it.

"At least it doesn't itch."

"It doesn't? I think it itches like hell – in a place where a priest should preferably not feel any itches at all." She briskly rubbed the lotion into her hands, her neck and face, and sat still while he finished with her hair.

"You need a new shirt," she stated, studying him through the mirror.

"Which is why you have made me one for Christmas," he laughed, tying a neat bow round her braid. He rested his finger on her locket, the one he'd given her some years ago. "And you, what is it you need?"

"Mr Angler himself," she said, but she couldn't stop herself from smiling. She swivelled round to face him, tugging him down to kneel before her so that she could cup his face. "You know, Matthew Graham, that all I ever need is you." She kissed him on his nose, ran her palms over his bristling cheeks. "Always."

"Always." He smiled.

Chapter 43

"On purpose," Alex repeated to the room at large, keeping her frozen backside as close as she could to the fire. "This date, to force us down here in the middle of the winter, it all smells of pettiness." Her whole body creaked in protest after the two and more days of hard riding through the wintry landscape.

"You can't believe that of Minister Walker or Julian." Matthew lowered himself onto an upholstered footstool. He extended his left foot and grimaced. "For a toe no longer there, it can hurt right badly."

Alex knelt and helped him off with his boots, rubbed blood and warmth back into his feet, and sat back on her heels, ignoring the twinge in her knee.

"Not of them perhaps, but definitely of Richard Campbell." She took off her heavy, damp cloak, shook it so as to send droplets of water all over the room, did the same with Matthew's, and spread them both to dry.

"The date was set before the weather turned this cold," Matthew said, "and they did show some consideration. They did allow time for Michael to recover his health."

"Not a trial?" Alex said next morning after having kissed Simon on both cheeks.

"How can it be?" Simon replied. "With no body, no witnesses, nothing but conjecture... I made them see sense on that, at least."

"So then, what's the point?"

"Ah." Simon fussed with his embroidered coat, adjusted his cravat, and inspected his ink-stained fingers before replying. "They might find against her, find reason enough to take it to trial." He looked at her, his light blue eyes bright with intelligence and anticipation. "It's Richard Campbell who's the problem. He and Gregor Macpherson go back a long time, he says, and he won't stand by and not see justice served on his killer." He made a disparaging sound, and patted Alex on the arm.

"Well, they're definitely men of the same ilk," Alex said. "About as much common sense as a frog in a pot." She glanced at Richard Campbell sitting on the opposite side of the room in his customary black garb.

"Frog in a pot?" Simon looked intrigued.

"You know," Alex said. "You place the frog in a pot of cold water, set it over the fire, and the animal will never notice as it's boiled to death."

"Not the most adequate of similes." But Simon's eyes rested for a moment on Richard, as if assessing the size of the pot needed to conduct a little empirical research of his own. "He has something up his sleeve," Simon muttered, a crease forming between his bushy brows.

Now that he mentioned it, Alex couldn't help but agree. Richard Campbell's smile was so wide one could suspect the corners of his mouth met somewhere at the back of his head.

"Ah well, there's a reason why I'm still well remembered in the Edinburgh courts." Simon beamed at Matthew and Alex, settled his long wig on his thinning pate, and went over to escort Sarah into the room.

Sarah looked demure. In grey, with starched apron and cap, a dark shawl over her shoulders, and her hair pinned back, she looked vulnerable, childish almost, where she sat on the stool accorded to her. Only when her eyes alighted on Richard Campbell was there a flash, a bolt of blue anger quickly suppressed. Michael followed her, carrying their baby son, and after a brief pat to her cheek, went to join Alex and Matthew among the spectators.

"It'll be alright," Alex whispered to him, concerned by his pallor. He shouldn't have come, not so recently recuperated from his illness, but Michael had refused to consider that an option. The door behind swung open, and among the men closest to the entrance a bout of elbowing and mumbling broke out, making Betty crane her neck to see.

"The Chisholms!" she hissed, and the whole room watched as the ten-man strong group, headed by Robert, walked down to sit in silent support on the bench behind Matthew.

"And look who's here," Alex muttered to Matthew, indicating the peg leg visible under one long cloak.

The door opened again, and here came the Leslies and the Ingrams, just as openly sitting down with their neighbours and friends, and the men of Providence murmured amongst themselves. And not only their neighbours, because there were Betty's parents, William and Esher Hancock, there was Lionel Smith, James the tailor, Kate Jones and many, many more. All of them were sitting like a bulwark around the Grahams.

"So many friends," Alex murmured to Matthew. "Look around you, Matthew, and count all your friends."

He didn't, he just squeezed her hand, but she saw how touched he was, how furiously he blinked.

Simon stood and in a loud voice demanded that this farce be ended before it began, saying that in his long legal experience, this was the first time he had ever encountered an attempt at accusing someone for murder when there was no corpse.

"Without undeniable evidence that Mr Macpherson is indeed dead, how can anyone be deemed guilty of his murder?" he finished, dusting at his sleeve before standing to the side.

"Are you asking us to believe that Minister Macpherson is alive and well, but chooses not to come forth?" Richard Campbell sneered.

"Stranger things have happened," Simon said. "I for one recall—"

"No, no," Minister Walker interrupted, "we have no time to go into your extensive recollections, Brother Simon. We will keep to the matter in hand."

"As it suits you, Minister." Simon bowed.

Richard Campbell might be a fiery orator, a man

renowned for his uncompromising sermons dripping venom and brimstone, eternal damnation and graphic description of the suffering sinners in hell, but he lacked somewhat in the courtroom. His description of the events as he saw them was incomplete, he reverted to a lot of blustering, and all the time Simon regarded him calmly, a shadow of a smile on his mouth that signalled to the audience just how ridiculous all of this was to him, a man trained in law.

"So, in summary," Simon said at the end, "you expect us to find Sarah Connor guilty of murder because Minister Macpherson was last seen mistreating her husband and pushing him in to roast in his home."

An uneasy ripple ran through the room, a shifting of woollen cloth against hard benches.

"No," Richard Campbell said triumphantly, "I have witnesses."

"Ah." Simon sounded unperturbed. He turned towards the bench, a stern expression on his face. "I would like to point out I haven't been appraised of these witnesses beforehand, which is, of course, in breach of all legalities."

Minister Walker glowered at Richard. "For shame, Brother Richard!"

"No matter," Simon said. "I'm sure I can handle it in my stride."

Richard first brought out a Mrs Mitchell, clearly confused as to why she was there, and quite intimidated by the minister.

"You saw her there, did you not? Saw her hiding the evidence of her crime!" Richard said once Mrs Mitchell had described seeing Sarah in the smouldering embers of her home.

"Her crime?" Mrs Mitchell blinked in surprise. "No, no, Mr Campbell, she was looking to salvage something of her home." She straightened up, and her watering eyes came to rest on a group of young men, among them Isaiah Farrell. "They are the criminals," she said squeakily. "To burn people's home to the ground like that!"

"We're not discussing them! We're discussing her,

a murderess!" Campbell pointed at Sarah, and Alex regretted not having brained him once and for all with her ladle the first time they met.

Mrs Mitchell's eyes grew very round. "She is? Who did she murder, then?"

"No one, Mrs Mitchell," Simon interjected, "but it seems the fact she was wandering around in the ruins of her house is evidence that she did."

"It is? But she was looking for her silver candlesticks." Mrs Mitchell said, and a rustle of laughter flew through the audience.

Then came a boy, who solemnly swore he'd seen Sarah throw something into the river, and Richard Campbell nodded with satisfaction at this undeniable sign of guilt.

"Disposing of incriminating evidence," he said, but the boy blinked and didn't understand.

"So what was she throwing? Bits and pieces of a corpse?" Simon asked scathingly.

"No." The boy fiddled with his hat. "I myself thought it was pebbles."

"Ah." Simon nodded sagely.

"She was weeping, the lady," the boy offered.

"Ah," Simon repeated, and for a moment, his eyes rested on Sarah's head. "Well, she would, wouldn't she? Her home burnt to ashes, her husband seriously hurt..." Simon thanked the boy for his time.

Alex felt herself relax. So far, Richard's witnesses had harmed rather than helped his case. The third witness was brought in, carrying something wrapped in cloth, and Richard seemed to dance on the spot, telling the audience that this was Mr Newby, former neighbour to the accused. Sarah's back tensed, hands tightening on her apron as she ducked her head, hiding her face from everyone. Shit. Alex dragged her attention from her daughter to the witness who produced a badly burnt boot that he'd found in his privy pit.

This, Richard said with a quavering voice, this was dear Gregor's boot, and what further proof did one need than this to see how he had ended his days? The audience leaned forward, staring at the charred piece of leather that was held together only by the sole.

"Gregor's boot? And how exactly can you prove that?" Simon sauntered over to a rigid Sarah, and patted his niece on her shoulder. She straightened up and widened her eyes at the remains of the boot.

"Is this not Gregor's boot?" Richard challenged her.

"I can't say," she answered. "I haven't had cause to study the minister's footwear." The women in the audience tittered nervously. Richard scowled them into silence, his eyes alighting on Patience.

"You recognise it?" he asked her.

Patience hitched her shoulders. "A burnt piece of leather – it could be anyone's."

"Does it have copper nails in a star pattern in the heel?" someone called out. Richard turned the object over, shook out a handkerchief to wipe the heel clean, and nodded. "Then it's the minister's," the voice said. "I set new heels for him some days before he rode out."

"And is it only ministers that get the star?" Simon asked.

The cobbler shrugged. "No, but you must ask for it. Very few do. At least here, in Providence."

The ministers on the bench all looked at Sarah, and, beside her, Alex felt Matthew shift on his seat, his thigh pressing hard into hers.

"So then," Simon resumed, "the boot, it seems, might be Mr Macpherson's – might be. But have you proof of how it got into the privy?"

"No, but it's no stretch of mind. The privies abut each other, and where else to dispose of something this conspicuous?" Campbell grinned, showing off a series of rotted teeth. "And now what?" he said to Simon.

Simon stood, arranged his sleeves, gave the boot a disinterested glance, and let his eyes scan the audience until he found what he was looking for.

"Stand up," Simon said, and the big man rose. "Of a size with Minister Macpherson, would you say?" Simon continued, facing the bench.

"Yes, more or less," Minister Walker replied.

Simon nodded. "Stand up, lass," he said to Sarah, who did as she was told. He indicated that the man was to come and stand beside her. In silence, he regarded the pair, let his eyes sweep over the audience and drift back to the bench. "And you seriously wish us to believe a young woman, with child at the time, could overcome a man of that size?" Someone laughed.

Simon waited a moment further, no doubt to let the image engrave itself in the eyes of the beholders, before indicating they should both sit down.

"So, gentlemen," he said, "what have we here? An accusation, no more. No body, no proof, nothing to show that Sarah Connor had anything to do with the unfortunate disappearance of Minister Macpherson."

"He's dead!" Richard Campbell interrupted. "You know as well as I do, he's dead!"

"I will go as far as to say he is probably dead, but how and when, well, that we don't know."

"And the boot?" Richard waved his hand at the dark lump still on display. "How did it come to be in her privy pit?"

"I thought you said it was the neighbour's pit," Simon corrected, "and as to how, I don't know, but you haven't proven it was Sarah Connor that placed it there, have you?"

"So why did she flee?" Richard asked. "Why not stand and protest her innocence?"

A rumbling of agreement flew through the room.

"She had just seen her man battered by a minister," Simon replied in a voice so low Alex had to strain her ears to hear. "She had seen him forcibly pushed back inside, seen the house set alight – by our proud militia, no less." He fleetingly looked over to where Isaiah Farrell and his companions squirmed. "Would you have put your life in the hands of such?"

"She—" Richard blustered, but Simon waved him quiet.

"She didn't trust you, and she was right. Had she not run, she would have hanged, no matter her innocence – and we both know that."

Alex wasn't sure how this was going. It was all too much conjecture, too little facts, but she could sense the ministers were vacillating, eyes resting for long stretches of time on Sarah. The single, irrefutable fact was that Minister Macpherson had last been seen alive just before walking into Sarah's backyard, and no one believed the minister had willingly left – why should he, with a pregnant wife and a comfortable home here in Providence? No matter that Sarah was a head and more shorter than the minister, no matter that there had been no body found, to most of the men in the room she was guilty – of something. And then there was the boot.

Julian rose to stand. "What time?" he asked Isaiah Farrell.

"Time?" The young man looked confused.

"What time was it when you and your companions, including Minister Macpherson, chose to amuse yourself by setting fire to the homes of innocent people?"

"Innocents?" someone called out. "They were papists."

Julian wheeled, sank his eyes into the speaker, who shrank together at the look of absolute disgust on Julian's face. The Chisholms turned as well, a phalanx of able-bodied men that silently reminded the audience that there were Catholics here, amongst them.

"Innocents, Brother Elijah. Misled, perhaps, but innocents nonetheless." Julian swivelled back on his toes to look at Isaiah. "What time?" he barked, and the young man jerked at his tone. He could be quite impressive, her son-in-law, although Alex had no idea what Julian was playing at.

"I don't rightly collect," Isaiah mumbled. "But we had as yet not supped, and it was dark enough that the fires showed up nicely against the skies." Simon made a sound that clearly conveyed just what a worm he considered Isaiah to be, and the young man flushed defensively. "It was the minister! It was him who said we might as well begin the cleansing of the city that same night, and why not start with the Connors?"

Minister Walker shook his head at this, and then asked Julian why the timing was important.

"I saw him," Julian said. "Just before midnight, I saw him." A mumbling ran through the assembled people.

"You did?" Minister Walker frowned. "And yet you haven't told us before?"

Probably because dear Julian was lying through his teeth, Alex reflected, sharing a hasty look with Matthew.

"Well, I wasn't sure when exactly this incident of uncalled for vandalism took place," Julian said, emphasising the word vandalism, "and so…" He shrugged eloquently.

Whatever skills Julian possessed, they weren't acting ones, and this was so far from an Oscar performance it almost made Alex embarrassed. Then she looked closer at Minister Walker, and in those experienced and sharp eyes she saw relief. Likewise in Mr Farrell's face, the man discomfited by his youngest son's loutish behaviour, and in Minister Howell's.

None of them were about to question the veracity of Julian's statement, all of them deeply ashamed of the atrocities committed against the Connors and others that evening back in April, all of them willing to give Sarah the benefit of the doubt.

The only one not in on it was Richard Campbell, and seeing as that man had not been overburdened with powers of observation, he just stared at Julian, mouth falling open when he realised that Julian's testimony had killed any circumstantial evidence tying Sarah to Minister Macpherson's potential murder.

After that, it all became a very hasty affair, with Minister Walker overruling Richard Campbell's bleating protests with a dismissive wave. "No proof, and I hope you're not insinuating Minister Allerton is capable of perjury."

"He's married to her sister!" Richard said, but that got him an even colder look from Minister Walker.

"May I remind you, Brother Richard, that Minister Allerton has been with us for near on ten years, a loyal and hard-working leader of our congregation." Minister Walker stood up, inclined his head in the direction of the assembled people, and left, the skirts of his long dark coat swinging round his legs.

Chapter 44

"Thank you," Alex said to Julian once they were back in his parlour. He looked so rattled she felt sorry for him – her minister son-in-law was very affected by what he'd just done.

"You did well." Matthew clapped Julian on the back. "So did you," he added, smiling at Sarah.

"Not that it was necessary," Simon voiced, coming in to join them. "On a burnt boot alone, they wouldn't have found her guilty of anything."

"Hmph!" Julian said. "That boot was an evocative piece of evidence."

Simon hitched his shoulders. "But impossible to tie to Sarah."

Julian gave him a cold look before focusing his attention on Sarah. "So, what did happen?"

Sarah shared a quick glance with Michael. "I don't know. I just shoved at him, and then the house collapsed, and I had to get Michael out, so I didn't see what happened."

"But you think he died there," Julian said.

Sarah bit her lip and nodded.

Julian seemed on the verge of further questioning when Ruth came in to ask them all to come to table. She handed Julian their infant son, and Julian's tight face relaxed into a wide smile.

"Quite a handsome lad, don't you think?" He held out his son for inspection.

"William?" Alex cooed at the child, not at all taken with the name.

"For my father – and the King," Julian said, before leading the way towards the promising smells of fish soup.

After supper, Julian firmly turned their discussions to matters other than the trial. All the while, he kept brushing at his arms, at his coat, as if attempting to rid himself of some sticky substance. His eyes wandered to Sarah, to Matthew, they darted to Alex, and then he was back at brushing at his sleeves. Alex guessed he'd be spending plenty of time praying for forgiveness for his perjury – a minor sin in Alex's book, at least in this particular case. The conversation turned to God and science, Alex throwing herself enthusiastically into the discussion.

"But that's the difference, isn't it?" Alex insisted. "Science can be verified, while God you have to take on trust. No one can prove He exists. No one can prove He doesn't."

"Do you doubt His existence?" Julian asked in an admonishing tone.

"Of course not, but to the more scientifically minded, God must appear a very vague concept." Well, to be quite honest, she still had moments when that hard-nosed, agnostic Alex of her long ago life vociferously argued that all this Bible reading, all this placing your hopes in the hands of an unseen God was downright ridiculous, but she had no intention of sharing this with Julian.

"Are you saying science and faith cannot coexist?" Matthew asked.

"I'm saying that sometimes they are contradictory," Alex replied. "After all, it isn't that long ago it was considered heretic to insist the earth rotates around the sun."

"Hmm," Julian said, frowning. "Galileo never questioned the existence of God."

"No, and nor does Newton. But others will, and the discoveries made in this day and age will ultimately change our collective perception of God."

Julian was silent, mulling this over. "How? What does Newton say that is so inflammatory?"

Alex found a ball of yarn and dropped it. "Why does it fall?" she asked Julian, who shrugged and said that was how things were ordered: if you dropped something, it fell.

"According to Newton—" Alex began.

"—an object falls due to the force exerted by a larger mass," Ruth finished. She blushed at the surprised look on her husband's face. "It's all there," she mumbled, pointing at a heavy book lying on her little table.

Matthew picked it up and flipped through it, giving his daughter an impressed look. "It's in Latin."

"Aye," Ruth nodded, "*Principia Mathematica* by Isaac Newton."

"Who gave you that?" Julian asked, now hanging over Matthew's shoulder.

"Mr Farrell lent it to me." Ruth smiled carefully at her husband, who frowned as he studied her reading matter. "I don't understand it all."

"One up on me," Alex said. "I don't understand it at all. Anyway, what Newton has done is demystify something. Before, an apple fell due to divine intervention. Now, it falls due to the laws of motion as formulated by Isaac Newton himself."

"Nothing has changed," Simon protested.

"No," Alex agreed, "the apple falls as it has always done. The difference lies in that we can now explain why. Once we can explain most of our existence through science, God becomes inconsequential."

Julian gasped. "Inconsequential? How can you say such?"

Alex sighed. "The march of progress, Julian. The more you know, the less you dumbly accept and believe." Both Julian and Matthew were scowling at her, making her smile. "But I know God exists." Of course He did, however irrational and inconsiderate He seemed at times – if not, how would she ever have met him, her Matthew? She met her husband's gaze, and his eyes softened into a golden green, his mouth curved into a smile. She lobbed the ball of yarn to Matthew, who caught it deftly. "If we'd been on the moon, the ball of yarn wouldn't have dropped. It would have sort of floated to the ground, this, of course, due to the much lower mass of the moon. And we'd be almost weightless, moving in huge, effortless bounds over the surface."

"How do you know?" Julian raised his eyes to the waning moon, barely visible through the small glass-paned window, and looked back at Alex. She couldn't very well tell him of grainy black and white footage, complete with astronauts.

"Anyone can see that. Look at how much smaller the moon is than the earth." Alex yawned exaggeratedly, told the room at large that she was far too tired to stay up much longer, and a few minutes later, she was making her way back to their lodgings, with Matthew and Simon.

"You left Julian agape," Simon chuckled, "wondering where you come by so much knowledge."

"And the reply to that is through my father," Alex said. "Not because I'm from another time." A barbed reminder of the time when Simon had shouted out to a room full of ministers that Alex Graham was not from here. No, she was from the future, a time traveller, no less.

"Your father," he agreed. He looked up at the night sky. "Is it true, then? That one day man will walk on the moon?"

"Yes, although I'm not quite sure what benefits that will bring. A cold and barren place, the moon is." She took a step closer to Matthew, liked it when his arm came round her waist to hold her close to his side. "They say Earth is beautiful from space, a twirling globe of greens and blues, a single sphere of life in an otherwise dark and forbidding universe."

"As God had ordained," Matthew said. Alex didn't reply, safe in the knowledge that for 300 years more, at least, this little globe would turn and turn.

Next day, Alex walked out to visit Kate, assuring Matthew she'd be quite alright on her own.

"Hmm," Matthew said, but agreed that she could walk out alone, but was not to walk back until he came to fetch her. She stuck her tongue out, gave him a quick kiss, and walked off briskly.

It was a bitingly cold day, so cold that the mud flats had an unusual lacing of ice around their edges, and the stands of dried reeds glittered and sparkled with hoar frost. Gulls wheeled overhead, complaining shrilly about everything from the cold to the lack of generous people to throw them bread crusts, and, further up, Alex could make out the silhouette of a large bird of prey – a wintering golden eagle, perhaps.

She stood for a moment admiring the view, the Chesapeake a flat expanse of silvered water bordered by grasses and tufts of reeds as far as she could make out. Almost as impressive as an empty moor, she decided, before drawing the cloak tighter around her shoulders and hurrying on.

Kate was delighted to see her, and in less than five minutes, Alex was seated with tea and hot biscuits, served by a silent house slave. Kate went on and on about yesterday, about poor Patience, little Joshua, commented that Michael looked somewhat pale and sickly, and every now and then replenished Alex's cup with hot tea.

Alex studied her lavish surroundings, noting that since she'd last been here the dining room had been further adorned by an impressive silver urn and what Alex recognised as being a tulip pot – with tulips, no less, Kate hastened to tell her, and Alex made adequately impressed noises, privately hoping the poor bulbs hadn't spent the whole year in their porcelain coffin.

"Still living in sin with Simon?" Alex asked.

"Absolutely, and very much sin at that." Kate winked. "I get the impression my daughter-in-law doesn't approve, or my son for that matter, but he's too canny to say anything that might push me in the direction of marriage."

Alex smothered a laugh, managing to keep a straight face when Kate's daughter-in-law entered the room, transparently not at all pleased to find Alex there.

"Mrs Graham." She curtsied, and her eyes sidled over to the window.

"Iris," Alex replied with a slight nod, wondering why the girl looked so shifty. Maybe it was just constipation or general unease on account of her pregnancy.

"Richard Campbell will not forgive you for yesterday," Kate said.

"Forgive us? What did we do? It was him trying to push through an accusation where there was none to begin with."

Iris muttered something under her breath and Alex turned sharply towards her.

"What?"

"Nothing," Iris mumbled.

"Iris here believes that there must be some truth in Campbell's accusations — don't you, my dear?" Kate's voice dripped with condensation. No love lost there, Alex concluded.

"Something happened," Iris said. "The Minister was there, and then he was gone, never to be seen again."

"Except by Minister Allerton," Kate reminded her. She poured herself some more tea, and returned her attention to Alex. "Campbell is vindictive, and persevering as well."

"And with the intellectual capacity of a snail," Alex said, making Kate grin and Iris look affronted. "Anyway, what can he do?"

Kate sat up a bit straighter, adjusted her well-fitting bodice over her bosom, and draped a shawl over her shoulders. Alex eyed the daring neckline enviously — to be quite honest, she eyed the entire outfit covetously, thinking that she'd do it better justice.

"Do? He can whisper and insinuate, Alex. And he's been asking a lot of questions about that unfortunate incident with Lucy and the painting."

Trust Kate to relegate the disappearance of four young women as an incident, Alex thought. Damn Mercedes for painting it in the first place. Damn Luke for sending the painting to Simon! Lucy had played with fire when she kept the little square of greens and blues, disobeying Simon's instructions that she burn it. Somehow, Lucy had discovered what the painting could do, and had used it to rid her life of women who had caught the eye of her husband, Kate's son — now so happily remarried to Iris.

"Actually," Kate continued, "he's been here too, hasn't he, Iris?" From the wave of red that shot up Iris' cheeks, he not only had, but the stupid girl had been forthcoming as well.

"Ellen Farrell told me," Iris said. "So I told the minister, about the magic contained in the painting, and how it was said Mrs Graham had painted them, and then how at the inquest, Mrs Graham was dragged towards it, and…" She fell silent, squirming under the look of disapproval in Kate's eyes.

"Mrs Graham is a friend," Kate said, "and we don't gossip about our friends. As to what happened at Lucy's trial, first of all, you weren't there, and secondly, quite a few of the people in the room were badly affected by the painting, including your dear uncle, Mr Farrell."

"But it was her it was trying to drag back! And her husband had to struggle to hold her, and had not Lucy snapped the picture in two, well then…" Iris made a very definite gesture with her hand. "Instead, it was Lucy – here one moment, gone the next, sucked into that little picture."

"And you told him all this?" Alex asked Iris. This was the kind of stuff that would make someone like Richard Campbell salivate – potential witches tended to have that effect on uneducated idiots.

Iris shrugged. She had been but repeating what everybody knew, and not a few expressed the opinion that Alex Graham had somehow been involved in the creation of the painting.

"But I wasn't," Alex told her flatly, and stared the young girl down.

Matthew arrived in the company of Simon, and together the four of them had dinner – or luncheon as Kate preferred to call it. Matthew's eyes kept on gliding back to Kate. In dark green, pearls around her neck and with her silvered blond hair, she was disgustingly attractive, creamy white skin rising out of that expertly cut neckline.

To further feed the jealousy in the pit of Alex's stomach, Kate preened, eyes glittering as she laughed and bantered. Simon went quite pink when Kate leaned to the side to kiss his cheek. Matthew, on the other hand, went stiff. Idiot. Alex kicked him, hard enough to make him wince. Two aggrieved eyes met hers, and she shrugged. That's what you get for gawking, mister. He coughed, asked Simon to pass the salt, and for the rest of the meal concentrated on fondling her under the table, his mouth quivering with a contained smile as Alex's cheeks heated.

"I think they make a nice couple," Alex said provocatively when they walked back to town together.

"You think?" Matthew shook his head. "Somewhat mismatched. Wee Simon is overly stout with at most five strands of reddish hair left to him."

"It's not all about looks," she told him icily.

"Mmm," he said, sounding quite unconvinced.

"Too bad they can't marry," Alex continued. Maybe then, Matthew could stop eating damned Kate with his eyes every time he saw her! She slid her eyes sideways, and with some surprise met his very green stare. He was smiling, and she seriously considered kicking him again. He was enjoying this, the bastard, enjoying the fact that she was twisting with jealousy!

"It isn't that they can't. It is that she doesn't want to," Matthew said. "Kate does not want to relinquish the control of her own affairs." He made a grab for her hand, neatly evaded. "Come here, lass." Alex shook her head. No way. His eyes shifted into a promising golden hue, a big hand darted out to close around her wrist and gather her to his chest. She glared at him, was summarily kissed. A very nice kiss, for all that he tasted of smoked pork.

"I wonder how long before Mr Richard Campbell starts bleating about their immorality," Alex mused once they came up for air. The other ministers chose to look the other way, wise enough not to meddle with Kate Jones.

"It won't serve him much, will it?" Matthew shrugged. He took her hand, adapted the length of his stride, his pace, to bring them into perfect synchronisation. "We ride home on the morrow."

"Home." She nodded, and they shared a quiet smile.

Chapter 45

Alex brushed the last of the snow from Jacob's tombstone, stuck her frozen fingers into her mouth to thaw them out, and sat down on the edge of the graveyard bench to take in the view before her. Late February, and the ground that flowed away from here to the river was a collection of browns: from the dark loam of the broken soil to the dull gold of the withered grasses, here and there interspersed with a vivid dash of green or a rapidly shrinking snowdrift.

Behind her, the mock oranges rattled in the wind, their long canes swelling with the promise of buds, and down by the river, last year's reeds had shrivelled into damp stands of rotting black. She liked these days when spring was still but a possibility, not yet a fact, and she drew in a lungful of the cold, wet air, holding it for a moment before expelling it. She repeated this exercise, and with each breath, her temper cooled a degree or so.

"Still angry?"

"Hmph!" she replied.

Matthew came over to join her on the bench. "What could I say?"

"No," she suggested.

"He has obligations, Alex."

"He's not even sixteen!" Alex exploded. "And how is he to support her out there?" She waved her hand in the general direction of the blue-green line of northern forest.

"He's a good hunter, you know he is. A right good trapper, as well."

Alex sighed. "He'll never belong fully, not there, with them, not here, with us."

"You could twist that. He belongs both with us and with them, a foot in each world. Not a bad thing, is it?"

Alex wasn't so sure. She could see it in Samuel's eyes at times, how he wasn't certain of his own identity. And it was their fault, for allowing Qaachow to claim him as a foster son, a brother to Little Bear.

Matthew gripped her shoulder and gave it a little shake. "You've said it yourself, how the lad by his own reckoning is a man and must live with the consequences. We can but be here when he needs us."

"Hmph," Alex said again, but with somewhat less heat. "Yet another grandchild we'll never know." Little Karen would grow up far away from them, an Indian girl through and through. Alex lobbed a pebble in the direction of Jacob's headstone. "Like his little girl, the daughter he left behind in England."

Matthew just nodded. From below came a loud shriek, young voices rose in anger, and Lettie came flying with Hannah and Maggie in determined pursuit.

Alex grinned. "Well, it's not as if we have a shortage of grandchildren, is it?"

"Lettie isn't a child. She's a pixie, a changeling."

Alex laughed, watching as Lettie, monkey that she was, made it safely to the oak and scrambled up into it, disappearing higher and higher.

Halfway through the morning, Samuel was ready to go, clutching Matthew's farewell gift, a musket, to his chest.

"I don't like this," Alex said. "You're my boy, and I want you to be here, with me."

"Doing what, Mama?" Samuel asked. "Being Ian's and Mark's unpaid help?"

"No, of course not." She ran her hand up and down his damaged arm.

"But that's what I would be. I don't want to live in a town. I have no skills except those of hunting and farming, so what then?"

Alex cupped his cheek. "Before all this, what did you dream of, Samuel?"

He smiled guardedly. "I don't rightly collect. Mayhap being a musketeer?"

She returned his smile, blinking angrily at the way her eyes were filling with tears.

"We failed you. We allowed you to be torn in two." Her son, and he was leaving her – them. Alex wasn't quite sure how she was to cope, her throat painful with suppressed sobs.

Samuel captured one of her tears with his finger and bent his head to lean his brow against hers. "It doesn't matter," he said, even if they both knew that of course it did.

"You're lying." She stood on tiptoe and kissed him on his cheek. "Wherever you go, and whatever you call yourself, you're my son, and I love you so very much. Go with God, Samuel."

He kissed her back, and disengaged himself from her arms. His hair hung loose around his head, held in place by a braided band, and the buckskin shirt he was wearing was new, decorated with beads and quills along the hem and cuffs.

"Will you bake me a cake for my birthday?" he asked as he turned to leave.

"What an idiotic question," she snivelled. "Of course I will."

Samuel smiled, and after giving his father one last hug, moved away to where his Indian brother was waiting for him down by the river.

Alex retreated to the kitchen, hoping for a piece of cake to take the edge off the gnawing grief in her belly. Her son, leaving them. Unfortunately, there was no cake. Instead, she found Carlos and Mrs Parson, one busy with her cooking, the other sitting at the table conversing.

"He's gone." Alex sat down with a loud sigh.

Carlos made a series of adequate comforting sounds. "He'll find his way. He's a very mature boy."

Alex wiped at her eyes. "He has to be. A father at his age!"

Mrs Parson looked up from where she was grating suet for the haggis, and snorted. "Don't fret, Alex. He'll be fine, aye?"

"Hmm." Alex slumped.

Mrs Parson chopped heart and liver, mixed it with the

suet, added oatmeal, onions and spices, before producing the rinsed stomach of the sheep they'd mercy slaughtered earlier, its leg badly broken. Carlos made a disgusted sound as she stuffed the stomach before setting the whole thing to simmer on the hearth.

"Will you be staying for dinner?" Mrs Parson grinned at the priest, who muttered something about unfortunately not being able to, he was only here in his pastoral capacity.

"I came to talk to Sarah – and Michael," he said.

Fat chance of any one-on-one. Michael did not as much as leave Sarah's side while Carlos was close, a somewhat excessive chaperoning, in Alex's opinion. Only during confession was she allowed to be alone with him, but what sins did a nursing mother have to confess?

"I just want to talk to her," he complained to Alex when she followed him outside to where his mule was waiting.

"Part of you does, but there's another element to it as well."

Carlos flushed and hung his head. "Yes, but it's something I'd never act on."

"But still," she said.

Carlos twitched at his coat. No cassock for him, not anymore. Instead, it was shirt and breeches, wide-brimmed hat and a hand-me-down coat that gave him the impression of being one nondescript working man among many others – until one saw his hands: white and uncalloused.

"Will you stay, do you think?" Alex asked as he swung himself into the saddle.

"Stay?" For a moment, Carlos looked confused. "Oh, you mean here, in Maryland." He smiled lopsidedly and gathered up the reins. "*Si*, I'll stay. After all, I have blood relatives here, don't I?" He tilted his head at her. "You don't look very much like Isaac."

"No," Alex agreed. "He took after the Spanish part of the family." They shared a quick, incredulous grin.

"Should I call you *tía*?" he teased in a low voice.

"I'm not your aunt!" she protested. "If anything, you're my age-old cousin."

Carlos just shook his head at the impossibility of it all,

and with one last wave set his mule up the lane.

"Expecting Thomas to swoon over your haggis?" Alex asked when she re-entered the kitchen.

Mrs Parson gave her a beady look. "He doesn't love me for my food."

"No, of course not," Alex snorted. "He loves you for all that." With her hands, she indicated a huge, swelling chest.

Mrs Parson laughed, peering down at her bosom with obvious satisfaction. "As you say, men are simple creatures." Her face fell together, a shadow of sadness flitting over it. "But then, so are we. All you really want in the end is a warm hand in yours."

"In the end?" Alex gave her a worried look.

Mrs Parson shook her head, holding up her latest knitting project to the light. "I don't plan on dying yet, not until my haggis is done." She sniffed with appreciation, making Alex laugh. "We plan on marrying," she added casually, "soon."

"You do?" Alex suppressed a smile at the thought. "So you love him, then." She went back to her turnips.

"Well enough," Mrs Parson replied.

"I can't start calling you Mrs Leslie," Alex grumbled. "It feels strange, somehow."

Mrs Parson burst out in laughter. "That's alright, lass, you can go on calling me Mrs Parson – even Thomas does."

"He does?" Alex asked, intrigued.

"I assume he doesn't want to be mixing us up." Mrs Parson shrugged.

"He could call you Gillian," Alex said.

"No one does," Mrs Parson answered sharply. "No one after Robbie." Her whole face wobbled, those normally so bright black eyes misted over, and Alex turned her back to allow her old friend to regain her composure.

"We were thinking of living here," Mrs Parson said in her normal voice a few moments later.

"Here?" Alex was surprised. Leslie's Crossing was a huge place, and even now with Adam Leslie married, there was surely room for Thomas and a new wife.

"You need me more than they need him," Mrs Parson

said, halfway between a statement and a tentative question.

Alex crossed the room to kiss her, wet hands held aloft. "Always."

Mrs Parson cleared her throat, patted Alex on the cheek. "Don't get dirty water stains on my knitting, aye?"

"They're very old," Betty said to Alex later that afternoon, sounding disapproving.

"Not too old to love each other," Alex replied, pouring the maple sap from the small container into the bucket Betty was holding.

"You think?" Betty's eyebrows all but disappeared into her bright, exuberant hair.

Alex moved over to the next tree. "I don't think they're setting the bed on fire, but, yes, I'm sure they're quite capable of getting the dirty deed done."

Betty made a disgusted face. "They're too old. It's unseemly, and besides, they wouldn't, would they? Not without being married?"

Naomi grinned, and asked Betty where she thought Thomas spent his nights now that he was a regular night guest.

"In the parlour nook," Betty replied, sounding confused.

"Of course," Alex hastened to agree, winking at Naomi over Betty's head. "If nothing else because Matthew would disapprove otherwise."

"You think I don't know?" Matthew yawned that same night. He shifted closer to her. "She's old enough to be my mam. I can't very well be laying down the law to her, can I?" He rolled her over on her side, slipped his hand in to rest where it usually did, between her breasts. "Do you think...? Nay, nothing."

"Do I think what?"

"Do you think she undresses?"

"Matthew!" Alex laughed. "Probably not," she decided after having thought his question through. She'd never seen Mrs Parson in her skin, suspected that not even Mrs Parson saw herself in only the skin.

"I don't think so either. But it is no great hindrance, is it? A shift, I mean."

An evening a couple of days later, Alex went off in search of Matthew, hurrying over the yard in clogs and with only her shawl over her shoulders. She was shivering by the time she reached the stables, the previously agreeable spring day having morphed back into a winter night.

"Matthew?" It was dark inside, dark and warm, the space full of the sound of animals.

"Down here."

She followed the weak light of his lantern to find him crouched by the farrowing sow. The pig flapped her ears at Alex in warning: one human, she could tolerate; two, no.

"Eight," Matthew informed her, using a wisp of straw to wipe the latest arrival clean.

"Good girl," Alex said encouragingly. The sow gave her a long-suffering look. "Did you talk to them?"

"Aye." He came over to Alex, and leaned back against the wall, one eye on the sow that was now busy producing number nine. "They won't stay. Michael insists he has a business to run down south." He stretched, grunting when his spine straightened out.

"To a point, he's right. He owns a substantial share in Nuthead's printing business. But won't it be uncomfortable for him to work with someone who brought the law down on them? Will Nuthead want him back?"

"If not, he expects to be reimbursed in full," Matthew said, "and, according to Michael, Nuthead doesn't have that kind of money."

"Who does?" Alex didn't like it. Sarah and Michael were safer here with them than down in St Mary's City, and what would people say about Sarah? Matthew went over to scratch the pig behind her ears. He held up the tenth piglet, studied the twisted foreleg, and with a swift motion broke its neck, tossing it to land lifeless in a pail.

"They can always come back," he said, "should things not work out."

Alex decided to try some convincing of her own, and went to find Sarah. Her daughter was sitting in her room, singing to herself while she worked her way through a sizeable pile of mending. She listened to Alex, but once she was done, Sarah shrugged.

"We'll be alright." She cooed at her son who was kicking his bare legs vigorously, happy to be freed of clouts and blankets. "It's important to Michael, to go back. He isn't much of a farmer."

From the yard came the sound of Michael laughing, a sound that made Alex smile in response. He hadn't laughed once since Joshua's death. Sarah's hand dropped to her belly, an instinctive gesture that had Alex raising both her brows.

"So soon?" she asked. Sarah just nodded, a glow suffusing her face. Alex gave her a quick hug. She'd done the same when Rachel died: created a new child to fill the void left behind. "A girl perhaps?"

"A lad, I hope." Sarah grinned. "We won't leave yet. I don't want to miss the wedding."

"Huh," Alex huffed, "almost unseemly this haste."

"I don't think she's with child," Sarah teased.

"You never know with her," Alex replied with an eye roll, making Sarah burst out in laughter.

"God!" Alex groaned, subsiding to sit panting and sweating on one of the benches that lined the makeshift dance floor, "Where on earth does that woman get her energy from?"

Ian grinned, stretched his right leg gingerly in front of him, and offered her his cup of cider. "Something she eats?"

"Yeah," Alex muttered. "She's probably high on some toadstool or other." Mrs Parson – no, Mrs Leslie – swished by, skirts flaring to reveal new silk stockings and bright garters.

Ian raised a brow. "Red?" He sounded impressed.

"I hope she's sharing whatever it is she's eating with her bridegroom," Alex said, "but it doesn't seem so, does it?" Thomas was a panting wreck on the opposite side of the barn, what little hair he had standing straight up. "He almost hanged Matthew once," she blurted, making Ian turn, surprised, in her direction.

"He did?" A slight narrowing of hazel eyes indicated Ian was more than willing to reconsider his present opinion of Thomas Leslie.

"May 1659, but luckily he didn't. Luke's fault, pointing Thomas and his men in the direction of that most dangerous escaped royalist, Matthew Graham." She snorted derisively. "Matthew a royalist! How anyone could ever believe that is beyond me."

"You haven't forgiven Luke, have you?" Ian asked.

Alex hedged, drinking down the cider in small sips. "No, I don't think I can. I try, though." Not overly hard, she had to admit, and since that incident up by the millpond...

Ian studied her thoughtfully, but didn't push. Instead, he took the mug from her, and led her out to dance.

Much later, well after bride and bridegroom had been allowed to retire without the normal ribald following all the way to their marriage bed, Matthew came to claim a dance from Alex. He was flushed after hours of dancing and drinking, had discarded his coat and was only in shirt and breeches, his height increased an unnecessary inch or two by his new shoes. His cravat he'd stuffed into the waistband of his breeches after having used it to wipe his face with, and in the glow of lanterns, he looked young, vibrant with life. He whirled her over the dance floor, lifted her high in the air, and Alex gasped and laughed, clutching at his arms when he swung her round and round. They stumbled and fell against one of the uprights.

"Alex," he murmured against her neck, oblivious to the people around them, "my Alex." He helped her to straighten up, and led her into the shadows, the hay rustling when he laid her down.

"Matthew!" she hissed when he began shoving her skirts out of the way. "Not here, not with all the people."

"They won't notice," he whispered back, his breath hot on her cheek.

"But—"

He kissed her into silence, unlaced himself, and then he was inside, a long, satisfied exhalation tickling her ear.

"So soft," he mumbled, "so warm." He kissed her again, and she could taste the whisky and the brandy, the beer and even more whisky. She felt like an errant teenager, biting back on a giggle.

"Aaah," he grunted, his buttocks clenching under her hands before he collapsed on top of her. Alex wriggled closer, hips pushing against him in a not so subtle reminder that she was here as well.

"Want more, do you?" he whispered in her ear.

"More?" she whispered back with suppressed laughter. "I haven't had any yet, have I?"

"Lie still, woman," he told her, and slid down to kiss her on the inside of her thighs, to breathe warmly into her curls, to tease her with his tongue.

"Jesus!" she gasped, all of her straining up, up. "Oooh," she added when he came inside again.

"Shh!" he admonished, covering her mouth with his, and now the whisky was overlaid with her taste, his taste, and he pinned her to the ground, moving very slowly until all of her shook beneath him.

"Wow," she said once her pulse no longer threatened to crack her temple open. He rolled off, smoothed down her skirts, and adjusted his breeches. Only yards away, people were still dancing, someone laughed out loud, and the fiddler increased the pace. In their primitive bed, Matthew clasped her hand hard in his and raised it to lie above his thumping heart.

Chapter 46

"What's the matter with them all?" Alex whispered to Matthew after yet another of the Providence matrons detoured to avoid greeting them.

"I don't know," he said, frowning at this blatant discourtesy. He placed Alex's hand in the crook of his arm, and continued up towards the meeting house. Someone tittered behind them, a hissed comment flew between a group of girls, and Matthew's frown deepened.

At the meeting house, they walked over to greet the Hancocks, standing in a little group with Ian, Betty, Ruth and Julian, and he felt as if he were Moses parting the Red Sea, people scattering to both sides in their haste to avoid them.

"Do we smell?" Alex asked Esther Hancock, sniffing at her own sleeve.

Esther shook her head, her mouth compressed into a thin line. "It's that minister," she said.

William said something long and colourful, glaring in the direction of Richard Campbell who stood smirking in the shadow of one of the plane trees.

"He has quite the tongue on him," William growled, "and now he has successfully planted the idea that Mrs Graham is a witch of a sort, for did not her own brother-in-law accuse her of that all those years ago?"

Alex paled, her fingers sinking into Matthew's arm.

"That man," Matthew began, but swallowed back on the rest. It would keep. First, he would go to kirk. Then he'd handle that despicable little man, once and for all.

Beside him, Ian cursed. "It's time that wee miscreant is taught some manners," he said.

"I'll not condone any violence." Julian frowned in turn at Ian and Matthew.

"Violence? Who said anything about violence? I aim to have a wee chat with the man, no more," Matthew said, fisting his hands a couple of times.

"We talk to him together." Julian placed a hand on Matthew's shoulder. "It's no great matter, a trampled pride, no more. We'll make him see sense."

"A contradiction in terms," Alex muttered. "Sense and Richard Campbell."

Matthew just nodded.

After kirk, Matthew and Julian succeeded in cornering Richard. It was a fruitless discussion. Yon maggot Campbell just smirked and tapped his nose, saying that he had a duty to the congregation – someone had to find out the truth about Mrs Graham and her potential dabbling in magic.

Matthew stared at Richard Campbell with dislike. "That matter was closed several years ago."

"Was it?" Richard asked blandly. "Was it truly?"

"Of course it was!" Julian put in.

"And her son?" Richard asked. "The lad Simon Melville accused her of having transported through time? Isaac, wasn't that his name?" He turned small eyes on Matthew and nodded slowly. "You said he was dead at the age of seven, Mr Graham, did you not? And yet now we hear the self-same Isaac died at Killiecrankie."

"Really? And who told you such?" Matthew asked.

Richard just shook his head. "Not telling, am I? But admittedly, there's something strange in all this, and I aim to get to the bottom of it." He flounced off.

"Isaac?" Julian said. "Is it true, Matthew? Isaac wasn't dead?"

Matthew ignored him. How on earth did Campbell know?

"Matthew! I asked you a question. Is Isaac not dead?"

"Aye, he is, very, very dead."

"When?" Julian asked. "When did he die?"

Matthew shrugged, moving to follow Alex, barely visible at the end of the main street. "Not now, Julian."

"Oh yes," Julian said, blocking the way, "now."

Matthew pushed past him. "Isaac died at Killiecrankie." With a curt nod, he walked off.

Matthew took a few turns round the little town looking for his wife, walked up and down the few streets that radiated like spokes from the central hub of the little town, the main quay. No Alex. He walked halfway out to Kate before recalling Kate was joining them for late dinner at Julian's, and so set off back to town, peeking round every stand of reeds in the hope of finding Alex sitting there.

He'd seen how frightened she was, and Matthew's hands closed tight in irritation that a charlatan minister should scare his wife like this. How unfortunate Richard Campbell had not remained forever up in Massachusetts!

He was almost at Julian's front door when he heard Alex's voice, high and loud with anger. When Matthew burst into the little study, Alex was on her feet, glowering at her son-in-law.

"What?" he asked, and Alex subsided against him like a pricked bladder.

"I'm requesting the truth," Julian yelled, "from both of you."

"What truth?" Matthew said. "With what right?"

"I have to know!" Julian hissed. "What is my wife if Alex is a witch?" The slap had him reeling back.

"How dare you!" Alex spat, her hand still held aloft.

"Julian?" Ruth stood in the doorway, looking from husband to mother. April sunlight filtered in from the window behind her, causing her hair to gleam like burnished copper where it peeked from under her cap. "Mama?"

"Never mind." Alex brushed past her, and made for the entrance.

"Alex," Julian pleaded, "I have a right!"

Alex swivelled on her toes. "I. Am. Not. A. Witch." With that, she left, and after throwing Julian a long look, Matthew hastened after her.

"A witch?" Ruth quavered. "Why do you say Mama is a witch?"

"I don't, but Richard Campbell does." Julian sank down

to sit, dragging his fingers through his few remaining strands of hair. After some moments, he lifted his face to meet Ruth's worried look. "I think there may be some truth in it."

Ruth gasped, took a step back from him.

"Your uncle once said your mother was from another time."

Ruth continued to retreat, her eyes wide with apprehension. "Witches burn."

"No, they don't, not anymore. They hang." Julian swallowed at the thought. "For now, you'll stay away from her."

Think, he had to think. Julian dropped his eyes to his half-written letter – begun well before breakfast when his world was still calm and orderly – raised them again to ensure Ruth would do as he said. The doorway was empty, there was a clatter from the other end of the hall, and through his window, he saw his wife hurrying after her parents. Julian groaned out loud, picked up his letter and tore it in two.

"Why, Matthew?" Alex asked, breathless after their enforced march up the slight inclination that led to Simon's office. "Why can't he just leave me alone? Or drop dead."

"Aye, that would be a neat solution to this whole mess."

"And how can people listen to him? Believe him when he spouts all that shit?"

"He has a silvered tongue, and people are easily swayed."

"It's not fair!" She came to a standstill, cheeks bright with anger. "How can anyone believe I'm a witch? What have I ever done to deserve that? Most of the people here in town don't even know me, do they?"

"Shush, lass," Matthew said. "It will sort itself."

Now that his mind was back to functioning logically, he was rapidly calming down. Richard Campbell might make accusations, but how well would they stick? Anyone present in that courtroom six years ago could swear to the absolute horror on Alex's face, and she hadn't denied having seen a painting such as the one used by Lucy. She'd even described how she burnt it. And as to Isaac…drowned – yes, that was it. They had presumed the lad drowned, and then all these years later, he had reappeared, miraculously saved by—

"Mama? Da?" Ruth's voice interrupted his thoughts. "Come back home." Her voice was unnaturally neutral, in severe contradiction to the way she kept on wiping her hands up and down her dove-coloured skirt. She put a hand on Alex's arm. "Please?" she added, her eyes a bright green.

Julian apologised profusely for calling Alex a witch before going on to insist they had to tell him the truth if he was to be able to help them.

"What truth?" Simon asked from the doorway.

"The truth about Isaac, for a start," Julian said, "and then maybe an explanation as to why you said Alex had fallen from another time?"

"That last you must discount. It was the weak attempt of a deranged father to save his only child." Simon shoved Duncan in the direction of the kitchen. "Go and find your wee cousins, laddie. And if you ask nicely, I'm sure Mary can find you something to eat."

Duncan skipped off down the passage, calling loudly for Edward and Faith. Simon turned back to Julian, smoothed down the cravat over his embroidered waistcoat – for the day a dark green decorated with white daisies – and exhaled.

"I said it back then to Minister Walker, I'll gladly say so again. How I lashed out blindly in an attempt to make my lass look innocent." He shook his head at himself. "I was right in one thing. Alex had seen a painting such as the one Lucy had before. So had I, and we both knew what it could do – that it was evil through and through."

"It's too late to retract," Julian said. "Richard Campbell has his teeth sunk into this particularly juicy bone, and he won't let go until it is cracked between his teeth."

"And what can he prove?" Alex's voice was high with rage – or fear, Matthew couldn't rightly tell. "What can anyone prove?"

"Nothing," Julian said, "but slander sticks. Like tar, it clings to you."

"I should accuse him of libel," Alex muttered. "Turn the tables on that little toad."

"Hmm." Julian frowned. "And Isaac?"

Alex inhaled, held her breath, and exhaled loudly. "I don't know." She looked at Matthew for help.

"We thought him dead," Matthew filled in. "One day, he was simply gone, and we couldn't find him."

Alex nodded, and took her cue from him. "The water, the millpond, we looked everywhere."

"Aye, one day there, the other not," Simon contributed gamely. Matthew threw him a warning look. Wee Simon did best to remain silent.

"And then, one day in 1688, he came to Hillview. I thought I'd die on the spot. All those years, thinking him gone and then..." Alex rubbed at a spot on her hand, frowning at it. "So, he came back, and I had him with me for eight months, and then he was forced to war and came back dead. Very dead." Her voice was bleak, stark in her sorrow, and Julian reached over to cover her hand with his.

"I'm sorry," he said.

"So am I," Alex whispered. "Poor, poor Isaac."

Over dinner, Matthew laid plans, and once the meal was concluded, Julian and Matthew set off to talk to Minister Walker while Ian was dispatched to find Campbell.

"You take care of Alex," Matthew said to Simon. "Make sure you're at the meeting house in an hour or so."

Ian looked about as dangerous as a starving catamount when he dragged a loudly protesting Richard Campbell into the meeting house. Over the head of the dishevelled minister, Matthew met his son's eyes and nodded his thanks.

"What's this?" Richard Campbell shook off Ian's hand and pulled himself up straight before his peers. "A trial?"

"Of a sort," Minister Walker said. "Brother Matthew here has come before us, most upset by the calumnies you're spreading about his wife."

From where he sat, Matthew nodded, eyes boring into Richard who, to his satisfaction, squirmed.

"Calumnies? What calumnies?" Richard looked at his fellow ministers, at the elders, at Alex who was seated in a corner, flanked by Simon. "I am but speaking the truth."

"Ah." Minister Walker regarded him over the rim of his spectacles. "If so, I presume you must have a long list of incidents to share with us, carefully annotated statements from witnesses that can prove these accusations of yours."

Richard twisted, muttered and mumbled, but he had no proof. He had no witnesses. There were no incidents.

"Nothing?" Minister Howell said. "You take it upon yourself to destroy Mrs Graham's reputation, and you have nothing to show us?"

"Of course I do!" Richard stared his younger colleague down. "I dare say all of you've heard of the strange, evil painting, haven't you?" He turned on his toes, pointed at Simon. "And you, Mr Melville, you were the one who accused her, your own good-sister, of being a witch."

"I did no such thing!" Simon said, leaping to his feet.

"Aye, you did! You said that she was familiar with that wee scrap of evil. You even said she'd used one! You called her a time traveller, man! A time traveller, gentlemen. Therefore, a witch."

"And, as I have admitted to Minister Walker, I lied," Simon said. "I perjured myself, and all because of my daughter, my lass. I said anything I could think of to save her. It was her, my Lucy, who spoke to me of travelling through time, probably because she was bewitched by that evil, evil painting. And I, God help me, I used what Lucy said in a feeble attempt to lay the blame elsewhere."

"But you all saw it," Richard nearly shouted, directing himself to Julian, to Minister Walker, to Mr Farrell, even to Kate Jones. "You saw Alex Graham being dragged towards the painting, helpless before it. The work of the devil, mark my words, and she its creature! Gregor said, repeatedly he said that—"

"What?" Matthew said.

"That it was wrong, somehow. And look at her now. See how she quakes in fear at the recollection of it all!"

All eyes turned to Alex, sitting pale on her stool.

"So do I." Simon sank down to sit, looking quite pale.

"That was a terrible thing to witness."

"Yes," Mr Farrell said, "a horrible experience, mark my words!" He mopped at his brow, looked as shaken as Alex did.

"No one disputes that painting was evil," Minister Walker said, "and Mrs Graham testified to seeing such a painting before. But that in itself does not make her a witch, does it? Alexandra Graham has never, by action or words, done anything that has led to anyone accusing her of witchery. Ever."

Richard grew desperate. His voice squeaked as he insisted that something was very strange about Alex Graham.

"Strange?" Matthew asked. "How strange?"

"She just is, and what about this Isaac?" There was a triumphant gleam in Richard's eyes. "Her son? First dead, then miraculously resurrected, and now what? Dead? Alive?"

"Dead," Alex put in, rising to her feet. "Very dead."

"Yes, now he is, but what about last time he went up in thin air? What then?"

"Not dead?" Minister Walker leaned forward. "But you said, Brother Matthew, that he'd died as a child."

"That's what we all thought," Matthew said. "The lad disappeared one day, and we couldn't find him – anywhere. All we found was his spinning top, just by the edge of the millpond. We looked for days, Minister Walker, we looked everywhere, but we found nothing. So we despaired and assumed he had drowned. The lad couldn't swim."

"But he wasn't dead?" Minister Walker asked.

"Of course, he wasn't!" Richard Campbell made a derisive noise, and seemed about to say more, but Matthew sorted that by rising to his feet and raising his voice.

"No, it transpired he wasn't. Snatched, he thought himself, but had no recollections of the events as such. All he remembered was being with us one day, somewhere else entirely the next day. And over the years, I reckon he forgot about us – he was a laddie when he disappeared – but one day, he happened to be in Cumnock, and something jogged his memory – or so he said. And so, one day he came home." Matthew slid his audience a cautious look, hoping he had managed to convey his story with sufficient sincerity for them to believe it. Out of the corner of his eye, he saw Simon nod discreetly. Matthew gestured at Alex, who had sat back down, eyes closed. "He was among the many that died at Killiecrankie. It near killed her, to have him back, and then lose him again."

"Hmm, yes…that must be difficult." Minister Walker peered at Alex. "So he wasn't magicked away through a painting? That's what Brother Simon said at the time, how little Isaac had been lured to look too deep into a painting – by her, by his own mother." He sent Simon a scathing look, and Simon hung his head, muttering that he'd already admitted he'd lied.

Julian cleared his throat. "Would any mother do such a thing? And anyway, if that was the case, how did he come back? Do you think such paintings exist elsewhere as well?"

"I sincerely hope not." Minister Walker shuddered.

"Amen to that," Mr Farrell said, dabbing yet again at his brow with his handkerchief.

"I'm telling you she's a witch!" Richard Campbell was on his feet. "She is loud and opinionated, she has her entire household under her thumb, and—"

"Well, that sounds like most women I know," Mr Farrell interrupted, making the assembled men chuckle.

"She doesn't belong here!" Campbell was near on jumping where he stood, raising a shaking arm to point at Alex. "She feeds her family strange things to eat, she insists they all submerge themselves – naked! – in water on a weekly basis, she—"

"She's Swedish," Simon interjected. "Swedish customs would seem strange to you."

"She hit me! She attacked a minister of her kirk!"

"Ah, so there we have it." Minister Walker sat back, steepled his fingers, and studied Richard. "Am I to take it these accusations of yours are simply an attempt to get your own back?"

Richard's breath came in loud, whistling gulps. "My own back?" He stuttered with rage. "The woman deserves to be whipped for what she did to me, but that's not why—"

"So why then?" Matthew demanded.

"Because I am sure she is a witch!" Richard licked his mouth. "And I can prove it to you. I will prick her, and you will all see!" He produced a long needle and threw himself at Alex, who was so taken aback she fell flat on her back, with the minister atop of her. She screamed as Richard tore at her clothing, yelling it was about time she was proved a witch before them all.

Ian beat Matthew to it. With a roar, he gripped the minister by the seat of his breeches and the scruff of his neck, lifted him, and threw him to the side. "You touch my mother again and I will slice you open from throat to groin!" Ian limped badly as he approached Richard, now cowering back against the wall.

"Help!" Richard bleated, waving his needle before him.

"Ian, no!" Alex sat up, arms crossed over her chest. Matthew felt a wave of ire rush through him. The damned man had torn her bodice, her shift, and she was bleeding from a number of small puncture wounds. He knelt beside her, shielding her from view as he helped her bring some order to her dress. She was shaking all over, her fingers incapable of sorting laces or buttons, and Matthew wanted to cradle her and shush her, hold her close and tell her things would be alright. But for now, he restrained himself to cupping her cheek with his hand.

"I'm fine," she whispered, trying out a wobbly smile. "Truly, Matthew, I'm okay." She got to her feet, swayed slightly, but steadied herself against the wall.

Richard was still sitting on the floor, Simon was holding Ian by both arms, and Minister Walker eyed Richard as if he were some sort of fat louse.

"Are you alright, Mrs Graham?" Minister Walker asked.

Alex nodded, no more, her chin trembling.

"I expect him to be punished," Matthew said, nodding in the direction of Richard Campbell.

"Punish me?" Richard was on his feet, glaring at Matthew. "For what?"

"For what? For attacking my wife like you just did, and for spreading lies about her," Matthew said. "Dangerous lies."

"Lies? They're not lies! I—"

"Enough!" Minister Walker had gone the colour of a boiled lobster. "You threw yourself at the poor woman, man! You have no proof. All you have is weak conjecture and some sort of misguided desire to avenge yourself on Mrs Graham for an incident that occurred years ago. You're a disgrace to our profession, Mr Campbell, and I will have you leave our town as soon as possible."

"But what about his punishment?" Matthew was not leaving until this vile worm of a man had been adequately chastised.

"I—" Richard broke off to adjust his dirty cravat. "I am a minister, Mr Graham. It would behove you to keep that in mind."

"And just as fallible as any other man," Minister Walker said. He looked Richard up and down, mouth pursing into a small, tight 'o'. "You will apologise, Brother Richard. In church, on Sunday, before the whole congregation."

"What?" Matthew and Richard said simultaneously. Not at all enough, in Matthew's book, but the look on Minister Walker's face made him swallow back on his protests.

"You heard," Minister Walker said, getting to his feet. "It best be a good apology, Mr Campbell. Contrite and humble. Even ministers can end up in the pillory. Or be caned."

"I still don't believe you," Julian told Alex when they made their way back from the meeting house.

"Believe what?" Alex would have preferred to walk back with Matthew, but Minister Walker had curtly told Matthew and Ian to accompany him – probably to make sure they desisted from doing Richard any bodily harm. Wise move, Alex concluded, having watched both husband and son study Richard as if he were vermin. Campbell himself had skulked off alone, eyes throwing barbs at the Graham family.

Alex shivered and suppressed the urge to scratch at her

chest and the itching pinpricks. She intended to do some serious disinfecting when she got back home, and hoped Ruth had some dried meadowsweet available. Alex dipped her head in Mr Farrell's direction and gave him a polite smile before returning her attention to Julian.

"Simon spoke the truth that day at Lucy's trial," Julian said. "I saw it in his face, but most of all I saw it in yours. You were shocked by his betrayal."

Alex opened her mouth to protest, but Julian waved her silent. "I've been a minister for twenty years. I've seen men – and women – in all walks of life, in despair and in joy. I know when I see the truth, and that day, it was written plainly on your face."

Alex closed her mouth before she succeeded in dislocating her jaw.

"I don't, however, believe you to be a witch – you're a good woman, Alex Graham."

"Oh wow, well, that's a relief," Alex muttered.

Julian gave her an irritated look. He was talking, wasn't he? "You know too much. You speak of Rome and Paris, of London and Seville. You casually refer to continents and seas. You mention in passing that this man will be king, while this one will not."

Alex's cheeks were prickling with heat. Had she really been that indiscreet?

"I can't help having had an itinerant childhood," she mumbled. "All that stuff you say I know, it is simply due to growing up surrounded by learned men, and—"

Julian waved her silent and chuckled, a bit sadly. "Stop it. I'll not press you. I'm not sure I want to know the truth – for my sake, or for the sake of my wife."

"There is no truth!"

Julian came to a halt. "Yes, there is. Circumspection, Alex. Something you need to practise."

Chapter 47

White Bear stood for a long time in the shadow of the trees. He slowed his breathing, closed his eyes, and allowed Samuel to resurface again, quietly trying out words in English after several months of speaking only Mohawk. It cost him, to change from Indian to white man, his identity once again splitting in two, all the uncertainties as to who he was welling up inside. He fingered his face for reassurance, swallowed a couple of times. Mama wouldn't be happy by this his final transformation, but he himself was elated that he had been accorded the right to be forever marked a man, despite his arm. On account of his aim, Qaachow had said, all those long hours White Bear had put in working only with his left hand were beginning to pay off.

A man – an Indian man. Once again, White Bear swallowed, no longer quite as sure this was who he wanted to be, not now that Samuel was springing into life inside of him, protesting that there, in the yard before him, was his family, his people. White Bear groaned. He couldn't be two people, two sons. He had made his choice, he reminded himself. He had an Indian woman and a child. White Bear was a brave, a man of the forests, not of the farm. He hefted his bundle of pelts higher up on his shoulder, gripped his musket and walked out into the open.

"It's Samuel!" Alex said, peering nearsightedly at the lone Indian that emerged from the northern slope. She wiped her hands on her apron and smirked at Mrs Parson. "I told you he'd be back for his birthday."

She danced out of the door, making for her son who was by now swamped by nephews and nieces. She saw Ian hurry over, come to an abrupt stop, and there was Mark, whooping as he bounded across the yard, and he suddenly faltered, his arms dropping back down his sides. Matthew appeared in the stable door and, even from where she was, Alex could see his mouth drop open, an instinctive expression of shock that he quickly wiped away, fixing a smile on his face instead.

By now, Alex was close enough to see for herself, and she had no idea what to say. It's not too bad, she told herself. It's actually quite pleasing in its design. Bloody hell! Her Samuel was sporting a huge facial tattoo!

"It's a bear's head," Samuel said to break the silence.

"Oh." Alex nodded.

"It looks nice." Malcolm smiled at his uncle. Samuel smiled back, two sixteen-year-old boys sharing a moment of exasperation with the strait-laced adult world.

"I want one too," Lettie piped up, standing on her toes to see properly.

"Lasses don't get tattoos," Samuel said.

"Well, thank heavens for that," Alex muttered. She took a firm grip of herself, decided that this was no big deal, and hugged her son. "Cake?"

Samuel nodded, and allowed her to tow him back towards the kitchen.

"What does it mean?" Matthew asked bluntly once it was only Samuel, Alex and him.

"Mean?" Samuel prevaricated, stretching himself after yet another slice of cake.

"The tattoo," Matthew clarified.

Samuel stuffed his mouth, chewed in silence.

"It means I'm an Indian man," he said finally, trying to avoid their eyes.

"Ah." Matthew sat back, stretched his long legs before him, and focused his attention on the scuffed toe of his working boots.

"I have an Indian woman," Samuel said, breaking a long, heavy silence, "and an Indian bairn."

"Not unless you want her to be." Alex served him some more beer. "She could be raised here, by us."

Samuel shook his head, mouth setting in a firm line.

"I don't want that. She belongs out there, with her mother and her people. And so do I." Samuel raised his chin, meeting Matthew's eyes.

"But you belong here as well," Alex tried.

Samuel gave her a rueful smile. "Aye, I do, and I'll be coming to see you often all the same."

Alex nodded, eyes travelling over her son. Tall and well grown, in buckskins and moccasins, a knife and tomahawk in his belt, he looked more Indian than white.

"And your faith?" Matthew said.

Samuel hitched his shoulders, saying that he saw no major difference between Da's God and the Creator of his Indian tribe. "It won't change, Da. I'm baptised a Christian."

"Raised a Christian as well, and I won't have one of my sons taking to heathen ways." Matthew stood up. "I have work to do," he muttered and left.

Samuel groaned and hid his face in his hands. "Why does it make such a difference? You knew already in February that I was going to live with my Indian people."

Alex stroked him over his long hair – too long, in her opinion. "It's repudiation, Samuel, and it hurts. Like hell, I might add."

Samuel shook his head. "Nay, it isn't. It's me trying to be whole."

"As an Indian, son. And we're not Indians, are we?"

"But you know I love you! You do, don't you?"

In reply, Alex opened her arms and hugged her son to her heart. "Of course we do, just as you know how much we love you."

Samuel wrapped his arms hard around her waist, and they sat like that for a long time.

Samuel spent the first couple of weeks at home tagged by a gaggle of admiring nephews and nieces. Patiently, he answered their questions, made them bows and arrows, let them finger his tattoo. He took Malcolm fishing, and they returned drenched to their skins, he sat for hours talking to Ian and Mark, and all the time, his eyes flew to his father, silently begging Matthew to come and be with him.

"Talk to him," Alex chided. "He needs your approval, Matthew."

"My approval? How can I give him that? And it's a wee bit too late in the day. Yon tattoo is already there!"

"It's not about the tattoo, you idiot!"

Matthew frowned at her, retook his hand.

"Matthew!" Alex grabbed at him, pulled him to a stop. They were returning from a long walk all by themselves, a Sunday ritual established since many years back. "You let him go in February, and he's right, isn't he? What life is there for him here, with us, except as an unpaid help to his brothers?"

"I can give him land! There's plenty."

"But Samuel can't work it himself. You know that."

"Neither can Ian."

"Ian is our eldest son. He's safe in his identity as your main heir. Yes, because of his back, he's also dependent on others, and you and I know just how much he hates it, but his place is here, and he knows it. Samuel on the other hand…" Alex gnawed at her lip, following the bright orange flight of an oriole with her eyes. "He has to belong somewhere. And you have to support him in his choice."

"I don't want him to be an Indian," Matthew said bleakly.

"Who does? But we owe him the opportunity to feel whole again, don't we? Besides, he'll be here often enough. As soon as I bake a cake, he'll come sniffing."

Matthew laughed despite it all, and gathered her close.

"And you?" he asked. "Doesn't it tear at you?"

"Tear at me? It's like having a sword plunged through my belly! But I…" Her voice trailed off.

"But you…" Matthew prompted.

"I want him to be happy, and he'll never be happy with us. Not anymore."

"And at least Matthew had a long heart-to-heart with Samuel before he left. So now, I suppose, we just have to let him go." Alex sat back on the bench, scraped at a stain on her apron. Almost a month Samuel had stayed, and the last week he'd been a constant shadow to his father.

"What else can you do?" Ian asked. "You can't keep him here by force."

"I should have let him fuck that little Ellen," Alex said, "and then he'd have been married to her by now."

Ian burst out in laughter. "Mama!"

"Well, I should. Then maybe he'd have felt as obliged to stay here, for her sake, as he does to go out there for his Indian wife!" She furrowed her brow. "Is he married to her, do you think?"

"I don't know. But best not let Da know he might be living in sin."

"Huh," Alex said, "somehow, I don't think he cares about that aspect of things – at least not right now." They were silent, sitting side by side in the fading June daylight.

"He blames himself," she added a while later. Matthew was twisting with it. Had he not promised Samuel to Qaachow for a year, none of this would have happened. On the other hand, had Matthew not done that then maybe there would have been no Graham's Garden, the homestead a smouldering ruin, the family killed or enslaved as had happened elsewhere during the Indian wars. "And I think it's my fault," Alex sighed.

"You couldn't do differently. Were you to leave the Indian wean to starve?"

Alex made a non-committal sound. Had she not nursed Qaachow's son back to life, the Indian would never have considered Samuel his foster son to begin with. Ian gave her a one-armed hug.

"He'll be fine," he said.

"Of course." Alex nodded. But he should be here, with her, not out there in the woods.

"I'm not sure," Alex said, scratching Viggo's head. The old dog rumbled happily and pressed his huge, hairy frame even closer, his tongue a garish pink against the grey of his coat.

"How not sure?" Matthew asked, coming over to sit

beside her. He flapped his hat in an effort to create some relief from the heat. Two weeks of haying behind them: a monotonous trudge up and down uneven pastures with the children and women following with rakes to even out the scythed grasses into long lines of drying hay. And tomorrow, they'd begin taking it in, and then… He stretched, feeling a creeping exhaustion between his shoulder blades and down his spine.

"Is it far enough?" Alex waved a hand in the general direction of the main house. "If you're going to go to the trouble of building us a little retreat, maybe we should be even further away."

Matthew shook his head. "Far enough." He was still rather doubtful about this whole enterprise, not at all understanding why Alex and he should have a need for a separate place to begin with.

"Daytime sex?" Alex said when he voiced this. "Long, slow mornings, only you and me?" She stood, came round to massage his shoulders.

"Ah." Matthew smiled up at her. "We can have that now as well. It's just a matter of closing the door."

"Let me rephrase. Daytime sex without everyone knowing exactly what we're doing." He chuckled. Aye, he'd like that. "And, anyway, it should be Mark in the big house, what with all the children and another on its way."

"Another?" He fidgeted under her hands.

"Yes, Naomi told me last week. Due in January, she thinks." Alex rolled her eyes at his pleased exclamation. "They breed like rabbits, Matthew!" She flushed when he held nine fingers aloft, one for each of the bairns she'd given him. "Mark will soon have six, Ruth is probably already pregnant again given Julian's craving for more sons, Sarah's—"

"Sarah is different," Matthew said sharply. His wife nodded, no more. "Why Mark? It should be Ian."

"Ian what?" Alex asked, confused.

"That moves into the big house."

"He does best in a house without stairs," Alex said, "and he knows that."

"Hmm," Matthew said, deciding then and there that his eldest son should have a new, expanded cabin as compensation. He got to his feet, extended his hand to her, and heaved her up. "I won't do any building this year," he decided, "but maybe next year. Swim?"

"Why is it that the moment you and I set foot on the shore, a bevy of children descend upon us?" Alex mock-grumbled an hour or so later. They were both still damp after a long, extended bath that had become somewhat of a romp when their grandchildren decided to join them, eagerly shouting for Matthew to throw them, for Alex to teach them how to dive.

"You like it." Matthew draped an arm around her. He studied the bairns that surrounded them in different states of undress: his blood, his flesh, and most of them so clearly of his get it made him puff up with pride. His eyes locked on Tom: Mark's son was a stringy boy with knobbly knees and dark hair. Just ten, he was the same age Samuel had been when he had been carried off to live with Qaachow. Samuel... He sighed.

Alex seemed to have followed his thoughts, eyes darting from Tom to him. She snuck an arm round his waist. "You okay?"

Matthew smiled down at her, nodded once. "Aye. He's right, isn't he? Nothing has really changed, and he'll be back for the harvest."

"He'd better be, given that he's got Malcolm with him. Ian won't be too thrilled if his eldest son isn't returned safe and sound in time for the real work."

Matthew's brows dipped. He'd not been glad to see Malcolm walk off with Samuel, had tried to argue Ian out of it – as had Alex. To their surprise, Ian had shrugged, saying Malcolm might fancy a few weeks pretending to be an Indian, but the lad was far too fond of his creature comforts to be in any danger of being permanently seduced into a life in the wilds.

They were just behind the barn when Viggo raised his head, floppy ears doing their best to rise into a point.

The dog stood absolutely still for some moments, all of him quivering, and then he shot off, sprinting up the lane for all that he was ten years old.

"Sarah," Alex said, already lengthening her stride.

"You think?" Matthew increased his speed, forcing Alex to run beside him. But he could hear the wean, screaming his head off.

"And Michael." Alex pointed at Pegasus.

"Fools, to ride alone all this way." But he was smiling as he said it, thinking that his youngest daughter was a bonny sight where she sat before her husband, her belly already rounding with the coming child.

"Here." Sarah handed down her grizzling son. "Do something, anything short of smothering him."

"He's wet," Alex said, shushing the laddie. "And hungry," she added when Matt attacked her knuckles.

"He's always hungry, look how fat he is!" Michael helped Sarah down, dismounted with a little sound of relief, nodding a thank you when Tom offered to see to the horse. "She was doing poorly in the heat," he said in a low voice to Matthew, "and I had to get away from my partner before I do something I would seriously regret – like force-feeding him type pieces." He scowled. "The partnership is to be dissolved. Simon is seeing to the legalities. Mr Nuthead has found himself other backers – men of impeccable Protestant background."

"And what will you do?" Matthew asked, following his wife and daughter with his eyes.

Michael shrugged and swatted at a fly. "I'm not sure. It's not as if I will receive a hearty welcome in any of the colonies." He shifted on his feet. "I was thinking horses."

"Horses?" Matthew turned to look at him.

"I'm good with them," Michael said, "and I have Pegasus to start with."

"How horses?" Ian asked.

"Breed them, break them to saddle, and sell them," Michael explained.

"Can you make a living out of that?" Matthew asked.

Any horseman worth his ilk did his own breaking.

Michael looked from Matthew to Ian, a slow smile spreading over his face. "Oh yes. Good horses are always in demand, and I have my eye on a couple of mares. Arabs."

"Arabs?" Matthew couldn't keep the interest out of his voice. He heard it himself, how eager he sounded. From the way Michael's smile widened into a grin, he heard it too.

"Beautiful, both of them. Of course," Michael added, "to breed horses you have to have land."

"We have land," Ian said. "Don't we, Da?"

"Hmm," Matthew replied, but in his head he was already seeing pastures full of brood mares.

Supper was a long, loud affair. On account of the heat, they ate outside, under the spreading branches of the white oak, and once they'd finished eating, the bairns escaped the table, leaving the adults to hours of conversation while the summer skies darkened into night.

At some point, Ian stood and suggested Mark and Michael accompany him to the river – the night was hot enough to require a late bath. Matthew smiled into his mug at the loud protests that met this suggestion – from Sarah and Naomi, mainly, who both insisted they wanted to come along. Ian rolled his eyes, muttered something about beer and women not mingling all that well, and asked if Matthew and Alex wanted to come along as well.

"No," Alex stretched, "I'm going to bed."

"Me too." Matthew rose and followed his wife inside. "I could do with a back massage," he said as he climbed the stairs, balancing the heavy water pitcher.

"Sure." She sounded distracted.

"What?" he asked.

"It's Sarah." Alex glanced at him. "She seems to think they're staying."

"Is that a problem?" An unnecessary question, as he knew Alex fretted like a mother hen at having Sarah so far away from her.

"Of course not! But what will Michael do for a living?"

"Horses." Matthew grinned. He undressed and flopped

down on the bed, telling her about Michael's plans as she worked out the tension round his shoulders.

"And they can live in Forest Spring." Matthew finished, grunting when Alex's strong hands concentrated on his lower back.

"All alone?" Alex asked, patting him on his warm and tingling back. He knew she wasn't overly fond of the neighbouring abandoned homestead – since several years owned by Matthew – this due to the fact that somewhere in the nearby woods were the remains of a rapist, hastily buried by Matthew more than fifteen years ago.

"Why not? And they will need a man or two to help, anyway." He looked about for his shirt, decided it was too hot to wear it, and rolled over on his side to watch Alex instead. He was quietly overjoyed at the thought of having Sarah back home, and as to Sarah, it was obvious she was just as happy, nearly skipping by his side when they'd taken a walk down to the river. Alex slid into bed beside him, nestled into him.

"Tomorrow," she said, patting him on his leg. "We can talk more about this tomorrow."

"There's nothing to talk about." Matthew yawned. "I've already made up my mind."

"Oh, well then," Alex replied with a slight edge. Matthew rubbed at her nape, the back of her head.

"You don't mind, do you?"

"No, but you could've discussed it with me first."

"Mmm," he replied, smiling into the night. They both knew these decisions were his to take. She pinched him, making him yelp.

"Supercilious bastard," she said, but without any real heat.

Chapter 48

Matthew woke well before dawn, propped himself up on an elbow, and studied his wife. On her back, quilts and sheets kicked into a heap at the foot of the bed, she slept deeply, her thin shift bunched around her waist. One arm was thrown high over her head, the hand curled into a fist, the other arm rested on her belly; vulnerable like a child, her mouth soft and half open in sleep. He catalogued her bit by little bit, from the odd toenail on her pinkie toe, to the pointed ears, the strand of startling white above her temple, the scar high on her arm after the wolf bite, the stretch marks she so hated that ran fanlike from her pubic bone and upwards.

Nine bairns she had given him: nine bonny, healthy children. It showed, of course it did, and when she slept like this, he could see it in her breasts, no longer quite as firm, in the way her flesh creased on her belly. They were growing old, he concluded, doing a cursory inspection of himself. There was a softness around his middle he didn't like, and even if he was fit and strong, there was no denying age. His body ached at times, muscles protested when he did things he'd done all his life, and every now and then, he suspected his hearing was going. Ah well, all in all, they were both hale and hearty, and the fire between them still burnt, a constant need for the other that, at times, made them behave like calf-sick youngsters.

She turned in her sleep, presenting him with her uncovered arse and the thick braid of hair from which a multitude of curls had escaped through the night. She was rosy and warm, her milky skin shifting to brown on her hands and forearms. On her feet as well, tanned after several months of walking barefoot or in sandals to save on stockings and shoes. So soft, her skin, so beautiful and smooth. He dipped his head towards her, drawing in the scent of lemon and lavender that always clung to her.

He closed his eyes and sniffed at the skin of her nape, where she smelled truly of herself – of winter apples and newly split wood, warm milk, and something else, a top note of pinecones and… He kissed her there, nibbled her, licked her, and with a humming sound, Alex buried her face deeper into the pillows, coming over on her knees. He rose behind her, the rope frame creaking in protest. Afterwards, they fell over on their sides, and Matthew spooned himself around her. He wasn't sure she had truly woken. He murmured her name into her hair, and dropped like a stone back into sleep.

Alex woke slowly. Beside her, Matthew snored, and from the way his shirt was pleated round his waist, and her shift pulled up to reveal most of her thighs, she concluded that she hadn't been dreaming some time earlier. She rolled out of bed, but after a quick stop at the chamber pot, she decided there was no reason to get up, and returned to bed with her precious letters from her sons.

Matthew made a series of satisfied sounds and pillowed his head in her lap.

She ran her fingers through his hair. "Hi."

"Mmmgh," he replied, still more asleep than awake.

"Adam should probably be a writer," Alex said, lowering the long letter. God, how she missed them! Her Adam, now fourteen, and, come next autumn, he'd be in Oxford, and with every day he grew away from them, became someone very different from the boy she'd left behind not quite a year ago. But in the letters it was still her Adam speaking, quick-witted and big-hearted, perceptive and considerate. She smiled at his description of walking through London with Hugin perched on his shoulder, and even more she chuckled at his description of Charlie's new wife: in Adam's opinion, not much of an improvement on Nan – even if Jane came with the benefit of not being branded.

She unfolded one of David's letters. Very short, a brief catalogue of successes, a small anecdote of a brawl in an inn

405

in which David – of course – took no part, a casual mention of a girl called Flora, yet another mention of this Flora, and then an apologetic sentence at the end, promising to write more at length next time.

"Huh," Alex snorted, and found letter number two. Just as short, a young man taking time out of a hectic life to pen his parents some dutiful lines before submerging himself in his day to day. And yet another little comment about Flora. "I wonder what she looks like," she said to Matthew, now quite awake. She hated it that this might be her son's future wife and, in all possibility, she, Alex, would never even meet her.

"He says, doesn't he? Brown hair."

Alex gave him a little shove. "That's like saying I bought a horse and it's got four legs."

Matthew chuckled into her shift. "Ask him, then."

"I will." She folded her youngest son's letter carefully. "One writes us a novel, the other a telegram."

"A telegram?"

"A very short message," Alex explained. "More along the lines of *I'm alive, goodbye.*"

Matthew burst out laughing.

She stretched for their latest missive, penned in Luke's distinctive hand. After a few general remarks as to Adam's progress, he gave a terse description of a Highlands still in flames, of a Stuart desperately holding on to Ireland, and a son with the intelligence of a newt.

> *Where does he get it, this knack for taking so many wrong decisions? A comely young man, a man who, God willing, will inherit a sizeable amount of money – in short, a catch – and the lad comes home with wee Jane, widow twice over, and God only knows what she's been up to in between.*

She waved the letter at Matthew. "Will you write him back?"

"I have to. For Adam's sake, if nothing else."

"But you don't really want to."

"Nay — not after what he did to you. And yet..." He twisted in her lap, raised a hand to her face. "I think he truly wanted us to be reconciled."

"For what it's worth, so do I, and you won't die from writing him the occasional letter, will you?"

The calm of the morning was shattered the moment Naomi opened the door to her cabin, releasing an exuberant Lettie on the world.

"Must she sing so loud?" Matthew muttered. "And what is it she's singing?"

"Massacred Swedish." Alex grinned. "Totally unintelligible, and she can't hold the tune either."

"Swedish? About what?"

"Oh," Alex said breezily, "this and that."

Matthew got out of bed. "Not lewd, I trust," he said, hunting about for a clean shirt.

"On the peg," Alex told him. "Of course not. It's all about frogs."

"Frogs?"

"Mmhmm." Alex poured some water from the pitcher, dipped a linen towel into it, and did a hasty wash. "My father taught me this when I was a small child, and he taught Isaac to sing it as well." She smiled at a very old memory of her father and son, Isaac two and a half or so, singing the frog song together while they jumped all over the garden. "*Små grodorna, små grodorna*," she hummed, and her eyes stung with tears.

In some weeks, it would be a year since Isaac died, and she hoped Rosie would remember to place a flower on his grave. My son, she thought, my firstborn son, and I never loved him quite as much as he deserved. He couldn't help his father, but Alex had indirectly made the baby, and then the toddler, pay for his resemblance to Ángel.

"Alex?"

"I'm okay," she assured him. "Just one of those moments." She touched him for reassurance, and he was solid and warm and very much here. His cheeks were covered with grey stubble, and he vaguely reminded her of Sean Connery in one of his later movies, even if Matthew had far more hair.

From below came the promising smells of ham and eggs, Thomas had evidently stepped outside to light his morning pipe, and she heard him saying something in a low voice to his daughter, Naomi. An angry squeal, and Matthew rolled his eyes.

"That child," he muttered, but the corner of his mouth twitched. He held out his hand to Alex. "Coming?"

It was hot, had been hot for days, with the noon hours spent in the shade to avoid being baked to a crust by the sun. And yet, every morning, they woke to glittering dew, to air that was fresh with the crispness of water. Today, the dew had evaporated by the time they made it outside, and once the beasts had been adequately watered, the family retreated to spend the day under the white oak, a lolling inertia that, for Alex, brought to mind picnics and barbecues, plaid-patterned blankets, and afternoons spent playing backgammon or cards.

They were all more or less asleep when the dogs began to bark, with Lovell Our Dog leading the pack at an exaggerated sprint up the lane. Mark and Michael were on their feet in an instant, Matthew and Ian somewhat slower. Muskets were found, hats clapped on heads, and by the time the dusty line of riders made it down to the yard, Matthew and his sons were waiting.

"Daniel?" Alex squinted in the harsh light. "Isn't that Daniel?" She hung back as the rest surged forward to greet Daniel, Ruth and their respective families. Her minister son, and in his arms was a boy who hid his face against Daniel's shirt, small pudgy arms tight around his neck. Still in smocks, but undoubtedly a boy, and undoubtedly Daniel's son, with the same blue eyes and dark hair.

"Magnus," he introduced, setting the boy down on his feet. Alex crouched before the child, extending a hand.

"Hi," she said. Little Magnus clung to his father's leg, blue eyes wide when he studied the people who surrounded him.

"Go on." Daniel unclamped the small hands from his breeches. "Bid your granny good day." Magnus clearly found all this intimidating, his mouth beginning to droop. Out of nowhere popped Lettie, and in her hand she held some squashed raspberries.

"Do you want some?" she offered. Magnus nodded shyly. Two minutes later, he had transferred his grip from his father to his cousin, smock flying round his bare legs as he ran to keep up.

"Don't drown him or feed him to the pigs," Mark said.

In reply, Lettie smiled sweetly and stuck up one waving middle finger.

"Lettie!" Alex gasped before bursting out laughing.

"Or teach him words and gestures a bairn his age shouldn't know," Matthew muttered, and shoved his wife towards their son to greet him properly.

She extended her hand to run down Daniel's arm, close around his wrist. They stood like that for some moments, reacquainting themselves with each other. Three years apart, and her son had become a man she didn't truly know, but his eyes were just as blue as they had always been, his hair was just as dark. She laughed, cried, cried even more, and Daniel drew her to him, enveloping her in a bear hug.

Julian cleared his throat. "Allow me to introduce our new minister." He beamed at Matthew, at Alex.

"Minister? Here?" Alex was not all that thrilled at the idea of having her own son entrusted with their spiritual well-being, but, from the way Matthew was grinning, eyes wet with pride, her husband did not share her opinion.

"In Providence," Temperance said, coming over to join her husband. She slid a hand round Daniel's arm and smiled at Alex. "Time we came home."

"Home," Daniel echoed. He shared a quick look with his wife, brows furrowing together in the slightest of frowns. Hmm. There was more to this than met the eye, but from the bland smile Daniel turned her way, Alex knew there was no point pushing – not yet. Instead, she turned to greet Ruth and the children, giving Julian a slight smile, no more. Since the incidents back in April, she wasn't entirely comfortable around him, seeing in his eyes a constant assessment, a barrage of unspoken questions.

In response, Julian gave her a crooked smile of his own and rolled his eyes. It made Alex laugh, and moments later, Julian had grabbed her in a strong embrace.

"A time warp, almost," Alex said to Matthew later, nodding to where Ian, Mark and Daniel were walking through the summer dusk, headed for the river. Mostly, she saw the young man that was missing: their tall, blond Jacob. She smiled though when out of nowhere, her sons were joined by their sisters, Sarah puffing and telling them to wait. Daniel snorted something about waddling ducks, and, for a moment, it was as it used to be with Daniel teasing and Sarah rising loudly to the bait.

"Soon she'll whack him over the head," Alex commented, and she was right because Daniel yelped. "Look, the Light Cavalry," she said, pointing to where Michael had now caught up with them, his arm snaking round to hold Sarah close. Alex smiled at how her youngest daughter and her man adjusted stride and rhythm to move like one. She reclined against Matthew, yawning after a long and emotionally draining day.

"Five of them here, imagine that." She snuggled closer to Matthew. "How does it feel then? To have your son become a minister down in Providence?"

"Wonderful," he said in a choked voice.

Not quite as wonderful two days later, when Carlos rode in on one of his regular monthly visits, only to break out in a joyous smile at the sight of Sarah.

"You look like a peach on legs," he said, and both Michael and Daniel clouded at his familiarity.

"How kind of you," she replied with a grin. "I'd have walloped you had you said a pear."

"What's he doing here?" Daniel inquired of Alex, a disapproving frown on his face.

"Visiting his friends," Alex said.

"He's a priest," Julian stated.

"Absolutely – just as he's always been."

"A papist priest," Julian said.

Not exactly news. Alex gave him an irritated look. "Michael and Sarah are Catholics, remember?"

Julian gave her an aggravated look. "My point was rather that Catholic priests are no longer allowed here, in Maryland."

Alex shrugged eloquently. "No one knows – unless someone tells."

Both Julian and Daniel scowled at her insinuating tone. Even more they scowled when first Sarah, then Michael, took the opportunity to have a private moment with Carlos.

"Confessing, no doubt," Daniel said in a voice loaded with disapproval.

"Mmm," Julian nodded. They cornered Carlos afterwards, asking him pointed questions as to how long he intended to stay in Maryland.

"I live here," Carlos replied.

"But…" Daniel gave an exasperated shake of his head. "You can't!"

"I can't? I seem to be managing quite well, thank you."

"It may be dangerous to you," Julian said.

"Life is dangerous, no matter where you are." Carlos finished folding away his stole, tucked his rosary beads back out of sight, and accepted the mug of beer Alex offered him. "I'm needed here."

Julian gave him a grudging nod. "You'd best be careful."

"Well, I wasn't planning on riding into town in my cassock." Carlos smiled.

Once Carlos was safely away, Julian steered Alex to the side and told her Daniel was right: these visits from a papist must stop. Alex raised her brows, crossed her arms over her chest, and waited until he fell silent.

"He's a friend," Alex said. "Even a very good friend."

"He's a priest! And you've already lost one daughter to him."

"So we're an ecumenical household – deal with it!"

"Ecumenical?" Julian blinked. "It's not allowed! This colony no longer holds with toleration, it—"

"Well, more's the pity, right? If it hadn't been for Lord Calvert's tolerant approach, there wouldn't have been a Presbyterian community in Providence, would there?"

Julian sighed. "You're right," he admitted in a surly voice. "But we weren't talking about ecumenism – we were talking about Carlos Muñoz, a Spanish priest."

"A priest and a good man. I'm sure God loves him." Alex disappeared into the pantry, but unfortunately Julian followed her, crowding her back against the shelves.

"God? How can you presume to know His preferences?" And she but a simple woman, his tone indicated.

"All women know God," she said. "We understand the preciousness and sanctity of life much more than most men do." She placed a hand on her stomach and smiled. "The miracle starts in here." She was very pleased by his reaction, a slow opening and closing of his mouth. "And who knows," she added, unable to help herself, "maybe God is a she?" With that, she ducked under his arm and skipped off – only to run straight into Daniel, all flaming blue eyes as he gripped her by the arm and led her off, insisting they had to talk – now – about spiritual matters.

"Sometimes children are a pain in the butt," Alex said to Mrs Parson before bringing down the meat hammer with a dull, slapping sound, "especially when they go all holier than thou on you." She was still angry after her argument with Daniel, him insisting it was eroding the moral fibre of the family to allow these regular visits from a Catholic proselytiser. It was important, he'd underlined, so important that the children be brought up safe within their faith.

"Otherwise…" he'd said mournfully, looking in the direction of Sarah. Just thinking about it made Alex's cheeks heat with irritation.

Mrs Parson chortled. "He's a minister, Alex. His wee sister is in danger of being consumed in eternal hellfire."

Agnes nodded concurrently from where she was washing vegetables. "All papists roast forever – everyone knows that. It is but a kindness, that Daniel attempts to save his family from this dire fate."

"You can't really believe that," Alex said, meat hammer frozen midway. Mrs Parson indicated that she shouldn't stop what she was doing, deftly filling the flattened slices of meat with parsley, finely chopped fat and dried prunes before rolling them together.

"No, of course not," Mrs Parson said. "Not anymore." Agnes muttered in disagreement but grumbled into silence when Mrs Parson frowned at her. "But Daniel is young while I'm old and wise, no?" She smiled, revealing all those startling white teeth. Agnes huffed, loudly.

"Old, definitely. Wise, I don't know." Alex pretended to study Mrs Parson. "You don't really look your age."

"Why, thank you," Mrs Parson preened.

"You look much, much older," Alex teased, ducking when Mrs Parson threw a prune at her. With a little wave, she escaped outside, making for her kitchen garden and Ian who was waiting for her.

"He isn't quite as uncompromising as all that." Ian grinned as Alex went on and on about bigoted ministers – all of them, damn it. "And he's young," he added loftily, making Alex smile.

"Well, it isn't as if you're hoar headed with age yourself, is it?" Gently, she poked him in the ribs with the shaft of her rake before going back to her work. Ian laughed, dislodged yet another piece of sun-baked earth with his spade, and in silence they finished the new bed.

"Garlic and leeks," Alex said once they were done.

He gave her an unenthusiastic look, muttering that he hated leeks.

"You like it in pies," she protested, using both hands to lift her sweat dampened clothes off her chest and let in some air.

"I like anything in a pie," he replied, and they both looked over to where the two apple trees they had planted together eighteen years ago stood heavy with unripe fruit.

"With custard," she said dreamily, her stomach rumbling

at the thought. "I don't like it, how he talks down to Sarah," she added, and Ian rolled his eyes at her shift back to the Daniel discussion. "He's been at her since he came, badgering her with questions about why she converted, four years after the fact."

"On account of Michael, I reckon."

Alex shook her head. "Not entirely. Very much on account of Carlos — her way of atoning for the heartbreak she caused him." Ian raised his brows, looking surprised, but nodded slowly.

"Are you happy?" she said some moments later.

"Happy?" His eyes drifted over to where Betty was walking across the yard. His face softened as he studied his wife, all that wild hair lying like a foxtail down her back. Betty turned, saw him, and raised her hand in a wave. He lifted his arm in response and Betty danced away, light as a feather on her feet.

Alex chuckled and patted his back. "You don't need to answer."

Chapter 49

"Forthwith, we will call this the month of homecomings," Alex decided when Samuel stepped out of the forest a week after Daniel's arrival, trailed by an exhausted but happy Malcolm who twirled to show off his new buckskin leggings.

"Forthwith?" Matthew laughed.

"Sounds more formal," she replied, before going over to kiss her son who was defending himself from the boisterous welcome of his older brothers, and in particular from Daniel. Firmly, she extricated Samuel from his siblings, took him by the hand, and led him off.

"Okay?" she asked. Samuel nodded, smiled at Matthew who came to join them.

"And the bairn?" Matthew asked after hugging Samuel. "Did you not think to bring her?"

"Next time," Samuel promised. But his eyes slid to the side, and Alex wasn't all that sure she believed him. She pursed her lips and studied her son.

"Do you speak English with Karen?"

"Some," Samuel replied. "Not much. Karen is a Mohawk, just like her mother, just like me. What need does she have of English?" The subtext was clear: his daughter wouldn't be burdened with two identities – not like he had been. Samuel gave her a defiant look, and Alex felt as if he'd slapped her. She retreated a couple of paces, wheeled and walked off, not wanting him to see she was crying.

Every day, she lived the loss of him; every day, she told herself he had to be allowed to make his choice, somehow become whole. It didn't help. Samuel was her son, but with each month spent with his Indian family, he was slipping through her fingers, and some years down the line, he

415

would probably stop visiting, having nothing in common with them anymore. Tears blurred her eyes, she pressed her hand to her mouth to mute the loud sobs she could feel tearing through her chest, and extended her stride, making for the haven of the forest.

"Mama?" Samuel caught up with her.

"If you're not teaching her English then how will I ever be able to talk to her?" she said, wiping at her cheeks. "But maybe you don't want me to, right? Maybe you'd prefer it if we all died, and you could pretend we'd never existed, that Thistledown was your real mother, not me."

He blanched. "Of course I don't want you to die."

"No, you just want to forget us. White Bear has no room for Samuel, but it isn't White Bear I love, it's my Samuel Isaac." When he made as if to hug her, she shoved at him. "Leave me alone, Samuel – sorry, White Bear."

"Mama," he groaned. "Don't be like this." Yet again, he tried to hug her; yet again, she shoved him away.

"It hurts," she whispered. "All the time, it hurts."

"I know," he whispered back. "I hurt all the time too." Tears stood in his eyes, the long mouth he shared with his father wobbled.

"Oh, Samuel!" She started crying in earnest, and this time she let him pull her close, resting her cheek against the supple leather of his shirt. "I don't want you to hurt, honey. I want you to be happy and whole, but I wish you could be that here, with us, not there, with them."

"I'm not whole there either." Samuel sighed softly. "But sometimes I am happy." He smiled down at her. "And sometimes I am happy here as well."

"Truly?"

"Truly." He stooped and kissed her forehead. "And I promise I will start teaching Karen English."

"And her Bible," Daniel said, stepping into the little clearing.

Samuel made a vague sound.

"It's important," Daniel said, nailing Samuel with his eyes.

"For you," Alex said. "Not necessarily for Karen."

"We can't have her growing up a heathen!" Daniel sounded so pompous Alex was tempted to kick him, even more so when her minister son narrowed his eyes at Samuel. "When was the last time you were catechised?"

"Umm," Samuel replied, looking at Alex for help.

"Every time he is here," Matthew said from somewhere behind Alex. "You need not concern yourself with Samuel's spiritual health – it is in good hands." Daniel pulled himself up straight. Matthew calmly met his eyes. "Go on," he said to his sons. "There's beer waiting for you – and work. Plenty of work."

Daniel groaned. "I'd forgotten how hard the farming life is."

"Aye well, you've gone all weak and pudgy over the last few years," Samuel said. "Is there any muscle left to you at all?"

"Weak? Come here, wee brother, and I'll show you!" Daniel pounced, Samuel emitted a sound somewhere in between a yelp and a laugh, and set off at a run, with Daniel chasing after, loudly promising he would have Samuel eat his words.

Matthew regarded them out of sight before turning his attention to Alex.

"Alright?" he asked.

"Better," she replied.

"Better is good." He tugged gently on a stray lock of her hair. "He will find his own way, lass. He has to."

"Why did you come back?" Alex asked Daniel some days later. He eyed her warily. They'd argued repeatedly over the last few days, heated discussions about Sarah and Samuel that generally ended with both of them glowering, refusing to back down.

"Didn't you want me to?"

"Of course, I do!" She took his hand and gave it a little shake. "But from a career perspective, Boston is better than Providence."

Daniel stopped to dislodge a small stone from under his bare sole. "I missed you."

"You did?" She was gratified – but unconvinced.

Daniel nodded, smiling in the general direction of where his pregnant wife sat with their son in her lap. "So did Temperance."

"Really? Now, why do I have problems believing that one? If Temperance missed anyone, it was Ruth."

Daniel laughed in agreement. "How is it that they don't run out of things to talk about? Since we arrived in Providence, those two have been talking constantly."

"They talk about you, a subject none of them can get enough of."

"Me?" Daniel came to a surprised and embarrassed stop.

Alex inclined her head gravely. "You don't stand a chance in hell. Between the two of them, they have you entirely figured out." She laughed at his expression, snuck a hand under his arm, and squeezed. "All women figure out their men. Rarely does a man figure out his woman."

"Oh aye?" Daniel looked down at her and grinned. "Da knows you inside out."

"It took him more than thirty years," Alex reminded him.

"So, why?" she asked again once they had reached the shade of the oak to collapse on the bench. She poured them both some barley water from the pitcher Agnes had prepared earlier.

Daniel gnawed at his lip. "Richard Campbell," he finally sighed.

"Richard?" Alex sat up straight. "That slimy worm of a man did something to you?"

"Not as such," Daniel said, "but he has a capacity for spreading rumours. We had words, nay, even blows. I couldn't let him get away with it, could I? Calling you a witch and all." He hitched his shoulders, adding that the incident had cost him a possible position at North Church, but at least it hadn't improved Campbell's expectations either, and last he heard, Richard Campbell had been on his way to some obscure place in Essex County.

"I'm sorry," Alex said.

Daniel smiled. "No great matter, Mama. Anyhow, Minister Walker offered me a position here, in view of having lost two ministers recently, and so here I am." He frowned. "It's unfortunate he hasn't died of something nasty," he muttered. "Richard Campbell makes for a enemy."

"Yeah, he's a narrow-minded bastard – but fortunately very far from here." Alex touched his cheek. "Will you be content, do you think, living here after so many years in Boston?"

"I don't know, but if not I can go elsewhere." He yawned, obviously bored by the subject. "Hot, isn't it?"

Alex grunted an agreement, her interest distracted by Lettie. What was the girl up to now? A bow in one hand, and was that an apple?

"Bloody hell!" Alex leaped to her feet. "Lettie!" she hollered. "Don't you dare, you hear?" Alex sprinted over the cobbles, making for where Lettie had placed Timothy against the barn door with an apple on his head.

"Holy Matilda!" Alex gasped.

"Nothing holy about this," Mark panted beside her, attempting to look stern.

"But you told us, Granma," Lettie said. "You told us about William Tell and how he shot the apple off his son's head."

Alex gave Lettie a little shake. "I don't recall suggesting you should try it."

Lettie hitched one bony shoulder. "I wasn't using arrows with real heads." She showed them the sharpened wooden points.

"Oh good, you wouldn't have killed him, just injured him," Mark said.

"I wouldn't have missed," Lettie replied, but sullenly promised not to try before sauntering off to find something else to set the apple on.

"See?" Mark groaned, turning to Naomi. "See all the grey hairs? On account of your daughter."

"My daughter?" Naomi gave him a light shove. "That child, Mark Graham, that imp, is a Graham through and

419

through." They both turned to look at Alex.

"A Lind," Naomi amended.

"Definitely a Lind." Mark nodded, grinning at his mother.

"Undoubtedly," Thomas put in, "same eyes, same hair…"

Alex snorted, but looked over to where Lettie was busy with her bow. The girl did look a lot like her, and that made Alex smile inside.

"It's Samuel's fault, teaching them to use bow and arrow."

Mark rolled his eyes at her. "It isn't Samuel that tells them stories about yon William Tell and Robin Hood, about Hawkeye and Uncas, is it?"

"Err…" Alex tried.

"Or about Legolas," Naomi said. She was a big fan of Alex's stories, in particular the ones about that magical Middle Earth.

"He's an elf," Alex protested. "He has magic powers."

"Lettie thinks she has as well." Thomas laughed, and nodded to where their common granddaughter was doing an interesting little dance, the neatly pierced apple held aloft.

Alex returned to the shade under the oak, drained her mug, refilled it, and gulped it down.

"That child…" she moaned, and beside her, Matthew laughed softly while Julian tsked and shook his head.

Daniel grinned. "I'd forgotten how entertaining life is here."

Julian choked on his drink. "Entertaining?" he wheezed. "Timothy is already half deaf, he doesn't need to lose an eye!"

"But he didn't." Alex studied Timothy and sighed. The measles had left him with a permanent hearing impairment, and it had taken a long time for him to regain his health. Even now, he looked frail, that mop of bright red curls sitting atop a pale and narrow little face.

"He could have died!" Julian said.

Alex smiled sadly. "Children die of many things, Julian, but rarely due to games."

Sarah made a strangled sound, and swayed to her feet. Alex shared a concerned look with Matthew, half rose to go after her, but Matthew's hand closed round her wrist urging her back down. Instead, Michael caught up with Sarah before she began to climb the hill to the graveyard, lifted Matt out of her arms, and offered her his free hand.

"He loves her," Daniel said as he watched his sister and her husband walk slowly up the steep incline.

"Surprise, surprise, even Catholics do," Alex told him.

"Alex," Matthew and Julian chorused.

"Aye, it would seem they do," Daniel replied, unperturbed.

"Tomorrow," Matthew said later that evening, sniffing the air. "We start harvesting the wheat tomorrow. This won't hold much longer." They were alone under the oak: Thomas, Mrs Parson, Alex and Matthew. The night was alive with the sound of crickets, a couple of bats did death-defying high-speed manoeuvres by the stable gable, and from the half-open kitchen door spilled a square of weak yellow light.

Thomas brought out a flask of whisky, drank and handed it round. "Beautiful," he commented, indicating their surroundings.

"Difficult to see," Alex teased, but nodded all the same. All along the western horizon, a glimmer of greenish yellow still lingered, a lighter band against which the uneven edge of the forest trees stood jagged. If she craned her head the other way, there hung a yellow harvest moon, and, in between, small glimmering points of light twinkled down at them.

Beside her, Mrs Parson exhaled softly. "So peaceful," she said. "I wouldn't mind, to lay myself down and die on an evening such as this."

"Forget it," Alex said, "not yet. You don't have time."

Mrs Parson made a gurgling sound of amusement. "Not yet."

The coming weeks were a flurry of work, men and beasts out on the field from dawn to dusk, with most of the children helping as well as they could. Mrs Parson became head chef,

Agnes took care of the cows and the pigs, and Alex and her daughters spent most of their time in the garden. This day was no different, so Alex grabbed a basket and set off up the slope.

Ruth was with her constant shadow, Temperance. A murmur of voices, a continuous sharing of secrets and experiences, and when Alex looked towards the further end of her kitchen garden she saw Sarah, silent and nearly invisible behind the exuberant bee balm. Alex detoured Ruth and walked over to Sarah.

"It's always Temperance," Sarah said in a low voice, "it's never me."

"They haven't seen each other in three years," Alex said, waving her hand at the buzzing bees that rose around her.

"She hasn't seen me much more, has she?" Sarah sighed deeply. "I miss her, Mama, but she doesn't miss me." Alex gave her a hug; it had always been like that, Sarah tagging after her older sister, her older sister far more interested in first Daniel, then Temperance and Julian.

"You have friends of your own, don't you?" Alex asked.

"Not like that." Sarah nodded over to where Ruth and Temperance worked head to head, straw hats bobbing in tandem.

"Neither do I," Alex admitted, "but I don't really mind. I have your father." Sarah made a disgusted little sound, but her long mouth curved into a reluctant smile. Her eyes darted to where Michael was standing in the yard, harnessing the mules. Alex elbowed her gently in the side. "He's enough, isn't he?" she teased. A soft blush suffused Sarah's face. She shifted Matt inside his shawl, and inclined her head.

"But at least you have Mrs Parson," Sarah grumbled, smoothing her hand over her distended belly.

"That's like saying you have me, Sarah. She's the closest thing to a mother I have." Alex gripped the small, rosy foot that suddenly appeared from within the folds of Sarah's shawl. "Give Matt to me, and then let's go and talk to your sister, okay?"

Ruth sat back on her heels and wiped at her sweaty face with a dirty hand.

"Beets tonight?" she said, holding up a couple of well grown specimens.

"I don't like beets," Sarah muttered. Ruth smiled up at her, the dark red braid come undone from its coil to hang heavy down her back.

"You know," she teased.

Sarah rolled her eyes, and together the sisters turned to their mother. "It's good for you," they mimicked. "You must always eat plenty of vegetables and keep clean."

Temperance giggled before saying that Daniel said the same thing – repeatedly.

"You forgot one thing, didn't you?" Alex grinned as the three young women spoke in chorus.

"And never, ever, go to bed without cleaning your teeth."

"Well thank heavens you've listened to something I've said," Alex muttered.

"Mama," Ruth groaned, "you've said it every day of our lives. You would have to be daft—"

"…or deaf," Sarah put in helpfully.

"…to not have learnt that by rote." Ruth finished.

"Huh," Alex said, and with a little backward wave left them to the harvesting, saying something about baking a cake instead – and maybe, just maybe, she'd save them each a slice.

Sunday, blessed day of rest, even in the midst of harvest. Alex woke in the grey predawn, slipped out of bed, and, without bothering to dress properly, made her way outside. The rosebush that flanked the kitchen door scattered wet all over her when she opened the door, and she stood for a moment on the stoop, surveying her little kingdom.

The barn and stables, the separate cabins, all of them had weathered to a soft silver grey, just as the main house behind her. The neatly cobbled yard, the stone flag walk that cut across it, it looked as if it had been here for ages, permanently rooted in ground that a couple of decades ago had been virgin forest.

If she made an effort, she could recall the first time

they'd seen this shallow, sloping valley, folding gently from where she now stood to the river: chestnuts and maples, grasses that had bowed and rustled in the wind, and nowhere anything that indicated man had ever been here before. And now…a sliver of domestication in a sea of trees, a fragile little existence that would disappear and be swallowed completely by the forest in less than a generation should they choose to leave.

The thought raised goose pimples all over her. Was there anything left of them in the twenty-first century? Would there be someone living here, in their place, and would that person's name be Graham? She hoped so: saw before her a line of descendants, tall, dark-haired men with Matthew's beautiful eyes – greenish-brown, dotted with flecks of purest gold. She smiled at the thought of him, still fast asleep upstairs. She stepped off the stoop, hurried over the chilly stones of the yard, and then she was swishing through the grass, her hems going sopping wet.

The graveyard was sunk in deep shadow, the roses on the sprawling bush a contrasting white where they snowed petals to fall on the ground and the headstones. Alex hesitated for a moment, not wanting to disrupt the somnolent peace of her dead, but then she laughed at herself and after a quick pat on Magnus' stone, went to sit beside Jacob, the main reason for her waking this early.

Having the whole house full of her children made his absence so much more painful. In the way Daniel turned his head, in Sarah's thick blond plait, how Ruth's eyes shifted to a light, light hazel when she squinted at the sun – in all of it, she saw Jacob. Her finger traced the carved fronds that decorated his headstone, lingered over his name.

"God, I miss you," she said out loud. In her head, she could see him smile, that signature slow smile that illuminated his face from within, and his eyes glittered in a shaft of celestial sun. His heavy fringe fell forward to hide his face, and then he was gone, melting back into her memory bank, and Alex sat for a long time caressing the little wooden baby Matthew had given her almost a year ago.

From her apron pocket, she extracted three smooth pebbles and placed them one by one on his grave: one for Jacob, one for little Rachel, and one for Isaac.

"Alex?"

She turned at the sound of his voice, and got to her feet. "I didn't mean to wake you."

"You didn't. I woke and missed you beside me, that's all." He held out his hand to her, and her fingers braided into his. "I don't like it, to wake up and find the bed empty of you." He nodded over to Jacob's grave. "They bring him back, don't they?" he said, a brittle edge to his voice.

"Yes, each and every one of them remind me of him." She waited while he did his own silent communion with their son, and then allowed him to lead them back down, this time over the kitchen garden. They stopped for a moment, and drew in lungfuls of herb-scented air, Matthew standing patiently while Alex broke off a few stalks of lavender, a pink stand of bee balm, some mint and catnip.

They resumed their walk, skirting the buildings on their way to the river, faintly visible through the trees that bordered the hay meadows. A long, silent walk, a quiet inventory of what they'd achieved together, carving out of wilderness a home, a farm, a garden.

Matthew showed her a dew hung spider web, clearly visible in the returning light, she pointed out a fresh cowpat before they stepped in it, and so they came down to the soothing murmur of the rushing waters. Yet another hot day in the making, another day of burnished skies that dulled to bronze with heat and dust. They stood together in the shallows, and Alex released her little posy to float away, an offering to her dead children, to God.

"Look." Matthew used his free arm to indicate the delicate pink of the eastern sky. Colour was returning to their world, greys morphing back to greens and browns, reds and blues.

Alex walked over to their makeshift bench. "Life is good," she said, resting back against the log. Matthew didn't reply, lowering himself to first sit then lie beside her, his head comfortable in her lap. Her hand drifted down to tug its way through his hair as it had done uncountable times since that first night they spent together, in a little cave on a Scottish moor.

"Very good," he finally said, and together they watched the sun rise over the treetops, welcomed by thousands upon thousands of birds that chirped and sang and warbled all around them.

He raised his hand to rest against her cheek. "Pancakes?" he asked, his hand moving softly over her face. She bit down gently on his thumb.

"Pancakes," she promised. Hand in hand, they walked barefoot back home.

Matthew tightened his grip on Alex's hand. My miracle lass, my gift from God.

Alex squeezed back. My man, the owner of my soul, the keeper of my heart.

At their heels walked a protective shadow, the outline of a tall young man glittering in the sun before it dissipated. On a cloud way up high sat a four-year-old girl who smiled down at Mama and Da, little specks on the ground far below. Higher up, further away, Isaac Lind was laughing as his Offa swung him round and round in a sky the deep, deep blue of his mama's eyes.

For a Historical Note and more information about Matthew and Alex, please visit www.annabelfrage.com

And for those of you that just don't feel ready to bid Alex and Matthew farewell, keep an eye open for a couple of short sequels. After all, we just have to know what Richard Campbell might do next, right?

For the readers who want something new, why not turn the page and meet Kit, the protagonist of Anna's upcoming series, set in fourteenth-century England...

Upcoming release from Anna Belfrage:

In the Shadow of the Storm

"Will she do?" The voice came from somewhere over her head.

"Do? She will have to, won't she?"

With a series of grunts, the men carrying her deposited her in a cart. Kit made as if to protest. A large hand gripped her by the neck, tilted her head, and held something to her mouth. No. No more. She spat like a cat, to no avail. Her mouth was forced open, sweet wine was poured, obliging her to swallow. And then there was nothing but a spinning darkness. Nothing at all.

When next she came to, a wrinkled face was peering down at her.

"Remarkable," an old woman said. "Absolutely remarkable."

Kit shrank back. Her heart leapt erratically in her chest, her gaze flitting from one side to the other in this unfamiliar chamber, taking in tapestries and painted walls, streaks of sunlight from the open shutters. Where was she? All she had were vague recollections of days on a cart, jolted this way and that. Days in which strong fingers pinched her nose closed until she was forced to open her mouth and swallow down that unctuously sweet concoction that submerged her in darkness.

"Not so remarkable when one considers that they have the same father," someone else said drily. A pair of light blue eyes studied her dispassionately. The eyes sat in a narrow face, a nose like a knife blade separating the two halves. A wimple in pristine linen and a veil in what Kit supposed to be silk framed a face that would have looked better on a man than on a woman – harsh, aloof, and with an expression which reminded her of old John back home when he'd cornered a rat.

"M-m'lady," Kit stuttered. She tried to sit up but was pushed down again.

"Oh no. You will not move until we have reached an agreement."

"Agreement?" Kit pulled at her hands, noting with a burst of panic that she was tied to the bed – a simple thing, consisting of a rough wooden frame and a straw mattress, no more.

"We are in a quandary," the lady with the blue eyes said. She pressed her mouth together. "Stupid, wilful child!"

"Me?" Kit's head hurt something awful. What had happened to her?

There was a barking sound Kit took for laughter.

"You, little one, will be anything but wilful. If you are…" The lady made a swift motion across her throat with her hand.

Kit cowered. What did they want with her, these two old crones?

The older of the women patted her hand. "It will be none too bad." From the homespun of her clothes and the coarse linen of her veil, Kit concluded she was not a lady but a servant.

"Where am I?" Kit asked.

"Where you are doesn't matter. It is what you are that is important." The lady stretched her mouth into an icy smile. "You are a soon-to-be bride. At noon, you will wed Adam de Guirande."

Kit did not know what to say. She didn't like the look in the lady's eyes, and for some reason she had no doubts that should she refuse to comply, she would end up dead in the latrine pit – the lady had that sort of air to her.

"Who are you?" she whispered.

"Me?" The lady cackled. "Why, I am the bride's mother, Lady Cecily de Monmouth."

Kit wanted to protest. Her mother was Alaïs Coucy – dead since two months back. Grief tore at her, and she turned her face towards the wall, not wanting these strangers to see the tears welling in her eyes.

"I know all about your whore of a mother," Lady Cecily said. "My husband's great love, no less." She sounded bitter. "But at least his bastard will come in handy."

"His bastard?" Kit tugged at her bindings. "I am no bastard!"

"What lies has little Alaïs told you? That your father is dead? That he abandoned her to pursue a religious vocation?"

Kit flushed. "My father—"

"Is my husband, Thomas de Monmouth. My husband, you hear?"

"But..." Kit slumped back against the thin pillow. For most of her eighteen years, she'd heard of her mother's sad story, how two young lovers fled the world, exchanged their vows before a priest, and hoped for an eternity together – except that her father had died of a fever. She didn't understand. Life as she knew it was caving in on top of her – all at the say-so of this unknown woman. "You lie," she tried.

"I most certainly do not," Lady Cecily said.

Kit closed her eyes to avoid that light blue penetrating gaze. She suspected the lady was telling the truth: every question she had ever asked about her father had been met with an evasion, or the sad tale of star-crossed lovers as trotted out by her mother. When she'd taken her questions to John or to Mall, they had looked discomfited and referred to her mother.

A hand on her shoulder shook her – hard. "No time for all that now. Those dolts I sent to abduct you took their time getting you here, and we have urgent matters at hand – first and foremost, your impending wedding. Mabel, call for a bath – the child is revoltingly dirty."

"No." Kit raised her chin and stared Lady Cecily in the eye, summoning what little courage she had. "I'll not wed on your say-so."

"No? Oh, I think yes." Lady Cecily's eyes descended towards her, filled with such menace Kit flinched. "If you don't, I will have you thrown out of Tresaints – and publicly branded a bastard."

"Tresaints? It's my home."

"It was deeded to your mother for life. And she is quite, quite dead, isn't she?" Lady Cecily smirked. "You have nowhere to go, little...Kit, is it? But here you'll respond to the full version of the name you share with your sister: Katherine."

A sister? Kit gaped.

Lady Cecily smiled wickedly. "What? You didn't know you had a trueborn half-sister? A girl who looks just like you?" She laughed as she straightened up to her full height. "So, what will it be? Destitution or marriage?"

Kit wanted to say destitution. She wanted to snarl and spit Lady Cecily in the face – accuse her of abduction, even – but she knew it would be futile. Women like Lady Cecily had power and wealth on their side. Kit had nothing. She swallowed back on a sob.

"If you say no, I will evict every single one of the tenants as well," Lady Cecily said, effectively nailing down the lid on the coffin that was already closing on Kit.

"And if I say yes?"

"If you say yes, your father will include Tresaints in your dowry."

Kit was trapped. She knew it, Lady Cecily knew it. She acquiesced with one single nod.

Lady Cecily patted her cheek. "Good girl."

CPSIA information can be obtained at www.ICGtesting.com
Printed in the USA
LVOW11s1546010715

444611LV00006B/666/P